THE RULE OF RANGING

BOOK 2

INTO THE VALLEY OF QUIETUS

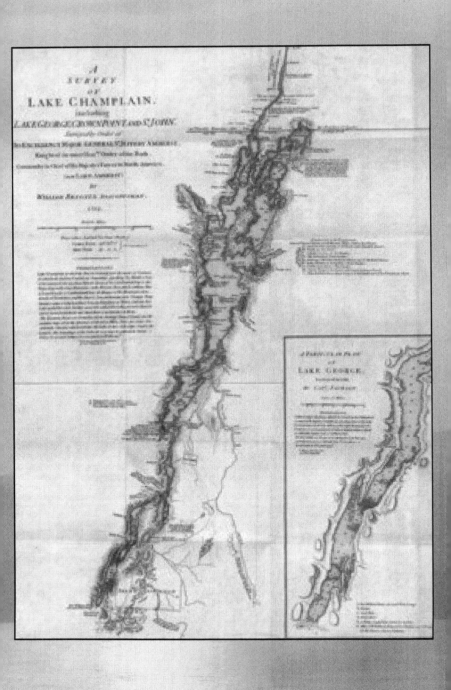

THE RULE OF RANGING

BOOK 2

INTO THE VALLEY of QUIETUS

By

Timothy M. Kestrel

TIMOTHY KESTREL ARTS & MEDIA, INC.

ISBN-13: 978-0-9886660-3-0
ISBN-10: 0988666030
Library of Congress Control Number: 2013922351

Book Cover desiign by Glen M. Edelstein
Book Interior design by Glen M. Edelstein

Timothy Kestrel Arts & Media, Inc.
1140 Avenue of the Americas, 9th Floor
New York, NY 10036, USA
http://timothykestrel.com

"Two things fill the soul with wonder and reverence, increasing evermore as I meditate more closely upon them: the starry heavens above me and the moral law within me."

—Immanuel Kant (1724-1804)

THE RULE OF RANGING

BOOK 2

INTO THE VALLEY OF QUIETUS

Chapter I

HENRY RAYMOND, a reporter from the *New-York Daily Times,* and the old man met in the lobby of the Catskill Mountain House for dinner. The old man was sitting in a custom-made wooden wheelchair, his fingers tapping the hand guard impatiently. As they shook hands, Henry Raymond noticed the velvety softness of the man's green smoking jacket as he assisted him toward the sumptuous dining room with banquet rooms in the back. Small groups of gentlemen gathered in quiet corners of the barroom to the side. The dining room tables were set with white linen tablecloths with earthy green placemats. Light from a row of crystal chandeliers reflected off exquisite china and the shining silverware on the tables (light seemed to annoy the old man). As they sat down, the old man picked up a knife as if by habit and scrutinized its sharpness closely.

Henry Raymond was surprised to find such a fine restaurant so far away from the city. He quietly noted that the old man looked out of place among the highbrow clientele. His gaze shifted to the spectacular view of the Hudson River Valley through large clear glass French doors on the long side of the dining room. Servants dressed in blue skirts, white aprons and red vests attended courteously to the guests, serving entrees and filling glasses.

The head waiter, his chin held high, keenly aware of his superior position among the dining room staff, received them. He led the two men to a sizeable table by large French doors overlooking the terrace. "Your customary table, Mister Morton," he said, pulling out a chair to the side to make room for his wheelchair.

The old man appraised the table setting, nodded and cracked his knuckles. "Alright, everything's in order, good." He waved away the menu the maître d'hôtel was handing to him. "The usual for me."

Henry Raymond, accustomed to selection in the city, measured the menu critically at length. He considered the rainbow trout, grilled with lemon sauce. He glanced at the old man and wanting to please him, he said, "Well, Finn, I suppose I will take the same."

The head waiter sharply clapped his hands twice, and one servant promptly fetched a bottle of Glen Avon single malt and two tumblers from the bar and brought them to the table while another servant filled water glasses.

"I hope you will enjoy the finest strip steak in the western hemisphere as much as I do, Mr. Raymond," the old man said before sipping the whiskey and savoring the earthy, smoky taste.

"I'm sure I will. You have excellent taste, sir," Henry Raymond replied. He snapped his briefcase, took out a notebook, and continued, "I genuinely appreciate the stories, sir, and your trust in me. I was hoping we could continue where we left off last time. I think you told me about the first fight on snowshoes."

The old man sneered, sipping his drink. "Raymond, memories can be a pain in the ass when you get to be my age. The day arrives sooner than you'd like when you realize that's all that's left," he said. He paused for moment, sighed and continued. "Anyways, where was I? Oh yes, that year ended badly, and the following year started even more fucked up. It was a cold, early summer day, and shivering wind blew across barren fields in the Hudson River Valley. The crops were destroyed by frost at night, and then, adding salt into injury, severe drought threatened the already frost–stricken fields. Roads and bridges collapsed or were washed away, thus cutting off main roads from other regions. The King in London was unwilling, and the aristocrats were ill prepared, to deal with emergencies. Dwellers of temporal shelters made from reeds and grasses were left to their own devices.

"In Fort Edward and the surrounding areas, townspeople and farmhands searched for sustenance in tree roots and pulled up grass. At the end of their tether, people converted dead vultures, buzzards, and animal bones found in the countryside into powder to be eaten as flour. Squalid specters wandered in search of food, the starving falling of depravity and hunger. Thin-as-rails militiamen collected corpses that were stiff as boards in wagons to be taken to the mass graves in the cemetery. To top it off, the survivors also had to worry about the pending military campaign, which the French were surely to start at any time.

"On the way to Fort Edward, an anorexic youngster, twelve years old, was robbed with blows of some corn he was carrying. Just down the road, a thief broke into a once affluent farm house and passed through the dining room without stopping where pieces of silverware laid on the table, went straight into the kitchen, and stole a pot where moist corn was cooking." He stopped for a moment as salads were served, and nodded when the waiter asked if he wanted fresh ground pepper with his salad. He poured the rest of his drink down his throat and wiped the corner of his mouth with a napkin. The old man ate with appetite as he continued, occasionally glancing at Raymond across the table.

"On the roads, mule drivers carrying corn were armed with fowling pieces converted to large caliber scatterguns, and for a good reason. When they arrived at the gates of a magazine, a scene of tumult occurred. Near the stores, people — driven by malnutrition — gathered to get at a chance at the food. A lot of women got into rumbling arguments and came to blows. The crowd grew as the creaking warehouse doors were opened, and those in the front were trampled by those in the rear seeking to storm the store. Three poor women were killed by the mob." The old man paused and ordered some wine to go with his zesty steak.

"You should have seen him, Raymond. There he was, standing tall and looking fabulous, shouting at us, poor buggers." Finn raised his voice and waved his arms. "All I want to see is your furrowed brows! Show me your true grit! Show me you grim determination! Show me you have the guts, and I'll show you glory! Show me that I'm wrong when I call you a bunch of yellow-bellied, faggot cowards!" Finn said as he cut and slashed the air with his dinner knife.

Raymond stopped with his fork half way up close to his mouth with some lettuce on it. "Who was that, sir?"

"Major Robert Rogers! Who in hell do you think I'm telling you about?" Finn snorted before emptying his whiskey tumbler.

Raymond began taking notes excitedly, his imagination painting vivid images in his head as old Finn continued to tell his story. The old man's voice sounded excited. Again, Raymond was mesmerized by the man's full-bloodied voice and felt like he was being drawn into a maelstrom and was whisked back across decades, back to the time when the events took place — in the old Fort Edward, New York.

§   §   §

Arriving in the Commanding Officer's residence, a very good example of the grandeur theme of Imperial glory, General Johnson walked through the front door and handed his quilted canvas jacket to the servant. He was dressed in an unusually striking, red uniform coat without any decorations. Behind him came Captain John Bradstreet of the provincial militia in a blue coat and Captain Robert Rogers in his green uniform with moccasins and rawhide leggings.

In the hallway, the two captains glanced around at the dazzling mansion. A large portrait of Lord Loudoun on the wall presented him as a young, dashing officer. Johnson turned to Rogers, and lowering his voice, he said, "I know of your sentiments toward the high command. Let me do the talking, Captain."

Johnson and Bradstreet handed their gear, muskets and sabers to the servants. One of the domestics extended his arm to Rogers to get his weapons, a musket and a cutlass (which he preferred in the close quarters of the thick forests instead of the standard issue sabre), but just one taciturn gaze from the captain sent a chill down the servant's back. The servant shivered, bowed, and hurried off as Rogers turned on his heels and cradled his musket on his left arm like a baby. He then followed the two other officers into the grand reception room.

Earlier that morning, Lord Loudoun woke up late in his grandiose, warm, comfortable bed and sneezed. He leaned on his side and let out an enormous fart. The Commander-in-Chief of the English forces in America, Lord Loudoun was a large and vainglorious man in a silk night gown, sighing in relief as he wobbled up from his grand four-poster bed, rubbing his hulking pot belly.

He motioned to an indentured servant, a young boy in a black uniform jacket and bright yellow coloring for the breeches and waistcoat, who stood by with a chamber pot in his hands. The lord lifted up his robe and filled the pot, spilling dark colored urine all over the boy's hands. *That fat bastard hasn't seen his tiny pecker in a decade, I bet,* the boy thought as he tried to hide his disgust and turned his head away.

A few weeks earlier, the young boy, twelve of age, had been robbed of his food on his way back home. He had then witnessed how his mother, who was trying to gather some meager pieces of bread and morsels tossed aside by the passing English soldiers, had been beaten with blows and kicks so hard that she fell head first into a puddle of muddy water. The boy was furious over the treatment of his mother by the brute soldiers. In anger, he picked up the first thing at hand for him on the ground, a pile of stinking horse manure, and hurled it at the soldiers. He was quickly apprehended and hit with musket stocks. The young man was strung up by his thumbs to a whipping post.

Just at that moment, Lord Loudoun happened to pass by, and he noticed the boy's youthful, fair complexion under a bruised and dirty face. He considered the boy for a moment (in fact he prized the boy's looks), and then gave his verdict: instead of flogging, the boy would serve as his indentured servant for a period of five years. The boy's mother watched in despair, completely helpless as her only son was led away, cuffed in chains. Loudoun's Chief of Staff ordered the boy to serve as the caretaker of his Lordship's waste, and that became his lot.

Loudoun's generous breakfast was served by two servants carrying plates and platters, which were full of enough food to provide for a large family. The chief servant reported to him the latest news.

"Sire, severe cold, summer frosts, drought, and famine have been reported in many parts of the colonies. An exceptionally remarkable meteorological situation has contributed to the scarcity of the maize. After an extraordinary drought, it was nipped by frost on the night of twenty-eighth, and the number of inhabitants carried off by this union of famine and disease throughout the colonies is estimated in thousands," the chief servant said, opening the curtains on the tall windows that overlooked a large, formal garden with water fountains and surrounded by tall, brick walls.

Another servant presented Loudoun with large plates of cold cuts, over-easy eggs, pastries, and tea. He sat down on a plush chair by the window, and the attendant placed the plates on a table next to him. The look on Loudoun's face was one of utter boredom and personally the incident did not affect him at all. Across a traditional, British garden that was in a rectilinear formal design, six well-nourished pedigree horses stood cared for by half a dozen workers at Loudoun's stables. The horses were led out for a morning walk, and the stablemen provided them fodder that was a rich blend of corn, barley, and wheat for breakfast. The horse's regular feed regimen was made of orchard grass and alfalfa hay. Most people in the colonies could only dream of such food.

Loudoun licked his fingers, syrupy from the delicacies, and toyed with the food on his plate while smacking his lips. "You know very well I do not want to hear any unpleasant news in the morning, Delbert," he said absentmindedly. He sneezed again and continued, "Particularly now since I have caught a cold, it seems. I have heard these rumors about starvation in the northern colonies. I don't see why. Judging by my own breakfast, there is plenty of food."

The servant knew it would be pointless to try to tell the lord any different, but he felt that he had to give it a try at least. "It is said that people have become scared of great mortality, pestilences, and hunger," he said, trying to sound convincing. "Wolves, ferocious beasts, and birds of prey appear in search of people to attack. Such has been the hunger that some people have been forced to sell themselves to indentured service in order to eat. Others have gone far into the hills trying to find places to plant. Certainly to resort to such measures, there is nothing to eat."

Loudoun stood up with a whopping, flavorful drumstick in his hand and looked out the window and off into the horizon. There was a scattering of dark clouds forming. "Well then, look Delbert. Things are looking better. See? It is going to rain soon," he said.

A servant came in to announce that General William Johnson, First Baronet and the British Superintendent for the northern colonies, had arrived for their morning meeting.

Lord Loudoun looked annoyed as he already guessed why the officers had arrived. He considered the provincials as a nuisance. Once again, they were going to request more troops for Fort Edward. Why didn't they just win the war as he had ordered them to do, instead of constantly whining and demanding for more men? And more importantly, why did they always want more expensive weapons and gunpowder?

Loudoun nodded a lukewarm welcome to Johnson who stepped forward from the doorway. He then noticed that Rogers was armed and raised his eyebrows. He was intimated by this rough looking, hardnosed pioneer. The actual basis was two-fold. First, he was petrified of weapons of all sorts. Second, he suspected (for a good reason) that there might be a conspiracy against him among the frontiersmen. Loudoun thought of them as devils who dwelled in the hills surrounding his residence and were covered in black roses and bloodied doves. Not only that, but surely they lived among wyverns that stalked the mountains. He had even heard firsthand accounts of a rabid deer feeding on the corpse of a slain huntsman.

"Why is this man armed?" Loudoun demanded with an unsteady voice.

"Sir, my musket goes where I go, and—" Rogers started to respond, but General Johnson gave him a stern look and cut him short with a wave of his hand.

"Sire, the French have offered a bounty on his head of 10,000 Livres in gold, dead or alive, and preferably impaled," Johnson said, giving Rogers a serious look to keep him quiet.

"Those cheap bastards could afford more," Rogers snorted, raising his chin.

"Furthermore, each ranger officer has 5,000 on his head, and even each and every Ranger's scalp is worth 1,000 Livres."

"Good. We must stand for something," Rogers said, and bit his lip as General Johnson raised his finger in a warning.

"Sir, I warned about Fort Oswego's vulnerability, but I have been all but ignored. Now our scouts report increasing French activity around Lake George. We have received numerous requests to send more troops to Fort Edward," Johnson said.

Loudoun remained silent for a moment, not knowing what to say. His mind raced in different directions. "But... but the main action is going to be in the Ohio Valley. That is the theater we have to focus on," he replied, and to the officers he seemed strangely absentminded. In fact, the gracious lord felt more gas building up in his stomach, and he squeezed his butt cheeks tightly together. He was not going to give these despicable provincial commoners the pleasure of humiliating himself in front of them.

Johnson remained steadfast in his position. "Sir, the reports are clear and numerous. General Webb insists more reinforcements are needed if he is to initiate a new campaign against Fort Carillon," he said.

Loudoun exhaled sharply. "General Webb should do what Webb does best and wait. It would be a reasonable expectation that this recently promoted officer would have some semblance of initiative, enough to at least find his own way to Fort Edward. But no, he stayed in New York for days on end and waited," he said annoyed.

Johnson motioned to Bradstreet to weigh in on the conversation.

"Sir, our long-term strategy is an attack against Crown Point and Fort Carillon. If Britain is to gain control of Lake George, a strike against the enemy fortresses on Lake Champlain is imperative," Bradstreet said.

"Yes, yes, yes. But wars are not won by rushing into things," Loudoun said, agitated. "I have it on my 'things to do' list. There are more pressing concerns, like politics, of which obviously you do not know, Captain. Fort Carillon can wait. We need a morale booster, and the military needs a face-lift. The provincials are to be incorporated into the regular units and position is to be subordinated to regular officers."

Bradstreet was taken totally by surprise. "But sir, these orders violate the very terms under which the militia has enlisted," he said.

Rogers started to say something, but an angry glance from Johnson silenced him.

Loudoun turned swiftly to face the two provincial officers. "Any resistance to my orders will be considered treasonous," he said, looking sternly at the two captains.

The three officers continued to present their arguments in a heated conversation. Loudoun felt he could not hold on any longer. The pressure in his belly was almost unbearable, and so he just wanted to get rid of the persistent officers, and finally he agreed to provide more troops. The three officers bowed and departed the room, leaving the Lord to his breakfast.

Once the doors were closed, they overheard Loudoun let off a colossal, roaring fart, sending the crystal chandelier tinkling on the hallway ceiling. Rogers chortled as he glanced at the other men. "We should have stayed a little while longer to witness his reaction."

Johnson turned to Rogers. "That was a valiant effort on your part, Captain. So far, the combination of General Webb, General Nanny Crombie, and Lord Loudoun, have managed to allow France mastery of the Ohio Valley and strengthen her lines of communication while at the same time they've lost a strategic fort and some of the best officers in the British army. Not to mention, they've alienated the provincials, sown the seeds for further discontent, and totally mismanaged Iroquois support. And they've done all this before a war has even begun," Johnson said, frustrated.

They went out to the court yard, and Bradstreet mounted his horse. "Sir, maybe even this cloud has its silver lining. I can only imagine what they might have accomplished if they had actually engaged the enemy. But they are, after all, the King's representatives in this forsaken country of ours," he said.

"You know why the King sends men like him over here? Ask yourself this: If you were the King, would you let his nasty ass in your fancy court?" Rogers said with a grin.

Johnson stepped into his private coach and leaned out

from the window. "This is His Majesty's domain and he rules as he pleases, and Lord Loudoun is his representative. At least we got him to send in a provincial regiment to Fort Edward. Get orders ready now. They are needed there as soon as possible."

Watching Johnson's coach depart, Rogers rubbed the stubbles on his chin. "To rule your own country... Now that's a thought," he said.

§   §   §

The farm, nestled under prominent, timeworn oaks and near a crystal-clear stream, was well kept. Inside the log building, Catherina Brett winced as she felt her tummy complain from hunger, and then sharp menstrual cramps hit her so hard that she felt nauseated. Irritated and exhausted, she could not decide which one was worse, and the indecisiveness maddened her even more.

She wore a short loose-fitting gown with a simple construction over her linen shift and pea-green skirt. A modest apron made of flax covered her jacket with only a few printed cotton cuffs as ornaments.

This morning she felt particularly stressed. She was not sure if she was more frustrated at using a piece of cheap Bohemian glass as a mirror or that she could not help thinking about that young, muscular blond man with his piercing blue eyes and long eyelashes. Every time he looked at her, she felt shamefully naked and yet strangely aroused. She bit her lip and made a center parting on her long, blonde hair. Completing the braids over the top of her head, she secured her hair with bobby pins made of bone and covered them with her unadorned cap.

Catherina worked the farm alone after her brother's death, disregarding the townspeople and neighboring farmers who pressured her to get properly married as any decent woman would. Scarcity of food made it difficult to feed her animals, and she was forced to add grounded bark from trees to flour and fodder in order to make them last longer. As she did, she was surprised to find that eating a certain birch bark actually made her feel a bit better.

She was feeding her cow one day when a man arrived on horseback. She thought she recognized him as he came closer, and it turned out that she did. It was James Robbie, a foreboding, wicked-looking man who wore a brown coat and had colored strings on the knees of his breeches a little above his dandy riding boots.

"I've come to buy your cow," he said.

"My cow is not for sale, Mister," she replied, still fixated on the man's odd strings about his legs. She then remembered seeing him around the fort at one time or another, and snapped her attention to the man as she recalled some of the rumors she had heard about him.

Robbie stared back at her for a moment, and then simply nodded and left without saying a word.

Catherine continued to tend to the farm and fixed a fence post. She attended to the animals, feeding the goose and the only piglet she had left out of half a dozen.

Hopping across the stream, she collected some more birch bark off the trees. She checked brushwood for any edible berries and also collected some blueberries and cowberries she found. She was then delighted to discover a bunch of chanterelle mushrooms with a fruity smell to add to her dinner. She enjoyed their mild, peppery taste and liked to sauté them in a pan with onions and cream.

Later that night, she returned to the cow shed to milk her only cow. To her shock, she discovered that the cow had disappeared. She searched everywhere, but could not find it. Devastated, she decided that the cow had to have been stolen.

Just then Finn arrived, smiling as usual, and took off his caubeen, revealing a short cut, dirty blonde hair that stuck up. He was unshaven and wore a green Ranger uniform jacket and fringed lace-up moccasins. He carried a Brown Bess musket and a worn, leather messenger bag slung over his back. Lifting his black leather strap that carried ammunition pouches, a tomahawk, and a dirk, he pretended that he just happened to be in the vicinity and decided to stop by for a visit. She rolled her eyes at his efforts to impress her and told him what had happened.

"Ma'am, that's so fucked up," he said. "How could anyone steal your cow? I will help you to get the animal back. What do you know about this Robbie character?"

"Not much, but I've heard some rumors about him. I only know that his farm is not far from here," she replied.

"Alright then, let's go and get your cow back. Don't worry. I know how to get into his place quietly, just like a recon into the enemy's camp. Trust me. I know what I'm doing. Just show me the way and let me handle the rest," he said as he urged her to follow him.

Catherina was skeptical and not entirely convinced about the plan, but she followed him anyway, eager to rescue her cow. She kept pointing the way to him as they took a short cut through magnificent pine trees. After they followed a slender back track across a clump of willows and hopped over a stream on a sequence of rocks, they arrived at the outskirts of Robbie's farm.

Stopping under a giant bird cherry tree, Finn took a knee and surveyed the farm. The sun set behind the trees, and darkness settled. He did not see anybody, and motioning her to stay close, he started his approach.

Once at the barn door, he carefully opened it, cringing as the hinges squeaked, and slipped inside. The air was thick, and it filled their nostrils with the noxious stench of manure wafting from the back. Catherina got excited as they found her cow tied and chained to the wall behind large, empty wooden boxes. Finn hushed her and started to untie the cow.

All of a sudden, the doors were pulled wide open-catching them by surprise and in a stream of light. Sheriff Jimmie Dick marched in with two deputies who held their lanterns. He was clearly drunk and held an open whiskey flask in his hand.

James Robbie, that scrofulous fox of a man, had been expecting all along that Catherina might try to get her cow back, and after a quick consultation with the sheriff, had arranged a stake out. Unknown even to him, though, was that the sheriff was in cohorts with the callous Hessian mercenary, Johan Kopf, also known as Totenkopf for the skull and crossbones emblem on his mirliton cap.

Kopf was assigned to the British general staff in North America to conduct covert operations, which usually meant dealing with the provincials by any and all means necessary. His and Finn's paths had crossed in the most unpleasant circumstances, each time forging a bitter resentment between them. As far as Kopf was concerned, it was all Finn's fault that he had been deprived of a career in civilized Europe and that he was sent to this cast off country. Now, upon hearing about this unexpected opportunity, Kopf immediately saw it as a scheme to get Finn away from the Rangers — his newly found band of brothers whose loyalty to each other was well known. Once in a stockade, who was to know when Finn would fall easy prey to twelve inches of dagger into his belly.

Catherina was wary of the sheriff because the townspeople said he was a raving lunatic. The old gunman was a well-known drunkard, and rumors were that he was, in fact, an opium addict as well. It was said that he frequented the opium dens in Albany because he persistently suffered from a gunshot wound to his ass cheek from a duel.

"Ha! The tip we received was spot-on! We caught you scoundrels red handed, attempting to steal Mr. Robbie's cow! Take these nasty thieves and throw them in jail!" Jimmie Dick said jubilantly and took a long drink from his flask.

Losing his temper, Finn clenched his fists and was just about to jump on the Sheriff when one of the deputies shoved the barrel of a musket in his face. Baring a row of rotten teeth, the deputy grabbed hold of Finn by the collar and pushed him roughly out of the door.

"Yes, it's stolen alright... stolen from me!" Catherina started, but she was cut off as the deputy slammed her hard against the wall and then took her crudely by the arm and pushed her out. The deputy tried to fondle her, but she managed to push his hand away. Finn took a step forward to help her, but the other deputy stopped him at gunpoint.

"Shut up both of you. I don't want to get a peep out of either one of you," Dick said between hiccups. He took a swig again from his worn, leather-covered flask and staggered. Finn and Catherina were bound to an old hay wagon with the cow tied up behind it and were led on the road toward Fort Edward. In his depraved mind, Dick already counted the money he was going to receive as a reward.

As they left the farm, hidden behind a dense willow thicket, two shadowy figures watched them leave. One of them wore a green uniform coat of the Hessian jaegers. Watching the event unfold according to his plan, Johan Kopf felt triumphant. He actually enjoyed playing a little game of cat and mouse.

Finn and Catherina were dragged through the gates at Fort Edward just as powerful, rolling thunder boomed and scaring the daylight out of the deputies. Dark clouds loomed over the palisades surrounding the fort, and a row of gleaming bayonets of the guards on top caught the last faint sunlight. The sheriff's office was located in a crude log building that doubled as town hall of sorts. It had window sills and a painted green front door. Animal skulls, antlers, and snakeskins hung from the eaves.

Finn and Catherina protested furiously as they were thrown into the jail in the back of the sheriff's office, and the man slammed the metal door shut with a loud clang. Grabbing the bars, Finn's lips pursed as he saw the deputy's face up close, and he recognized the man. He was the same young cretin he had seen on the road when the wagon train had been ambushed and Kopf executed a French prisoner.

The imbecile grinned at him, revealing dark, creamy teeth in shriveled gums.

Dick slouched behind his desk. "Judge Lynch will be taking care of you two in a due manner when he is in town next time," he said, before rummaging through the desk drawers for another bottle.

Finn was fuming, pacing back and forth like a caged animal. Feeling insecure deep inside, he fumbled absently with the moose-head locket around his neck. Catherina watched him anxiously, feeling guilty for getting them into trouble. She did not understand why he was so irritated, but she was afraid to ask what was wrong. Finn appeared to be angry at her for some reason, probably because he was now in jail for helping her out, she guessed.

"So, where do you come from? You have an accent," she asked softly, wanting to ease up the tension between them.

He stopped pacing and looked out of the small window with bars in it that sat high on the back wall. Outside, it started to rain, and lightning flashed. The thunder storm grew louder, rumbling like cannon fire.

"Finland," he said as heavy rain poured down and wind blew water on his face through the cell's open window.

She liked his accent and responded eagerly. "Oh, Finlay. Where is that? I keep dreaming about traveling to see new, strange places at least once in my life," she said, dreamily wrapping her arms around her for warmth. "I have heard stories about the monumental water falls to the west. I heard someone say that the man who discovered them, Peter Kalm, was from some place called Finland.

Maybe you know him? Anyway, Daniel says that the Niagagarega also talk about this sacred place," she said.

Finn frowned. "Not Finlay, I said Finland. Anyways, all this will be sorted out as soon as they see the branding on your cow," Finn replied, pounding his fist against the wall and wincing slightly. He was worried what would happen when his commander, Captain Rogers heard of his arrest. "Hey Sheriff! Check the stupid brand!" he shouted.

Catherina grimaced and looked away, biting her lip. "There is no branding—" Her voice faltered.

Finn spun around to face her "What? The cow is not branded?" he said. "But people around here know you, don't they? They'd testify that it's your cow, right?"

"I forgot all about it. I mean it's not a big deal, not around here you know," she said looking back apologetically.

"You forgot about it? And now I'm in jail because you forgot about it," Finn said, his face blanching.

Catherina's eyes flared, and she straightened her back and lifted her chin. "How dare you accuse me. It was your brilliant idea to recon his farm. Yeah, right. Recon my arse," she replied as she folded her arms.

Hearing her words, Finn's eyes lit up as if he just heard a great idea, and he grinned. He was about to retort, but she realized that he had misunderstood her (intentionally too, most likely), and pointed her finger at him with a look of don't-you-even-dare-say it.

They were interrupted as the tomfool deputy opened the door. He came in holding a massive skeleton key that hung from a rattling, heavy chain. They saw through the open door that the sheriff was passed out behind his desk in a wooden chair, feet on the table and snoring. "Your neighbors have corroborated your claim, Miss Brett. While the sheriff is taking his usual nap, I think it's only fair that you are free to leave," the deputy said.

Without saying a word, Catherina barged out, presumably to find her cow and return home. Finn, who had to stay and write a release paper, soon came running after. He caught up with her as she was trying to pull her cow on the muddy road in a pouring rain.

"Stop being mad at me, will you? I'm the one who is supposed to be mad. Besides, it's only a cow. People are starving, and you could take many steaks out of her," Finn said as the rain soaked him to the bone.

Catherina stopped on her tracks in the middle of the road. She was enclosed by the rainy spray, standing drenched in a puddle of muddy water. She looked furiously at Finn, clenching her fists.

"It is not just any cow. It's my cow. It is my only cow. She gives me cream and milk to churn into butter that I can trade in the market. What a nitwit you are. Didn't they teach you anything in Flintland or where ever you came from?"

"Never mind, crazy woman. Let's just get this old cow back," Finn said, shrugging his shoulders.

"She's not old," she retorted, stomping her foot in a puddle.

"Call it what you like," Finn replied. He moved behind the cow and started to give it a push as she pulled it by the leash. Unfortunately, Lady Fortuna was not kind to him, and he slipped on the wet ruts and fell face down in the reeking sludge. Catherina gaped at the sight of him stretched out in the muck, and then she let out a sidesplitting laugh.

§   §   §

In Fort Edward, a cold wind blew, dusting leaves across iced fields as Finn rushed through the gate. He jumped over piles of droppings and dodged a bucket full of human waste somebody had tossed out a window and onto the street. He crossed the bridge at the back gate by the river, and he was still fuming when he arrived on Rogers Island. He met Fronto, Gus, and Daniel at their bunkhouse made of timbers. The logs had filling between the chinks and gaps in an attempt to insulate the building.

Gus sat on the steps outside the hut and rubbed his short black hair, which had a lot of natural curl and body. It was closely cropped, forming lightning patterns on the side. He was enjoying smoking a long, clay pipe carved from meerschaum that was shaped in the form of an elderly black man's head, a shaman or a king. As Finn walked by, his clothes sloshing and foul, Gus waved his hand in front of his nose and pointed at a watering trough. "Look at you. You need a bath."

Finn tossed his gear on a bunk bed. "No. I need a stiff drink. That crazy woman and her crazy cow drive me nuts. We're starving, and all she cares about is her stinking cow. You know, I could really sink my teeth into a nice, thick, juicy steak. But no thanks to that pig-headed woman," he replied, tearing open his rucksack to get his last bit of beef jerky and stuffing it in his mouth all at once.

Fronto, Gus, and Daniel, trying not to laugh out loud,

glanced at each other. Finn glared back at them and felt like the odd-one-out in his circle of friends. Olaudah "Gus" Equiano was a former slave. Daniel was the Wappinger Chief, and Fronto was an outlandish wanderer. Finn realized that these three outcasts were not only his brothers-in-arms and friends, but his only family. In this hut with them, he felt safe and his anger mellowed out.

Daniel wiped clean his decorated, multi-notched war club. His tattooed and war-painted face was gleaming, but he pretended to be serious. "Young chief, I'd rather be a crazy, wild man rather than under a squaw's moccasin. But maybe you'd like to buy a pair from me to wear when you visit her?" he said, smirking.

Fronto, wearing a necklet made of beads, clam shells, and coins around his neck, was cleaning his musket meticulously while he sat on the bunk next to Finn's. He was amused, and as he leaned closer, he narrowed his eyes at Finn. "Temperance, whippersnapper. You shouldn't be so quick to jump to conclusions. She may be right, you know. Slay the cow now to get your steak one time, but there would be no more cow, steaks, milk, or butter," Fronto said.

Finn looked back at Fronto and noted his steady features and weather-beaten skin with a short stubby grayish beard, which he had not noticed before.

Finn dismissed the others by waving his hand and jumped up to clean himself at the trough. While they were talking, a troubled couple arrived, dressed in worn out work clothes. They started telling them that more items, trapping gear, and hunting supplies had been stolen in the fort and the surrounding farms.

"Where's the sheriff? You should talk to him about it," Fronto asked.

The woman, who had a gaunt face and troubled eyes, made a drinking motion with her hand. "Snoozing, as is typical this time of the day. He doesn't care at all," she said.

The man stepped closer. "Something strange is happening," he said. He fearfully glanced over his bony shoulders and lowered his voice to a whisper. "I saw a black figure place something in a hole on the side of an oak tree."

Finn turned around, his hair dripping wet. "Show us where this happened," he said.

The woman led them toward the site. As they traveled through the fort, other townspeople, curious to see what was happening, followed.

They crossed some meadows and clumps of aspens. After a couple of miles, the woman stopped. She hesitated and looked scared. The woman pointed out an oak tree with her a raw-boned finger.

Finn cautiously approached the tree, and he saw a gaping black hole on the face of it. He rolled up his sleeve and reached inside.

The old, towering oak was not just any tree. Many superstitious beliefs remained among the people of who, or what, dwelled in the pits of its many cavities. The townspeople gasped at his daring move and backed away. Finn pulled out a bottle with a string tied around it. Opening the bottle's sealed lid, he discovered a map of Fort Edward and the surrounding countryside inside, complete with notes and avenues of approach that an advancing force might use.

Fronto took the bottle and inspected it but could not

read the worn out label on it. The dark brown bottle was old, scratched, and covered in mold. The cork had a noose in it to carry the note and a thick layer of wax to seal the bottle. "Catherina was right. Do you remember her talking about this?" he said.

"Could it be that we're afflicted by a thief and a spy at the same time?" Finn asked, looking at the map.

"It's probably not just one and the same individual, but different people doing their dirty work to bring about our demise. We've found their drop off point. The spy has left his findings for someone else to pick up and will obviously receive further instructions in return. But the whole town knows about this place now. No way would a spy use it again, knowing he has been compromised," Gus said.

"Spies don't work alone, ever. They report back to their master, whoever it is in this case. I must get this to Captain Rogers," Finn said. He took the map and the bottle, and they returned to the fort with a long line of distressed townspeople trailing behind them.

Once they arrived back on Rogers Island, Finn rushed to the command post to report the map. Robert Rogers inspected the items closely and decided he had to take them to the commanding general for further analysis. He slapped Finn on the shoulder in praise and commended him for a job well done. Rogers placed the items in a brown leather messenger bag, which he slung over his shoulder. Grabbing a musket that leaned against the wall, he headed out to the headquarters.

Finn appreciated praise for his work because it made him feel being accepted and worthy, but as he stepped out in high spirits to tell his friends about it, he noticed that

Fronto had become detached and had wandered off. Later, Finn found him leaning on the bar in the Silver Star tavern with a set-apart look on his face.

Finn felt sorry for him and wanted to cheer him up. He had always wanted to ask Fronto about his tattoo depicting a stork and some strange looking letters on his arm, but the look on Fronto's face seemed unpleasantly familiar. Finn was all too acquainted with loneliness, and he made a mental note that he must write to Rosie. By now she must be worried sick over what had happened to him, but right now, this eccentric old man needed his help.

"Hey Dog, what is it that troubles you?" Finn asked.

"Memories." Fronto answered, absent minded as he toyed with his tumbler filled to the brim with golden whiskey. He pinched and pulled the tiny hairs from his earholes. "Where are the seats at the feast?"

"You talk strange again, old man," Finn said and motioned Mary Brant to bring him a drink as well. "But tell me about these memories."

Fronto let out a sigh. "If you must know, there was a time when I was in the company of a priest named Giles and a girl named Isabel. Turning a street corner, we ran into a nasty surprise, an ambush. She turned out to be a spy for my enemy, one Thomas Hardy, a master of false-hearted arts, who was with a priest, Philip Sherman. She had sold me out for a few lousy nickels. A scuffle broke out, dirks were drawn, and Hardin, who was threatening and attacking me, drew the first blood, but I got him with a dirk-thrust in return and also a strong blow with a stone, which struck him down dead," he said.

"Sorry to hear, my friend, but anyways, we all have awful memories." Finn said, and downed his drink. "I know I do."

"Tell me, whippersnapper, what have you learned from them? Nothing it seems. But I tell you this: a silver skull watch tells you the minutes. They all hurt, and the last one kills."

Taking a look at his companion, Finn got an impression of an older man who seemed to be a stranger in a world where others saw him to be one as well. Just then his mother's advice flashed through his mind. *When an older man offers his advice you must listen to him.* Finn felt a surge of kinship to this odd wanderer and slapped him on the shoulder. "Dog, as far as I'm concerned, your skull could be made of silver. Now snap out of it. We want you. Let's go," Finn finished the drink, tossed a couple of coins to Mary Brant, and urged Fronto to follow him outside.

Outside, they met disturbed townspeople who had gathered in the square. Standing on some wooden crates, Robert Rogers addressed the people as he held up the map and the bottle in his hand. "Stay calm, but be vigilant. More than likely, the spy has already packed and is running with his tail between legs, but you should report any suspicious activity immediately to me. We will have roaming guards to keep everybody safe. We'll find that groveling, no-good son-of-a-bitch and put an end to him," he said. Stepping down, he summoned the officers and ordered Ranger patrols out to search the surrounding areas.

§ § §

Throughout the following weeks, there was a flurry of activity on Rogers Island. Work parties and the Rangers expanded the existing buildings and erected new ones in the camp. In the evenings Finn was dog tired, but he managed to write a letter to Rosie, his hands shaking from excitement and exhaustion. He explained what had happened since he was seized by the press gang in Bristol. Wanting to spare her and to avoid making her even more worried, he did not mention the goriest details of his exploits.

More supplies had been brought in the canteen, and the supply sergeant handed out gear and equipment. Weapons were issued from the armory, and Robert Rogers walked around, highly motivated, barking orders. His younger brother Richard, always so vigorous and athletic, had just arrived back from Massachusetts with a line of nervous recruits following him.

"Richard! Can you see what all this means, brother? We're getting stronger. We're going to be the most powerful, new fighting force in the world, and you'll be one of my captains, I promise you that," Roberts said. "I want to raise even more companies, and then we'll bring James and Tiny back to join us for the new campaigns. By the way, have you heard any news of them from Mountalona?"

"Yes, I see what you mean," Richard replied as he looked around the camp and slapped his older brother on the shoulder. "The boys are doing great, helping Mom and Pa run the farm. But they can't wait to join us. And Bill and John Stark are as excited as we are."

Robert turned serious and lowered his voice. "I must tell you, we're in pretty poor shape right now, and we're short on supplies. The French are planning something disgraceful — that is certain. But they're just as much affected by this dreadful weather as we are," he said.

On the training field, new privates were surrounded by stone-faced Ranger sergeants. The privates trembled, anxiously waiting what would happen next. Tension mounted as Lieutenant Moses Hazen marched in front of the formation. He was a tough looking man with pocked marked and scarred face, and his reputation for cold-bloodedness preceded him. The privates were certain they were done in.

Hazen spat tobacco on the ground. "All I see is raw meat. Cannon fodder at best. Stand straight, you sorry-ass yellow-belly slimes of the earth! My commander has forsaken me and given me the responsibility to try and make fighting men out of the lot of you. Now I look at you and see this business is impossible. I've never seen such a sad bunch of maggots in my life," he said.

Robert Rogers pointed out to some large timbers hanging from the trees by chains. "Start them on the tomahawks first."

Training started immediately, and the new recruits practiced close quarter fighting with tomahawks. The Ranger officer swung the logs, first slowly, and showed the privates how to move around them and hit the logs with their tomahawks, using a combinations of high and low blows. They learned how to block and tackle the tough logs with their shoulders, and finished the job with a double blow to the front and back. Working in pairs, Ranger privates learned quickly to form a line of scrimmage and strike the log from two sides at the same time. As their skills improved, the speed of the swinging logs was increased.

Robert Rogers loathed staying in the office doing paper work or running from one staff meeting to another. He preferred to be where the action was, training with his men in the field. "Remember men, dance, wrestle, and strike, all in one swift motion! Let 'em have it! That's the way to do it! That's how you'll survive and can return to your Molly's chamber at night!" he said.

Then the recruits were taken to the firing range few hundred yards outside the gates. Lieutenant Donald Mac-Curdy addressed the new privates who were preparing for target practice.

"I can't repeat this enough: Discipline, men. Discipline is the key word. In the heat of battle, the winners are the ones most disciplined. Well-aimed shots. Forget fancy stuff. Center mass. Aim at his belt buckle, hold your breath and pull the trigger. Then, learn to reload before his dead body hits the ground and his buddy takes his place in line so you'll be ready to take him down, too." Donald Mac-Curdy barked, marching back and forth.

With all the new arrivals, Robert Rogers decided to re-organize his expanding command. He always felt cramped inside any building, and therefore, he had his desk brought outside. "Officers, gather around. There are now enough Rangers to create more than one company. Our Mohawk allies included, I have decided to construct three new companies," he said.

The Rangers were reorganized so that the A Company was commanded by Robert Rogers with 1st Lieutenant John Stark, 2nd Lieutenant John MacCurdy, and Ensign Jonathan Burbank. Finn, Gus, Fronto and Daniel, found themselves in the headquarters section and became responsible for scouting, communications, and security details.

The new B Company was commanded by Captain Richard Rogers with 1st Lieutenant Noah Johnson, Ensign Nathaniel Abbot, and Ensign Caleb Page.

The company of Mohawks was commanded by Captain Jacob, who was dressed in tanned leather breaches and a green military coat. The Mohawk warriors, with war paint on their faces, stood in line behind him as Daniel greeted them and turned to Captain Jacob.

"Captain Jacob, too many Iroquois brothers have joined the French ranks, and it makes me proud to see you and your brethren joining us in this fight. The problem is, they are not accustomed to a white man's disciplined way of parades and drills," Daniel said.

Captain Jacob sharpened his tomahawk and wiped it clean with a piece of cloth. "It is a sad day when the mighty Iroquois nation cannot find a common cause. The French and the English both treat us like scum, but we can't stay out of the fight. Friends of my enemy are my enemies, and I shall eat their hearts. We're free men and warriors, and we have chosen to be with Captain Rogers because he knows how to fight like us. We will count many victories and take many scalps."

The guards on the main gate shouted that marching troops approached the fort. Soldiers appeared from the woods, marching on the dusty road and following wagons to their bivouac site outside the gate. Captain Israel Putnam, eager to find adventure, arrived in front of his Connecticut Provincials, dressed in blue uniforms with red facings and leggings.

Israel Putnam, with his rugged, blue-eyed and wholesome looks, was flamboyant and famous for his reckless courage and fighting spirit, and he was well aware of it. "Here are the boys with the mighty uppercut from Connecticut," he said in a loud voice that sounded across the fort.

Robert Rogers heard the commotion and rushed out to meet with Putnam. "I'm glad to see you, Captain Putnam, you bad ass, gun-toting, mountain-climbing, fast-marching, knife-wielding, ass-kicking, name-taking grunt!"

"Good to be here, Captain! Splendid little war you've got. I've heard terrific news about you. They say that you can present us with some lovely action against the French."

Grinning from ear to ear, Rogers was excited to see his old friend from the eastern provinces and led him to his command post. He pulled out a bottle of whiskey and two glasses, along with some tobacco, clay pipes and a few maps. The two men spent time in reminiscence of good old times, in the scouting companies back in 1746, guarding New England frontier. Then they started planning how to deploy their troops for the forthcoming operations.

Later in the evening, Robert Rogers, tipsy from his organizational session with Putnam, came out to address the Rangers who were cleaning weapons and equipment in front of their bunk houses. He looked at the men approvingly as they gathered around him. The tools of the soldiers' foreboding trade, muskets, cutlasses, daggers, tomahawks and gear, were clean and oiled, ready for action in a moment's notice. He thought, *This is the most unforgiving, ruthless bunch of mother-fucking, steely-eyed destroyers of French dreams I have ever seen.* However, well-hidden inside, he had a gnawing anxiety that the events of the previous action on snowshoes might repeat themselves.

Pushing his dreads aside, Rogers nodded in satisfaction and took pleasure at the opportunity to speak. "Men, war isn't a picnic, poem, pretty painting, or piece of fancy embroidery," Rogers said. "War cannot be advanced kindly with a velvet glove, or care, consideration, respect, politeness, or modesty. War is an insurrection — an act of violence by which one army defeats another. In war, your mission is to let the other side die for his cause so that you can go home to a warm bed to be hugged by your woman." As he continued, his voice rose, "The pathetic French don't have what it takes to win this war. We shall crush them because we love to fight! We, the Rangers, thrive on the sting of battle!"

§   §   §

The French stronghold, Fort Carillon, was perched on a commanding position on Lake Champlain and surrounded by water on three sides. It was strongly fortified by high battlements and bastions made of ashlar. Over the turrets, eight colorful regimental flags flapped in the breeze. In the center was the colonel's standard, an all-white *drapeau blanc*, that had a large, white cross stitched upon it and three large, golden fleur-de-lis, surrounded by unique *d'ordonnance* colors, each representing the king's sovereign authority vested in the commander of the regiment. In the inner ward, young drummer boys wearing the Royal Livery, a blue coat lined red and with red cuffs and a waistcoat laced with golden braid, beat cadence for the soldiers in parade drills.

In the oriel room on the top floor of the keep, General

Louis-Joseph De Montcalm pranced around in his gray-white uniform that was laced blue and gold. He had inspected the gate house and the defensive works in preparation for his attack on Hudson Valley and found them to be in excellent condition.

General Montcalm turned to his *aide-de-camp*, Captain Bougainville. "*Le mieux est l'ennemi du bien,*" he said, taking off his black tricorn laced gold with a black cockade. "Better is the enemy of good, and we are the best! I'm ready to deal with the English station at the far end of the lake since it provides the English a launching point for attacks against us. But before we dedicate our forces against the pathetic English fort, we must know more about the disposition of enemy forces."

General Montcalm was a controversial man among his officers and troops. When he was still young, on the death of his father, he became the Marquis de Saint-Veran, inheriting the honors, rights — and debts — of the title. His precarious financial situation improved soon after by his marriage to Angelique Louise Talon du Boulay. According to persistent rumors, eventually they became a loving couple despite a marriage arranged only for wealth and power.

Bougainville was not certain of his commander's abilities. He knew that Montcalm entered the army at the age of nine. He received an excellent, private education and served with distinction ever since. As far as Bougainville was concerned, the general's capabilities as military leader in all affairs regarding the war and the administration of his men remained to be seen.

After his father had purchased a captaincy for him, Montcalm saw action in several campaigns in Poland and

Austria before being captured in Italy. After being released, he was wounded in action. He received several medals for valor, and to his utter surprise, he was transferred to New France as the head of French troops in North America.

Montcalm paused for a moment to think. "*Sacrebleu!* Is it possible for the Canadians to be more pathetic than the English? I was sent to this shithole of a country because I botched court politics. It is a dirty castigation for something I did not make. But I'm a professional soldier, and I intend to carry out my mission and charge for the King to the best of my abilities. I will not let anyone stand on my way. No one, not a single petty Canadian or English dog will stop me."

Ever since his arrival in Nouvelle-France, Montcalm clashed with the governor, the Marquis de Vaudreuil who constantly complained about the lack of support in terms of staffs and provisions from France. Besides, Montcalm insisted on the European form of fighting while the governor favored hit-and-run stratagems that worked well in the vast Canadian wilderness.

Montcalm dismissed the Canadian's penchant for guerrilla tactics. He developed open hostility to Vaudreuil and labeled the entire administration corrupt. His dispatches to France showed exaggeration of his own efforts to the best result and were damaging of Vaudreuil.

Captain Bougainville did not say anything but handed some papers to the general. "*Alors*, I have four thousand men, but I don't know enough about the English forces. I'm tempted to surprise them and use it to my advantage," Montcalm said, reading the lists.

Bougainville counted the troop roster. "Sire, we have

been able to procure close to two thousand warriors from different tribes. *Parbleu*, together with the marines and other support troops, the full force we have amounts to eight thousand men," he said.

A spy came in, dressed in a long, black cloak over his disguise and handed the General a green bottle with a cord wrapped around it. Montcalm pulled out the wax covered cork, opened the bottle, and drew out a rolled-up piece of parched paper with blackened edges. He rubbed his chin as he read the secret message.

"*D'accord*, this is interesting. This intelligence says the English goal is probably Louisburg. The enemy's troop levels might now make an attack on the English fort feasible," Montcalm said in contemplation.

"Sir, this notion is reinforced by the questioning of deserters and captives taken during scouting and raiding expeditions," Bougainville replied.

Suddenly, musket fire rang out from the camp, just outside the fort, and the two officers jumped. An Abenaki warrior shot and wounded a militia prisoner trying to run away. The man collapsed on the beach at the water's edge. He was immediately seized by the Abenaki warriors.

The French officers stopped the warriors from making the prisoner run a gauntlet, but they had difficulties controlling the warriors from fighting over the prisoner's uniform jacket. There was not enough loot for everyone.

A group of old Abenaki, Mi'kmaq, Ojibwa, Ottawa and Caughnawaga Mohawk chiefs sat down in a semi-circle and smoked their pipes. General Montcalm watched young warriors who were praying, dancing, and chanting around a fire. The prisoner, kicking and screaming, was dragged and tied to a stake. General Montcalm, indifferent, turned and walked away. "*Je suis baba*, I need to relieve myself," he said over his shoulder, unbuttoning his pants.

At the river's edge, warriors' shrilling howls and blood thirsty war cries were mixed with the agonized screams of the prisoner. The French leaned back in horror as the most harrowing scene, straight from the depths of hell, was revealed in front of their eyes. Wyandot warriors burned the prisoner with hatchet blades heated in a fire. Lenape warriors hit him with a ceremonial club and pulled out his fingernails. Two Ottawa warriors removed prisoner's skin at the wrists and ankles. An Abenaki warrior slashed the prisoner's throat and collected the warm, gushing blood to drink it. A Shawnee warrior slashed the prisoner's stomach open, right below the rib cage, and a Mi'kmaq warrior pulled his heart out to eat it. The prisoner's body was butchered with knives while the warriors hunkered down in a circle around it and yelled out their horrendous calls.

A horrified, young French lieutenant witnessed the brutality. "*Grâce à Dieu!* We must stop them!"

Bougainville turned look away, feeling ill. "*Ètonne!* Repulsive behavior, but I'm afraid that any attempts to curb this act would result in the loss of some of these warriors. We cannot afford it. We want them against those cursed Rangers," he replied, tasting a rancid vomit in his mouth and barely able to hold off throw up.

Montcalm returned, and with contempt, he watched the warriors engage in a frenzied, horrid dance. "*Tant pis*, harden your mind and drive all doubt aside. We shall move out. We shall prove the world the power of the French regulars. Since we do not have enough boats for the whole force, the advance guard shall leave a day earlier and move over land along the western shore. I shall sail the next day with the remaining force, and we will rendezvous five leagues from our objective. When you get there wait for further instructions," he said.

Hidden from the French only a hundred feet away and camouflaged by shrubbery, the Rangers in green coats and buckskins blended in chokeberries and dogwood. The patrol was led by Donald MacCurdy and Moses Hazen, who used telescopes to observe the French camp and the inhuman slaying of the prisoner. Remaining expressionless, MacCurdy gave hand signals for men to pull back. Not a blade of grass moved as the Rangers slid off.

§   §   §

In Fort Edward, some time had passed without any action, and the guard detail on the palisades by the gate leaned lazily on the logs. Two guards were smoking pipes while the third man walked to the side to take a leak. All of a sudden, he stopped and started whooping and hollering, pointing to the road ahead. Alarmed, the two guards jumped on their feet and quickly grabbing their worn-out muskets rushed to get a better look. They saw a series of colorful wagons in red, white, and blue and adorned with golden ornamental lettering on the side. The procession of wagons appeared one by one from the woods on the road to the fort. The wagons were driven by women with a few men riding shotgun.

Under the guard's watchful eyes, the wagon train pulled up to the field next to the gates and formed a square. The lead wagon facing the gates had high, red and golden letters painted on the side that proudly presented *The Best Traveling Candy Box in America*. Helen of Magdalena and her entourage had arrived in Fort Edward.

The women, dressed in chemise, girdles, and push-up corsets, climbed down to stretch (and to promote their merchandise) after a long journey, and the men started building camp and setting up rocks in a circle for a fire pit. Once that was complete, they placed steel rods over the fire for cooking. Side openings on one of the wagons were propped up and a large, flat board was positioned to serve as a bar on the windowsill while a few log benches and rough tables were brought outside. The burly bouncers armed themselves with truncheons under their belts, and thus, as a sign of proper American ingenuity, the whore house was open for business within minutes of their arrival to the frontlines.

On Rogers Island, General Johnson discussed the situation and upcoming missions with Robert Rogers and other the officers in the command post. They were interrupted upon hearing the commotion outside. Robert Rogers opened the door and asked what the hell was going on. A junior Ranger ran by, who was counting his coins and blushing with pleasure, replied that a convoy of whores had arrived and had set camp right outside the gate.

Rogers turned back in. "Great. This is all we need. More whores!" he said. Johnson jumped up from his chair and hurried to the window.

Rogers coughed to get the General's attention. "Ahem, sir. Where were we? Oh yes, as I was saying, now we find ourselves again, challenged by our perennial enemy, to protect what is rightfully ours," he said.

Johnson wiped the window clean with his sleeve to get a clear view. "Captain, we shall leave no doubt as to our supremacy in the area. We shall do whatever it takes to enforce that," he said.

Rogers waited until they were alone and turned to Johnson. He lowered his voice. "Sir, I heard that the Mohawk call you *Waraghiyaghey*, which means Big Business. Once we have settled this matter with the French, sir, I'd like to discuss some darned attractive property investments with you. My bet is that vast tracks of land will become available in these parts, and a gentleman such as you would do wisely to seize the opportunity," he said, almost whispering.

Johnson started to respond, but he was interrupted by the guard. Rangers Donald MacCurdy and Moses Hazen had returned from patrol and were removing the remnants of their camouflage made of common ninebark. They reported directly to Rogers. "Sir, Colonel Parker has lost approximately two hundred and fifty men, with nearly one hundred and sixty men killed or drowned. The rest were taken prisoner at the Sabbath Day Point," MacCurdy said.

"What happened to the Colonel?" Rogers asked.

"He was lucky to escape the onslaught and led what was left of his men back to Fort William Henry," Hazen said, spitting out some dirt.

"We followed them from a distance when the French and the Abenaki loaded their prisoners and plunder into boats and headed north. Along the way, they sang songs and indulged on the rum taken from our men. Once back at Fort Carillon, the savages, drunk on rum, tortured, boiled, and ate one unlucky prisoner," MacCurdy said.

"Young warriors do that sometimes when they're getting ready for war. The spirit is called *Aireskoi*, the most powerful of the guardian spirits for young men training to be warriors," Rogers said.

"It was disgusting! Those savages! There is only one way to deal with them. Kill them all." MacCurdy was still disgusted by what he saw.

"That's why surrender is not a Ranger word. I'd strongly recommend that you do not get caught alive," Rogers said, pounding his left palm with his right fist.

Johnson shuddered at the thought of being captured and placed a small tin can containing a pre-measured paper packet of black powder and a single round of ball ammunition in his breast pocket. It was to be used for a last quick reloading, if required. "Our resolve will not be deterred by the enemy who enjoys such demonic things. They will not catch my soul," he said.

"The French are bound to try to capitalize on their victory and drive forces south from Carillon. I'd send two units actually, one naval force on Lake George and another chopping through the dense forest on the west side of the lake, if I was in their shoes. With their recent success at Sabbath Day Point, they probably expect little to no opposition from us. Clearly, their objective is going to be Fort William Henry. Gentlemen, prepare for battle," Rogers said.

"Yes sir," MacCurdy replied, and pulled out the hunting knife he carried inside a raw hide legging and a sharpening stone from his pocket.

§ § §

In Albany, above the Chinese opium den in an alley behind the *Stadt Huys* town house, Johan Kopf woke up in a Tudor style, full tester bed. His three day furlough was over too soon. He tasted the hard, sour aroma of rum in his mouth, and he still felt drowsy from the nights before. He shook his head to clear it, but the past two days remained a blur after prodigious quantities of booze, absinthe, and opium. Lifting the covers, he discovered two naked Chinese whores snoring beside him. *Not too shabby,* he thought. *It seems like I had fun. I wish I could remember it.*

Glancing at the women's small, youthful bodies, round butts, and perky breasts, Kopf was tempted to continue his wild escapade. He then collected himself, deciding that duty called first and fun had to be second.

Kopf forced himself up. Steadying himself naked, he wobbled over to an old wash basin with a porcelain enamel water pitcher. He leaned on the counter under a large, ornate mirror with a gilded frame and a black glaze. He smiled and winked at his own reflection in the mirror, rubbing his strong, dimpled jaw. The ladies were attracted to his exceptionally handsome looks, and given an opportunity, they also felt that he was particularly well-endowed, too.

After washing and shaving, he took a small bottle labeled *Kölnisch Wasser* and splashed it on his face and breathed out with joy at the bite on his skin. He took a dump in a chamber pot in the corner. All the while, sneezing, coughing, and fanning his face with his hand because his creation stank so badly. He started to feel much better as he put on his shirt and buttoned his green jaeger uniform coat. He prepared a spoonful of absinthe by placing a brown sugar cube on it and pouring a generous amount of green liquid on top.

Kopf told himself again that he must write a letter to his mother and detail all of the fabulous opportunities he had discovered on the new continent. He then noticed a worn out picture lying on the table and picked it up. It was a study of the Order of the Black Eagle, the highest honor a Hessian could win on the battlefield. It was not just a medal to him as it would mean a title, fame, and noble status, as well.

He admired it for a long time, softly following the edges of the cross with his fingers, feeling the slightly ribbed surface. He then gently folded the picture and tucked it safely in his breast pocket. His resolve was fast and decisive. One day he would get it, and then he would belong. He would no longer be "Nobody from Marburg". Putting on his woolen mirliton cap with skull and crossbones emblazoned on its front, he marched out and mounted his horse.

Riding along the Hudson River, Kopf whipped his horse mercilessly and drove the spiked wheels on his spurs into the horse's side, drawing blood. The animal galloped until its sides started foaming. With the sturdy horse straining under him and the wind blowing in his face, he imagined himself as the rider of the apocalypse and took pleasure from thinking that people called him Totenkopf. He adored his nickname and considered it his mission to keep up his reputation.

Arriving close to Fort Edward and the surrounding farms, he soon discovered that the Rangers were gone again. They were constantly patrolling the forests north toward the Canadian border. Kopf rode around, asking for information from the townspeople and farmers. He claimed that many Rangers, particularly Finn, Gus, Fronto, and Daniel, were suspected spies for the French. People did not like the Hessians and listened to Kopf more out of fear than courtesy, but when he wanted to be, he could be outgoing and convincing. In any case, to support his claims, he described many unexpected events that had taken place in the area recently. After Kopf departed, some people started having second thoughts that maybe there was a hint of truth to his allegations.

§   §   §

In the Catskill Mountain House, Henry Raymond and the old man were served their dinner. As their main course arrived on a lacquered goatskin and brass serving cart with oval shaped meat domes made of silver, the old man continued his story. "I remember that day well when the Helen of Magdalena and her column of whores arrived in Fort Edward. At the age of nine, Helen was apprenticed to a seamstress in Aldgate, in London. After losing a valuable piece of lace, she was scared of her lover and ran away and took to living on the streets of the slum district of St. Giles. She became well known in London as the pretty little wench who charged the schoolboys half a crown for a moment of her time in Pope's Head Alley.

"She was making decent money, and so she was taken in by her mentor, Mother Westbourne, whose whorehouse in the red light district of Covent Garden was among the most expensive brothels in the city. Because nobody knew where she came from, her dark complexion and black hair earned her the name Helen of Magdalena.

"Under the Madame's protection, she was celebrated for her youthful beauty and wit and attracted many aristocratic customers who wanted to spend the highest price for the greatest sins in her chambers. Soon, she was boasting that she had half a dozen of lords as clients. Even dukes and the future king were said to be amongst her lovers.

"Then one night in the Three Tuns Tavern, a man by the name of Colonel Francis Charters was so smitten with her beauty that he attacked her and tried to rape Helen in one of the private dining rooms. There were no witnesses, and Charters' servants in the next room later testified that they heard nothing. During the struggle, Helen of Magdalena snatched the knife she had been given with her meal and stabbed the horny fella in the heart. The jury found her guilty of assaulting and wounding the man, but there was one but — the judge happened to be one her most loyal customers — and he acquitted her of intent to murder, and so she was promptly deported to the American colonies.

"In America, she landed in Philadelphia and decided to change her life around. She became an entrepreneur who made substantial money in importing olive oil, which was quite a lucrative small business at the time. Olive oil was preferred over whale oil because it was much cheaper and had more uses. But eventually she found her new civil life boring. Then the war started, and she saw all those new regiments full of young men being formed. At the same time, she met by chance with Selous Claymore and heard about his plans to set up a lumber operation in the middle of nowhere on the Hudson River. Smart as she was, she realized that she was onto something.

"With profits from her olive oil business, she bought a dozen used, horse-drawn, flashy showman wagons and painted them in assorted bright colors: red, white and blue. She even had little stoves installed in them for heating. She hired some whores, a cook who doubled as a bartender, and a couple of burly bouncers as body guards, and they followed the New Hampshire regiment to Fort Edward.

"But she also had a big secret too, which I heard of only much later. She was a lesbian who dominated and abused her young prostitutes. Her own wagon was filled with bondage items, and underneath her bed, she kept a chest with a satanic altar in it. Or so I was told," the old man said with a wink.

Raymond continued taking notes on the side while he was eating. "How did the locals get along with the natives in the area? The relationships weren't always amicable and quite to the contrary, right?

"Aye, the relationships were strained. But on occasion, the people got to know each more and even marriages were possible. For example, Daniel and Shelagh," the old man said.

"Really, can you tell me more, sir?"

"Well, if I remember correctly how things happened, at the time, we were busy patrolling the surrounding areas, and Daniel spent most of his time in the woods with the Mohawk warriors. One day, running across the fort toward the gate and going around a corner, he bumped head on into Shelagh Bella Brotherton, who dropped her bits and bobs. He apologized profusely and helped to save her effects scattered on the ground. Getting back up and seeing her up close, he fell in love with her at first sight, like lighting striking from a clear blue sky. One smile from her disarmed him, melting and healing his heart that had been toughened by years of brutal combat.

"Can't blame the man, you see, Shelagh Bella Brotherton was an exquisite, petite woman with black hair and an hour-glass figure, and a curious, enigmatic smile. Her forefathers from Ireland had arrived in Hudson River Valley centuries earlier with the Italian explorer Verrazano. Proud of her Old World ancestry, she covered her dark hair with a hair-net made of golden threads and silk. She looked tiny and vulnerable standing next to Daniel's massive frame of solid, battle-hardened muscles, but she was not afraid of him at all.

"That one day Daniel was of no use in the field. He was distracted and paid no attention to what was happening. Other warriors wondered what might be wrong with him, as he usually was the one leading the efforts.

"From then on, when Daniel came back from patrols, he started to frequent the places in Fort Edward where he hoped to catch a glimpse of Shelagh. There were a couple of times he managed to catch her from the distance, but she never spoke to him until much later.

"Then one day, he saw her dressed in a white muslin gown, walking down a street, accompanied by the two older women who were her chaperones. Keeping a respectful distance, he followed the women. He turned to look at a shop window when any of them happened to look back at his way. Then, to Daniel's great surprise and the older women's shock, Shelagh turned around suddenly, walked across the street, and greeted him. She had noticed his reflection on a shop window. He was impressed and smitten with her bold move because usually English women were afraid of his tattooed and scarred body.

"Shelagh's decisiveness filled Daniel with such joy that he retreated to the woods to think about her in his secret retreat. He sat under a big, weeping willow tree by the Hudson River that quietly flowed under a green canopy. Daniel had once declared that poets and artists could get him only up to the heights of a mountain. It was from that time onwards that only Shelagh could guide him to paradise. Only Shelagh made him feel invincible, and to honor her, he decided to write her a sonnet better than any man could ever hope to create," the old man said.

§   §   §

From the early in the morning fog, near the shores of Lake George, a bow of a canoe appeared, cutting a duckling off from the brood. The cute little duckling panicked as it became trapped between the hull of the canoe and paddles. Before it had a chance to call out to its mother, a tattooed hand swooshed down and grabbed the little duckling by its throat and lifted it out of the water. Abenaki Chief Colonel Louis snapped the duckling's head off like a cork from a bottle and squeezed the life out of the tiny form, drinking the blood squirting out of the neck, and then tossed the drained body away.

As the sun rose above the horizon, the fog lifted and revealed the French advance parties moving on the shore ahead of the armada of gun boats and troop carriers that glided along the lake on a mission of destruction.

Watching the invasion force pass from his command post, General Montcalm slammed his telescope shut. "*Regardez*, we shall advance and reduce the petty English log structure to burning ruins and rubble at the south end of the lake. Captain, tell our allies that after pillaging and burning the enemy fort, they are allowed to collect as much loot as they can handle," he said.

The French regular battalions secured the shores in advance of the main regiments on the lake. The French regulars, wearing pure-white wool interlaced with royal blue wool on the edges, were augmented by an almost equal number of Canadian militia and a large contingent of active Abenaki, Mi'kmaq, Algonquin, Lenape and Ottawa allies. Their warrior allies, painted for war, were thirsty for blood, ready to unleash their razor sharp knives on the loathed Rogers Rangers and any others unfortunate enough to fall into their hands.

The French marines were usually issued with a musket, a sword, a bayonet, a cartridge case, and a sword belt on which to fix all their gear. The veterans found out pretty quickly (usually the hard way) that their short swords were of poor quality and, in fact, they were nearly useless in the northern forests against the Ranger's cutlasses, which were made by Harold Ferrara. The French sold or traded their swords for tomahawks or hatchets, which were better weapons in the woods. Sometimes, however, they would simply leave their swords behind.

The French knew well that the famous sword smith Harold Ferrara lived in Fort Edward, and they had placed a bounty on his head for his live capture. By no means was he to be harmed. He was a wanted man for his skills in forging the Damascus steel into masterpiece weapons of war. One distinguishing feature displayed on his blades was a prominent fuller, or blood groove.

Montcalm watched with content as two hundred men of the artillery units, with their thirty-six cannons and four mortars, passed him. They made the French force almost unbeatable. The French forces came down the lake and silently broke from the early morning fog and into view of Fort William Henry.

The French artillery was soon off loaded from the barges and canoes and was deployed to firing positions. Captain Bougainville reported to General Montcalm. *"Par excellence!* The artillery is ready. Distance to the target is eighteen hundred yards!"

Montcalm observed the English fort through his telescope and saw an officer standing on the wooden palisades watching him through a telescope. The two men stared each other for a moment, and then General Webb blinked and lowered his spyglass. He quickly stooped down and scurried to the yard for cover.

Montcalm calmly judged the distance to his opponent and decided to try his luck. "Get ready for *succès fou*! See that northwest bastion, Captain? Let that English son-of-bitch bear the brunt of our first artillery barrage. Open the fire!"

Bougainville turned and conveying the command, shouted over his shoulder. "Artillery, fire!"

The French artillery fired a thunderous, ear-shattering volley. Massive clouds of smoke erupted from the roaring barrels, spitting deadly cannon balls, smolder, and flames. The carcass shells and bombs from field mortars whistled through the air and hit the British palisades, ripping them apart like match sticks in a series of massive explosions. Shards of wood impaled defenders and hot razor sharp metal shrapnel whizzed through the air, tore gaping wounds into flesh and bone. Men screamed in agony as cannon balls tore limbs off their bodies. Big geysers of dirt were thrown high in the air, and the earth shook. Detonation blasts hit some British regulars who were ripped apart, and their bodies were slammed hard against the ground like rag dolls.

The wounded, with their legs and arms torn off, screamed in agony and choked to death in their own blood. General Webb watched in horror as a razor sharp heavy steel fragmentation severed a head that rolled across the yard like a bowling ball and landed at his feet.

Across the battlefield, Montcalm took a deep breath and enjoyed the black powder smoke in the air that drifted from the beleaguered fort. He was pleased to see the effects that the bombardment had on the fraught enemy, and he turned to his officers. "Ha! Do you smell that? Black powder smells like victory. We caught the bastards with their pants around their ankles. Captain, keep up the cannon fire. Then begin a series of entrenchments to get closer to the fort walls." He then turned to Colonel Louis who was standing nearby and anxiously waiting for orders. "Colonel Louis, commence the attack to block the road between the fort and the enemy camp on the other side."

The warriors launched their merciless attack, descending from the surrounding hills like swarms of monstrous demons, screaming for blood and shooting on the run. The French marksmen followed them, positioning themselves

between the entrenched camp and the fort. The attacking
forces soon straddled the main road, and continued harassing and killing the frantic British in the camp and the fort.

Most of the couriers dispatched to other British forts
for help were cut down in cold blood by the French or
killed and scalped by the Abenaki. A few unlucky ones
were captured alive. At night, the shrieking screams of tor-
mented souls echoed in the woods, and the air was thick
with the nauseating smell of burning human flesh. The devilish bonfires on the shores cast demonic displays of images
that would have made Dante sick. That night, it seemed as
if Satan rose from the depths and his face flickered on the
pitch-black glass surface of Lake George. Terror reigned
supreme in the black abyss of the night, and many heads
turned gray from sheer horror.

At sunrise, inside the Fort William Henry, General
Webb was visibly shaken while trying to assess the fort for
damage. Alarmed by a guard, Webb reluctantly climbed
to the tower and saw the attacking French forces and their
commanding General calmly observing his destruction
through a telescope. General Webb felt a sharp tremor in
his stomach and squirted a little rivulet of wet ooze down
his tights. He climbed down quickly and paced back and
forth. He saw Lieutenant Colonel George Monro approaching for orders.

"Sir, the French are closing in, and I need orders—"
Monro said, but Webb cut him short.

"Colonel Monro, take charge. I must ask the headquarters in Fort Edward immediately. Don't worry, you'll
be fine. I will send reinforcements," Webb said as mounted
his horse and then galloped full speed out of the fort and

past the entrenched camp with his coat tails flapping. His body guard of Light Dragoons in light blue tunics and ceremonial roman-style crested helmets swiftly followed him, trying to keep up with the General, trying to protect his escape. They punched through the enemies with their lances and slashed left and right with their swords.

The men in the fort and the camp could hardly believe their eyes how the lucky bastard got through the enemy lines. Earnest, brave soldiers were being tortured to death, and this peacock just rode off like on a picnic to the park. For the rest of their lives, the survivors kept telling about the General's departure as a prime example of inequity in life.

Monro realized that the fort had fallen into his authority as he helplessly watched his commanding officer disappear into the relative safety of the forest. Across the battlefield, he saw the ruthless enemy forces creep closer and closer. He let out a sigh. "There goes the General, leaving me to clean up this mess," he said. Turning to an officer nearby, he continued, "Captain, give me a head count."

The captain was dazed and at a loss, and wore a bloody bandage around his head and was breathing in short gasps. "Sir, I think we have a total of two thousand men, counting the campsite and the fort. Maybe a maximum five hundred able-bodied man the fort. The French has already cut off and blocked the way to prevent our troops from joining forces."

Up on the remaining palisades, Munro tried to determine the enemy's strength, but he had difficulties to see anything due to the thick smoke drifting across the battlefield. "Alright, that may well be, but we're in a well-fortified position and the French are limited in numbers far away from their main camp. I can only hope that General Webb will act wisely and will send a reinforced Ranger element behind the French forces to harass them and cut off their supply lines. That way we could use a typical hammer and anvil action. Right now, all we can do is to wait and see what the French will do," he said.

"What are your orders, sir?" The captain asked, once again. He looked resigned, not expecting an answer.

"I'd guess that the main attack will come from the west because the east side is swampy and fortified by the camp," Monro said.

The British never made any attempts to thwart the French forces landing on the shore in increasing numbers. They simply decided to wait and see what would happen next.

As the bloody siege went on, the French artillery inched closer and closer and the bombardment became even more accurate, every cannon ball finding its target with unpitying accuracy. The British casualties mounted, and any hopes of strengthening continued to plummet quickly.

§   §   §

After careening twenty five miles through the wilderness, General Webb reached Fort Edward and rushed through the gates with his shattered horse. For a moment, the magnificent thoroughbred stallion, direct descendant of The Darley Arabian, stood head down with the nostrils flared, heaving and staggering, and then it collapsed in the yard. There was only one last thing anyone could do for the poor animal. One of the soldiers somberly cocked his musket, but a Ranger cook in a bloody apron ran out from the canteen with a pipe in his mouth and a butcher knife and a meat cleaver in his hands. He pushed the soldier away and slaughtered the horse while it was still kicking in convulsions.

Without paying any attention to his mount, Webb rushed inside the commander's office, and with shaking hands, he grabbed a crystal whiskey jug. He tossed the golden colored liquid down his throat before spitting up. Once he regained some of his posture, he reported about the ruthless and merciless French capture at Fort William Henry.

General Johnson started immediately to rally the troops ready. "We must help them. Send more troops now. Captain Rogers, have your Rangers go out immediately," he said.

Unfortunately, the officer corps of the British army was riddled with commanders at the highest levels who felt serious personal inadequacies. Now it was Webb's turn as he waved his arms in objection. "It's no use. Nothing can be done. It's all hopeless. Send out messengers. Colonel Monro must be told that there is no hope," Webb said, sniveling.

Robert Rogers noticed the dark brown stain in the seat of Webb's pants and pointed it out to Johnson. Rogers breathed out, fanning his face with his hand.

Johnson was furious, and urged Webb to move. "General Webb, we must send reinforcements immediately. Maybe all is not lost yet. The Rangers are ready to march on moment's notice," he said.

Webb looked back at him, wide eyed and visibly shaking. "I forbid it. As the commanding British army officer, I'm in charge here. It's no use, and the enemy is far superior in strength," he said, voice juddering.

Rogers let out a groan and snatched some maps from the table. He stepped forward to present his improvised plan to save the fort in distress. "Sir, I can get my Rangers to enemy's rear and cut off their supply lines. At the same time, you'll send reinforcements from here, and Colonel Monro can cut out from the garrison in force. We will overcome them in between our forces. We can still win this!"

Webb walked up and down, scared stiff, wringing his hands. "Captain Rogers, you and a couple of raggedy companies of provincial amateurs can hardly be a match against the regular French forces with artillery en masse! They are so intense. Any attempt at relief is futile, given the proper military forces available to us."

Rogers' head tilted downward and his eyebrows pulled down. He forcefully rubbed his neck and let out a long breath. He then straightened his back, putting his one arm behind his back and grabbed his wrist with his other hand. "Sir, we're wasting oxygen here, blabbering while good men are dying out there."

Johnson was furious, but they could not do anything. "It's of no use, Captain." He then pulled Rogers to the side and said, "He does not understand modern warfare."

Johnson scribbled some notes on a piece of parchment and handed it to Rogers. "Captain, we have to act decisively. First, send a couple of men out to take this message to Colonel Munro," he said and turned to Captain Dugald Campbell, "Captain, have the Black Watch ready for action."

Dugald Campbell of the Black Watch tossed the rest of his glass aside, stood up and belched. "Aye, by the time we go and pay a visit with those bastards!"

Rogers nodded and rushed out, motioning to Moses Hazen and Finn who stood outside. "Hey you two. You have just volunteered to take this message to Fort William Henry. Beware, it is besieged by a strong enemy force. Your task is to find your way in. Use your initiative," he said as he handed them the rolled up paper. Hazen grabbed it and without a word, the two Rangers took off running.

Seeing them leave the gates, Johnson was comforted that something was getting done. Then, as he turned back to Webb, he felt disgusted and grabbed him by the collar. "Stop your whimpering, General. Pull your shit together for crying out loud," he hissed between his teeth as he shook him forcibly.

§   §   §

Running in short, vigorous strides, Moses Hazen slung his musket over his back and headed out. Finn followed his example and managed to keep up. They kept up a steady pace, following ridge lines and crossing streams, going down and up, hands-and-knee-climbing ravines, and running through the woods for four hours without stopping. Hazen raised his hand, signaling to stop as they heard the gunshots and the cannons, and knew that when they were getting closer.

They advanced warily up and across a long slope of backwoods, breaking a course in from head to toe scrub. Following a ravine down to a small stream coming out of the hillside, they ran almost head-on to two French guards. In a swift movement, Hazen and Finn fired almost simultaneously from the bushes without stopping and killed both of them, then sprinted through the French skirmish line, taking the enemy by surprise.

Hazen fought like a madman, killing several French and Ottawa warriors with his dirk and tomahawk. Finn watched in disbelief as the dead men fell backward, blood spurting from gaping wounds and slit throats, their bodies hitting high tussocks of moss. The corpses' feet juddered in spasms as the men bled to death.

Hazen and Finn were covered by the smoke drifting across the battlefield. But the concealing effect worked both ways. A fledgling Abenaki warrior, with a hunting knife in his hand that caught the light, jumped in front of Finn and charged him. Finn parried his blows. Stepping rearward, he did not hear himself scream as he felt the warrior's blade slice a cut on his forearm. Finn tripped on a body and landed on his back, losing his musket.

The warrior let out a war cry and jumped on top of Finn, straddling his chest and victoriously raising the enormous hunting knife to take his scalp. Finn thought it was his last hour and prepared to take the final blow that would end his life. For a fleeting moment, still fighting for his dear life, Finn thoughts rushed through his mind. *This is it. I'll never see her again.* Just as the warrior was ready to deliver the deadly blow, he saw Finn's moose-head necklace and stopped. Surprised, Finn looked up at the warriors painted face and saw that the man had blue eyes.

Finn was panting heavily as he used the opportunity — kicking and pulling with his elbows — he backed away from the warrior. The warrior stared back at him with a curious expression, tilting his head slightly. Finn then remembered he had heard some stories about a kidnapped boy, years earlier. "Is that you, Dorie?" Finn said.

The warrior listened to him, still looking puzzled, and his hand holding a knife glittered in the sun. Then, turning his head up, the warrior shouted out a war cry and disappeared into the smoke.

Moses Hazen fought in an uncontrollable, trance-like fury, killing enemies left and right with his cutlass. Covered in blood, intestines and dirt, he rushed from the smoke to Finn's side. He grabbed Finn by the arm and helped him up. Without a word, Hazen kept moving, and Finn followed in his wake, walking in a ghastly tunnel of pink mist and flying bits of intestines and brain matter. He covered Hazen's movement, shooting other enemies and dodging falling bodies. Bullets hit the logs and trees around them, sending splinters hurling through the air like daggers. Out of sheer luck, neither one of them was hit as they threw themselves over the remaining log defenses into the fort.

Hazen and Finn were covered in soot and blood and spat dirt as they collected themselves. Hazen used his hands as ladles to drink from the trough, but Finn plunged his head straight into the water and drank until he came up coughing and sputtering.

Colonel Monro viewed them in amazement as he received and read the message they delivered to him. "General Johnson wants to know what the situation is, but General Webb is telling us that we might as well surrender because he cannot support us," he said, astonished.

Finn looked around the fort and witnessed a disheartening sight. Bodies lay everywhere. Empty black powder flasks and cartridge pouches littering the ground told him that ammunition was running low, and seeing the limp, unfocused stare on the survivor's faces told him that their spirits were even lower. The overpowering stench of fear, bile and shit hovered over the wretched spectacle. The thousand yard stare on the men's faces showed no hope at all. When war marches in through the door, glory flies out of the window. No more regimental balls, no more shining metals, no more pretentious parades, just enough time left to feel the pain and die. The bodies of four British officers and forty men killed in action were collected and placed haphazardly in rows on the parade ground.

Finn climbed up to the fighting positions on the palisade, and as a breeze shifted the heavy gun smoke, in front of him opened an empty, unspeakable, godless, hopeless cavity filled with craters and corpses.

He could have sworn he saw the foreboding manifestation of Beelzebub hovering over the battlefield, laughing insanely, in the black smoke, and the demonic flies that were with him. Petrified, he inhaled sharply and turned his head to look away.

At that moment, from the corner of his eyes, he caught a glimpse of some Hessian troops in their blue uniforms and long bright colored caps. Then and there he noticed that one of the officers was wearing a green Jaeger uniform, and as he looked closer, he realized that it was Johan Kopf.

Finn felt a freezing numbness run through his veins, and he tasted a tart brass in his mouth. But just like that, the fear of perdition was gone. Pulling the pistol from his belt, he jumped down from the palisades and grabbed another pistol from one of the dead officers. He saw Johan Kopf go around the corner behind a log house, which had been blown apart and scuttled after him.

Kopf was taking a leak against the smoldering logs, when Finn appeared out of the smoke behind him. Feeling surprisingly calm and ready to collect his revenge, Finn aimed the two pistols at his nemesis. Both pistols aimed at the back of Kopf's head, he felt his flesh crawl. His trigger fingers itched, and he fired, but he was too far, the bullet hit a log. Then a realization held him back: execution like this would be too easy for Kopf.

Finn fought the urge to shoot the bastard in the back. Sweat was running down his forehead, and the sun shone in his eyes. Steadying his hands, he wanted to make sure he would not miss and walked toward his archenemy. *I'm a better man than that scumbag. I must do this honorably*, he thought and took a better aim at the hazy figure. He felt a jarring frisson of sweet revenge on his tongue.

"Totenkopf, turn around! You butt-plugin, scrotum-squeezing, cross-dresser, this is the end. You killed my family, and now I will have my revenge," Finn shouted.

Kopf heard him alright, but pretended to be relaxed and whistled softly. Shaking himself, he calmly glanced over his shoulder, wary of Finn's every move. "*Du verdammtes Arschloch*, if you just knew how many wayward privates and russet-coated brigands like you have crossed my way," he said.

"Let me refresh your memory, scumbag. There was a village in Finland years ago. You killed my family!" Finn shouted, almost choking, his eyes filling up with tears.

Kopf dropped his show and buttoned his pants. As he

turned slowly, the sun caught the skull and crossed bones badge on his cap. He looked warily at the pistols in Finn's hands and put his hands palms down in a calming fashion. "Listen boy, I'm a professional soldier. I do what must be done, and what others fear to do. I obey the King's orders, and command men in a battle where quarter is neither asked nor given, and I get paid well for being skilled at it. I have no time for children or mercy," he said in a quiet, menacing voice.

Finn heard a noise, like the wheels rumbling on the track and a powerful whooshing rumble but did not pay attention to it. "I'll bring heaven down and hell up on you, cock sucking son of a bitch!" Finn shouted and pulled both triggers.

At the same moment, a colossal barrage of shells from the French artillery landed in the fort. Massive geysers of the earth were thrown up in the air, and the palisades and log buildings were blown apart by humongous explosions. The earth shook as one of the buildings nearby housing the powder exploded, throwing Finn off balance. He covered his head with his hands, as he was buried under rubble and burning logs, losing the death grip on both of the pistols.

Kopf had heard the horrid sound, and not thinking twice, he ducked just a fraction of a second before Finn pulled the trigger. He hit the ground and only one of the bullets winged him in the arm. He cried out, and grasping his injury, he spun around and crawled toward a crater before disappearing into the smoke.

With his clothes torn and smoldering, Finn crawled out from the pile of destruction, bruised, battered, and spitting dirt. His blond hair stuck out in every direction and was blackened with soot. His ears rung and he could barely hear the wounded crying and wailing in agony. The barrage ended, and the last shell, a dud canister shot, hit a towering log right next to Finn's head and fell on his foot, sending him hopping on one foot while holding the other.

"Fuck! Fuck! Fuck! Why, oh why did I wait?" he said. Sitting down to examine his wounds, he came to the surprising realization that he was not afraid of Kopf any longer, and only a hollow feeling, remained toward the man.

Cowering behind his command post, Colonel Monro had watched the French artillery pound the fort into smithereens. He winced as the deafening explosions shook the ground, and he crawled like a lizard into a shallow hole in the ground under heavy logs. Then, just as fast it had started, the bombardment stopped and silence settled in, leaving the fires burning and black smoke lingering over piles of dead bodies. The British survivors were shaken and distressed, but they were relieved to be alive.

Ignoring the painful wound, Johan Kopf crawled over the palisade remains, and slithered into the wet grass. He came by a dead French soldier in a ditch and grabbed the uniform coat from the body. Using the enemy coat as a disguise under cover of smoke and confusion, he calmly stood up and strode off the battlefield.

§   §   §

In the meantime, across the battlefield at his command post, General Montcalm smiled broadly as he saw the fort's reduction into a pile of rubble and burning logs. He spun around and around in a victory parade, flapping his arms and humming a marching tune. His smile subdued as Captain Bougainville arrived to inform him of the rapidly dwindling stacks of cannon balls. He realized the artillery was running dangerously low on ammo, but enemy's condition was still unclear and his supply lines were stretched to the limits. Always a rationalist, he soberly ordered Bougainville forward, under a flag of truce, to offer surrender to the beleaguered English.

Walking across the scorched ground, Bougainville approached the British gates under a white flag. Colonel Monro in his blackened and torn uniform appeared to try to keep up the appearances in appropriate British fashion.

"My commander, His Excellency Montcalm offers you an honorable surrender and to protect you from his allies," Bougainville said. In no uncertain terms, he informed Monro that General Montcalm knew darned well that there was no hope for reinforcement, reciting one of the intercepted letters from the British couriers. Furthermore, the French trenches were already only two hundred yards outside the fort wall. Any further resistance would be dealt with deadly force.

Monro took a defiant stance. "Captain, tell your lord that we're still well armed and willing to achieve glory," he replied.

"*Chien de l'enfer*, there will be hell to pay. But if you surrender, the entire unit will be allowed to progress off in a military parade, colors flying, to Fort Edward, or whatever hell hole you choose. Cannon will even be allowed to attend the procession, but no ammunition," Bougainville said.

"I must admit, this is unusually generous offer, sir,

and I'm concerned for the well-being of my troops" Monro replied, pretending to consider the offer, but fully knowing that he had no other choice. Dying for his King was not high on his list of accomplishments to do.

"You have no room to negotiate, *en têcheur*. In return, you will not bear arms or fight against France for the next eighteen months. No ammunition will be granted to your men, just in case," Bougainville insisted.

"What about the sick and wounded?" Monro said and motioned toward the field hospital.

"The sick and wounded will be returned when they are well. In addition, one English officer shall stay here as hostage until our escort, attached to the retreating English column, returns safely from Fort Edward, *c'est ça*," Bougainville said and turned on his heels ending the conversation.

Monro summoned the officers for a quick conference. "Since General Webb refused to send help, I see no other way but to accept the terms. In European terms, all is well. We have, though defeated, retained our honor. The avaricious French soldiers have hardly earned their victory. But once we leave, there will no longer be a British post on the shores of Lake George," he said and ordered a flag of surrender to be hoisted to the pole flying over Fort William Henry, or what was left of it.

On the French side, the warriors from the various tribes stood by restless, wanting to plunder the fort because it was their only reward. They saw plenty of valuable clothing, arms, ammunition, supplies, and rum for the taking in the fort. Many felt deprived of their prize as the tense situation lingered and tensions mounted.

Finally, the British assembled by companies, and with Colonel Monro on horseback, they were ready to leave the fort. The last British unit assembled and marched out of the gates, and left about seventy wounded in the care of the French. A French escort of two hundred troops was on the scene, ready to escort them out.

Almost immediately, a group of warriors entered the fort to loot what baggage the British left behind. Finn heard the cries and screams for help from outside the fort, as resisting troops attempting to protect themselves were killed.

A French missionary, Pere Roubaix witnessed the sacking of the fort. He saw a warrior step out of a log house, proudly waving a severed, bloody head.

Bougainville witnessed the killings. *"Merde!"* he exclaimed and turned to Montcalm. "Sire, torturing natives is one thing, but allowing them to execute English soldiers and civilians under our protection is a totally different matter. It will not look good on you in the courts of Europe," he said and nudged the general by the elbow. Montcalm froze without replying, and he just stared at the captain's hand touching his arm. Bougainville withdrew his hand and bowed in apology.

The British march from the entrenched camp to Fort Edward was halted by hostile warriors who gathered by the road and blocked the British from leaving. The warriors pestered the soldiers, butt-stroking and harassing them and demanding their baggage. Montcalm posted French soldiers to protect the British, but the violent warriors forced them out of the way.

It was a long, tension-filled day of yelling, pushing,

and shoveling. The British regulars formed a long line and started out, and at the rear of the column were militia men from the Massachusetts regiment, some New Hampshire militia, and camp followers. Finn ignored the hostile warriors around him, and kept searching the file for Johan Kopf.

Moses Hazen warned him and the other troops. "Don't resist them, or they will kill you. Just keep your eyes fixed straight ahead and keep moving."

Suddenly, they heard a frightful whoop, and the enemy warriors fell upon the column from all sides. The warriors were cruel, pawing, grabbing, poking, pushing, and robbing bag, baggage, and clothing from the terrified soldiers. One soldier resisted, stiffly holding on to his only possessions, and he was swiftly knocked down by some Abenaki warriors, hacked to death with tomahawks, and scalped. Panic-stricken camp followers, including women, children, and some soldiers, fled into the woods. Warriors gathered loot, and herded women prisoners to be taken with them. It was a place of utter chaos and panic.

Monro kept his eyes fixed straight ahead. "March steady, a soldier is worth more alive than dead. The French pay handsomely for the return of prisoners alive."

As the soldiers broke and ran, the warriors pursued them. Escaping soldiers were killed and scalped. Moses Hazen talked to Finn. "A scalp is not worth as much as a prisoner, but it's still better than nothing," he said.

Bougainville had pulled the right string by pleading on the general's vanity. Montcalm realized that perhaps he was right, and unnecessary bloodshed could tarnish his reputation as an officer and gentleman — his political enemies would see to it — and that could prevent his return to the court in Paris. He rushed to stop any further killings. His greatest triumph was about to be marred by the performance of his warrior allies who kept attacking the British soldiers as they marched out of the fort under negotiated terms of surrender. Disgusted, Montcalm intervened in an attempt to halt the slaughter.

With considerable effort, Montcalm was able to gain control over the warriors. He demanded, pleaded, invoked their gods, and even begged the warriors, but only after he promised more prizes and loot, they agreed to listen to him. Finally, the French were able to restore some semblance of order, and the rest of the British fort was set afire before they departed back toward the French stronghold on Lake Champlain, Fort Carillon.

Montcalm turned to Bougainville, and lowering his voice, he told him that he could forget the captain's insolence earlier if he drafted a report of the event that portrayed the general in most favorable terms.

Accordingly, Bougainville (who, under some other circumstances, perhaps should have been a dramaturge) drafted a dynamic report, which depicted heroic Montcalm, boldly throwing himself in harm's way to save the English prisoner's lives. As a second thought, Bougainville added that the general even had brazenly bared his own chest, and declared, "Kill me, but spare the English!"

Following the forsaken British column that stank of sweat, urine, and blood, Finn's feet skidded painfully on the ruts left by the wagons. He grimaced, and trying to stay Spartan, he ignored the intense aching of his bruises and cuts. "You would need a poet to make a hero story out of this clusterfuck of a battle," he said, before cursing and spitting on the ground. As they marched on, he never looked back.

Chapter 2

AS THE SPRING ADVANCED, rivulets of melting snow filled the streams and rivers. The forests turned into many shades of green, from light to dark. The ridge lines and mountains were colorful as well and bathed in warm sunlight. The forests around Lake George swarmed with Rangers on regular patrols, screening, ambushing, and taking every opportunity to harass the enemy to their best abilities.

On the home front, trying to ignore the raging struggle around their homesteads, farmers around Fort Edward were working at the planting of meager crops. Spring was an uncertain time. The food stores had been depleted over the winter, and the outcome of the new crops remained to be seen. Hunters shied away from venturing too far after elusive prey at the risk of getting captured by the hostile warriors. At the mill, people mixed pine bark to the little flour left from the previous year. In the town markets, people were dying over the high cost of foodstuff. They were haggling and bargaining, and complained that the rude city residents were ripping off the poor farmers whom they mockingly called country bumpkins.

On the eastern seaboard, the ocean glimmered in the distance. It sat calm and down after stormy winter season.

Yet the waters were deep black and difficult, and there were remnants of storm clouds on the horizon, keeping the fishermen in suspense. Seagulls hovered over the waves breaking against rocks on the shore and called out to one another.

Boston harbor was busy, hustling and bustling. Seamen, fishermen, and savvy entrepreneurs bartered while drunken Marines and whores argued over prices. The start of the new sailing season brought in long waited ships, new people, and valuable cargo from Europe, the Caribbean, and Africa. Among the merchant ships lay a Royal Navy man-of-war. She was the double decker, 72-gun, *HMS Grafton*, anchored some distance from the pier.

Commodore Gayton approached the ship of war on a dinghy to bring new orders. He climbed the pilot ladders and landed on the quarterdeck where the crew was busy scrubbing the decks. On the stern deck, a sergeant was drilling a squad of Royal Marines.

Gayton walked briskly past the gun crews stocking ball, chain, bar, grape shot, rammers and sponges. Taking off his tricorn hat and stooping his shoulders, he ducked and stepped through the companionway and into the aft cabin that was lit through a row of sternlights. In Admiral Francis Holburne's command post, Gayton handed the orders from Lord Loudoun to the Admiral, ordering his squadron ready for an expedition to Fort Louisburg.

Admiral Holburne did not like what he read in the orders. "Is he sure? We have bloody little intelligence on the French forces in the area," he said.

Gayton stood statuesque with his hat under his arm.

His eyes were fixed in the distance. "Yes sir. He was very specific."

Holburne watched the busy harbor with his hands behind his back. "The fleet is still at anchor from the winter. He must have gone bonkers and totally overboard. Does the noble Lord know anything about naval operations? It takes time to prepare the fleet for operations," he said, tossing the report on his desk.

"Yes, sir, but he gave detailed instructions," Gayton replied. He was an experienced naval officer and knew well that the fleet should have been operational already. The Admiral was certainly inefficient, lazy, or both.

Holburne turned, and measuring Gayton with a quick glance, he sighed. "So, Louisburg it is then. My fleet consists of fifteen ships-of-the-line and three frigates with eight battalions. That amounts to about five thousand on board. Tell me Commodore, you have been to Louisburg before, haven't you?"

Gayton remained expressionless. "Yes sir. I served under Captain Douglass on board *Vigilante* in 1745. For this effort, Lord Loudoun has prepared ninety transport ships and has five ships-of-the-lines, ready to sail. He shall meet you in Halifax."

"Well then, we have nothing to worry about, right? We know exactly where we are heading," Holburne replied sarcastically and turned his attention to some papers on his desk. He waved his hand at Commodore Gayton, dismissing him.

Gayton bowed slightly. "One more thing, sir, you are to take on board a company of Rangers. Their mission is to land and reconnoiter the surrounding country side for potential landing sites," he said.

"You are dismissed," Holburne said and turned to a stack of papers on his desk.

Gayton turned stiffly and marched out, closing the squeaking door behind him.

§　§　§

Among the provincials and the British, days of chaos followed in the aftermath of the Fort William Henry disaster. People were in emotional turmoil, showing anger, guilt, and sadness, with unpredictable reactions. They felt uncontrollable insecurity about the fear and distress the disaster caused. Sometimes the anger was directed at family members or at strangers in random.

Robert Rogers led the Rangers who had expressions on their faces fierce enough to cause nightmares. They marched at a fast pace toward the sounds of gunfire. He could not stand still and do nothing, and thus he had ordered the men to move out as soon as the news of the devastation reached Fort Edward.

Chasing the enemy across the wilderness, they discovered two enemy soldiers, the rear guards of the French Army, one of whom was posted on the trail leading into the woods from the dirt road. Robert Rogers gave the hand signal to his patrol to stop and motioned the closest team to follow him.

Rogers marched close to the road in broad daylight with five Rangers until they were challenged by the French guards. The guards heard gravel crunching under a careless foot.

In great surprise, one guard called out. "*Qui etes*

vous?" The man asked nervously, grasping his musket. Robert Rogers, in a calming tone, answered in French, signifying friends, and the guards were deceived until the Rangers were there, too close for comfort.

"*Mot de passe?*" The guard demanded a password.

"Rogers," Rogers replied.

Realizing his mistake, the other guard mounted his horse and galloped off, attempting to escape. One of the Mohawks quickly fired an arrow, which made a twanging sound as it penetrated the man's neck and stopped with half of the shaft sticking out of his throat, and the body fell into a muddy pool by the road. The other guard's horse was seized by the Rangers, and Rogers swiftly pushed the man out of sight from his post.

Behind a clump of black willows and arrow wood, the French prisoner struggled in vain against his captors, but he was callously beaten and interrogated. He spat blood and teeth, but he remained defiant. "*Fils de pute!* Our forces are over eleven thousand strong. You will never beat us."

Rogers recognized the firm bearing on the man's face and realized that as a prisoner, he would only cause problems and possibly jeopardize the entire patrol. Rogers nodded to his men, who dragged the prisoner away. A Mohawk warrior put his hand over the man's mouth and ran him through. Forcing the dying man to bend at his waist, the warrior yanked the man's head back, exposing his throat. As the Mohawk stepped back to avoid the spills on his moccasins, another warrior stepped forward and slit the man's throat with his knife, sending long gushes of blood over the brushwood.

The warrior let the body go, and it fell in the undergrowth, still gurgling and kicking in spasms. The big hunting knife flashed in the sunlight as three quick cuts removed the bloody scalp from the body.

Just then Moses Hazen and Finn appeared, coming in fast from the woods. Finn felt blood running down his side from an aching wound and he spat wearily, tasting blood in his throat. He told himself to learn to dress wounds better. Hazen, breathing heavily from exhaustion, told Rogers that it was all over, and Fort William Henry had been totally demolished. Rogers pursed his lips and hit a tree with his fist.

Unknown to them, a few miles across the forests, Johan Kopf marched alone through orchard-bushed hills and around a grade of woods to the top of the cavity wall where he could look down on the Hudson River and check his wound. He was furious because he realized that Finn was getting stronger and would not be such a simple character to play around any longer. Finn had become a formidable enemy to be reckoned with, but Kopf was determined more than ever to break Finn's neck.

As soon as he got back in Albany, Kopf reported to the secret operation's headquarters. He had devised a plan that, on the surface, was intended to flush out any enemy spies in the vicinity. However, his true intentions were to plant evidence in Fort Edward that would implicate Finn and his friends for collaboration with the enemy. To his dismay, the commanding officer, General Cage, dismissed his plan and ordered Kopf to report forthwith for a cleanup operation along the headwaters of the Allegheny River. For the first time in his career, Kopf was truly tempted to disobey his orders and go after Finn anyway. In the end, his sense of duty and eagerness to please the General overcame his more primal instinct.

In the meantime, Finn was the point man leading the Ranger patrol back to Fort Edward. When he got within a couple of miles of the fort, he cut through a downward tunnel of foliage. Coming out on a shoulder of a high hill, looking down on the river valley below, he saw a dark figure wearing a heavy coat and standing under an age-old box elder. He gave the hand signal to stop and ran crouching back to Robert Rogers.

"Sir, there's a man under a tree. Obviously, he is observing road traffic. I think it could be the spy," Finn said.

"Right, take few men and seize him," Rogers replied.

Finn moved out, followed by Gus, Fronto, and Daniel. They moved around a giant ant hill to find a good vantage point, but Finn could not see much in the thicket of swamp rose. They advanced cautiously another hundred yards and heard a muffled cough from the figure. Finn motioned the others to stop while he sneaked close, first crouching low, then going down on all fours before finally lowering himself on the on his belly.

Finn crept behind the figure. Taking a deep breath and holding it, Finn jumped up and grabbed hold of the man by the arms.

They struggled, and first Finn seemed to get the better of him. But then, the figure rammed his knee into Finn's groin three times in a row. Finn went down. But instead of making a run for it, the figure stepped back, fists raised and ready to fight. The hood came off, revealing a long blonde hair. It was not a man — it was Catherina. "Finn, it's you! Jesus! You scared the living shit out of me!" she said, catching her breath.

"What the hell is this? Catherina, what are you doing?" Finn panted and tried to get back up while holding his crotch at the same time.

"I'm standing guard in case this spy should try to come this way. Captain Rogers did not enlist me, but I can help. I'm not any wall rose. I'm going to organize a women's home front," she said, chin up.

"Catherina, you should be staying in the fort and taking care of the wounded. You should be preparing food and cleaning up and doing other chores like that," Finn countered. In truth, he was more concerned for her safety.

Catherina's eyes flashed, and she was about to unleash an all-out, spirited retort on him when Gus, Fronto, and Daniel appeared from behind the swamp roses and walked up to them smiling.

"Well, well. What have we here? A little lover's argument, is it?" Fronto said, leaning on his musket and winking his eye to the others.

Catherina stepped up to him and poked his nose with her fore finger. "Watch it, Dog, or whatever they call you. Dead men don't tell tales," she said, eyeing him angrily.

Out from the bushes, Robert Rogers and the rest of the Ranger patrol appeared. Rogers smirked at Finn as they walked by. "Can't you control your woman, Ranger?"

Catherina gasped and was about to explode at him, but Finn pulled her back, and Daniel calmed her down. Finn sprinted after Rogers.

Catherina turned to Gus, Fronto, and Daniel, who all stood side by side and trying to look like they had not seen or heard a thing. She paced in front of them. "Does he know anything? It's all about being able to decide for myself. But he doesn't get it, does he?" she said, glaring at the men. They all looked up or sideways, everywhere else but her.

Fronto gathered enough courage, coughed and said, "Excuse me, ma'am, but the man is wounded."

Catherina spun around on her heels to look the way Finn had gone. "What? Is he alright?"

Finn caught up with Robert Rogers and kept up beside him while talking and dodging low lying branches. "Sir, no matter what, she is right. We still have a spy lurking around here somewhere," he said. "We know his drop off, and I'm sure he is now reporting back to the enemy our reactions to the fall of the William Henry. My guess is that this would be a good time to prepare a stake out."

Rogers was walking briskly, thinking of various scenarios in the aftermath of the recent tragedy. He stopped and motioned the Rangers to file past them. "Perhaps you are right. We have been busy fighting, but now it is time to deal with this mongrel for once and for all."

§   §   §

The next morning before dawn, moonlight cast eerie shadows in the pine trees as the Rangers moved toward the site where the enemy spy had been sighted. A troop of British regulars followed them, nervously clutching their rifles. They were city boys, former thugs and thieves from London, unaccustomed to the woods at night. Robert Rogers had opposed their presence, but General Johnson had insisted Rogers let them to come along, or perhaps have Hessians joining in the stake out, which had been even more unacceptable.

Catherina had been doing morning chores when she saw the Rangers move past her farm. She dropped what she was doing and quickly followed the men, realizing what they were going to do from the way the men were heading.

The Rangers formed a circle around the old knotted oak tree that was the drop off point, hiding in the nearby dogwood bushes. The forest turned silent, and a few killdeer birds started singing. Everything seemed to be perfectly in order.

After a couple of hours, as the sun rose above the tree tops, a dark figure appeared and proceeded cautiously, glancing left and right as he came. The gray form placed a bottle into the gaping hole, in the side of the tree. Just at that moment, the Rangers sprang from their hideout and seized the spy.

"Captain, we caught the spy red-handed!" Moses Hazen shouted.

To everybody's surprise, the spy turned out to be one of the townswomen dressed in a petty coat. The woman looked small and vulnerable. She was surrounded by the burly Rangers and frisked, but she did not seem to be afraid. She stood in front of them, resigned and expressionless.

Interrogation did not provide any information. Robert Rogers pulled Catherina aside. "Do you know her? I need something, quick. The Brits want blood. She's lucky the Hessians are not present. They'd do much more to her than the Brits," he said.

Catherina shrugged her shoulders, feeling bad for not being able to help Rogers or save the poor woman. "No, but I have seen her around the fort. I think she works in the canteen as a cook."

"She did not have any stolen items on her. But at least we're safer now," Finn said, searching the woman's belongings.

"We intercepted her this time, but more than likely, Abenaki scouts have picked up the earlier messages," Daniel said.

Moses Hazen pulled out a hunting knife, its razor sharp blade catching the light, and turned it under her eyes. "Why did you do it, woman?"

She looked past the blade and directly at him. "They have my family."

Rogers pulled Hazen back and stepped in front of her. "We all have lost family members. Do you have anything else to say in your defense before I have to turn you over to the British?"

"I know no more of the matter than you do or half as much," she replied.

Rogers looked at her with a squint of an eye. They stared each other for a moment, and she raised her chin defiantly. A drop of glistening sweat ran down his temple, and time appeared to stand still. Fighting the enemy in combat was one thing. Condemning a civilian, a woman no less, to death was something totally different. The silence was broken by someone's muffled cough.

"Alright then, may God have mercy on your soul," he said finally, and stepping aside turned to others. "I bet she knows nothing more".

The burly British regulars eagerly stepped forward and with bitter, vengeful smiles on their faces, took her away. They grabbed her by the arms and marched her off behind a barn, pushing and shoving, and forcing her to lean against a big tree.

Finn took off his caubeen, tense and disturbed as firing squad commands echoed in the woods. Catherina turned to look away. Rifle barrels rose, and the woman stared at the gaping black barrels aimed at her. All her life, she had been an object for men's whims and desires one way or another. The war that took away her family was started by men. The gross, last thing she saw was a line of ruthless men, aiming at her. She felt a shiver ran down her spine, but no remorse or fear, and then surprisingly, calmness upon the realization that all pain and suffering was over, finally. She took a deep breath and holding it, closed her eyes and recited a silent prayer.

A volley fired, and bullets ripped through her chest and hit the tree behind her. The woman slowly slumped down on her knees, and then fell back against the blood soaked tree.

The shots echoed among the pines, and the smoke from the musket muzzles lingered. Silence fell. Nobody moved. The sight of the dead woman and the implications of it were brutal even for the battle-hardened Rangers. Finn was devastated, feeling a terrible, growing coldness settling in his inner self. "I don't understand. Why anyone coerce a civilian to spy on us? A woman spy, no less. That is so dishonorable," he said.

Fronto sat down on a stump. He was tired and weary of life, having seen too many events like this one. "Men do not always respond to meet our hopes. Events transpire as they do. Folks act as they are. Hold what you in fact get," he said, fighting against rising resentment.

Finn picked up a bristly, dark blue, woolen blanket with red and white stripes on it and walked over to cover the dead woman. He knelt beside her, shook his head, and gently closed her eyes with his fingers.

§   §   §

Benjamin Franklin and John Morton summoned George Washington, William Johnson, and Robert Rogers to a meeting in Tun Tavern in Philadelphia. The agenda was to seek different ways how the provincials might be able to work together in order to present unified demands on the British overlords. Rumors circulated, and new, dangerous ideas of democracy had been voiced. Any open manifestation of such ideas would have been dealt with quickly and harshly, resulting in instant death sentence, and so they were kept quiet.

The men gathered at a corner table in the back of the lounge for privacy. A broad-shouldered bouncer stood by to keep other interested people — and informers — away and warn of any British. Rogers and Washington kept eyeing each other warily, unsure why the other one had been invited. Both men were apprehensive of each other's motives and intentions. Washington disdained Rogers' abilities and saw him as an obstacle to his own ambitions in the British regular army. Rogers, on the other hand, considered Washington to be another upstart without any real martial skills, who only managed to get promotions through family connections. Drinks were served, and Benjamin Franklin, in his usual manner, spoke first.

Franklin threw back his long mullet and wiped his high forehead with a handkerchief and raised his glass. "Here's to beer! It is the living proof that God loves us and wants us to be jolly." He took a long drink, burped, and wiped his mouth to his sleeve. "Gentlemen, without further ado, let me shortly describe the issue at hand. As you already know, I have proposed m-my Albany Plan that calls for a union of the colonies under one government as far as might be necessary for defense and other assorted overriding purposes."

John Morton looked skeptical. "Perhaps so, but there is a serious glitch in our plan. You see, in order to proceed with our plans for the unity we must first rectify our issues with the Iroquois nation," he replied.

"Yes, cunning, blood thirsty savages as they m-may be, my goal has been inspired by the Iroquois Confederacy. However, they m-must make their decision. Whose side are they on in this war? We cannot form any league if we have unresolved issues with them," Franklin insisted.

"We all know that there are deep divisions among the various tribes," Johnson commented.

Robert Rogers touched a scar on his cheek. "I happen to know something about the warrior way of thinking. There are many chiefs, but some are more powerful than others. We need to build an alliance with the key chiefs, then others are more likely to follow suit," he said.

"This task is of outmost importance to our cause and our war efforts. It must remain confidential," Washington urged them.

Rogers, taken by surprise, looked miffed at Washington and the other men. "Mission? What mission?"

Franklin was keenly aware of the tension between the two men and intervened in order to prevent any arguments. "Yes, Captain Rogers, as you already pointed out, we need to reach some key individuals within the Iroquois confederation. You shall hold a party to negotiate with them. And as Washington already pointed out, this is truly sensitive m-mission," he said.

"I happen to know one prominent person. I think we should take her with us. Her name is Mary Brant. She is the older sister of Joseph Brant," Johnson said.

"Take her with us, you say? With all due respect, sir, but it may be a better idea if I talk to the chiefs directly first, and then you seek the support from her separately. That way we will have two avenues of approach to get this help from them, and it leaves her more space to create the back channel within the confederation. Plus we may gain valuable intelligence that way otherwise not provided to us. That is, if you have her under control, sir," Rogers said to the General.

"I have her under control alright," Johnson replied as he winked at Rogers.

"That you do, sir. Your reputation precedes you. You do have your way with the ladies," George Washington said.

The men laughed, and a servant girl sidestepped Johnson's groping hands as she brought more whiskey. Glasses were raised in a toast.

"Mr. Franklin and I will leave the military details of this matter to you, gentlemen. Rest assured, you will have our whole political support," Morton said.

As the evening wore on, the waitress started a fire in the hearth and lighted lanterns. Drinking and spirited debate went on late into the night. Franklin, who was in his usual, jovial mood, placed himself in the center of attention throughout the party.

§　§　§

The following day, Finn heard the news that the mail wagon that had been carrying his letter had been ambushed and destroyed by a renegade band of Iroquois. Disheartened at first, he then bought another sheet of old paper and wrote a new letter to Rosie, and sealed it with a kiss for good luck.

Upon learning of the attack, Robert Rogers did not waste any time. He ordered Finn, Gus, Fronto, and Daniel to accompany him on the quest to meet with the Iroquois chiefs.

"Ranger Nimham, you will take the lead. When we talk, you'll sit next to me, but you'll only speak when I tell you to. Is that clear? I'm representing all of the colonies, and so it must be absolutely clear to everybody there that I'm in the position of authority," Rogers said.

They followed ridge lines and circled around highland tops. The lush, green tree line directly below them was covered in a mist from nearby river falls. They negotiated the terrain to the other side on top of the falls by hopping on wet rocks. They descended to a large meadow nestled among the hills. They arrived at a wide open area with regular berms around it like bleachers. There were huts along the wood line, and large crowds of Mohawks and Mohicans were yelling and hollering.

Finn had never seen so many warriors in one place and grabbed a better grasp of his musket, looking wide-eyed at Fronto and Gus.

Looking straight ahead, Daniel led them directly onto the field. Rogers followed him, not paying any attention to the warriors around them. Young Iroquois warriors were playing some sort of game on the field. Each team consisted of several hundred men carrying long sticks, on a mile-long range, running after a large ball made of furry deerskin.

Finn stopped to watch the warriors play. "What are they doing?" he asked. "The women seem to enjoy watching it."

Women and children were cheering on the side lines, urging their teams to win.

"It is called *baaga'adowe* or *baggataway*, the Creator's Game. White people call it lacrosse, or the staff," Daniel said.

"You call that a game? Looks like mortal combat to me," Finn said, astounded. The players crashed in a massive tackle, leaving the men spitting blood. The crowd cheered and hollered. A warrior landed hard on his back, bleeding and knocked unconscious.

"Yes. The game lasts from sunup to sundown for three days straight. It is played to give thanks to the Creator as part of ceremonial ritual," Daniel continued.

"It is played to resolve conflicts, heal the sick, develop strong, virile men, and to prepare for war," Rogers filled in. Women tended injured players on the side, taking care of broken bones, bloody teeth, and bruised eyes.

"You got that right. Who needs war after playing a game like that?" Finn said, amused.

Daniel smiled. "There is more to it, young chief. The warriors consider it as deep spiritual link, fitting the spirit of fighting in which it's undertaken. Warriors who take part do it with the purpose of bringing glory and honor to themselves and their tribes," he said.

Groups of old warriors and chiefs were sitting on a knoll, smoking long pipes and enjoying the game. Rogers recognized King Uncas of the Mahican among them and walked up to him and offered him a fur belt. "Brother Uncas, here is a belt of wampum. For the advantage of King George, we'll have a large amount of Rangers for the next campaign, and being thoroughly convinced of your attachment, I want in pursuance of my orders to gain your support here early in the spring," he said.

Chief Uncas appraised the belt and nodded in agreement. He knew Rogers and the reason why he had arrived. "It is advantageous to see you again, Captain. Chief Nimham, take a seat and enjoy the game with us," Uncas replied.

Rogers sat down facing Uncas with his legs folded under him, and Daniel sat down beside him. Finn, Gus, and Fronto, were seated behind them.

Uncas motioned for more pipes, and three women brought pipes and loaded them with tobacco, handing one to Rogers and Daniel, and then to Finn, Gus, and Fronto. The men smoked in silence until Rogers cleared his throat.

"We must speak, Chief Uncas. There was a war on Lake George, and to our surprise, Iroquois warriors fought on both sides," he said in a dry voice.

"Yes, it is a sad day when our Nation is divided, and a group of Mohawk and French ambushed a Mohawk-led English column," Uncas replied.

"I'm here to talk with you how we can stop that. My commanders sent me here to request your help to decide whose side the Mohawk are on," Rogers said.

Uncas thought for a moment. "Tell me what you have in mind."

Rogers shifted for a better posture and leaned closer while lowering his voice. "Should you choose to join us as a captain, you shall have a commission. You can choose your own ensign and sergeants. The company should consist of fifty men or more. In the event that the deserters from Brewer's Corps will join you, the General will pardon them. You may hire a clerk who shall be allowed the regular pay. I wish you success in raising the men, and shall be glad to have you with us as soon as possible. But we need to confirm our union, Chief Uncas," he said.

Uncas sat quietly, enjoying smoking his pipe. "Chief Aupumut said when it comes time to die, be not like those whose hearts are filled with the fear of death. When their time comes, they weep and pray to live their lives again in a different way for a little more time. Sing your death song and die like a hero returning home. I say we must do so together as one nation for our common interest," he said.

Finn noticed a beautiful woman standing on the side line. She smiled coyly at him, and Finn poked Gus on his side. "Gus, that's her! Remember? Her name is Spotted Bear," Finn whispered, exited.

Gus patted his arm, telling Finn to calm down, but it was to no avail. Finn looked for an excuse to leave the discussions because he saw something much more interesting close by.

"I want to try this game. It can't be that difficult," he whispered to Fronto and Gus.

The players, wearing red-and-blue breechcloths, picked up ball sticks and a leather ball stuffed with deer hair. Finn walked by Spotted Bear flexing his muscles and picking up a game stick. He smiled confidently again to her and got ready and the game started. He was promptly run over, landing heavy on his back. Finn got back up, shaking his head, and was tackled and knocked down several times. Stunned and spitting grass he cleared his head.

While Rogers was talking, Uncas nodded to Spotted Bear motioning toward Finn.

The ball was tossed up, and the warrior who caught it straightaway set out at full speed toward the opposite goal. Being closely pursued, he threw the ball in the direction of his own side, who took up the race. Always a quick learner, Finn noticed that the swiftest players engaged at the center of the field and the slower arranged themselves around the goal posts. The heavier players held the ground in between. He realized that his best chances were in speed, quick changes of direction and dodging. *Actual life is really hard, too,* he thought, *there are no soft falls, but those falls make me who I am. I can do this.*

Hearing a war cry behind him, Finn peeked over his shoulder to see a giant of a warrior charging him at full speed. He jumped around the man and moved swiftly on the edge and headed toward the corners. He jumped high and intercepted a pass and snatched the ball in the net, surprising even himself. Blocking for him, a warrior smashed an opponent with an elbow to the face, sending the man sprawling onto the ground. Finn dodged another opponent, and ran out in front. He swung the ball behind his back, over his shoulder, and made a nice, long pass to a warrior who quickly scored a goal.

The warriors were impressed by Finn's devil-may-care attitude, quick stops, turns, and backward steps. He survived in the game for several minutes, but then came the inevitable big hit, right from the faceoff, that left Finn stunned, bleeding and motionless on the ground for several moments. Coming to his senses, Finn heard faintly how Robert Rogers ordered the Rangers to get ready. The powwow was going to end soon.

Getting up, Finn was not accustomed to praise, which was done so publicly by these wild looking, fierce warriors.

Fronto saw his plight from the sideline. "You must ensure that you don't turn into a Caesar. You do not want to get dipped into the purple dye — for that can happen," Fronto quipped as Finn was brandishing his game stick over his head.

Bruised and battered, Finn walked toward a stream to bathe and went across a clump of elms and a lilac brush with an aromatic, haunting fragrance. He wiped blood from the corner of his mouth. He came around a giant snowball bush and stopped in his tracks. Spotted Bear was waiting for him, standing tall and proud, beautiful and sexy in her buckskin dress.

"I remember you from the woods. I watched you play," she said and came close to him. He admired her long, shining black hair and tanned skin with yellow and red colorations. He could not help noticing that the leather strap on her dress had come loose. He gaped down her open buckskin shirt that revealed her ample cleavage.

She took his moose necklace in her hand. "I see you have a powerful protector. You must be a reliable provider and on the field you are a mighty warrior. But what kind of man are you?" she asked and stepped close to him. She pressed her body against his and gently fondled his crotch.

"It brings me good luck," he said and leaned back, not knowing how to respond.

She pushed him behind some large boulders and pulled a leather cord on her shoulder. Her deerskin garment dropped down on her belly, bearing large, firm breasts. It then slowly fell to the ground, leaving her fully naked. She was lean and stunningly beautiful.

Finn felt his blood boil and surge through his veins so hard that it made him dizzy. There was soft moss and brushwood on the ground, and he reached for her, trying to pull her down with him. She spun around and leaned down against the rock, looking at him over her shoulder. Just one look at her perfect, pear shaped buttocks and the wet, alluring vulva between her shapely tights, drove the hurt and any remaining sense out of Finn's head. A primal urge took hold of them both, and they engaged in unrestrained, wild sex in the woods.

For a fleeing time in the wilderness, Finn felt that he was not alone in the world and that someone, this gorgeous woman no less, actually wanted him.

§ § §

The pow-wow ended, and much to his satisfaction, Robert Rogers noted that his wampum had been accepted, but he wasn't quite sure if an alliance had been sealed. Heading out at a brisk pace, but avoiding any trails and open areas, he led Gus, Fronto, and Daniel back toward Fort Edward. Finn came running out of the bushes and caught up with them, while closing his belt. He had grass and twigs in his hair. Fronto winked his eye to Finn, and Gus shook his head.

Daniel stopped to wait for Finn and slapped him on the shoulder. "My brethren gave you a name, Finn. They call you Most True. You played. You won, and you claimed your prize. They think you a warrior now," he said.

Rogers stopped to wait for them. Seeing Finn, he guessed the rest, and he was all excited. "Did you have sex with that woman?"

Finn pulled straw from his hair and tried to hide the stains in the front of his pants. He looked chagrined. "Look here, I can state unequivocally that I did not have..." his voice faltered, seeing the other's faces. "Well, what the heck. Yes, I did."

"Sealed with a kiss, I see. Great," Rogers said. He turned to Daniel and continued, "Ranger Nimham, you're next. Now, we must provide the news soon because Chief Uncas on our side. Fortune can turn in our favor on all our future operations. I might even get promoted for this."

Gus patted Daniel on the back. "Well Ranger, you got yourself a difficult mission. Take one for the team."

Several hours later, as they drew closer to Fort Edward, they heard whiplashes and horses on the road. To their surprise, they discovered the fort in turmoil as delegations of high level officials were pouring into the fort from three directions. Two of the carriages almost collided as they tried to get through the gate at the same time. General

Johnson was caught off guard and appeared from Helen of Magdalena's wagon. He buttoned his trousers and hurried to the fort.

The meeting had been prepared in the greatest secrecy, and the locals were never informed of it due to concerns over poor security around the fort.

"What the fuck is going on here?" Rogers asked. "I've got a war to fight. I don't have time to go from one meeting to another for crying out loud."

The British set up their command post across the fort from the provincials. Messengers hurried back and forth between the groups. The Iroquois were left out from the negotiations, and they gathered in front of their quarters, left out only to watch as the fate of their nation was in strangers' hands.

The central meeting place was agreed to be in the Silver Star tavern. Johnson cleared the house by throwing out all customers and declaring it closed to the public. "I hereby commandeer this venture to be the meeting place for these negotiations. Everybody get out and stay out!" he shouted, and tossed a purse on the bar in front of Mary Brant.

Rogers posted sentries at the door because he knew from experience that all sides deployed secret agents to eavesdrop on the others. The provincial delegation consisted of Benjamin Franklin, John Morton, and George Washington, as well as Thomas Pownall, Governor of Massachusetts, and James De Lancey, acting Governor of New York.

Lancey was elected to be the chairman for the locals. "Gentlemen, we're gathered here to settle an urgent matter with the British. I represent New York, and Mr. Pownall represents Massachusetts, Mr. Franklin and Mr. Morton represent Pennsylvania, and Colonel Washington represents Virginia. That, I think, makes us fully capable of making imminent and relevant decisions in this regard," he said.

Across the fort, arrogant British officers were in panic, expecting further orders from Lord Loudoun who was in charge of the British delegation. Loudoun turned to the officers. "Do I have to remind you that it is my reputations at stake in London?" He said.

Unified, they marched across the fort with their body guards to meet with the provincials. Without further ado, the British blatantly blamed the locals for the failed war efforts, General Braddock's failure, Fort Oswego ambush, and the Fort William Henry disaster, everything.

"The Braddock Expedition defeat was largely due to the inadequate provincial support," Loudoun charged.

General Abercrombie eagerly supported him. "The ambuscade of Fort Oswego package train resulted purely because the provincials did not obey orders given to them," he said.

"Fort William Henry was lost due to the local militia's incompetence," General Webb added.

The provincials were insulted and outraged. Exchanging horrified looks with Franklin, John Morton stepped forward. "How dare you to insult us like that. We have been most trusted British subjects and carried more than our share in this struggle," he said.

Franklin was extremely disappointed after hearing the accusations from the British. "Provincial military has carried its burden in battle. Our casualties are significantly heavier than the regular British army."

Washington tried to talk, convinced that he could find ways to amend the situation. He made appeasing gestures and hoped to find a way to impress the British, but the uproar in the room only got louder.

There was some pushing and shoving in the back between the British and the provincial aides. Rogers assumed a mediator's role and tried to get some sort of consensus among the quarrelling factions. He stepped forward in the middle of the room and raised his hand.

"Hear me out. I know the local tribes around here," he said, but nobody paid him any attention nor heard him over the yelling and shouting. Rogers glanced around and pulled out his pistol and fired it at the roof. People were showered with saw dust, and one British troop made a move toward Rogers, but Finn blocked him, shaking his finger in front of the man's face. Shocked, everybody quieted down.

Rogers stood in the middle of the stunned, crowded room, holding the smoking gun in his hand, and his eyes snapped from man to man. "At ease! Now listen. I have reached an agreement with Chief Uncas. By and large, the Iroquois will join our side. He will urge other warriors to fight alongside us, and that will help our cause," he said.

Rogers continued on, feverishly trying to convince the British about new ways of fighting the war. He insisted it should be fought in the Mohawk style, with hit and run tactics.

The British listened halfheartedly because they had their own internal power struggles that were a higher priority to them. Conniving Abercrombie convinced Loudoun that in order to cover their own participation and to pacify the provincials, Webb was to be blamed for everything. Seeing a potential opportunity to blackmail favors from Abercrombie later, Loudoun agreed, and Webb was made the scapegoat. Webb was relieved from his duties, and indignantly he got on his horse and galloped off in shame.

Abercrombie was extremely pleased after managing to get Webb's post. Secretly, he had even higher ambitions. Unaware of all this intrigue behind the scenes, making a last effort, the provincials finally managed to convince the British that more Rangers were needed, and Lord Loudoun hesitantly agreed.

The British seemed to lose all interest in the petty, local affairs, and they prepared to leave the fort and return to their more comfortable headquarters.

To conclude, the meeting was closed, and the delegations departed. The fort quieted down, and Finn found Fronto sitting in the tavern, hitting on one of the waitresses. He was tossing a coin in his hands and said to her, "This game is acutely like the one that was just played out by the British, my dear. The rules are simple. I'll flip a coin, and you have to guess which side it lands on. Heads, I get tail. Tails, I get head. Okay?"

After a while, Gus and Daniel joined them. Catherina arrived as well, looking for Finn, hoping to talk to him, but for some reason unknown to her, he averted his eyes and turned to the Rangers.

At the bar, Finn was downing a drink after drink, thinking of Rosie and feeling guilty and embarrassed of his own act earlier. Now, seeing Catherina made him acutely aware that he had betrayed both of them, and himself, because he had not been able to control his urges in the woods with Spotted Bear. He felt lonelier than ever before.

§   §   §

The war offered no breaks. In Fort Edward, the gates flung open, and Robert Rogers marched in from yet another patrol, closely followed by his brothers, James, Richard, John "Tiny", and Bill Stark, who was flanked by a hulking wolf-dog Sergeant Beaubien. Their uniforms were dirty and most the ammunition spent, but their weapons were clean as a whistle, oiled and ready. Right behind them followed a band of fierce Mohawk warriors in war paint and covered in enemy's blood, and then another group of grim Rangers accompanied by Finn, Fronto, Daniel, and Gus.

Seeing the handsome, hard-nosed frontier fighters, older women blushed, gathered their squealing daughters (who wanted to see more too) and shepherded them away out of sight before daring to steal a bashful glimpse of the Ranger's eyes.

The husbands and fathers turned away in haste, pretending to be busy fixing something that did not need fixing.

General Johnson arrived to inform Robert Rogers that the Rangers were needed on a special naval expedition. He met Rogers in front of the supply room, where he was counting sacks of beans and boxes of bullets. When Johnson approached him, Rogers motioned the civilians to leave them.

"Captain, I'm about to tell you about the Louisburg

mission. The Rangers are needed to recon the area around the French fort for possible avenues of attack. The navy will be there in a supporting role," Johnson said.

"My Rangers are perfect for that mission, sir. They can operate both on land and at sea. If we had wings, we would attack from above as well. My men will blow everything up after marching all day, then drink all night, and screw all the women in town so hard they'd walk funny for a week," Rogers said.

"No doubt about that, Captain. Consider this your warning order and wait for further instructions. I'd recommend additional training in the meanwhile. Captain, I appreciate what your Rangers are capable of, and the question is how we convince the higher headquarters about it," Johnson replied.

Rogers studied the roster and stopped to ponder for a second as he noticed that a man by the name of Sergeant Beaubien was drawing a regular pay marked in the same company with William Stark. He did not recall any French turncoats, or even Canadians, joining his ranks. He made a mental note to ask Bill Stark about this. He then decided to put Joseph Gorham in charge of the naval detachment. "I will assign this duty to Joe Gorham. He is a second generation Ranger. The first Ranger unit assigned to the regular establishment of the British Army was formed by his father, John Gorham, who is a legend in his own right around this neck of woods," he said.

"Yes, I remember hearing about Gorham," Johnson replied.

Rogers pulled Johnson aside for more privacy and lowered his voice. "Sir, you remember our contract on our strategy regarding the Iroquois allies? The first step has been played out according to plan. Now we need complete the second part," he said.

Johnson looked around to make sure they had privacy. "Yes I do, Captain, and you shall begin the second stage right now. Now if you forgive me," he replied and stood up to leave.

Rogers grinned and winked his eye. "Yes, sir, and good hunting," he said and waited as Johnson pulled his hat down over his eyes and departed. Rogers gave Daniel Nimham a hand signal.

Daniel walked across the bridge to the fort and toward the Silver Star lounge. On the way across the fort, he politely greeted some ladies on the sidewalk, but the women did not return the greeting, being afraid of the warrior's brawny and tattooed, battle-scarred figure. There was a man and a female side-by-side in the stocks on the square next to sheriff's office. Passers-by shook their fingers at them, and a man spat on the ground in front of them.

Daniel sat down under a tree near a large barrel that acted as a table and ordered some food and a drink. While he was eating, Shelagh Brotherton came walking by as he already knew she would do at that time of the day. She was closely followed by two older ladies, her two chaperones. Daniel admired Shelagh, who was a strikingly beautiful, petite woman with short black hair and wide set eyes. She was dressed in a colorful skirt, a buckskin top, and moccasins. He smiled at her and was pleased as she returned it.

Just then, around the corner came four sturdy Rangers who, as if by chance, blocked the old ladies from passing, and cutting them off from Shelagh. Daniel jumped up, and taking Shelagh by her elbow, whisked her around the corner, out of sight. He gently pressed his finger on her lips to keep her quiet. She looked at him hulking over her, wide-eyed, more out of surprise rather than out of fear. She nodded silently and let out a sigh of excitement.

"You are Shelagh. I have noticed you several times," Daniel said.

"I know who you are too, Chief Nimham," she said.

"My status with the British ladies precedes me. Perhaps ladies speak the truth, perhaps not. Perhaps you would like to find out?" Daniel said.

"Most certainly not, but I'm not scared you either. What can I do for you, Chief Nimham?" Shelagh asked. She looked at Daniel, trying to gauge his intentions. He was, after all, a prominent figure in the Iroquois nation.

There was a practical side to Daniel's interest in her. After all, love, at that time and age, was just the icing on the cake. Robert Rogers and Johnson convinced him that a close relationship with Shelagh would boost the Wappinger's public and personal dealings with the British and the provincials. "I go straight to the point. We need to make a pact, Shelagh. I need your help in our war effort," he said with all the trustworthiness in his voice he could muster.

"What could I do? I'm only a woman. This is a man's war," Shelagh replied.

Daniel learned something in his youth while running after young Iroquois women who were not the easiest ones for a young man to catch. He knew how to be forceful with eagle-eyed ladies. He placed his hand on Shelagh's arm.

"You have a mother and sisters, and a father and brother. They are all affected by this war, just like everybody else. Think about them. Most importantly, you have authority among the British. Help me to develop my dealings with them. You could make a significant difference, Shelagh," he said.

Daniel was an excellent judge of character and people's motivations under certain circumstances. Shelagh had, in fact, felt a lot of stress and was scoffed at by the villagers because she did not care for any of the young men whom they expected she should marry. Girls were usually paired with potential grooms at an early age by their parents in accordance with the custom. The deciding factors were the size of dowry and family honor, which usually went hand in hand.

At the age of eighteen, the clock was ticking for Shelagh to make her decision, or her parents would make it for her. Shelagh, however, simply considered the entire collection of beau's to be too immature, and she wanted a real man. A man that would protect her — and ravish her on occasion. Quietly, she had made up her own mind to find a reliable provider and secure financial security. In secret, she had begun taking notice of the handsome Wappinger chief, and she had been enamored with him.

Nevertheless, Shelagh was not an easy girl, and she knew well what the stakes were. She proudly raised her chin up. "Perhaps so, but the best way I can help my family and my people is by hard work and prosperity," she said, stealing a glance at Daniel from the corner of her eyes.

"I can provide you all that," he replied.

"I know what you can do," she said, unpretentiously.

"Bargains like this, between a man and a woman, should be sealed in the appropriate manner. I shall be the custodian of our relationship, Shelagh."

"No."

"I can provide you with status, property, and wealth."

"No, means no," she said firmly, but her breathing was getting heavier, and he noticed it.

Daniel stepped closer and slid his hand up her thigh. "No means I shall try even harder," he whispered. "Shelagh, I must admit that I have a dream where I surprise you while you are washing under the water falls. Imagine, where I would aim a powerful stream of warm water? Besides, this could lead to a verbal marriage contract," he said.

His exact come-on perplexed Shelagh, although she found his hard, warrior demeanor devilishly sexy. She was now thoroughly intrigued and roused. "You mean a hand-fasting?" she asked.

"Yes, Shelagh, I am talking about a spousal," he nodded at her.

"Are you sure? No trickery?" She said, still somewhat guarded.

"No, not at all. Take my word. I promise," he replied.

He slid his hand higher and squeezed her thigh firmly, taking her breath away. She nodded, excited, shy, and itching all at the same time.

"Is that a yes?" He asked.

She nodded again. "Yes," she whispered.

Without ado, he took her hand and led her by the back fence into a barn. They climb into a hayloft, and he slid his hand up her skirt, following her upstairs.

"I'm not ready for babies, but seed-spilling is a sin. To white men it is, anyway," she said, her back turned to him. She pulled the cords of her blouse open.

He pressed himself against her back, cupping her breasts. "Don't worry, I'll be careful. Trust me," he said slipping his tongue in her ear. Pulling her skirt up, he propped her up on the rafters.

§   §   §

The next morning right before day break, there was much yelling and shouting on the Rogers' Island. A rooster was startled out of its slumber and almost fell off the fence. The dazed and tired Rangers woke up to shouting and loud banging. Moses Hazen and Donald MacCurdy threw the doors open and barged in yelling and screaming. "First call! Drop your cocks and grab your socks! Get your head out of bed, now! You walk like ladies!"

Finn, Gus, Fronto, and Daniel scrambled outside, pulling on their clothes and grabbing their equipment. Out on the assembly area, they met Robert Rogers, who was incensed as usual and barking orders. "What the fuck have I told you? We train as we fight. Always be ready to march at a moment's notice. No time to slack off. Lazy men get killed. No pain, no gain."

In the adjacent hut, Hazen kicked and punched the new recruits and threw the slowest ones outside through the door. "Pain is weakness leaving your miserable, girlish bodies!"

Thus began all day and all night training missions for the Rangers. Finn was at ease in his element in the northern frontier forests. His excellent navigation skills were noticed after he led a patrol for twenty miles without a map or any other aid across unfamiliar terrain. He was told to take the patrol to a road intersection, and after marching all day, they arrived dead on at the objective in the afternoon.

"Young chief knows his trails," Daniel said with an approving nod.

"How do you find your way in the wilderness so well?" Gus asked.

Finn shrugged his shoulders. "I don't know. I just do. It's like I have a compass inside my head. Anyways, when I'm in doubt, the trees, ants, and birds show me the way," he replied.

"What about life? Can you find your way just as easily?" Fronto asked.

"What the fuck do you mean, Dog?" Finn replied, puzzled.

Before Fronto could answer, Robert Rogers arrived. "You sure know your way in the woods, Ranger Finn. As such, I will make you my pathfinder," he said. Turning to look at Daniel, he asked, "So, Ranger Nimham, did *you* accomplish the mission?"

Daniel affirmed by nodding his head. Rogers seemed to be extremely pleased as he marched off and gestured to a runner. He was instructed to take a message to Chief Uncas that said that the coalition had been consummated.

The Rangers continued training for hours on end, moving long distances, reconnoitering, raiding, and then moving again to a new location and practicing ambush tactics. As they lay at an ambush site, John Stark walked on the trail along the firing line. "We will lie down quietly, until birds and animals return to their normal behavior. This way, any approaching French or Injuns will not see anything out of the ordinary," he said.

Moses Hazen paced back and forth behind them. "There are two types of ambushes. A hasty ambush is done quickly when the enemy is approaching but unaware of our presence. Today we will practice a deliberate ambush, which is set up in a planned and orderly manner, hours ahead of an expected enemy moving along his known lines of communication," he said.

Rogers stood on the road, his right hand on his hip, and cradled his musket on his left arm. "This is the kill zone. I call it the French Promised Land. When they arrive on this piece of property, they shall meet their maker, I promise," he said, pointing out the section on the road.

On the other end of the firing line, Donald MacCurdy positioned the three-barreled pole cannons, each manned by the gunner and assistant gunner. "The pole cannons are set up at the end of the firing line so that they will have a clear oblique field of fire into the kill zone! But always remember to put one hand for flank security!"

The sun rose higher, and by noon it hovered high above their heads. The Rangers lay motionless in the ambush site all day. Men kept nodding, almost falling asleep in the high temperature of the day, and their buddies poked them in the ribs with their elbows to keep them awake.

Finn rested his cheek on the butt of his musket and tried to stay awake, but the heat made it difficult. He was watching a trail of ants carrying bits of leaves and grass right in front of his face on top of a tree root. His mind kept wandering, and he dozed off. He dreamt about sweet, blue-eyed Eva in his home village, and their moment of passion in the barn. Then red-headed Rosie pushed her aside and led him to the stables at night. Abruptly, exotic Prudentina from the slave ship, her skin like chocolate, pushed her butt against his groin. But then, out of the wildflower bushes, Spotted Bear appeared naked, and Finn let out a soft sigh, dreamily smiling. Then, beautiful blonde Catherine appeared with her hands on her hips, glaring sternly at him as the images of the other women vanished. Finn noted with satisfaction that she was indeed a blonde, catching a glimpse of her pubic hair and tight, voluptuous buttocks. Seeing all of these curvy female forms, eyeing all the breasts and butts, he felt his manhood start to get hard, and... A whippoorwill startled him from his slumber.

Finn shook his head to wake up, feeling a surge of intense loneliness. Then, he was alarmed as he heard a Ranger to his right gasp. Then another Ranger gasped, and a third. Then a fourth — bewildered, Finn wondered what was happening.

A fifth Ranger gasped, and then Fronto, next to him, gasped too. Finn was baffled. Just then, Finn's eyes almost popped out as an enormous snake slithered over his legs. He gasped. Gus to his left gasped. Finn chuckled trying not to laugh. Daniel and the other Rangers to his left inhaled one by one as the snake moved over their legs as well.

Quiet and stillness returned. Mosquitos buzzed, and birds sang in the trees. Late in the afternoon, scattered clouds covered the sun and a fuzzy nippiness fell over the forest. The last rays of the setting sun twinkled behind tree

tops, and Finn heard muffled noises in the distance —
squeaking leather and hooves. Someone was approaching
the ambush site on the road. The Rangers got ready and
quietly cocked their muskets.

Everybody was surprised to see Bill Stark and a woman
arrive on a horse carriage. They stopped dead in the middle of the kill zone. Bill Stark helped the woman to step
down as they laughed and teased each other. The Rangers
glanced at each other; a situation like this was not in any
training so far.

The couple started having hot foreplay, right in front of
the Rangers. Bill Stark pushed the woman against the wagon and raised her skirt to her hips. He was getting ready,
intent on dropping his pants, when the younger Rangers in
the ambush could not take it any longer and started snick-
ering, and the lustful couple on the road heard them.

"Hey Ranger, don't let us disturb you. The young ones
need the class," Fronto quipped, and the Rangers laughed
out loud.

The girl let out a little scream, and Stark, snapping angry glances at the woods around them, pulled his pants up.
"You're fairies and low lives. What the hell do you think
you're doing? You just compromised the mission over the
unexpected," he shouted, waving his fist. Stark helped the
woman to get back in the carriage, and they drove off rapidly in a cloud dust. The entire firing line burst out laughing and hollering.

Robert Rogers was not amused. "At ease, men. Ranger
Stark was on it and he's right. What if this was a real ambush and you started laughing because of the scene and
doing so gave your positions away? Always expect the un-

expected, remember that. Now get ready to move out," he said.

"No time to eat. You have already rested. Now get going. Form two lines on the road, each individual five yards apart. Intersperse the lines so that no two men are level. This way, should we be ambushed, a single ball will hit only one target," Hazen said, taking the lead.

Rogers took them on a forced road march with full packs, moving them twenty-four miles in eight hours.

"Remember the Thermopylae, Rangers. The Greek runner ran twenty-four miles to deliver the news. We will do the same tonight. Get ready for a tactical road march. We will cover the same distance by sunrise. March or die!" Rogers shouted.

The Rangers marched in silence, leaning forward under heavy packs and gear, carrying muskets at the ready. John Stark stood by the road as the Rangers marched past him. "Rangers will move farther and faster, and fight harder than any other soldier. If you fall by the wayside, may the devil take you," he said.

"Drink water, men. Squad leaders, make sure your men drink enough water. I will not accept any heat casualties today," Rogers barked.

Two lines of men dressed in green snaked along a forested road, nearly blending in with the surrounding plant life. The Rangers took turns carrying heavy pole cannons, but Finn refused to hand over his, determined to carry it all the way through.

Silhouettes of marching men, hunched under heavy rucksacks, advanced toward the setting sun. The sun fell beyond the horizon, and the Rangers continued a fast paced march into the dark woods and non-stop through the night.

During the road march, Donald MacCurdy approached one of new privates who was whining and staggering on his feet and falling behind. Fat Murray, a chubby man with sandy hair, red whiskers, and large protruding ears, was ready to fall out.

MacCurdy hardly believed his eyes and regarded the man in front of him with contempt. "Do you feel tired? Are you hungry? You look like shit, private. If you want to quit, all you need to do is say so. Just say one word, asshole, and you can get on those wagons that will take you to Molly's chambers where you can eat, drink, shit, fuck, and sleep to your heart's desire."

"I wanna be a Ranger but — but I'm so tired!" Fat Murray wailed and wiped his runny nose.

MacCurdy looked thoroughly disgusted. "You cockgobbling, cum-guzzling, butt-pirate! Molly will pat you in the head as she'd cared for you because she wants your money. But I don't give a damn, you sloppy son of a bitch!" He roared and gave Fat Murray a swift kick in the ass. He picked up speed and caught up with the others in front of him.

Robert Rogers ran up to Fat Murray and yelled into his ear. "What's your major malfunction, asshole? Listening to your incessant drivel is making my shit lumpy. You don't like it here, do you? Then join the British regulars, where the confusion of officers and subtlety of sergeants abound!" He shouted.

"March or die!" Hazen barked at Fat Murray and gave him a hard push, sending him tripping and wobbling down the road.

This encouragement from the officers proved to be futile, however, since after just a few miles, Fat Murray was done. He stumbled and fell head on into the ditch, sniveling and holding his knee. MacCurdy stooped down to look at him. "You're all fucked up, scum bucket."

Fat Murray burst into tears, and Rogers, his face twisted in loathing, spat on the ground in front of him. "Another wanna-be bites the dust. Throw this sorry-ass, potbellied, motherfucker out of my beloved Rangers!"

§   §   §

Vivid rays of sunlight streamed through the oak leaves and cast playful shadows on Catherina's farm. She sat outside on a bench, reading and churning some raw milk into butter and buttermilk. Working the plunger was hard, tedious work, and she had to keep switching arms to do it. Finally, she drained the buttermilk into a wooden bucket with metal ring supports and placed the hard butter clumps in a round, stilted cheese box, covering it with a linen cloth. Planning to barter the goods for some items she needed from the store, she borrowed a horse and an old wooden farm wagon from a neighbor and drove to Fort Edward.

When she arrived in the Helming Brother's Trading Company, she found it bustling with hunters and trappers and warriors, trading their wares and telling tall tales. Two of the earliest arrivals in the fort, Carl and Gustav Helming, were Jewish twin brothers from Virginia. People could not tell the twins apart and always got mixed up between them. The business savvy brothers devised a plan where one acted polite while the other drove a hard bargain, and they kept switching the roles. People, on the other hand, tried to receive additional discounts by referring to the other brother's promises when he was not around.

Catherina finally managed to conclude her business just as Bill Stark was passing by with Sergeant Beaubien, his massive wolf dog. He stopped to help her load some sacks of flour and rations on the wagon.

Finn happened to come by on his way to Rogers Island and grabbed the last pouch to throw it on the wagon.

"That's okay, Finn. We got it, but thanks anyway," Catherina said, pleased that he had offered to help.

Bill Stark offered to drive the wagon back to Catherina's farm. They got on the wagon, and she sat in the middle close to him. Sergeant Beaubien jumped in the back. Finn hesitated at first, but then he jumped on the bench next to Catherina.

Growing up in a remote farm with her strict, deeply religious parents and overly protective brother, Catherina was not used to dating young men or courting anyone for that matter. But she wanted to get Finn's attention, and so she started flirting with Bill Stark and laughed at his jokes just a little too loudly. Despite her good intentions, her plan backfired, and Finn grew jealous. She was taken quite by surprise as Finn suddenly jumped in the back of the wagon and sulked. Finn rubbed Sergeant Beaubien's oversized, furry ears, and after a little while, he cursed silently and jumped off, walking away.

Stark realized what had happened and stopped the wagon. He ran after Finn and grabbed his arm. "Hey, Ranger, she is not coming between us. I'm not interested in her. I've got someone else in mind."

Finn shrugged him off. "Yes, yes, you can be funny to her, but leave me alone," he said, turned around, fuming, and snapped at Catherina. "And you are flirting with disaster, Miss," he said and walked into the woods.

Sitting on the wagon and watching him go, Catherina cursed quietly, biting her lower lip. *Well, that did not go so well*, she thought. *Men can be so bizarre.*

Finn wandered in a large colony of Aspens, ruminating on the quirks of the opposite sex. After a while, he came to the realization that his own behavior had not been very respectful, particularly considering his encounter with Spotted Bear earlier and how guilty he felt about being disloyal to Rosie. But after all, he was a red-blooded man. What was he supposed to do when a dazzling woman offered herself to him like that? But what would Rosie think and say? And Catherina must think of him as a jerk, although they were not actually dating or anything. And why was she constantly intruding on his thoughts like that? It was infuriating him.

In the end, he just could not figure out women, simple as that. They could be so strange. He kept thinking about how he might be able to make amends and apologize to Catherina when he came to a stream with some willows. He took out his knife and cut a twig, then began carving a small notch into the wood to make a whistle. As he was cutting a circle around the twig, he cut his finger. He watched as the blood drops fell on a bed of white sand by the stream. He stared at the blood drops, lost in thought.

Fronto showed up, looking for him. Seeing his dark stare, Fronto covered up the drops of blood with dirt to allow Finn to recover his wits, and then walked with him back to Fort Edward. "Come on, whippersnapper. Snap out of it. I know what we could do. Let's go and catch us a villain," he said, poking Finn on the side.

Finn cheered up, and they fetched Gus and Daniel to join them. A plan was drafted and soon they found a suitable place outside of the fort, close but out of sight. Finn placed a musket on a pine tree as bait, and they hid in a thicket of willows and riparian trees, ready to pounce on an easy to fool thief. Late in the afternoon, as the daylight started to fade, they saw a man dressed in a long, black oilskin duster coat and a black tricorn hat approach the musket from the woods. Just as he reached to pluck the musket, the thief heard four metallic clicks from flintlocks being cocked. Raising his arms and slowly turning around, he faced four gaping barrels aimed directly at his head.

"One false move and you'll meet your maker," Finn said.

Unknown to them at the time, it was a fluke chance that they had caught the man. He was a wanted highwayman on the lam from Nottinghamshire, England. Folks called him Major Oak, and he was a raw-boned and wily man. He had just happened to be passing through the area, seeking a new place to practice his questionable trade after a robbery gone sour back in the old country. Now, seeing an opportunity in the form of an abandoned rifle, he merely followed his highwayman's instincts and grabbed it.

Daniel and Gus grabbed Major Oak by the arms, and held him tight as Fronto frisked him. The corner of Major Oak's mouth twisted in condescension as he brazenly regarded Finn. "Who's this scared little puppy?" he asked and spat tobacco on the ground.

"Catching a low life like you was easy. You are but a

stabber in the dark, a spineless nasty rat," Finn said. It felt good to let out some of the bottled-up anger inside.

"Temperance, whippersnapper," Fronto said, but Finn had worked himself beyond listening.

Major Oak snarled back at Finn and spit in his face. "Fuck you all. You're nothing but bloated buffoons."

Finn snatched a riding glove from the man's belt and slapped him in the face with it. "I demand satisfaction," he said and stepped closer, his face only inches from Major Oak.

Gus sighed and spreading his arms in a helpless fashion, shook his head at Finn. "I wish you would listen to Fronto just once. I guess you want me to be your second now. It is my responsibility, above all, to try to reconcile the parties," he said, and took another look at Major Oak. "Oh, what the hell, let's take this ass-clown to the field!"

Holding the man tightly between them, Daniel and Fronto walked him into an open field. Gus pulled out two steel-hilt belt pistols and checked each one. He handed one to Finn, and after a moment's hesitation, he handed the second one to Major Oak.

The two men walked across the ground and turned to face each other twenty-five feet apart. Major Oak acted like this was an everyday happening to him. Then, without hesitation, Major Oak raised his gun and aimed at Finn's hip, as was the dueling custom. He fired and missed, but the ball nicked Finn in the shoulder.

Finn cried out, holding his shoulder. "What the fuck was that? Did you miss me on purpose? Do you think I'm not worth shooting? That was a terrible mistake, sir!" he said, incensed.

In one swift motion, Finn raised his pistol, hardly aiming, fired and hit Major Oak in the forehead. The back of his head was blown off and he fell backward. The lifeless body landed on the ground with a thud, his legs twisted under his body and dead eyes staring into eternity.

"Nice shot. Young chief's hand is steady!" Daniel exclaimed.

Just as Finn's shot rang out, Bill Stark and Catherina pulled their wagon up to the scene. Sergeant Beaubien was standing in the back with his front legs on the railing and his bushy tail wagging. Catherina realized what had taken place and was shocked to see the dead man on the ground. She pointed her finger at Finn. "Don't you know the rules? You were supposed to wound only, not kill," she said.

Finn looked back at her, startled. "What are you talking about? I don't play any games. I shoot to kill," he said, shrugging and spreading his arms.

"Listen, buster. You should learn some manners like a gentleman. I'm a woman, but I could put an end to any man's life with three mighty blows, cut off his head, and cut him into quarters. But what you just did had no honor in it whatsoever."

"I did it for all of us. Besides, that's probably the guy who stole your cow, which I helped you to get back, for crying out loud," Finn said, pointing at the body with the pistol.

"You have no soul! You should cover your right hand in a tissue when entering a church, for you don't want the hand that has killed a man to offend God!" She was shouting now and clearly enraged.

Bewildered, Finn stared at her. "But I don't even go to church."

Fronto rubbed his chin. "Hmm, maybe you could say that the soul is like a spider in a web. When the web is disturbed by an insect, the signal is transmitted through vibrations to the spider sitting at the center," he said.

Catherina gave him an angry look. "Oh, and you can bugger off, too," she said, storming to the other side of the wagon.

Bill Stark took the pistols and glanced at the dead man lying on the ground. He told Finn to report to Captain Rogers.

Gus had inspected the dead man's belongings and pulled out a folded piece of paper from his pocket. It was a warrant for forty pounds to catch a felon. "Well, well, it seems that right there is the outlaw Major Oak himself. We caught a notorious thief and poacher. Bad news is that we have to travel to Nottinghamshire to collect the reward."

Finn let out a sigh and glanced at Catherina again. He turned to Bill Stark, "And I'm rightfully angered by her unjust words. Sir, I shall volunteer for the next mission, whatever it is," he said and headed toward Fort Edward.

Gus, Fronto, and Daniel loaded the dead man onto the wagon and urged Catherina to turn the wagon to following Finn so they could keep him out of more trouble.

On Rogers Island, Finn stormed into Robert Rogers' command post. "Sir, I need a mission. Any job as long as it is far away from here," he said.

Bill Stark arrived and explained what had taken place. John Stark was ready to take disciplinary action against Finn. "You could be tried for murder and sentenced to death," he said as his brother Bill placed the pistols on the table. "In this case, killing a known robber, the sentence could be commuted to a fine, upon the grounds that the offence only amounted to manslaughter," he said, mulling over the incident.

Robert Rogers took a burning twig from the fireplace and lighted a long, decorated, clay pipe. He smoked in silence, glancing at Finn, Gus, Fronto, and Daniel. He took the warrant and folded it in his pocket. "I'll take that and collect it for you. I bet that Sheriff Jimmie Dick would be more than happy to string him up on a tree limb," he said and thought for a moment. "But, I need all the Rangers I can get, and men are required for the Louisburg mission. It will be beneficial to send him out of here for a while until things calm down a bit. You four, report to Captain Gorham in Boston," he said.

Moses Hazen looked at Finn and then at Rogers. "Out of sight is out of mind?"

"Exactly, and perhaps a short distance between the two lovebirds will help to sort things out. Ah, and what could be a better chill down a young man's head than some rigorous naval engagement in the fresh ocean air?" Robert Rogers said, chuckling.

John Rogers laughed, "Good choice, brother. That freaking Hessian Totenkopf keeps bugging me to death about our hero here. I'm running out of excuses why we don't turn him over to the Hessian," he said.

§   §   §

A big blue moon, hanging low on the horizon, cast a dancing, golden bridge of light on the waters of the Massachusetts Bay. On the dark water's edge, with capes and headlands, a few city lights flickered in the blackness. Off the coast, in the entrance to the Boston harbor, lay a group of small islands that formed natural breakwaters. The Rangers glided silently across the water on boats and used rope ladders to climb aboard the troop transport ships. Finn, Gus, Fronto, and Daniel gathered at the railing to look out at the vast ocean while the fleet prepared to sail to Halifax.

Anchors were raised just as the sun rose above the horizon. Finn noticed curiously how the rats jumped off the ship en masse. Quietly, without a sound, the animals hurled themselves into the cold waters and swam toward the shoreline in the distance.

The Rangers were not used to having the heaving, up-and-down movement of the ship deck under their feet. Some of them soon became seasick and leaned over the railing, spewing profusely while leaving the rest gagging and gasping for fresh air.

Sailors, Marines, and Rangers watched each other warily. Captain Gorham was leery of the sailors. "A perversion of sailors is a given," he said softly.

Sailors gathered in a circle, bowing their heads as a priest gave a sermon on the deck. He held his finger up in the air. "Mathew 17:27, Notwithstanding, lest we should offend them, go thou to the sea, and cast a hook, and pick up the fish that first cometh up, and when thou hast opened his mouth, thou shalt find a bit of money. Those receive and give unto them for me and thee!"

Luckily for the seasick, after only a few days of sailing, the fleet arrived on the shores of Newfoundland. On the flagship, Lord Loudoun delayed matters and ordered the fleet to drop anchor off the coast of Fairview Cove, near the Narrows. He planned that the combined force should proceed directly to Louisburg. "The troops need to be exercised first, especially those who have just come in from a long sea voyage," he said.

Troops landed and encamped on Citadel Hill, which rose a hundred and eighty feet above the sea, and training for siege began.

In the evening, the men were served salmon cooked over an open fire, which was a rare treat. The fires were built on the cliff overlooking the North Atlantic. The Rangers admired the sea as the sun set behind them and cast colorful spikes of light over the dark blue waters.

Finn gazed at the distant horizon, but then he felt a twinge of homesickness. The delicious smells from the fish cooking over the fire and his grumbling stomach reminded him where he was. As they were eating, Finn picked his fish with his fingers and dropped the pieces in his mouth. The sweet and tasty fish, perked by brown sugar, also had hints of chili, soy, and lime.

Finn started chatting happily. "Way back home, my friends and I used to go fishing all the time. We caught salmon like this, and trout, and pike." His voice wavered, and his expression darkened. "Those were happy days, with my friends and my family. My mom. Uncle Otvar, Padric—" His voice faltered, he stopped eating and turned to face away. He felt as if the misery would suffocate him.

"What happened to them?" Gus asked. Finn did not answer, but instead got up and walked away to the cliff and sat down alone, staring across the ocean.

Daniel was going to go after Finn, but Fronto stopped him. "Let him be. He needs to be alone for a moment. He has yet to accept the fact that he is alone in this world, and until he does he can't start building a new life," he said.

On the flagship just off shore, Lord Loudoun received Admiral Holburne and Captain Gorham in his fancy aft cabin. The three men enjoyed vintage port wine and sweet biscuits served by a cabin boy who was bruised, trembling, and trying to maintain a distance from His Lordship.

"Sir, the provincials have been restless, and there have been outbreaks of small riots," Holburne reported to Lord Loudoun.

Loudoun kept a lecherous eye on the cabin boy as he served more wine. He sucked air through his thick lips and caught a bit of saliva in his handkerchief. "As you are well aware, I have laid a general embargo on all outward-bound ships in American ports. My objects have been, firstly, to prevent the communication of intelligence to the enemy. Secondly, I'm to obtain the necessary transports, and thirdly, to obtain additional seamen for his Majesty's ships. What is our order of battle?"

"Once combined, our fleets count seventeen ships-of-the line, fourteen frigates and sloops, two bomb ketches, and one fire ship escorting one hundred and seventy-nine transports," Holburne replied.

Captain Gorham, in a green Ranger uniform, his face grim with determination, stepped forward to report on the land forces. "Sir, the combined land forces consist of fifteen regiments, five hundred men of the train, five hundred Rangers, and one hundred carpenters, amounting to nearly twelve thousand men," he said.

"Admiral Holburne, your primary goal is to land a

Ranger force close to Louisburg in order to maintain the siege operations on land," Loudoun ordered.

"Yes, sir," Holburne replied.

"Captain Gorham, you shall take parties of Rangers to patrol the surrounding woods and seek possible avenues of approach to the enemy fort. Meanwhile, vessels are being sent to reconnoiter the harbor of Louisburg," Loudoun said to Gorham.

"Yes, sir," Gorham replied and saluted sharply.

Loudoun took the most steadfast stance he could muster. "We shall make every attempt to learn the state of Louisburg."

The following night, under cover of darkness, the ships sailed farther north toward Cape Breton, approaching the enemy occupied territory. The waters seemed to get darker, colder, and more shadowy by each nautical mile. What kind of evil French sea monsters lurked in the deep, just waiting for an opportunity to guttle entire ships at any time?

The Rangers went about their business as usual and guided their landing craft past the perilous underwater rocks and precipitous cliffs, leaving only narrow passages on the shore. They made a quick landing on the windy shores in the gloom, and several patrols spread out into the woods and countryside around the French fort.

The Rangers set up a patrol base and defensive perimeter on a wooded knoll that resembled a large gravesite, or perhaps remnants of a long forgotten Viking expedition. Finn saw a large, old fishing boat with oars dangling from a rope tied to a tree nearby and got an idea. "We could commandeer that local fishing boat, and disguised as fishermen, we could take a closer look at the ships under cover of darkness, sir," he said.

Captain Gorham thought about it for a moment. "Alright, that's a nifty idea. Let's go and see what they're up to in the port," he said and led Finn, Gus, Fronto, and Daniel to scout the fort and harbor.

Cloaked by the blackness, the Rangers rowed their boat amongst the enemy ships. Fronto leaned over, putting his mouth to Finn's ear. "Into the heart of darkness we go."

Torches lit by guards on the ship decks illuminated the waters around the ships. The Rangers were just outside the light in the veiling fog. Gus and Daniel rowed the boat while Finn and Fronto aimed at the guards, ready to shoot. They slipped in and out of shadows among the large ships. Gliding silently on the murky, still waters in the night, they counted the French war ships.

"The French have scores of ships and thousands of troops here," Gorham whispered.

Their small boat was hemmed in amongst the vast enemy ships, the masts hovering high above them. Muffled voices of the French guards, cussing and cursing as only sailors can, carried across the water.

Gorham was busy taking notes at the stern while Finn and Fronto covered him with muskets at the ready. Gus and Daniel kept rowing, taking extra care in placing the oars in water silently. Once they had seen enough, Captain Gorham motioned for them to get out.

The Rangers landed back on the shore and jumped from the boat into knee-deep water. Finn gave the boat a push and sent it back toward the sea before running to the patrol base. As they approached the patrol base, Finn was in the front, running up the cliff. He stopped suddenly, staring down a musket barrel aimed directly at his face. He was an instant from oblivion. A chill ran down his spine and his scrotum tightened up.

"The running password?" The harsh voice in the dark demanded.

"Hell if I know. Anyways, we didn't set up one, duh!" Finn replied.

"Oh, it's you," the voice said, and the musket barrel was lowered.

After a quick, meager meal of field rations — venison jerky and a thick slice of half-rotten pork lard on hard biscuits — Gorham gave new orders. "Ranger Finn, I will take the main patrol back and report our findings to Lord Loudoun. In the meantime, you will stay here and set up an observation post to watch for any enemy activity," he said and took off to see the commander.

On the flagship, Lord Loudoun received the intelligence with satisfaction. Regardless of Gorham's succinct account, his Lordship was resolved to proceed to the attack of Louisburg.

§ § §

The blue and gray of the overcast skies and the Cypress-dotted grassy hills provided concealment for the Rangers. The air was filled with hazy moisture off the ocean which gave softness to the rugged land. They had to move slowly and steadily, because Egrets and Herons nesting in the area made it difficult to move around without disturbing them. Finn, Gus, Fronto, and Daniel set up an observation post in a hidden enclave overseeing the enemy port. They saw schooners and clippers scurrying back and forth as privateers were slipping in and out of the port.

Finn saw one of the crews leave the boat without a guard. The enemy was being presumptuous. "Let's find out what our French friends are up to," he said and motioned the others to follow him.

Sliding over the railing on their bellies, they got on board one of the boats left unguarded and rummaged through it. Finn discovered a messenger bag with some letters, and he kept turning them in his hands.

Gus grabbed the papers from Finn and turned them the right way. "Let me see these, I can read some French. They appear to be lists of troops and ships, and some orders," he said, looking at the papers.

Finn looked pleasantly impressed. "Man of letters, huh?"

"Shit, it looks like an additional twenty-four French warships have settled in at Louisburg. We did not count those earlier. These letters must be taken to Captain Gorham immediately," Gus said.

"The enemy ships must have been anchored farther out since we didn't see them earlier," Fronto said.

Seeing the letters, Gorham cursed and promptly delivered them to the flagship. Lord Loudoun was not happy as he received the disturbing reports about their intended target. "Blimey!" He said, and for a moment he seriously considered having Captain Gorham shot for bringing such lousy reports.

"Sir, we counted three full French squadrons now united in the harbor of Louisburg. I'd estimate that around four thousand regulars beside its base of three thousand men are available for its defense," Gorham said.

"That is quite a problem for us, sir. But how reliable are these reports exactly?" Admiral Holburne asked Lord Loudoun. Hearing the thinly veiled allegation, Gorham's glance snapped at the Admiral angrily, but he bit his tongue.

In a heated debate that lasted for hours, Holburne argued in favor of direct naval assault on the enemy fortifications. He pleaded and begged, but in vain. In the end, Lord Loudoun called the strike off and ordered the invasion force to return to Boston.

However, after Loudoun departed, Holburne decided it was time to take some initiative. He was resolved to reconnoiter Louisburg for himself and to earn himself a ribbon and some fame in the process.

Holburne's arrival at Louisburg with his fleet did not go unnoticed. Near the harbor's mouth, some of his ships got so close that the big guns on the Louisburg walls took shots at the large, fluttering sails.

Cannon balls hit the ships and tore gigantic holes in their sails. Ships fired back, but the British cannons were no match for the French artillery, and their shots fell harmlessly into the sea. Nevertheless, having proven himself worth of a medal under murderous enemy fire, the Admiral was thus able to conclude that the strength of the enemy had not been exaggerated.

Gorham reported the dire situation to Holburne, hoping to convince him to return to Boston. "Sir, we can't find any usable land routes that could help us, and we're hopelessly out gunned. I strongly recommend a tactical retreat to fight another day, sir."

"The French commander did not take the bait. He did

not come out," Holburne said, nervously drumming the railing with his fingers.

It was quickly becoming apparent to everyone at the scene — excluding the Admiral — that success was now impossible, and the attack should be abandoned at once. Holburne continued to argue. "No guts, and no glory!" he said, demanding guts from the men, and reserving all the glory for himself. But in the end, he too was forced to admit that perhaps the effort was futile.

At the French port, the commander Dubois de la Motte estimated the situation and called his opponents cards. He signaled his fleet to unmoor, whereupon the British tacked and stood off. At dusk they finally sailed away.

The troop transport navigated closer to the shore so that the Rangers could get on board. On the shore, Gorham told his men to get ready to depart. "Ranger Finn, you will take a dozen men and provide a rear guard for the rest of the Rangers to embark. Once we're safely offshore you will follow us, is that clear? I will send you a signal."

In order to secure the withdrawal from the beach, Finn, Gus, Fronto, and Daniel set up their men in fighting positions to engage any enemy approaching from the land. The rest of the Rangers filed past them and loaded onto the boats.

At first, everything went smoothly, but then the troubles started when an unusual, easterly storm formed. During the night, it veered to the south and rapidly escalated into a gale. Holburne watched in horror as his fleet was struck with tragedy, and there was nothing he could do about it.

On the rocky shore, cold, howling winds battering his

face, Finn watched how the fleet struggled to stay afloat. Then, the *HMS Tilbury* was struck and went to pieces with all of her crew. Sailors tried to get to other boats, but the mast fell and crushed them all.

The *HMS Grafton,* bearing the broad pennant of Commodore Charles Holmes, was also struck. She lost her mainmast, fore-top-mast, and rudder but survived. Giant waves washed the deck and wiped screaming sailors off into the deep, blue sea. Finn winced as he saw the men drowning, fighting against the merciless tug from the deep, reaching out for an invisible ladder that was not there. But their screams were carried off by the howling wind.

The *HMS Ferret* foundered with all hands. Terrified Royal Marines threw away their weapons and jumped into the sea, and promptly sank to the depths under their heavy equipment. One brave soul tried to save his comrade from drowning, pulling him from under the chin to keep his head above the water. Finn trembled as he witnessed a wave hover over the two men for a moment, and then both of them were washed away into the depths.

All the other ships of the fleet were severely damaged, and no fewer than twelve were either partially or wholly dismasted. Holburne sent his most damaged ships directly to Great Britain under Sir Charles Hardy and Commodore Charles Holmes and departed with the rest to Halifax.

"Look at that! Not one left is fit for immediate action!" Daniel exclaimed, looking at the sinking ships and over-loaded boats that were filled with desperate sailors and Marines who struggled to save themselves.

Amid the chaos, Gorham leaned against the rolling deck to stay on his feet. He waved a lantern toward the beach, hoping his men would see the warning light. On top of the cliff overlooking the bay, Finn, Gus, Fronto, and Daniel were watching as the ships fought the giant waves. Then they saw the faint signal light and rushed down the embankment to the shore where the boats were.

The Rangers were determined to make it to the ship and paddled hard to get over the waves breaking on the beach.

Fronto assumed the coxswain's position as the most natural thing to do. "Row, row, row your boat!" He sang out loud and cheerfully, dangling his hand in the water over the side, just as if they were punting on the River Cam in Cambridge. When he saw a gigantic, roaring wave approaching, he grabbed a paddle and steered the boat head on toward it at the last minute. The wave threw the boat upside down like a piece of cork and sent them flying into the freezing water.

On deck on the transport ship, Gorham saw what had happened to their craft and shook his head in desperation. Yet another team was lost for sure.

Sitting at the bow, Finn flew off into the ice-cold water and was dragged under water. He struggled to get to the surface, his lungs bursting, but in the dark water he did not even know which way was up. He felt a panic run down his spine, and he became painfully aware that he might actually drown. Around him, bodies of drowned troops from other boats sank toward the bottom, and Finn realized he must go the other way. He was running out of air and had to fight desperately through the sinking bodies to get to the surface.

Finally, Finn popped up underneath the boat that

had turned over. He found a pocket of air and gasped for breath. A split second later, he was hit in the head by the boat and then thrown under again as a massive wave crashed into the capsized boat. He struggled frantically amidst the sinking equipment and bodies.

On the ship, Gorham shook his head in desperation after having lost so many talented men, or so he thought. Out of sight on the beach, the waves cast Finn, Gus, Fronto, and Daniel on the gloomy shore, along with bits and pieces of the boat. Finn was surprised to find his cap floating right next to him. They had barely survived the storm and were exhausted and soaking wet.

"Keep going! We must get off the beach and past those cliffs!" Finn shouted, pointing to a wuthering, sandy bank maybe a hundred yards from the water line.

The Rangers crawled and stumbled across the frosty beach that was littered with broken pieces of boats, wreckage and bodies and climbed through the tufts of Marram Grass to higher ground. From the relative safety of the top of the bluffs, the Rangers watched the ships struggle to set out toward the emerging light and calmer seas.

Finn, Gus, Fronto, and Daniel glanced around, searching the desolate seashore, and they all realized at the same time that they were on their own, deep in the enemy territory, a long away from home.

§   §   §

The darkness fell like a heavy drape across a scene in a tragic opera on a stage. The Rangers lay down, hidden in a thicket and listening to the ocean waves in the distance.

The men checked their gear in stout silence while Gus went from man to man. "Redistribute the ammo. Drink water, men," he said in a low whisper.

Only Fronto seemed to be able to maintain a positive attitude. "Look at it this way. We have no young ensign holding the map," he quipped.

"You're right. There are no ensigns here, Fronto," Finn replied and looked at the young Rangers around them. He was hardly any older than they were. *They are all so young*, he thought. *We're the seniors. When in hell did that happen?*

Then and there, the faces of so many fallen Rangers flashed through Finn's mind, and he felt traumatized and clueless as to what to do next. Now, on this windswept, God-forsaken end of the world, the young Rangers kept glancing back at *him*, convinced that he would know what they should do.

Pushing his own qualms and self-doubt aside, Finn motioned the men closer, although he had no idea what to say. He wanted to encourage them. "Rangers, huddle up. We're a long way from home, and we're cold, wet, and tired. We have no food, devilish little ammo, and we're totally surrounded by the enemy. I can't imagine any better time to attack," he blurted out, the gruff confident tone of his own voice sounding strange in his own ears.

"A journey of a thousand miles starts with one daring naval raid," Fronto replied.

"If we stay undetected, we might have a chance. Maybe the French will think that we all perished when they find remnants of the boat," Daniel said.

"Who dares, wins," Gus said and slung his rucksack on his back.

"Right, but first we head south and then turn southwest. We hold a steady pace and stop only to eat and sleep at daybreak," Finn decided.

The Rangers, miserable, yet indomitably unwavering, stayed in a clandestine patrol base for a day, drying their weapons, themselves, and what little gear and assets they still had. Finn threw some additional pieces of articles on the shore by the remnants of the boat. He dragged the body of a drowned Marine farther ashore so it would not be dragged back out by the waves. He used branches to wipe out any footprints on the wet sand. He was hoping to divert any potential pursuers and to make them think that all Rangers had been destroyed by the waves. Then, in the last remaining light of the evening, they started on the long and dangerous journey back to Fort Edward.

The Rangers moved guardedly for the first five miles, and after being convinced that there was no immediate danger, they broke into a dog trot that would eat away the miles. They avoided any contacts, staying in the undergrowth away from any paths and clearings, moving silently and using hand signals. They advanced swiftly through the fog like ghosts, moving around villages without being noticed and then disappearing into the fog again.

Several hours later, they came across a farm where a longhaired wolfhound was tied to a post in the yard. Ears alert, the creature lifted its gargantuan snout, smelling the air and staring into the dark. It growled softly and anxiously but did not bark.

In the darkness, Finn aimed his musket right at the

snarling dog's fangs. A connection between the beast and the man was set, along with an understanding of who would die first if the dog barked and someone came out of the house to investigate. With his other hand, Finn gave the Rangers a hand signal to move on, and the patrol quickly snaked behind him past the farm.

The moon began to rise just as the Rangers made it past the yard without incident. Finn followed them, baring his teeth and snarling at the dog, which tucked its tail between its hind legs and scampered around the corner to safety.

Silent, dark figures of men marched at a quick pace through the moonlight. An owl observed them, tilting its head and peering down at them as the Rangers came across an enemy outpost. Fronto was walking the point when he noticed the danger and dropped into a crouching run back to the patrol.

Finn snuck closer to take a look, and seeing a single, sleepy guard leaning against a fence, he realized there was no safe way to get past the enemy guard position. They would have to go right through it. It meant that they had to kill the guard silently — an extremely hazardous task even under the best of circumstances.

Finn returned to the patrol. "There's a river gorge on one side and steep cliffs on the other. Buggers put their outpost in the right place; there's no way around it without alerting them. But there is only one guard awake. The rest are sleeping some distance away in a tent," he said.

"We must go right through. I will take care of the guard," Daniel said as he pulled out a large hunting knife.

Finn put his hand on Daniel's arm. "Wait. We must do

it together. We must be silent. If you try it alone, he could get a shot off with his musket to warn the others. We'll sneak up to him, and you get his musket when I grab him. We must drag him away, so the others think he deserted. We have only one shot at it. If something goes wrong, we will kill them all and make a run for it. Rally point is 500 yards in that direction," Finn said, pointing.

Keeping their bellies off the ground in order to not make noise, Finn and Daniel crept toward the guard. They followed a wooden fence until they came to a gate with a bar across the road. Under a flickering light from a single torch, the guard was leaning against a wooden fence and sleepily nodding his head. He almost dropped the musket from his hand, causing Finn and Daniel to freeze for a moment.

Maybe fifty yards away, there was a lean-to with a small fire in front of it and some muskets leaning against each other. Other than a faint sound of snoring, the camp was quiet. Fronto and Gus covered Finn and Daniel with their muskets as the two snuck closer and closer to the guard. The rest of the Rangers were a short distance behind them, ready to spring into action if required.

The sole drowsy guard, sleepily yawning and stretching his arms, did not realize that Daniel and Finn were right behind him. In a flash, Daniel leapt from the grass and snatched the musket from the guard's hands. At the same time, Finn hit the guy from the rear with a forearm strike to the neck and carotid artery. Finn wrapped his right arm around man's neck, making sure he locked the throat and pharynx in the V formed by his elbow. Finn grasped his left bicep and wrapped his left hand around the back of the man's head. He pulled his right arm in and flexed it and at the same time pushed the man's head forward. Finn kicked his legs out and back, maintaining a block on the man's neck, and pulled him backward until his neck broke with a crack. The man's life was snuffed out instantly, and the Rangers heard only the silent scuffle of the dead man's feet in convulsions on the leaves.

Finn held the body tight until it went limp. Daniel grabbed the body by the arm, and they dragged it off into the bushes. Daniel hung the guard's musket on a fence post and threw the guard's hat in the direction they had come from. As the Rangers passed through the camp, Daniel snatched a bag of supplies.

The Rangers hurried in single file past the French lean-to. The soldiers inside the tent continued sleeping. Finn was the last one to go through the camp, so he covered their tracks. Musket at the ready, he made sure nobody woke up.

Finn had to walk right next to the sleeping French, silently stepping over their legs. His musket muzzle hovered only inches from a French sergeant's face. The man twisted his handlebar mustache and rubbed his nose as the musket barrel had tickled his nose hairs.

Finn stepped back and to his horror, knocked over a rattling kettle. He froze and raised his musket, ready to shoot. He aimed right at the piece of hair sticking out of the man's left nostril.

The French sergeant yawned and rolled over on his other side, smacking his lips. When he stopped moving, Finn's aiming point was right at his left ear. Finn took three steps backward slowly and disappeared into the night after the Rangers, leaving only swirling fog behind.

Sometime during the night, exhaustion started playing tricks on Finn's mind, and he stopped and gaped into the fog. He saw a flickering image of Catherina dressed in a flimsy, sheer nightgown that outlined her shapely breasts and pubic mound. She wore a sword belt around her waist. She was standing a little ahead, waiting for him, holding Marlyon the falcon on one arm and stretching her other arm toward him. He rubbed his eyes and looked again, but she was gone. He was startled as the Rangers kept moving, and he had to catch up. *Damn*, he thought. *Seeing stuff like that out here could be fatal.*

§   §   §

Unfortunately for the war effort, there was no method to the British madness, only firmness of purpose to the rapacity. The splendid formal garden around Governor Lawrence's residence was from another world. Lawrence entertained two tittering ladies of ill repute in the over-elaborate carriage drawn by a team of six horses and escorted by two British dragoons.

Johan Kopf, in his jaeger uniform and followed by a group of Hessians, met them on the outskirts of the vast grounds surrounding the palace. The horse skidded in the loose gravel as the rider yanked on the reins. Lawrence ordered the driver to pause and stepped out of the carriage and motioned the captain aside.

Kopf motioned his Hessians to halt and form a perimeter around him and the Governor, but out of hearing distance. He took off his mirliton cap and reported to the Governor Lawrence. "These greedy Acadians have enriched themselves during the recent disorders and now they boast that they have done much damage to us. The Mi'kmaq and Abenaki have obtained valuable furs from the local tribes, which they sell for a considerable profit," he said.

Lawrence admired the rough texture of a massive trunk of an old oak tree. "Continue the expulsions as ordered, Captain. They shall fear the King, for he is of the Lord's appointment."

"Their leader, Joseph Broussard, so called Beausoleil, has major charges against him. Charges such as assault and battery, consorting with the hostile tribes, a land dispute and a paternity claim," Kopf said.

Lawrence's lips pursed as he turned to face the captain. "We know well that this dog Beausoleil has given support to the French. Governor Shirley has declared him and eleven others as outlaws for having provisioned the French troops. Tell the men that there is a bounty of fifty pounds sterling for the capture of each of these scumbags and vermin," he said.

Kopf stepped closer. "Sire, I request permission to take care of a personal issue. I need to finish a job I started a long time ago, and now the little nitwit is close by."

Lawrence would not hear any of it. He gave Kopf one opportunity for a quick check to find Finn, but he was to set his personal undertakings aside and focus strictly on the mission at hand. Kopf detested his job as a secret messenger between the governors; it made no matter to him that he was selected for it due to his reliability. He had to force himself to calm down and wait for an opportunity.

Kopf was right in that his counterinsurgency skills

were wasted, because at that exact moment, on the west side of the bay at the foot of the Caledonian Hills, Joseph Broussard and his brother John were busy organizing a resistance movement. The brothers had been fighting for the Acadian independence for decades, actively resisting the British incursions in the area, raiding settlements and destroying farms. They took great pride in being two persistent thorns in the English flesh.

The Acadian's old allies, the Mi'kmaq, had taught them the rudiments of survival in this harsh country and helped them to settle in the area. They showed the Acadians good hunting grounds and which plants were edible and which ones had medicinal powers. With their help and support, the Broussard brothers planned to overcome the English.

Now once again, they went from village to village in the area, asking for money for their insurgency from the villagers, and gathered supplies, black powder, and weapons for the freedom fighters.

The men in the village of Chipoudy gathered around them. John Broussard addressed them, taking a close look at each man in turn. "Again our lives are threatened! It is permissible to kill the aggressor in self-defense. The legitimacy of private war rests on this fact. We must accept the principle of self-preservation, which nature has given us and not from the exploitation of the aggressor," he said.

Joseph Broussard noticed that the crowd was receptive to hearing what they had to say, and he stepped forward. "War is the father of all and the king for all!" he said.

John pounded on a box with a clenched fist in the air. "The English, captivated with the appearances of vain glory, give the names of virtues to their crimes!" he shouted.

"When the power of law ends, war begins!" Joseph said.

One of the older Acadian men stepped forward, his angry glance snapping from man to man, and shook his fist. "There are those wars that are unjust and are made without sufficient cause. And then there are those that are just wars and are made to punish injuries," he said.

"Gods and men honor those who are slain in battle," John replied. The men replied with shouts and war cries. The brothers exchanged quick glances as they noticed that the men and the Mi'kmaq warriors around them were getting agitated, just as they had planned.

"English souls smell in Hell," Joseph Broussard said, fervently.

"Wars are made to punish not only oppression, but also to protect against fraud and deception!" John shouted.

Joseph hopped off the pile of boxes and started handing out ammunition pouches. "Man's character is his fate! Join us, and become the wakeful guardians of the quick and dead!" He shouted, waving the musket above his head.

The Broussard brothers were surrounded by a large group of young men, all zealous to do something about the desperate situation. Soon, they led a sizeable force of Acadian fighters and Mi'kmaq warriors and headed out into the hills and tablelands beyond, brandishing tomahawks, knives, and muskets, and ready for war.

§   §   §

The situation in Fort Edward was not much better. Catherina and the town women were worried, and the whole village was anxiously waiting for any news from husbands, fathers, and sons. Shelagh Brotherton was the most troubled of all.

"Before we marry, we're worried about our future husband. When we're expecting our first child, we worry about the baby and how we will look after childbirth, and how it might affect us and if he will still want us. Then we're worried over whether our children have enough clean water to drink. Will our husbands come back from the war path? When they do come back, we're worried sick they will have some hidden trauma in their souls. Worry never ends. I wish I could stop worrying," Shelagh said, looking vexed and wringing her hands.

"Just because we haven't heard anything from them doesn't mean something awful has happened. Many times, no news means good news. I'm sure they are all right. They must be," Catherina said, trying to remain positive, but she looked just as anxious as all the other women. She could not stand still, so she went to check for any news from Robert Rogers.

"No, ma'am, I have no more news than what you already know. We must be strong-minded. My men will come back when the operation has been accomplished and not a day sooner," Robert Rogers told her.

There were many rumors circling in the fort, and Catherina wanted to put an end to them all by trying to calm the people. "Listen. Stop thinking the worst and stop spreading rumors. We will know soon enough. I'm sure they will be back as soon as possible," she said, encouraging the townswomen.

Then, everyone turned on their heels as the guard

shouted from the palisades, "The Rangers are returning! I see them in the distance, coming down from the hills!"

The villagers assembled at the gate, anxiously straining to see the Rangers return, finally. Catherina joined the women, searching for familiar faces as weary and tired Rangers filed past them. Robert Rogers arrived to receive the Rangers with his brothers. He saluted and shook each Ranger's hands as they walked by him.

"Good job, men, good job. I have received excellent reports from Lord Loudoun," Rogers said.

"Sir, we did what was ordered," Captain Gorham said.

"We will discuss that later, in private," Rogers replied.

Catherina saw no signs of Finn or the others. She noticed Gorham talking to Rogers and rushed to see him. "Captain Gorham, where are the rest of your men?" she asked.

"I'm sorry to tell you the news, ma'am. They were lost on the beach in Acadia. Their boat capsized and was lost with all hands. I'm so sorry," Gorham replied.

Johan Kopf galloped in, looking arrogant. Catherina thought that he possessed the bearing of a soldier and the manners of a courtier. In her eyes, that rude manner and his striking dressy looks — tall and lean with a dark and handsome face correct in every line — made him spurious and apocryphal. The green uniform certainly fulfilled his penchant for pomp, and quite clearly he pursued further glory.

Kopf sneered. "Has anyone seen any signs of the little *Schwanzlutscher* I am looking for?" he asked, and the townspeople turned away from him, but Catherina confronted him.

She was furious. "How dare you, Totenkopf! No use looking for him any longer. He is dead," she said, fighting the tears.

Looking down from his horse, Kopf gave her a long salacious look from head to toe and licked his lips and smiled, revealing a gleaming gold tooth. "So you already know my name," he said and leaned closer. "He is dead when I see his corpse!" Using the spurs to control his horse, he spat on the ground and rode off.

§   §   §

The Rangers followed a wide river, keeping a safe distance from any open areas, and tried to find a place to get across. Daniel figured that the river was the River St. Croix. It was relatively shallow, but the current ran swiftly as it flowed over the rocks. Daniel was walking point, twenty feet ahead of others, when he saw a bridge in the distance and gave a hand signal to stop.

Crouching down, Daniel ran back to the patrol. "Things are too quiet. Birds are silent. I don't like it," he whispered.

Finn gave each man a quick look and made his decision. "Alright, let's go and see this bridge. I'll take Daniel, Gus, and Fronto with me. The rest of the patrol can wait here," he said and turned to one of the young privates. "Ranger, you are in charge here. If we make contact, we'll fall back to this location. If you make contact, proceed due south away from the river. We will then join up three miles from here on the southern bank, is that clear?" he asked, pointing directions with his hand.

The private nodded, and Daniel led Finn, Gus, and Fronto toward the bridge. They low-crawled closer in the high grass and observed a British work party cutting firewood. Just then, from the nearby hills, a volley was fired, and the British regulars were caught in a deadly fusillade by Acadian and Mi'kmaq fighters, commanded by the Broussard brothers.

The British were hit by the enemy fire, sending the survivors scrambling for cover. A lance corporal was about to give orders when a bullet hit his open mouth. The back of his head was blown off, and another trooper's stomach was ripped open by a separate shot. Screaming in agony and clutching his belly, he tried to hold in the bloody mess that was his intestines.

The rest of the British sought refuge behind the river bank. One man, jumping toward safety, was hit several times right in the face in mid-jump and fell into the river.

From the high cliff above the Rangers, the Acadian fighters started throwing makeshift bombs down below. Finn was changing positions and one of the explosions landed close to him, forcing him to fall behind large logs and boulders. He tried to see what was happening across the river, but he could not hear or see anything. Then the smoke drifted away and he saw the English wavering under fire and that the only way out was across the bridge. He hesitated, seeing the bullets hitting the railing and sending dagger-like shards of wood flying.

Finn took a deep breath. "We got to help them! Follow me!" he shouted. He then got up and was at once forced back down by withering enemy fire. The British on the other side rushed toward the bridge.

"What the hell is happening? Who is going which way?" Gus was confused. The Rangers tried to cover the British retreat and they reached almost to the middle of the bridge.

Finn realized what was about to happen. "Beware!" he shouted, but he was too late.

The Broussard brothers and Mi'kmaq warriors stood up from behind a stone wall and fired a volley at close range.

On the bridge, the British soldiers were slaughtered as bullets tore through flesh and muscle, and dead troops fell in a pile of blood-spattered bodies. Streams of blood ran through the cracks to the river below. The awful stench of fear and shit and the vicious killing by the large caliber bullets at close range made even the Mi'kmaq warriors grimace.

Finn dove for cover, wood splinters from bullets hitting the logs all around him. Bullets made ugly, buzzing sounds as they barely missed him. Finn, Gus, Fronto, and Daniel all realized at the same time that they were cut off from the main patrol.

"Get back! Get back!" Gus fired and waved frantically. Falling back to the bridgehead, they reloaded and crouched behind the stone wall back to back.

"We must get to that farm!" Fronto shouted, pointing to some farm buildings nearby. They moved under fire and passed a henhouse as they sought shelter behind a cowshed. Firing and reloading in turns, they were covered in dust from bullets hitting all around them.

"Bloody hell, are we going to make this place our last stand?" Fronto said as he reloaded.

"We've got to get out of here." Finn looked around to find a way, but the only option left was to spring from the frying pan directly into the fire.

Daniel waited until everyone had reloaded. "Cover me!" he shouted and started running. Instantly, Finn, Gus, and Fronto jumped up and fired to cover his advance. Daniel made a dash across the bridge but was forced back by withering enemy fire.

"Next time, tell us first what you are doing." Finn was angry at him. Fire arrows streaked through the sky across the river as the enemy musket fire forced everyone to seek cover. They failed to see the improvised portable mortar that the Broussard brothers had hauled to the position, ready to fire.

The Rangers heard the dull metallic thuds of the mortars firing. They ducked behind whatever cover they could get when all of a sudden thunderous explosions shattered the henhouse next to them. Pieces of dead chickens, intestines, blood, and feathers flew all around, covering the Rangers. Mortar rounds and fire arrows hitting the ammonia-filled chicken manure had caused the devastating chemical reaction.

"What the fuck..." Gus said, his ears ringing from the blast. He eyed the billowing feathers flying around them like snow. He made wild hand gestures, driving off any evil spirits. Daniel saw all the dead chickens and looked like he was ready to throw up at any time.

"Oh Lord," Fronto said, wiping goo off of his coat.

A hay wagon caught on fire, and clouds of thick smoke drifted between them and the enemy, giving them a short break in the fighting. Daniel shouted across the river. "Hey Mickey Mack, you shoot like squaws!"

The answer came at once. A fierce volley was fired at him, sending pieces of wood, rock, and dust flying.

A herd of panicked, noisy geese stormed past them across the bridge, which was still covered in a thick smoke. Finn realized there was a moment of confusion on the other side. "This is our chance! Run!" he shouted and ran out.

Finn ran down into the smoke after the geese. Gus, Daniel, and Fronto fired their muskets and followed him, hopping down onto the river's edge. They were covered with the river bank on the other side and ran several hundred yards before stopping to take cover in a hollow. More explosions from makeshift bombs and mortars threw rocks and dirt on top of them as the French and Mi'kmaq warriors launched another attack.

Gus peeked from between the boulders, trying to find a way out. "The patrol has taken off by now, just like they were told. But we can't follow them. We're on the wrong side of the river. We must find a new crossing point," he said.

Retreating several more miles, they looked for a safe place behind a rocky hill. Suddenly, they encountered a teenage Acadian girl herding a flock of Llanwenog sheep with black faces. She was shocked to see them and tried to run away, but Finn chased her and brought her back. She kicked and struggled, biting his hand. He yelled in pain and threw her on the ground. Frightened, she looked up at them.

"Fuck!" Finn said, holding his hand.

"If we take her with us, she will slow us down. We will get captured, and Mi'kmaq will show us no mercy, you know it," Daniel said.

"We can't let her loose either, she would alert the enemy. Same results," Fronto added.

"If we tie her down and leave her, she'll die of exposure." Gus shook his head.

"Stop blabbering. Keep moving. We'll figure it out later. We got to get the hell out of here," Finn said.

The Rangers managed to escape into the thick woods until the firing behind them quieted down as they went deeper into the forest.

"We need to find a place to regroup and rest for a while. It seems like they are not going to follow us. They are probably too busy chasing the patrol," Daniel said.

The Acadian girl noticed the moose-head locket around Finn's neck. "*Traverse des bourgots*, there is a cave ahead," she said quietly and pointed toward a rocky cliff ahead.

They stumbled across the rock-strewn ground in the direction she had indicated. Finn helped the Acadian girl when she fell down, shivering from both cold and fear.

Inside the cave, they found a fire pit with embers, and Daniel inspected it. "The wood is dry and won't smoke much. We can use some fresh spruce branches to fan out the little smoke that is produced," he said and quickly got the fire going. The flames warmed the group and threw shadows on the walls.

Finn took off his gear and his wet coat. He sat down on some straw and hay that was scattered on the ground.

In the back, there was a large, flat stone laid out like an altar, and Finn saw a small, worn-out box on top of it. "That chest looks familiar. I think I've seen it somewhere before, maybe in a dream when I took an oath of some sort.

There was also a spear with a multicolored rod that I took with me. It seemed so real at the time, but now it seems so vague," he wondered aloud.

"Maybe it wasn't a dream, but something that really happened," Fronto replied.

"Time seems to go so fast. I have no idea how long it's been since we met in the tavern. So much has happened since then," Finn said.

"It has been a long time, whippersnapper."

Finn had difficulties focusing. His thoughts kept shifting between Rosie and Catherina. His hands shook, though he was not cold any longer. "All my joy is nothing but a dream, and I must carry a heavy burden of my memories with me. And never in all this time have I sought my way back to Rosie?" Finn said, his head hanging.

Fronto looked at him and let out a sigh. "I can see how it bothers you, and I can only hope you will not let it take you down. You must remain fully alert."

"Dog, you can hardly blame me for feeling like shit sometimes, can you?" Finn said.

Feeling Fronto's reassuring hand firmly squeezing his shoulder, Finn felt somewhat better. "I didn't know. I did... not... know...." Finn breathed out heavily, drained of all hope and feeling utterly condemned. "I will never outlive my shame. I'm responsible. I killed my family, my whole village," he said and looked away, forlorn.

"You are only responsible for your own actions. You had nothing to do with that. It speaks volumes on your behalf that you're not seeking blind revenge, but that you are here, with us," Fronto said.

Fronto, scruffy and with terrible smelling breath,

rubbed the bristles on his chin and said, "You should honor your family by continuing to live. She would have told you those exact words."

"Who is she?" Finn asked.

"She's right over there, behind your left shoulder. The lady in black."

"Huh?" Finn was stumped.

"There was nothing before birth," Fronto replied. "And there's nothing after death. Only what you do in between, matters."

Gus had been listening, preparing his gear. "Any man who seeks only revenge with arrogant talk also denounces himself, as well," he said.

Fronto hit his chest with his fist. "Damn right, to live a good life requires strength. Earn it."

"Young chief, there are two types of men. Great Manitou shows kindness to one while the other sees nothing but His anger," Daniel commented.

Finn was quiet for a long time. "I thank you all for your kind words. All my life has been a struggle, and I tell you, crossing that bridge today was hard for me," he said, feeling grateful, for these men were more than his brothers in arms.

"Life is more like wrestling than dancing," Fronto replied.

"My biggest worries and desires and longings are for my sweet Rosie," Finn said and stopped, hesitating as his thoughts bounced to Catherina again. "I wonder if I will ever see her again," he said.

"Yearning for your woman is honorable, but you must bear it well to do her justice!" the Acadian girl said and came closer to the fire for warmth. She did not seem to be so afraid any longer.

Finn gave her an inquiring look. "What would you know about it?"

"There are many things that I don't know, but then there are many things that I do know," she replied.

Gus sat down on a big rock and pulled out his knife and some hard, black bread from his backpack. "Strength and honor, whatever that means, just like Fronto said," he said.

"Perhaps we all need to learn not to endorse ourselves too highly in this life. Arrogance will take us nowhere," Fronto told Finn.

Finn felt that he needed to confess something in order to get it out of his mind. "Long time ago, I got into a fight and killed a man. I was an idiot and ignorant. Then I robbed his clothes," he said.

The Acadian girl spat on the ground and glared at Finn furiously. "*Ostie!* Beware, or you will experience the final judgment. Repent, or dragons and devils will come to take you away."

"Be quiet, squaw," Daniel said, gesturing across his throat with a knife. The Acadian girl shut up and backed away from him, eyes wide in shock.

The girl looked at him and pulled back. "Don't hurt me, just a fortnight ago my dear brother was brought home pallid and promptly lost all his power. Doctor found parts of the stem and arrow head in his wound and pulled them out. We prayed for him, and I promised the King that if he saved my brother, he would not give up soldiering. I said happily I'd forgo meat, wine, and fresh bread if he didn't take my brother away from us. But when others heard he was going to give up soldiering they cried. They wanted to know who would stand guard and protect them. Then my brother said he cannot die because my commitment to abstinence and poverty would throw our family into peril," she said.

"What happened to your brother? Did he survive?" Gus asked.

"His wound started festering, and doctor applied all his skills to alleviate his suffering. He tried every cure known to man against strong poison from aspis, to ecidemon, to echontius, to jecis, and meantrix — all to no avail. He then treated my brother against every nasty malicious worm there is. We sought help from wild herbs and all sorts of ointments. But Manitou did not smile upon us that day," she said, looking terribly sad, and Gus felt sorry for her.

"We shall move out at dawn and get some food to eat. Maybe we'll find some yew and roots that we can chew on to sustain ourselves. Now let's get some rest," Fronto said. Packing his rucksack, he got it ready to use as a pillow.

"Sleep well now and maybe you'll dream about twenty-five fine-mannered and pure virgins," Gus said.

Wide awake that night, hearing only the girl snoring in the darkness, Finn kept thinking about his friend's words. Having them around was like seeing a spot of light in the darkness of ignorance.

The following morning was quiet and cold. They moved out before daybreak. The girl's hands were tied to a leash, and grumpily she followed Finn. They marched swiftly, and she had trouble keeping up with them. The sun rose from behind the hills, and they kept moving fast. Hours later, Finn estimated that they had traveled far enough. He raised his hand to stop the patrol and turned to the girl and pulled out his knife. She looked at him, scared stiff, and took steps back and tripped on a tree root.

"Relax, I won't hurt you," Finn said and leaned over to cut the cord. After he freed her, he turned to the others. "We're far enough that it will take her several hours to get back, and she is too tired to move. We'll get another twenty miles behind us before she reaches anyone," he said.

Finn turned back to the girl. "Listen, I could leave you here without anything, but I will give you some food if you promise to wait until the evening before you head back," he said, holding his musket close to his chest.

The girl rubbed her wrists and looked at him without saying anything. She heard edginess in his voice, but saw firm determination in his eyes. She glanced over her shoulder back the way they had come from and then nodded to him. Finn knew that in her mind, she was estimating distances. He took off the sash from his shoulders and handed it to her. She did not make a move to take it, so he dropped it on the ground and parted with her, following the others. The girl calmly watched them disappear into the woods.

As soon as they were out of sight, Finn dropped off at the wood line and cocked his musket while the others kept moving. He turned around and waited to see if the girl would follow them or start running away. He very much hoped the girl would not do anything stupid. To his immense relief, she stayed put and sat down on a tree stump to eat. After concluding that she was not going to make a run for it, he thought, *Good girl,* and lowered his musket and turned to catch up with the others.

Finn reached the others, and Fronto gave him an approving nod. "There are times when you discover how strong you are when being strong is the only choice left," he said.

They came to a stream and followed it downstream for a couple of hundred yards and then on the other side, made a sharp ninety-degree turn and headed in another direction. They crossed miles and miles of gently rolling hills, speckled in maple trees.

§   §   §

The farmers around Fort Edward headed back to the fields, fearing that the crops might fail and there would be a severe shortage of food once again. Fear of food shortage kept the farmers, townspeople, and hunting parties active. Worrying about lost souls was useless because there had already been so many of them.

In the fort, to everyone's great surprise, a guard from the palisades shouted, "More Rangers are coming back!"

Hardly believing their ears, the townspeople dropped what they were doing and rushed out to the gates. Catherina felt a surge of hope as she rushed to greet the Rangers. Dark clouds gathered on top of the trees behind them as the young Rangers from the Bloody Creek massacre returned. They reported that Finn and the others were cut off from the patrol and had been killed by the Acadian warriors.

Upon hearing this terrible news, Catherina felt crushed. She was miserable and confused, and she turned away from the people. She sought privacy and found a stone bench under a small tree. She struggled not to cry and talked to herself, trying to find solace and comfort.

"I cannot ignore my feelings, or I will regret it years later. I have known people who seemed to sail through the death of a loved one, and then had many troubles later," she thought out loud.

Feeling miserable, Catherina noticed two ferrets playfully chasing each other around a large rock. *Where is my rock?* She kept asking. A chilled wind blew leaves around her, but she did not notice the cold. She wrapped her hands around herself and felt as if she were being drawn into a powerful circular current of time.

She saw the world in a blur, twirling around her. She felt emptiness, but after a while, she focused on the solid rock and clenched her fists. *That horrible man was right. Not until I see Finn's body.* She saw the two ferrets again, sharing a morsel, and that helped her to snap out of it. *I must fight thoughts like that and not allow myself get drawn into apathy*, she thought.

Catherina returned to her farm, determined, and started working hard to keep her thoughts away from the loss. It was not easy under the circumstances. She needed to get herself resupplied from Albany, but there was no money. Without any help, the fort could face famine and even starvation. Rumors told that some of the prisoners were slain and cannibalized, adding to the fear of the people.

Catherina went collecting wild mushrooms in the forest near her farm when she caught a glimpse of three figures appearing from the wood line in the distance. She shaded her eyes with her hand to see who they were, but the figures had disappeared.

Catherina shook her head and continued to search for more mushrooms. Then she saw the figures again, and looking more closely, she recognized Daniel, Gus, and Fronto. Relieved, she smiled and looked eagerly for the fourth character to come, but saw no one. Her heart sank into her shoes.

Catherina let out a sad sigh, but still she was glad to see her friends alive. She hurried across the field to meet with the others.

Just a short distance away, one of the farmers was working the fields with his son, Copp. All of a sudden, two Lenape warriors rushed out from the woods and seized the boy and started leading him away by the shirt sleeves.

A shot was fired from the woods, wounding one of the warriors. Catherina could hardly believe her eyes as Finn appeared, running after his friends. He had been covering their back. Copp's cries had caught his attention, and he rushed to fight the warriors. He snatched the boy away from them, leaving the shirt sleeves in their hands.

Daniel, Gus, and Fronto chased the Lenape, firing their muskets at them, but gave up after the warriors managed to disappear into the thickets.

Seeing Finn, Catherina was ecstatic at first. He just stood there, alive and well, with that dummy grin on his face as always. Her feelings had been left in turmoil, and unable to control them, she felt an anger beginning to build up inside her.

"The situation seems to be dangerous around here. What can we possibly do?" Finn asked.

"A virtuous human life is possible if we follow nature.

Following nature means being able to figure it out," Fronto replied.

"Dog, you are talking in strange tongues again. People are starving around here," Finn said, just as Catherina marched up to him and pounded his chest with her fists.

"How dare you!" Catherina shouted in tears and then turned on her heels and ran away.

"Take a few deep breaths, woman," Finn said, astonished. Daniel glanced at a stunned Finn and ran after her.

Finn was bewildered, asking Fronto and Gus what the hell had just happened.

"She has been under a lot of stress," Gus said.

"She must learn to make her anger work for her, rather than against her," Fronto said.

"Oh yeah, but what about me? I could write a book on pucker factor. I have had to endure exploding chicken shit and all kinds of nasty stuff, you know. Why doesn't anybody care about that?" Finn said. Puzzled by Catherina's act, he watched her disappear toward the farm.

Chapter 3

THAT YEAR, adding to the hardships on both sides across the entire frontier, winter arrived early. The sun glimmered on the fields that were blanketed with snow. A brisk air stood still in the forests which were frozen in time. Red rowan berries under their icy glazing stooped down over a stream that ran over ice-covered rocks.

Sebastian Rasle, a Jesuit missionary in a worn-out cloak and wide brim hat, led Captain Lignery of the French provincial militia to the Abenaki winter encampment. The village was about an acre of ground, taken in with timber and set in the ground in a circular form with ports gates and about one hundred houses.

"These bloody savages are hard of hearing when I teach them the truths of Christianity," Rasle said.

Captain Lignery pulled his heavy woolen scarf over his collarless gray-white coat to help shield himself from the bitterly cold weather. He was carrying a rucksack with a kettle hanging from it. He cursed silently as he had left his thick fur coat in the barracks.

"The Abenaki are adroit warriors and—," he lowered his voice, "they know dozens of ways to deal with the English mad dogs," he replied.

The two men entered the village through a barrier

fence gate. The houses were conical in shape and covered with birch-bark or with mats, with each family occupying a single dwelling.

There was a meeting house of considerable size, oblong in form and roofed with bark. Other structures were used by the males of the village who preferred to band together in social fellowship.

One of the young warriors approached a young woman and offered her presents. She smiled and accepted the gifts. He grabbed his belongings and together they moved in.

Rasle found them a spot to sit near one of the cooking fires. "The Abenaki confounds repeated efforts by both the Iroquois and English to overcome them. They just melt away, regroup, and then counterattack. Your timing to visit is superb, Captain. You see, they have two councils, the grand and the general. The former consists of the chiefs and two men from each family. It determines matters that are of crucial importance to the tribe, such as the sentence of death on those deserving it. The general council, which is taking place now, is composed of all the people, including males and females, and decides matters relating to war," Rasle said.

"I believe that each tribe has a war chief and also a civil leader whose job it is to preserve order, though this is accomplished through guidance rather than by command. But I must say that Abenaki leaders have difficulty controlling their warriors," Lignery said.

Rasle heated some wine in a cup over a fire. "It is my solemn duty to protect the rights of my few Abenaki converts, and I'm reluctant to admit any French Catholics to see them, and there should be little doubt as to my thinking about any contact with the English heretics. My approach has been particularly useful now and has served to isolate and protect them," he said.

Bands of Abenaki warriors arrived and gathered in groups in front of the conical, bark-covered dwellings. Hunters brought birds, squirrels, and rabbits to the encampment. Young men brought fish, and the women prepared corn stalks.

Unruly children ran around the camp, shouting and laughing. They toppled a stand and foodstuff was scattered on the ground. One of the warriors, Colonel Louis, grabbed a boy by the arm.

"Behave. I will tell you all a lesson story to give you advice. The foolish deeds of Gluskonba and Azeban, the Raccoon, whose greed and boastfulness provide you negative examples," he said, looking sternly at the boy, but his voice was forgiving.

Colonel Louis led the children closer to a fire. To hear his story, they gathered around him. "Now listen. I will tell you 'Finding One's Way'. It is a story of a budding Abenaki boy discovering his roots," he said.

Proud chiefs dressed in full regalia arrived and warriors, with their faces painted, escorted them to a little knoll in the middle of the village. They also wore colorful shirts, capes, and blankets around their shoulders. Complementing their outfits were flashy jewelry and headgear made of feathers, beads, silver, and copper. In their arms they carried their most prized weapons. Three chiefs wore red, white (or worn light grey actually), and blue uniform coats, and sat down side-by-side by the fire. European clothing was a prized possession. Pipes made of animal bones and wood were filled from leather pouches.

"The war parties have arrived for counseling. Who are the chiefs?" Lignery asked.

Rasle nodded discreetly at the chiefs while handing a steaming cup to the captain. "The chief wearing the red coat on the right is Orono, a Penobscot chief. His father was a Frenchman and his mother half French and half Penobscot. He has none of the physical characteristics of a Penobscot, save that he is tall, straight, and well proportioned. He embraced the Roman Catholic religion while relatively young. The Abenaki believe in the immortality of the soul. The old man wearing white in the middle is Grey Lock himself, or Wawanotewat, meaning 'he who fools others'. He left Schaghticook and joined the Sokoki at Missisquoi. Unable to capture Grey Lock or discover his secret fortress near Missisquoi, the English asked the Iroquois to help, but they refused to get involved except as possible mediators," Rasle replied. "And then there is the ruling sachem Passaconaway, in blue coat. He is a celebrated magician, a famous war commander, an eloquent speaker, and a wise ruler. He has the reputation of being a spiritual leader and is influential in these parts. He has prudently maintained close relations with the Massachusetts and New Hampshire colonies for over a decade."

Lignery sipped the hot wine. "But I heard that the spirit of hostility frustrates Passaconaway. There is a strong prejudice in the English mind against these tribes, which brings them and the Abenaki into conflict in many different ways. Injury is retaliated by injury, and blood is avenged by blood. Murders are followed by wars," he said.

"The wide-ranging frontier between Quebec and New England, a no man's land, contributes to the confusion, but no clear dominion is also a convenient excuse for seizing it. If you want to hire these warriors, you must learn something about them first. The Abenaki call their homeland *Ndakinna,* meaning 'our land', and *Alnanbal* meaning 'men'. The name Abenaki originates from a Montagnais word meaning 'people of the dawn', or easterners. The traditional homeland of the Abenaki is *Wobanakik,* or Place of the Dawn," Rasle replied.

Lignery regarded the warriors indifferently. He was not interested in Abenaki customs or traditions, just on what they could do for him. "We call them what they are, the Wolf Nation," he said.

"These people are Sokoki; the English call them the Saint Francis tribe. There is another large population in Becancour near Trois-Rivieves," Rasle said and focused on his hot wine.

The two men stopped talking as Chief Orono raised his hand and handed the pipe to chief Passaconaway. "Our people have suffered two major epidemics since the early contacts with European fishermen," he said, addressing Gray Wolf.

Gray Wolf took the pipe and smoked. "The English support our enemies the Iroquois, and they are hungry for our land. They spread like locusts throughout and steal the valuable farmlands in the river valleys," he replied.

Chief Passaconaway filled the pipe and lit it with a burning twig from the fire, then spoke. "We can hardly feed thousands of refugees from the south," he said.

Chief Orono let out a sigh. "New Englanders have

never understood our case. We have never been interested in helping the French. We don't even always get along with the French. We have our own fight with the English to avenge past wrongs and to keep them from taking our land," he replied.

Grey Wolf's eyes flared. "For generations we have watched in shock how the English and the French fight several wars over who owns our homeland," he said, angrily.

Passaconaway nodded heatedly. "And not just that. To trade with the French in Quebec, our people have to cross an area controlled by the Montagnais who are over and over again unfriendly and charge high tolls for passage," he said.

Sebastian Rasle and Captain Lignery were sitting a short distance from the chiefs, observing and listening.

Rasle drew a rough map on the frozen ground with a stick. "I've been increasingly alarmed that the fur trade is corrupting and destroying our local allies. But since this places me at odds with more acute economic concerns, my complaints are usually ignored by the government in Paris, at least until a glut of fur on the market caused the prices to fall. With the support of the French court, the fur trade was restricted, and then I was able to convert and separate my converts from further contact with the Europeans," he said.

Lignery leaned over to Rasle, whispering, "Father, we're not truly interested in the Abenaki because we get all the fur we need from the Great Lakes through the Huron. But we also need warriors. We need the Abenaki as a shield to protect Quebec from the English. We will provide weapons and promote hatred toward New England."

The chiefs were ready to complete their meeting. Orono stood up. "Grey Lock, we did not see you at the treaty in Montreal, but shortly afterwards you honored the request of the Sokoki and ended the war, but never signed any agreement with the English. Many years of peace followed fifty years of war. But now, we are on a war path once again," he said.

§   §   §

Preparing her farm house for the winter, Catherina stuffed some straw and grass in between the logs for added insulation. She added a couple of blocks of wood in the fireplace and took her falcon Marlyon outside to flex her wings. There was a pole with a cross member on the other side of the field, maybe a hundred yards in the distance that she used for training the falcon. She raised her arm, and upon command, Marlyon swooshed across the field to the pole. Catherina wore a thick leather glove, and she took a dead mouse in her hand. She called Marlyon and the magnificent bird flew back, landing on her outstretched arm and grabbing the dead rodent in her beak.

"Go on, one more time," Catherina urged her falcon, and she flew with the mouse to the pole to feed. Then her head perked as she heard something. She dropped the rodent and took off, flying higher and higher.

"Hey, where are you going? Marlyon, get back here!" Catherina called after the bird of prey, but her calls were in vain. The falcon rose higher and flew over the forest.

Five miles across the winter forest, Finn was riding

alone, lost in thought, when Catherina's falcon swooped down and started following him. He came upon a clearing in the woods where there was a herd of wild geese. The falcon dove past him and attacked one of the geese, but could not lift it into the air. Instead, the bird dragged its prey under a soaring spruce tree.

Dismounting his horse, Finn leaned in to take a closer look at the falcon. The blood drops from the dead goose on the snow made Finn uneasy for some reason, and he started to speculate that his experiences had been a deception of some sort, fabricated to trap his soul by malicious spirits. Now he thought he saw his mother's features drawn in blood in the snow.

"Who has drawn your features with such vibrant color? In his goodness, is it the Creator or the Devil, who let me to see your dear face again? Glory to the handiwork, in blood brightened by snow, and snow reddened by blood, I see your face, my mother," he thought out loud. He regarded the blood without moving, deep in thought.

Finn did not hear a faint ruffling in the woods as somebody approached. Luckily for him, it was not the enemy. Fronto, Daniel, and Gus, dressed in fur coats and winter moccasins and on a hunting jaunt, found him staring into the snow.

"Snap out of it. It's time to go hunting. Bear hunting," Fronto said, pounding on Finn's shoulder.

"A blast of hunters and the sound of wild boar are such splendid sounds," Gus said, wanting to cheer up Finn.

Daniel pointed direction, calm and matter-of-factly as usual. "There is a bear cave by the Prospect Rock. You better leave the horse here, young chief. We can come back to get it once we have bagged the bear," he said.

Finn followed, though not very enthusiastically as they headed out in bone-crushing air, searching for dense covers that they knew deer would move into during frigid temperatures, and bedding near a food source. They found some tracks, but no animals.

Hours later, Finn was feeling much better when they arrived at a cliff, and climbed over the high rock with Fronto leading the way. Finn followed him only a few steps behind as they scaled the crag. Stones from under their feet dropped down to the treetops far below. On the other side, they set up a camp in a small opening.

Daniel pointed toward the bear's lair. "The cave is over there, maybe fifty yards," he said.

Finn led the others in approaching the cave. Gus and Fronto took aim at the cave entrance while Finn started poking the burrow with a long pole. Nothing happened.

Finn leaned closer into opening to have a better look. He got back up and turned toward the others. He leaned on the pole, still in the opening.

"Sure smells bad, but I'm not sure if anything's in there!" Finn shouted, waving at the others to come closer.

All of sudden, a gigantic cinnamon-colored bear charged out of the cave, roaring and snarling. The staff was knocked out of Finn's hands, and he flew backward, landing heavily on his back in the snow.

"Holy shit!" Fronto shouted and just stared, stunned, at the five-hundred-pound beast.

"For once I understand you, old man! Don't just stand there, shoot that fucker!" Finn yelled, scrambling to his feet.

Snapping out of their surprise, Gus and Fronto fired. Gus's musket misfired due to wet black powder, and Fronto's shot ricocheted off of the bear's skull. The wounded bear reared up on his hind legs, roared in pain and ran into the woods.

The men reloaded as quickly as they could, but the bear was faster and disappeared into the thick bushes.

With a few hand signals, the men spread out and started chasing the bear. They had to advance slowly through the dense forest, expecting the wounded animal to bounce on them at any moment from behind the trees. While they followed the tracks, the bear was smart and ran in a wide circle and came to their camp behind them.

The bear threw things around and found a canteen and started drinking from it. Soon, its eyes turned red, and it got even madder. Just then, Finn, Gus, Fronto, and Daniel came trotting into the camp, skidding to a stop. They were surprised to find the bear in the camp and scrambled back.

"Whoa!" Gus shouted.

Holding the flask in his paws, the red-eyed bear rose up on his hind legs and roared. Daniel moved to the side, trying to get around it to a better position. Sunlight glinted from the animal's enormous fangs, and the beast raised its mighty paws with humongous, scimitar-like nails. The bear let out a deafening roar, and Daniel got a full discharge of its breath on his face.

"The bear is loaded. Somebody gave him whiskey," Daniel said.

"What kind of an idiot would give whiskey to a wounded bear?" Finn said, looking sternly at Fronto. It was his flask the bear was holding. The drunken bear shook its long, coarse fur and spun around on its hind quarters. It reared on its hind legs again, roared, and charged Daniel.

With not enough time to reload, the three of them fought the ferocious bear with only clubs and sticks, trying to stay out of its reach. Gus was knocked down, and Fronto leaped on a rock and jumped on its back with a knife in his hand. The bear shook him off like a rag doll and sent him flying while Finn was frantically trying to find a musket loaded with ball and buckshot.

"Where is it? I can't find the damn gun!" he shouted and finally found it under piles of snow — unloaded. Cursing, he fumbled with the heavy slug rounds as he loaded the gun. The adrenaline rush made his hands shake badly from excitement and terror, and he dropped the rounds in the snow.

Dazed and bruised, Gus and Fronto rose, shaking their heads. Daniel, alone, was fighting the bear back with a long stick. "Kill the beast any time you're ready! Like right now!" he shouted.

Finn went on his hands and knees, frantically searching for the rounds. The bear turned its attention to him just as Finn found them and loaded the gun. The bear seemed to realize his intentions and charged. *Oh fuck me, oh shit*, Finn thought, but at the last moment, he leaned back, stuck the barrel in the bear's gaping mouth and pulled the trigger. The gun blast blew the back of the bear's head off, spraying Finn with blood, bits of skull and grey brain matter. The bear fell to the side, its legs twisting and kicking.

Finn wiped his sweaty brow. "Damn, that was close. Luckily, back home we learned to deal with drunken bears from the east."

§   §   §

Temperatures plummeted and the people in Fort Edward suffered in the bitter cold. Some of the British regulars became rebellious and demanded the commander abandon the fort and retreat to Albany for better winter quarters. General Johnson was jeered by his own troops as he looked at them from the frosty window. There was a large fire crackling in the big fireplace. "They know nothing. All this has been well worth my efforts. The King made me a baronet and Parliament voted me a reward of five-thousand pounds in sterling."

Johnson poured himself and Robert Rogers some more whiskey. He glanced at Rogers who kept his glass out for more and filled his glass to the rim.

"We see the manipulative hand of the Catholic France being directed against our Protestant colonies," Johnson said.

Rogers admired his half-full whiskey glass with pleasure. "A key reason for the fall of the Stuarts was because they were on the verge of restoring the Catholic Church. Because of this, the Jesuits have been secretly entering England on behalf of the Vatican for years. Here in New England, we hardly fail to see how members of this same religious sect are living among the Abenaki on our northern frontier," he replied.

"When the savages commit a murder, or perpetrate a massacre, it is obvious that the French have incited them to it, or at least approve of the act. Accordingly, the Massachusetts governor has offered bounties of fifty pounds for a male Abenaki prisoner, forty pounds for a male scalp, twenty-five pounds for a woman or child prisoner, and twenty pounds for a woman or child scalp. You should make sure your Rangers know this," Johnson said.

"We have been victims of unprovoked attacks since the King Philip's War and refuse to accept any Abenaki title to the land. It is clear that the continued raids by the Abenaki are French aggression, plain and simple," Rogers said.

Outside, the church bells tolled the alarm, and people shouted. A house in the fort had caught on fire, and thick billowing smoke poured out from the windows. Panicked residents ran outside, coughing and almost overcome by the smoke.

The fire had started from the Helming Brother's storehouse, and it was Christina Helming who first noticed the thick smoke rising from the barn roof. Soon the whole of Fort Edward was in danger, and people rushed about carrying buckets of water. Flames were threatening the entire town, and the Rangers rushed to help from Rogers Island.

Finn, Gus, Daniel, and Fronto returned from their hunting trip and saw the commotion, panicked crowds, and flames. They followed the Rangers and grabbed some buckets. Finn took off his mittens and placed them on top of a box.

Then people saw sparks flying from Helming's neighbor's house to the roof attic where hay was stored. The wood was tinder-dry and the roofs, being made of shingles and mulch, ignited easily. Lofts in the stables and cowshed were also filled with dry hay and feed, which only made the problem worse.

Helen of Magdalena drove her wagons hastily away from the fort to a safe distance. The Scottish gunsmith,

Harold Ferrara, threw buckets of water on his gun shop walls to keep it from the flames.

Mayor Trevor Glock rushed to the scene, watching in horror as the town hall was threatened by the flames. "The town hall is on fire! Save the town hall!" he shouted.

Robert Rogers rushed out and made a quick assessment of the situation. "No! We must stop the fire from spreading to the saloon first!" he shouted back.

"What? Are you crazy? We must protect the town hall," Trevor Glock said.

"Mayor Glock, the town hall is almost empty, but the saloon is filled with whiskey."

"The town hall is more important than your whiskey, Captain!"

"The distillery in the back might explode," Rogers replied.

Glock turned to the townspeople. "The saloon is on fire! Protect the saloon!" he shouted.

The spectacle was horrifying but fascinating. The whole Helming store was wrapped in smoke. Multicolored flames threatened other buildings.

Over the crowd and through the smoke, Finn saw Catherina carrying buckets of water. Then to his horror, a burning roof collapsed and she disappeared in thick smoke and sparks. He leaped frantically forward, searching for her.

"Where is she?" he kept asking people who were carrying buckets full of water to fight the flames.

Then he saw her, unconscious on the sidewalk, overwhelmed by the smoke. Finn rushed to help her and found her breathing. He lifted her up and carried her away to a safe distance and laid her down on a tarpaulin. She gained consciousness slowly and looked up at Finn hovering over her.

Catherina coughed. "If you try to kiss me, I will kill you. We've got to stop meeting like this. People will start talking," she said.

People screamed as the distillery behind the Silver Star caught on fire. The saloon keeper, Molly Brant, was almost killed by the inferno as the still exploded, and the violent ethanol blaze sent white and blue flames and scorching sparks high into the air.

The situation worsened. The distillery had been close to the church and suddenly the church roof caught on fire. Flames were visible in the bell turret hatches. The red-hot bell stopped its tolling as the building was covered in a mass of flames. The blazing turret could not be saved, and people withdrew to watch in horror as the tower came crashing down. The bell fell into the burning timbers and planks and was melted into a shapeless mass.

As the flames died down, only a smoldering, black structure was left of the town hall. "We will build a new town, and a much better one. Until then, we can keep our meetings in the saloon," Glock said.

By dawn, Helming's house, the church, and a couple of other buildings had been destroyed. Several people were hurt, and three charred bodies were discovered.

Shocked and enraged, people searched for a fall guy and they found one. Carl Helming's handmaid, Maria Vass, was a suitable wrongdoer because, just before the fire started, she had been seen kneading dough in the backyard with the wood-fired clay oven wide open under the shelter. She was rough handled by the townspeople, pushed around and spat on. Harold Ferrara grabbed a coil of rope and started making a noose.

Luckily for her, Daniel found some tracks leading off into the wilds and following them, where he soon discovered an unused fire arrow dropped in haste. He handed it to Robert Rogers who inspected it. "It's a fucking Abenaki arrow. We will fight fire with fire," he said and snapped it in two.

John Stark brought up a thick worsted glove he found. "We found this mitten and some footprints. It could belong to whoever fired the arrow," he said.

§   §   §

In the British headquarters, General James Abercrombie was hesitant and kept grumbling that he did not get enough ins and outs from his officers. He claimed he could not arrange for operations because he did not have sufficient numbers.

The officers commonly thought that General Abercrombie was a genius at organization but wavered in his leadership to the point that his troops began calling him General Nanny Cromby. He managed the remarkable feat of assembling thousands of troops and moving them and their supplies through the backwoods, but afterward he was completely inept at soldiering.

Behind his strong-minded façade, Abercrombie shilly-shallied between positive and negative emotions as his mood changed from elation to despair and back again. His emotions were never stable: feelings went from calm to awful, then from negative to positive, and from spirited to blue. All this left his decision making capability paralyzed. He was not able to respond to the operational crisis at hand. Robert Rogers and General Johnson attempted to step in and make the decision for him, but he prevented them from doing so.

"Sir, we must act now," Rogers addressed the General with a strong, determined voice.

"How dare you raise your voice to me," Abercrombie replied and threw a temper tantrum of pride, arrogance, and intellectual superiority. He withdrew behind excuses and demanded more details.

Rogers excused himself, nudged Johnson aside and whispered to him. "How in hell are we supposed to wage a war when we have leaders like him?" he said, but Johnson just shook his head, not knowing what to do.

The officers deliberated over the upcoming operations, and finally, Abercrombie hesitantly gave an order. "Lord Loudoun plans a strike at the French forts at Fort Carillon and Crown Point, early this spring. We shall begin now by a sequence of reconnaissance patrols to the vicinity of the enemy forts," he said. "Captain Rogers, I already have ordered an advance scout under Israel Putnam. Upon his return, his Connecticut provincials shall work together with the Rangers. The original plan calls a force of four hundred Rangers to attack the French forts."

Upon hearing the numbers, Rogers' eyes lit up. Immediately in his mind, he started planning for the best possible route across the dense wilderness.

Israel Putnam's patrol returned, soaked and filthy from the long trek, and he reported to the headquarters. "One of my men, John Robins, is missing in action. We must assume he is captured or has deserted. In any case, he is able to reveal our intentions to the French. Worse yet, a convoy of sleighs bound from Fort Edward to Albany on the frozen Hudson river was ambushed by a raiding party of French and Abenaki north of old Saratoga. Edward Best, one of our sutlers, was carried into captivity. He, too, might have heard talk of our intentions and would be able to repeat them to the French," he said.

Rogers threw his hands in the air. "Fuck! This is a serious breach of security. The mission has been compromised before it has even begun," he shouted and turned to Abercrombie. "Sir, we must abandon the operation immediately."

Abercrombie leaned back, lit a pipe and raised his feet on the table. "Lord Loudoun will have none of that, and we shall continue to prepare for the mission. As a matter of fact, Captain, your job is to scout the French forts, not with a group of four hundred men as was first given out, but you will take only one hundred eighty men, officers included, with you so that you have fewer chances of being detected," he said.

Rogers stopped pacing, totally taken by surprise. His gaze snapped from man to man. "But sir, with the elements of secrecy and surprise already lost, we need the additional fighting strength!" he said.

Abercrombie enjoyed smoking the pipe. "Captain, you have your orders and are dismissed. Carry on," he replied.

Rogers stormed out and returned to Rogers Island. He ordered the Rangers to get supplies and equipment ready for their mission.

Finn took a white linen sheet and cut a hole in the center and tried it on a like a poncho. "Snow is white, and so should we be white as well. I think sharpshooters wearing this could get close to the enemy and use their shooting skills to deadly effect," he said.

Rogers issued his warning order. "Rangers, we're to proceed to the neighborhood of Carillon, not with four hundred men as was at first given out, but with a hundred and eighty, officers included. Now we have every reason to believe that the prisoners and a fugitive, under torture, have informed the enemy of our planned excursion. Yet my superior, fully knowing all this, is sending us out with only one hundred eighty men. Prepare for a tough mission, men, and bring along extra ammunition and supplies," he said.

Getting their gear ready, Finn was searching for his gloves. "Hey, old man, have you seen my mittens? I can't find them. I need to borrow yours if you have an extra pair," he asked Fronto, who threw him a couple of heavy woolen gloves.

Privately, Robert Rogers confided to his brothers. "I must confess, unskilled as I am in politics, this mission fills me with doubt, but my bet is that the commander has his reasons and is able to justify his decision."

§   §   §

The Rangers gathered for the operations order and listened in silence. They had no misconceptions about the odds they faced on this mission, and each man knew what to expect. They were going into harm's way, outnumbered and outgunned. The men wrote letters home and prepared their last wills and testaments. Many young men jammed their knives on walls and hung wedding bands and letters home on them as a final message to their loved ones. Then, weapons were cleaned and loaded, and knives and cutlasses were honed razor sharp in stony silence and resolve.

Robert Rogers did the final inspection of the men and equipment lined up in front of his command post. He took a detailed look at the three-barreled pole cannons and ordered each Ranger to carry more ammunition for them. The rucksacks were heavy enough already, and Rogers decided to take a few sleds to carry extra supplies and ammunition.

The sleighs were pieces of cut wood, shaved thin, about sixteen inches wide and six feet long, and turned up in the front. The sleighs glided easily over the snow, with two arms and a cross bar to pull them.

At sunset, Robert Rogers' facial features dimmed at the last light. "To be or not to be, that's not even the question," he said.

Richard Rogers grabbed his rucksack and musket, and gave hand signals for the Rangers to move out. The Rangers marched out quietly in a single file through the palisade, each man tossing a coin in a bucket. Robert Rogers, looking concerned and anxious, watched them file past.

The Rangers passed burned out ruins of a farm with blackened charred logs sticking out of the snow. Robert Rogers divided the patrol into three columns, each one headed by an officer. Dugald Campbell and the Black Watch flanked the main patrol on the left on the west shore. The Scots wore long rawhide leggings and, as could be seen whenever they jumped over logs and stumps, fur underwear under their kilts.

The columns marched in separate files, the ones to the right and left keeping about fifty yards distance from the center line when the terrain permitted it. Scouts were kept in the front and rear, and flanking parties at a due distance with orders to halt on all high ground, to observe the area where the patrol was heading. They advanced as far as the first narrows of Lake George and then set up a patrol base on the east shore in the evening.

Four sentry points consisting of six men each were posted around the base camp. Six Rangers were sent three miles down to establish a forward listening post just in case the enemy was coming toward the Rangers' position.

Scouts checked the vicinity and returned without discovering any enemy in the area. Nevertheless, the Rangers stayed on their guard upon the lake all night, the men taking turns to sleep a couple of hours.

Prior to the first light of dawn, the entire patrol was awakened, that being the time when the enemy warriors usually chose to fall upon them. The Rangers got ready to receive the attack. As the hazy light increased, the forest remained silent, and the Rangers left their camp at sunrise, moving in extended order up the lake, using ice creepers and snowshoes.

"Men, stay close to the eastern shore," Rogers whispered as the men passed him by on the ice.

Having made about three miles, Bill Stark grabbed Sergeant Beaubien by the neck as he saw a dog running across the lake. He motioned three Rangers to reconnoiter a small island ahead, expecting the enemy to be there in ambush. The island was found to be empty, but Robert Rogers took no chances.

"Rangers, remove your ice creepers and put on snow-shoes. We're going into the woods to move parallel to the shore," he said, pointing to the woods.

The Rangers halted at a place called Sabbath Day Point and swiftly formed a defensive perimeter. Rogers conferred with his officers. "The men are exhausted. We put up now for the remaining daylight hours. Officers, keep the lake under observation through telescopes while the men rest," he said.

John Stark positioned the pole cannons and set guards. "Keep formation closed up," he instructed the men.

Rogers ordered the men to lie down upon the ice and wait, as Phillips and six Rangers proceeded down the lake on ice skates. Two hours later, Phillips came back to inform Robert Rogers that he had discovered what he thought was a fire further north on the eastern shore, but was unsure.

Rogers sent Phillips back, accompanied by Ranger White, to double check the first findings. They returned three hours later, fully persuaded that a party of the enemy was encamped at the place.

"Maybe they saw a patch of snow or rotted wood turned phosphorescent in the darkness, but we can't take the chance," Rogers told the officers.

The advanced guard was called in, and the Rangers moved across to the western shore where they took defensive positions in a thicket to conceal their sleighs and rucksacks.

Richard Rogers informed the officers of the meeting at the command post. Robert Rogers laid out his plans and drew a rough map on the snow. "We must push inland to the west, circling behind Bald Mountain and keeping out of sight of the French observation post there," he said.

Leaving a small guard with their baggage, the Rangers kept advancing along the western shore, keeping to the back of the mountains. They discovered a road, not much more than a wide foot path in reality, which the French used for supplies and halted to wait for any resupply parties. Rogers intended to ambush the French on the road leading to the fort and ordered the men to eat cold rations while waiting that night. Three hours after sunrise, the area remained quiet and Rogers decided to move on.

"We'll continue further inland and then march down the Trout Brook valley," Rogers said.

The Rangers advanced in three units, Captain Blakeley leading the way, and the main body in the center was led by Robert Rogers. Ensigns White and Waite led the rear guard. On their left, at a small distance, the Rangers were flanked by Trout Brook, and by a high Bald Mountain on the right. Their main body kept close under the mountain so that the advanced guard might observe the brook.

§   §   §

Two nights before, under the cover of darkness, the French at Fort Carillon were reinforced by three hundred Marines, two hundred Abenaki, and various Nipissing warriors. The warriors held council, and their medicine man prophesied that an English war party was out.

Then a group of warriors returned from scouting and reported that they had crossed the tracks of two hundred men on snowshoes at the place where the Rangers had struck inland from the west shore of Lake George. When they heard this, the warriors could hardly be restrained.

First, a group of ninety-five men, mostly warriors, set out heading south along Trout Brook. Fifteen minutes later, another group of two hundred men plus a quick reaction force of French marines, Canadian militia, and more warriors followed them.

Out in the wilderness, the snow was four feet deep and the movement was difficult through the dense forest, even with snowshoes. Alert and with five yards between men, the Rangers advanced two miles. Then Daniel, walking the point, informed them that the enemy was in sight with a force consisting of about one hundred warriors.

The Rangers threw down their rucksacks and prepared for combat. Robert Rogers assumed that the enemy's main force was approaching on their left, and immediately took action giving new orders. "Ensign McDonald, take command of the advanced guard and make it a flanking party to our right," he said.

The Rangers turned left and crawled within a few yards of the crest of a ridge. Observing the land slowly descending from the rivulet to the foot of the mountain, they extended their position along the bank, far enough to oversee the whole of the enemy at once.

Waiting until the enemy's front was nearly opposite their left wing, Rogers fired his gun as a signal for a general discharge. The pole cannons opened up with buckshot and cut down warriors like grass. Firing and screams of dying men echoed in the woods.

The Rangers barrage killed more than twenty warriors and sent the survivors scrambling. Some young

Rangers followed them in hot pursuit, cutting down enemies with their hatchets and cutlasses. Some of the Rangers began searching and scalping the dead at the first ambush site.

Rogers saw the surviving enemies running toward the fort. He was still convinced that they had destroyed the main enemy force. "McDonald, kill 'em all!" his shout echoed in the woods.

Two hundred yards away, the French veteran Captain Langdale, a somber and most assuredly ugly man, heard the firing to his front. He deployed his two hundred men in skirmish lines and advanced swiftly across the woods in a rough line of battle.

Within minutes, Langdale's force received the fleeing survivors of the ambush that were being hotly pursued by Ensign MacDonald's Rangers. They were followed closely by nearly the whole of Captain Blakeley's company, including lieutenants Increase Moore, Archibald Campbell, James Pottinger, and Ensign James White.

The Rangers ran straight into Langdale's volley that was fired at close range. Captain Blakeley and all his officers were killed or wounded in the lethal fusillade, heavy slugs tearing through muscles and bones.

Moore and MacDonald, both mortally wounded and bleeding profusely, managed to gather the survivors and fall back, hard pressed by Langdale and Durantaye, to Roger's main body before they succumbed to their wounds.

In the melee, Rogers realized that the enemy unit they had routed was only the advanced guard of Canadians and warriors who were now supported by the French regulars.

The enemy was coming in force to attack the Rangers on their right.

In the confusion, Rogers was unable to establish the remaining Rangers into a firing line facing the attacking French and warriors. The Rangers were scattered too far through the woods where they had followed Blakeley's men in pursuit of the defeated warriors.

Seeing the gravity of the situation, Rogers broke out in a cold sweat. "My flank has been turned and we're in danger of being surrounded! Fall back toward the high ground of Bald Mountain!" he shouted.

Under constant fire from the superior enemy, the Rangers did what they were best at and regrouped. They began retreating, fighting toward the high ground in an orderly fashion. Several men were killed in action, providing covering fire while the others moved. One Ranger single-handedly attacked a group of Abenaki with a cutlass and killed three of them before being cut down and hacked to pieces. One of the pole cannon crews was lost as the crew's position was overrun, and the men were bayonetted without mercy.

The jubilant French and their warriors saw that the destruction of the insufferable Rogers Rangers was at last within their grasp. The French pressed on in their vicious attack, and the Rangers could not break contact.

Langdale's face was distorted in a contemptuous, victorious smile. "*Je t'emmerde!* Rogers, you English son of an ugly whore! There is no mercy this time! Your hides are mine, all mine!" he shouted.

John Rogers, taking cover behind a stump to reload, shouted over his shoulder across the clearing. "Langdale, shut your cockholster! You're a walking, living, breathing crotch sore of a goat-fucking, three-bedroom, cave-dwelling, motherless, sheep-herding, and salad-tossing, aborted three-toed tree sloth of a douchebag!"

Bill Stark, on the other hand, was calm and collected under fire. Sergeant Beaubien followed close behind him, like a shadow. He directed the fire of his men. "Men, fire at intervals. One shoots, another is ready while the third reloads! Well-aimed shots, men, make every shot count. Remember, aim at the belt buckle, and let him have it."

The Rangers took up positions in proper order, and fought with steady and well directed fire, causing the French to withdraw a second time.

Due to the high casualties, the Rangers were not able to follow up their success, and the enemy rallied again. Recovering their lost ground, the warriors made a frantic attack against the Rangers' front and both flanks, but were forced back again.

Both sides were exhausted by now and needed a moment to regroup. Finn put on his white poncho and crept closer to the French. He took careful aim and made a cuckoo sound – *coo-coo coo coo-coo-coo* - to lure the enemy out of their cover. To their demise, curiosity got ahold of three young city boys. Within a couple of minutes, changing his positions between shots, Finn had killed three French regulars who stuck out their heads. "*Turkeys*," he mumbled to himself and reloaded.

Waite and the ten men of his rear guard on the left were cut off from the rest as the Rangers scrambled up toward the high ground. Hand-to-hand combat was fast, ruthless, and lethal. Only Waite and another man succeeded in escaping the carnage and making it into the woods.

The Ranger's two remaining pole cannons roared in turns. The attacking French took heavy casualties, buckshot tearing into the French ranks at close range. The trees were painted in red. The French were thrown into chaos and retreated again, but the Rangers' ranks were thinning too quickly for them to explore the enemy's weakness.

The French and Abenaki warriors were infuriated by the sight of scalped corpses, victims of the first ambush. It took them only minutes to regroup and attack the Rangers a fourth time, throwing themselves into repeated assaults.

The Rangers position became more and more perilous. Phillips talked to Rogers. "There are two hundred warriors ascending the mountain on the right, attempting to fall upon our rear."

Rogers nodded grimly. "Take eighteen men to gain possession of the hill," he said.

Phillips jumped into action in front of his men and succeeded in gaining the summit first and repulsed the warriors by a well-directed fire in which every shot killed its target.

By then, the Ranger perimeter was strained to the breaking point. Rogers was patching and filling everywhere. "Crofton, take fifteen men and cover our left flank!"

Crofton rushed out with his men and immediately came under intense musket fire from the French. To get a better view of the situation, Rogers jumped on a large rock. "Pringle, take Roche and eight men to assist Crofton," he ordered, standing boldly on the rock in plain sight.

From his vantage point, Rogers saw that the enemy and

the Rangers were not more than twenty yards apart and sometimes intermixed. Rogers face twitched nervously as he counted that the enemy was much stronger than he had anticipated. "*Fuck, fuck, fuck! Not again!*" He spat out and hit his left hand with the right fist. *Those motherfucking French!* He thought, and jumped down for cover, sparks from enemy bullets hitting the rocks around him.

Finn blinked in the bright muzzle flashes and his ears began ringing as the sounds faded. Looking over his shoulder, he caught a glimpse of Rogers' hard, scarred face, damp with sweat. Rogers darted back and forth, trying to assess the situation. Finn noticed that Rogers looked strangely nervous, and beads of sweat ran into the lines of his face.

Then Finn remembered the similar events of a year before and realized why Rogers was so anxious. He felt sweat break out on his skin, his glance snapping to each man in turn. There was no way out, it seemed.

James Rogers came running low to meet with his brother. "We have lost eight of fourteen officers and over a hundred men. Our only chance is to hang on until nightfall and then make a run for it," he said.

The wounded Rangers lay dying, but before they called for God or their wives, before they called out for their mothers, they called out for their fellow Rangers. The surviving Rangers comforted their dying comrades, quietly exchanging the last few, private words, spoken quietly man to man. "I am honored... to have walked... with you... we'll meet again in Valhalla. See you on the other side, brother."

Rogers darted around between the fighting positions to assess their situation. "Waite holds the center with some thirty men still strong. Phillips holds the right flank with eighteen men — not nearly enough. Crofton and Pringle hold the left with twenty men. There's only one thing left to do," he said with a grim expression on his face.

Richard Rogers grunted and cupped his mouth with his hands. "Get ready to meet your Maker! Kill them all and let the devil sort them out," he yelled, and the Rangers came alive with fury.

The enemy, expecting surrender, was shocked to see the Rangers mount an attack in such a situation. The surprise was a success, and the enemy broke and ran. This time, the Rangers did not follow, but instead held their ground. The Abenaki did not run and instead rushed forward.

"Fall back!" Bill Stark shouted to his men.

Rogers charged up the hill, followed by twenty men, toward Phillips and Crofton. They got to the top where they stopped and fired at the warriors who were pursuing in large numbers, killing several and wounding others.

Archibald Campbell Senior saw his son get hit and go down. "Archibald!" he shouted and rushed out to save his dying son. He picked him up on his shoulders to carry him to safety. As he turned, they were both hit in the back several times. Father and son fell on top of each other in a final embrace.

"Hold the line! Do not break the line!" Bill Stark commanded.

Phillips' twenty men were at this time surrounded by three hundred screaming warriors. Rogers got close enough to him that they could talk. "If the enemy would give good quarter, I think it best to surrender — otherwise we will fight while we have even but one man left to fire a gun," Phillips said.

The last French attack came in from all sides, but Phillips on the right was the first to be cut off and over-whelmed. Phillips' Rangers ran out of ammunition and made one last daring attack with knives and tomahawks. In the end, badly wounded, the survivors were forced to surrender. Once in enemy hands, scalps were discovered on some of the survivors. Without further ado, the Abenaki tied them to trees and hacked them to pieces in the most barbarous and disgusting ways.

Colonel Louis was ecstatic, waving bloody scalps in front of Phillips' bruised face. "I will take this officer and the three others as prisoners and collect the reward in Montreal!" he shouted.

Up on the hill, the enemy got so close to the Rangers that fighting was practically hand-to-hand and muskets were used as clubs. The French regulars used bayonets, and the Rangers fired pistols at point-blank range and then fought with tomahawks, cutlasses, and dirks.

Rogers smashed a warrior's skull open with a tomahawk so hard it got stuck. "Rangers, fall back upon Crofton and Pringle!" he shouted as he used his foot to pry the tomahawk loose off the skull, making a sucking noise.

Finally, the Rangers were able to retreat to the summit behind them. They saw that it was impossible to retreat any farther.

James Rogers turned to Robert. "I will take this part of the hill. You go ahead and take the other side, brother," he said and took positions on one side of the hill while Robert defended the other. Their platoons consisted of only twelve men each.

Pringle, with blood running from several wounds, dove over the logs, utterly exhausted and barely able to talk. "Sir, a large party of warriors has ascended the hill on our right. Roche's snowshoes and mine are broken. We can't move in deep snow fast enough to escape. Sir, we will cover for you," he said, reloading his musket. The two men leaned against a rock, getting ready to fight to the death.

Rogers had to make a quick decision. "We must disperse and evade the enclosing enemy individually. The designated assembly point is the ORP on the west shore," he said. "Wait for my signal."

Rogers threw off his uniform jacket and put on his snowshoes backward, in order to deceive the enemy. He urged the men to do the same as they dispersed in the dark woods, their tracks showing as if they had come running to the cliff and gone right over it.

At the same time, the enemy overran Pringle's Rangers position. The Rangers were bayonetted against trees, and the wounded were shot where they lay. The jubilant warriors discovered a discarded uniform coat, and in the breast pocket they found officer's commission papers. Langdale read the papers, announcing that the loathed Robert Rogers was dead. Triumphant shouting and war cries echoed in the woods. The Ottawa pointed down below to figures on Lake George, and seeing the tracks, they figured the Rangers had escaped by sliding down the steep side of the mountain.

Robert Rogers and his men made it to the lake with difficulty. Battered and bruised from running over slippery rocks and stones down the mountainside, the Rangers reached Lake George in the evening. They were joined by several wounded men who were assisted to the place where their sleighs had been left.

"Two Rangers, on ice skates, head south for Fort Edward with request for a relief force to bring in the wounded," Rogers said. Two able-bodied Rangers ran out immediately. He turned to the others. "Put the four severely wounded men on sleighs, with two men each to pull, and head south!"

The wounded were placed on sleighs, and they moved out on the ice and disappeared into the darkness. The remaining Rangers formed a perimeter around the rally point where they waited to meet other evaders as they came in.

The Rangers passed the night without fire or blankets.

The night was extremely cold and the men suffered but behaved in a manner consistent with their conduct in the action.

In the morning, the Rangers proceeded down the lake, and at Hoop Island, six miles from the shore, they encountered the reserve force coming up for rescue. They were led by John Stark who brought with him provisions, blankets, and horse-drawn sleighs.

§ § §

Straight from the mission, Robert Rogers grabbed his brother's jacket and headed out to the headquarters. He was informed that the commanders were busy — at a ball. He rushed to the governor's mansion just as servants were making final preparations for a dance and dinner party.

Rogers insisted to meet with George Howe, 3rd Viscount, and a Brigadier General in the English army. A snooty servant led him to the library, but he went too slowly for Rogers, who pushed him aside.

Howe was discussing tactics with George Washington and several other officers. Rogers almost took the door off the hinges as he barged in. He nodded to Washington and walked up to Lord Howe, ignoring the other officers in the room.

"Sir, with all due respect I must protest. My last operation was a failure due to the piss-poor planning and lack of resources. We suffered numerous casualties because of this."

The staff officers gave him a disapproving look and then turned to Howe and Washington. Rogers paced back and forth and grabbed a white handkerchief from a servant, wiping his dirty hands and face with it. He tossed the soiled cloth back on the butler's tray.

Washington cleared his throat. "Captain Rogers—" he began, but Howe cut him off with a raise of his hand.

"I have heard reports that the Rangers have served impeccably and have brought back a lot of useful intelligence," he said as he turned to a bowl and washed his hands.

"My Rangers deserve much better respect than this. They fought gallantly, as they always do, and yet we suffered over sixty percent casualties!" Rogers said and kept pacing with his hands behind his back. "Besides, you must be fully aware, sir, that I have used my own funds to hire them. I expect reimbursement in order to recruit new Rangers if I'm to continue my missions effectively."

Howe nodded, fully aware of the poor planning, which he intended to use as leverage against Abercrombie. He walked around a large table and moved some tin soldiers and cannons around. There was a chess game on a side table and Howe took one of the pawns, weighing it in his hand.

"Well, yes. Maybe you are right," he said and paused. "Captain Rogers, I will recommend your promotion to the rank of Major of the Rangers in His Majesty's Service. You are also set about the task of reconstructing your shattered force. Stand by for further orders." He turned to see the effect his words had.

Rogers stopped pacing and looked at Howe, startled, right as Howe's aide brought him a rolled up paper with a stocky red Royal seal on it.

Washington coughed loudly and looked stricken. "But sir—" he started protesting, but an angry look from Howe shut him up.

"That is your new assignment, Major. It should alleviate some of your losses, don't you think? Congratulations," Howe said.

Rogers took the scroll and opened it slightly, looking at it in disbelief. "This is excellent, Lord Howe. I knew I could count on your assistance. I will return to the fort immediately and get ready for the next mission. You can count on me, sir," he said.

Rogers turned on his heels and calmly marched out and closed the door softly behind him. Outside, he forced the horrific images of dying men out of his mind for the time being. He took a drink from his flask and braced himself. *Rangers never die, they just go to hell and regroup*, he thought and jubilantly kissed the new commission paper in his hand.

§   §   §

On Rogers Island, the former storehouse was turned into an infirmary for the wounded Rangers. A doctor in Boston had been given orders to report for duty and supposedly was on his way to the fort. In the meantime, Catherina and Shelagh Brotherton tended the wounded men, washing wounds and changing bloody dressings to the best of their abilities with the negligible means available to them.

Donald MacCurdy released the Rangers. "Now it is time to celebrate Major Robert Roger's promotion."

Seeing their wounded comrades in capable hands helped to ease the pain, but many of the surviving Rangers still felt a ferocious wrath and needed a way to release some of the stress. A number of them originated from Ireland, and they planned an extravagant Saint Patrick's party, painting their faces green and scaring the townspeople, as many of them regarded it as a pagan ritual.

While going through the rounds in the evening, John Stark overheard the Rangers planning the celebration. Immediately, he commanded the sutlers to carry no rum to them without a written order. The supply sergeant nodded but the order was never followed (he had been paid off by the Irish Rangers), and casks of whiskey were distributed to the Rangers.

Fat Murray lurked in the back alley, having brought in another load of illegal rum. He could not stay away because he wanted to be seen with the Rangers so he could keep bragging. He walked around the bar cowering in the back, trying to stay away from the Rangers, hoping they would not take notice of him. He blinked in shock as he felt his sweat making his armpits slap wetly. The horror of the idea that any of the Rangers would smell his sweat was embarrassing. That exact moment, he felt a trickle of piss running down the wrinkles in his fat thigh, and he hurried to the corner table to cover it up.

A few Rangers stayed sober for reasons of conscience, but many more drank heavily in the Silver Star lounge. One Irish Ranger called Fionn MacCool, a giant of a man, raised a toast. "Here's to Niall, one of the greatest Irish kings! He marched south with his Scot and Pict allies against the Romans in Britain. It was there that Niall's forces took prisoner one Succat, one that you now call St. Patrick!"

The Rangers drank boisterously. In a corner table, Fat Murray had gathered a few young boys around himself. "I was selected for Rangers," he told them, "but in a tragic training accident my knee was injured. Now, let me tell you a story of a real Ranger, a mean motherfucker..."

MacCurdy, taking a drink and walking around the bar, overheard him. "Shut your face, Fat Murray! You seem to know more faggoty details about the faggots before the faggots even do, you faggot!" he said as he walked past him and joined the others.

Another Irish Ranger named Brian Boru raised a toast as well. "And now we find ourselves, lads, far away from our fathers' land, just like Saint Patrick did so many years ago when he was a young man. Let's drink to Saint Patrick, who tells us in his confession how he heard a voice in his sleep compelling him to leave his cruel master and find a boat that awaited him, and after the six years of slavery, he fled his cruel master. And it was there, of course, that one night in his sleep he heard a voice saying to him, 'You do well to fast. Soon you will depart for your home country'. And again, an extremely short time later, there was a voice prophesying, 'Behold, your boat is ready'. So here's to Saint Patrick!"

The bar was filled with much yelling and bellowing. Daniel leaned closer to Finn. "Young chief, tell me if true friendship is even possible between people whose ultimate concern is not for each other but for their own good?"

Finn thought about it for a moment. "I don't see why seeking my own pleasure would prevent me from doing well to others, because that feels good, too," he replied. Fronto overheard them and raised his eyebrows, not sure if he had heard Finn right.

"Once, I found myself having to answer that very same question," Fronto said. "Remembering our little naval expedition, that if there are two shipwrecked sailors who find themselves clinging to a plank that will only support one, what should they do? Should they produce lots to choose between them? Should they struggle to stay on the plank, or should the less valuable let go? Or would it be appropriate for both of them to jump off so that neither survives?"

"Randomness by drawing lots seems absurd," Gus said.

"Old man, you ask some crazy shit. What is notable here is not to survive, but to act rightly," Finn said.

"But who defines what is right?" Fronto asked.

Finn shrugged his shoulders. "I don't fucking know! All I know is that I would not refrain from helping others when it is the right thing to do, or fail to do what justice demands," he said.

Hearing Finn's comments, Fronto looked pleasantly surprised, and without saying anything more, he nodded his head in agreement at Finn and raised his tankard in a toast to him.

More drinks were poured, and even more overflowing sorrows were drowned. Servant girls were groped and teased, and a woman ran across the bar screaming and laughing, chased by Ranger MacCool. The Rangers started singing, "As I was a-walking round Kilgore Mountain!"

The Irish troops could not forget the ancient custom and poured out copious libations in honor of St. Patrick.

As the night went on, Fronto was in his element. "The thirst of the Irish is terrible and must be properly taken care of. If not, I cannot guarantee anybody's safety within miles!" he shouted over the noise.

The doors burst open as Johan Kopf entered the lounge followed by half a dozen Hessian troops. He marched to the counter and threw a mitten on it. "Somebody here is missing a glove like this one, which was found near the place fire arrows were shot to start the fire!" he said with a victorious smile that lit his face as a candle might light a skull.

The Rangers went silent, not knowing what to say. John Stark walked up to Kopf. "Totenkopf, what are you implying? Whoever started the fire is now missing this mitten?" he said.

Finn came in from the backdoor, buttoning his pants. He saw the mitten and grabbed it. "There it is. Where did you get it?" he said with a hiccup.

Stark turned to face him. "The Hessian claim it was

found near the spot fire arrows was shot. Where did you lose yours?

Kopf pointed his finger at Finn. "By the powers vested in me by the commanding officer, arrest him!"

Finn's face turned dark from rage as he noticed Kopf standing at the other end of the bar. "Totenkopf, you're a lying sack of shit," he spat out and turned to Stark. "That reptilian vulture is trying to frame me. I threw my mittens off when we came in from the woods to help fight the fire."

The Irish Rangers hated the Hessians for many reasons of their own and with loud yells — *Fág a' Bealach! Músclaígí an t-iarann!* — charged them across the bar. Tables and chairs were smashed. Tankards were spilled, and men wrestled on the floor. Finn moved through the drunken crowd toward Kopf.

"Totenkopf is mine!" Finn shouted, but before he reached Kopf, he was knocked down by the Rangers clashing with the Hessians. John Rogers picked him up and pushed him away from the melee, leaving Finn behind a wall of brawling drunken hulks.

Outside on the palisades, Catherina and Shelagh Brotherton brought hot drinks to the guards. The French were aware of the rumbustious drinking practices of the Hibernians and decided to use it for their own advantage. Captain Langdale endeavored to arrange a surprise attack in the night while the Irish portion of the garrison was engaged in drunken carousing.

From the corner of her eye, Catherina caught a glimpse of dark shadows approaching the fort, advancing from tree to tree. She looked closer and shouted an alarm, picking up a musket.

The French militia and Abenaki warriors launched their night attack. Musket fire erupted from the wood line surrounding the fort. The fort was saved by the vigilance of the guards, who returned fire and repulsed the French while the other troops came to their senses.

Sober Rangers rushed to help and Catherina fought gallantly alongside them on the palisades. She fired her musket at the enemy muzzle flashes. Finn, Gus, Fronto, and Daniel hurried out from the saloon, stumbling to help with the rest of the Rangers.

"Where have you been? Drinking with your buddies, I see, while I held the fort," Catherina said as they climbed onto the palisade. The Hessians, outnumbered and too sober, decided it was better for them to wait for another time to fight the drunken Irish savages and quietly disappeared into the night.

Shelagh stood beside Catherina with her arms folded in front of her. She drummed her fingers on her arm and tapped her foot and looked angrily at Daniel. Then the unimaginable happened. It was the first and only time anybody ever saw the mighty Wappinger warrior afraid of anyone. Daniel gulped and picked up his rifle to fight.

Seeing now that their effort was hopeless, the French ceased their attack and withdrew into the woods. Finn turned to look for Kopf, but he had again disappeared, and no one knew where his billets were.

§   §   §

The following days, an early spring melted the snow away, and the forests turned light green. After the surprise night attack against the fort, the British and provincial commanders were not satisfied with the conditions. Lord Howe arrived in Fort Edward and summoned General Johnson and Robert Rogers to discuss the situation.

"The Frogs are up to no good that is for sure. We need more intelligence to prepare a preemptive strike at their main bases," Howe said.

"The latest attack was repelled, but the reports tell of increased activity all across the frontier. They are planning something vile," Johnson said.

"Major Rogers, get ready to take your Rangers in a new attempt to take an engineer to Carillon to make drawings of the fort," Howe said. Rogers protested, but Howe simply dismissed him, expecting nothing but unquestioning loyalty in return for the recent promotion.

Johnson supported Rogers' argument. "You are right, Major, that the war party attacking the fort on St. Patrick's Day was only a prelude," he said.

"But sir—" Rogers started to reply.

Howe remained adamant. "No ifs or buts about it. Now get a move on, Major," he said, departing without further ado.

Rogers was keenly aware that the Rangers needed rest. He hesitated, but he could not disobey direct orders and so he summoned the men. He faced them, and seeing the determined mindset behind their exhausted expressions, he decided to cut to the chase. "Alright men, we will do a recon mission. But we must take some packages with us on this movement," he said.

The Rangers were astonished. They had just come back from a challenging job where they had taken heavy casualties, and now they were being sent back into harm's way. To them, one measly St. Patrick's Day party did not count as rest.

"I know. I know. I don't like it either, but orders are orders. Look at this way, it is our chance for revenge," Robert Rogers said.

That motivated the Rangers and soon they moved out with some militiamen from the fort and the engineer from the regulars. A couple of British officers gathered at the gate to watch them depart. One Ranger with a hangover threw up while marching past the officers and almost soiled their boots.

The officers looked at the man in contempt. "Barbarian!"

Robert Rogers walked by, cradling his musket on his left arm. "That may be so, but they are *my* barbarians," he said.

During the movement across difficult terrain, two militiamen suffered bone fractures, and they were sent back to Fort Edward. The Regulars bitched and moaned about them moving too fast and wanted to rest. In fact, they were scared of the dark forests around them, and the Rangers whose menacing bearing appeared like the wrath of Mars to them.

Dugald Campbell and Donald MacCurdy stopped the moaning Regulars. "Now shut the fuck up, you pukes. If you don't stop babbling like idiots, I will discharge the enemy from their misery and kill you myself, maggots! We Rangers have a saying: March or die!" MacCurdy hissed between his teeth.

The Regulars were horrified and shut up. The patrol

reached Sabbath Day Point nearly overcome with the cold of the night. The scouts returned, and they reported that two working parties were seen on the east side, but none on the west of the enemy fort.

Rogers judged this a suitable time for the engineer to make his observations. The patrol moved another five miles toward the enemy fort and then stopped. Rogers did not want the noisy Regulars near him when closing in on the enemy. "Captain Williams, you are in charge of the Regulars here. I will take the engineer, forty Rangers, and forty-five Mohawks with me to the objective," he commanded.

This time, Rogers was not going to get taken by surprise. It took six hours for the Rangers to advance the last five miles to the ridge that overlooked the enemy fort. They crawled the last two hundred yards. Behind cover and concealment, Rogers and the engineer, using their telescopes, started their observations and began drawing details of fortifications.

Four hours later, Rogers returned to the objective rally point. Preparing for the patrol to return to Fort Edward, he sent five Mohawks and one Ranger to monitor the lake crossing from the east side. But before departing, he sent the engineer out one more time to the fort, with Finn, Fronto, Gus, and Daniel as security. They returned at midnight, the engineer having finished his duty to Rogers' satisfaction.

"Alright, let's get moving, but maybe we'll find targets of opportunity on the way back, like the working party we saw earlier," Rogers said.

MacCurdy's face lit up, and he winked. "Aye sir, this sure is the land of opportunity, all around us."

Rogers ordered Williams and the Regulars back to the patrol base. "Captain Williams, get your regulars back to the Sabbath Day Point. Your men are too distraught with the cold to advance them any farther. I will continue the mission with my Rangers and set up an ambush," he said.

Without the extra baggage, as the Rangers called the Regulars, the movement was faster and stealthier. Rogers marched the point with Captain Putnam pulling security for him close behind. The Rangers and the Mohawks followed to attack the French working party. Early, in the morning fog, they crossed the lake at South Bay, eight miles south of the Fort Carillon. At dawn they arrived opposite of it, within half a mile of the French parties employed in cutting fire wood.

"Ranger Nimham, take a couple of men to see the size of the enemy element and their exact location," MacCurdy ordered. Daniel nodded and led Finn, Gus, and Fronto on a scout. Two hours later they returned.

"The enemy is forty in number, and at work close upon the lake shore, nearly opposite the fort. All the boats are on the other side though," Daniel said.

Rogers smile was so cold it made budding wildflowers shrivel up and die. "Fuck it. It'll take the French fifteen minutes to cross the bay. This is it, men. Just don't kill them all. I want prisoners, too. Now, let loose the dogs of war," he said.

Throwing off any lingering civility, the Rangers descended onto the enemy. Not a single shot was fired, as the Rangers used cutlasses, dirks and tomahawks to wreak their grisly revenge. Screams of the dying were quickly muffled by the butchering thuds and whacks and thwacks.

Each Ranger, soaked in bloody muck, thought someone else would keep at least one prisoner, but none actually did. The element of surprise was lost only when a running enemy was gunned down mercilessly.

Musket shots echoed in the forest, and the fortress across the water was alarmed. Soon, the French sent out a war party of eighty Canadians and warriors, backed by a hundred and fifty regulars, to hunt down the Rangers. War cries and hollering sounded across the water.

The Rangers retreated, and the moment they disappeared into the steep hillside, warriors and Canadians appeared on canoes in hot pursuit.

Turning to take a look behind, Finn caught a glimpse of Colonel Louis who was leading the warriors.

The Canadian militia and warriors landed on the shore just as the Rangers ran up to the summit and halted upon the rising ground. They turned around and fired a volley, killing five warriors who were too eager to get too close too soon.

The Rangers resumed their retreat, moving quickly cross-country. A couple of miles later, Finn stayed a little behind and took a stand, and waited. When he heard the approaching enemy, he made a cuckoo sound again. "Come here, little turkeys. Come to Daddy," he said softly and breathed out.

At the same time, Colonel Louis jumped on a tree stump two hundred yards away. Finn immediately shifted his aiming and fired at him. Colonel Louis saw him move and dove for cover, but he was too late and was hit in the shoulder. He yelped in pain and rolled into the bushes. Finn cursed and took off running after the Rangers.

The Rangers proceeded five miles farther, at which point the enemy was getting closer and closer. They turned around and took advantageous positions upon a long ridge. "Steady, aim...," Rogers said as he reloaded.

The Canadians and warriors rushed out of the woods right into the Rangers' and Mohawks' volley. The dying had hardly time to fall down when the Rangers launched a counterattack. "Beat 'em, bleed 'em, and kill 'em!" MacCurdy shouted, leading the charge. The enemy survivors had no time to escape and were cut down before the French regulars appeared a couple of hundred yards behind. Dead enemies were scalped quickly by the Rangers on the run.

The idea of getting caught alive kept the men running up and down the hills and ravines. "Dog, I can't make it any longer. I'm finished," Finn said, exhausted.

"Quit moaning and groaning. If you think things are so bad, go ahead and kill yourself and be done with it," Fronto yelled at him.

"Whatever crawled up your ass?" Finn asked, and kept going.

The enemy continued chasing them along narrow crests, across streams raging with melting spring water and down slippery mountainsides. The running fight continued as the Rangers reloaded and shot without stopping. The enemy started to hesitate and began to fall back as their numbers were thinning fast, and the Rangers gained distance.

Another five miles later, the forests behind them were quiet as the Rangers reached Sabbath Day Point, fifty miles from the place they had started. Men were completely exhausted. Robert Rogers slumped beside his men. "I'll say it myself, men, that was a long fifty miles."

§   §   §

A couple of days later, the people enjoyed pleasant spring weather in Fort Edward. The sun came out, encouraging Fronto and Daniel to find Finn and Gus. They were all stiff and aching from the last mission.

"Finn is probably the only one who doesn't mind the winter war, but the rest of us need a little rest and relaxation," Fronto said, stretching his shoulders.

"We should go fishing. What say you?" Daniel said, massaging his thighs.

Gus rubbed his arms and was really interested. "Sure. We're losing the war but why not? I don't know about you, but my morale is exceedingly low right now," he said.

Finn did not say a word as he followed them, walking stiffly and rubbing his back. As they passed Catherina's farm he wanted to reconcile with her, so he sauntered (or more like wobbled) over to her front porch. "We're going fishing on the river. Would you like to go with us? It's a beautiful day," he said, hearing her moving inside the house. There was no answer, and Finn looked worried for a moment.

"Sure, that would be nice. I'll get my coat," Catherina finally replied. Hearing her voice, Finn smiled in relief.

Other townspeople were at the river too. There were some women washing clothes on a pier and men inspecting fish nets. Abijah Hort took his wife Hester and their two kids fishing. They launched a boat, although some onlookers warned them that the boat was unfit for use.

Hester was remarkably small and feminine. "Dear Lord, be merciful to me. The river is so vast, and our boat is so small. Protect me, oh Lord, for our boat is so small," she prayed in the boat.

The Hort family proceeded on the boat out to the river. Abijah got his fishing rod out and gave it a cast, but he did not notice that a vessel was approaching from upstream. Two men, Colonial Bill and Hopper, were descending the river on a barge loaded with timber.

The two men on the barge saw a deer that stood at the edge of the water for about ten seconds and then started swimming across the river, bobbing up and down on the waves.

"Look. There's a deer. It seems dazed," Hopper said.

"Quick, take a musket," Colonial Bill said. Hopper reached for his musket and stood up to get a better shot at the deer.

On the shore, Finn noticed the deer as well. "Look, a deer is swimming," he said. The deer was now swimming frantically almost in the middle of the river.

People gasped as a huge back tail of a giant fish broke the surface near the deer.

"Look! What was that?" Catherina said.

"It is a giant fish. It is too far out to see clearly, but it is a fish. I can't believe how big it is," Daniel said. The predator's massive back was now seen just below the choppy waves as it launched its attack.

From his boat, Hopper had seen the giant fish, too. But he could not decide if he should aim at the deer or the fish.

Suddenly, Hopper's barge collided with the Hort's boat.

Hopper was standing on the bow of the barge, and as he turned to see the boat, he tripped and grabbed at Colonial Bill for support, causing both of them to fall into the river. Hopper hit his head on an oar falling into the water and was so dazed he had a hard time staying afloat. The much smaller Hort boat was upset, and the occupants were plunged into the water. Poor little Hester was screaming for help before she was drawn under.

"Quick! We must launch a boat to rescue them!" Finn shouted and ran toward some rowboats nearby. They launched the nearest boat successfully and after considerable exertions, they rescued the sufferers who were hypothermic from the cold water. They pulled Colonial Bill from the water barely alive, but Hopper was found drowned.

Another boat rescued Abijah Hort and the kids, but Hester could not be found. The Mohawks assisted the provincials in bringing the bodies to the shore. Just then, on his way to Fort Edward, Doctor Barrett arrived, dressed in black, and immediately attended the victims as soon as the bodies were recovered.

Doctor Barrett took a box from his horse. "Ladies, move aside, this is not for your eyes. Men, make a fire. Pull down his pants and turn him over on his stomach. I will do my best to resuscitate him," he said.

When the fire was started, Doctor Barrett opened the box and took out a rectal tube which he inserted into Hort's rectum. He then took out a fumigator and bellows and threw some tobacco leaves onto the fire. He filled the bellows with the smoke and connected the fumigator to the rectal tube.

"The warmth of the smoke will aid his respiration." The doctor said, working the bellows and blowing smoke up the poor man's rectum. People shook their heads, hoping for a miracle.

"I believe it is obvious by now that Hort is beyond earthly help. Hopper is not faring any better," Fronto said.

The efforts were futile, and Hopper and Hort were beyond all aid. The traumatic event cast a dark shadow over the community, and the council meetings were postponed.

"Mr. Hopper was one of the earliest and most ardent members of the community. He was also a large land proprietor who was widely respected, and his untimely demise is severely felt and deeply regretted," Carl Helming solemnly said.

Shivering under a blanket, Colonial Bill, a superstitious man, had a strong opinion as to what had caused the accident. "All this happened because of that witch Hester. She is a woman who acts strangely, as if she fancied other women, or worse than that, Satan himself. She is always argumentative with her neighbors, and is cantankerous, feisty, angry, and quick to take offense. I tell you the truth, she is a witch," he said, his voice shaking. The people thought he was out of his head and did not listen to him.

"I will initiate the funeral as is appropriate. All the townspeople are urged to attend," Doctor Barrett said.

"The Pickwick Club will hold a meeting to consider the erection of a tombstone in memory of the deceased," Gustav Helming said.

Solemn people departed the site, following the wagon carrying the bodies. Colonial Bill stayed behind and after the others had disappeared he turned toward the river. He made pagan gestures and recited some strange rites. "You are now indicated by that name of Hester Hort that not having the fear of the Lord before thine Eyes you have of late years provided entertainment of Satan the formidable Enemy of King and humans and by his guidance have killed the body of Mr. Hopper, besides other witchcraft, for which according to the law of the Lord and the established law of this commonwealth you deserve to die."

§   §   §

In the Catskill Mountain house, Henry Raymond watched in amazement as the old man poured himself more whiskey. He placed a hand over his glass as Finn looked at him and asked if he wanted some more. Henry could hardly believe his eyes as the old man took a long drink and let out a sigh of pure joy. He didn't even seem to get drunk at all. Finn looked back at him and winked. "I see what you're thinking, Raymond. I can tell you're not a drinking man. That's good. I tell you, those Irish guys are just a bunch of pussies circling a saucer full of warm milk when it comes to drinking whiskey."

The old man turned quiet and solemn, and after a moment of hesitation continued, "Anyways, Raymond, if you had seen what six tomahawks can do to a man's body in a manner of seconds, you'd be pouring that stuff down your throat like a wild man from Borneo, as well." He tilted his head back and emptied his tumbler in one swift gulp.

"Doctor Josiah Barrett was an intriguing character as he rode over to his large congregation on horseback, his saddlebags filled with drugs and medicines, surgery tools and a bible, for he was also a preacher and a teacher.

"In Fort Edward, most families used domestic remedies for their ailments, and it was part of Doctor Barrett's teaching of a good housewife to understand the different herbs, leaves, roots, and tree bark, what ailments they were to be used for, and where to find them in the woods. Catnip was soothing to the nerves. A bouquet of blue mountain thistle, common mullein, and orange jewelweed, randomly picked and grouped together, and wrapped with a patterned ribbon, acted as a tonic. Boneset was beneficial for fevers, and skunk cabbage was used for rheumatism. Aromatic plant teas of all kinds were used for most of the common ailments.

"The good doctor did not know a great deal about handling different kinds of sickness, and bleeding and a purge were both used in case of sickness. If the patient recovered, the doctor got the credit for it, and if he died, it was charged to Providence.

"When Doctor Barrett was younger, he studied surgery with butchers and barbers in London and Boston. He relied on herbs and primitive instruments to make potions and hand out cures. He held strongly to the ancient Greek belief that the body contained four fluids, or humors, which must be released during infection. The way to let out humors was to bleed the patient.

"The doctor carried his tools for his appalling treatment in a leather saddlebag that rolled out on the side of his horse. Tools of his profession were mortar and pestle, small knives called lancets, bowls used to collect the blood, and leeches in a jar that he applied directly to the skin. Leeches can suck up to ten times their weight in blood. Small saws were used to remove limbs, and hot pokers were applied to cauterize the wound after amputation.

"The Doctor's fee for a visit in the region was one shilling. For more than a mile distant he charged three shillings. For a night visit, four shillings, and for an all-night visit and medication, the price was nine shillings and sixpence. As was true of the pastor's salary, the doctor was paid mostly in farm produce. I remember one invoice of nine pounds, seven shillings that was paid in sundries, apples, flax, pears, timothy-seed, beans, clams, fish, eels, pigs, watermelons, and geese.

"Once, a particularly serious epidemic of smallpox swept over Fort Edward and many were the deaths among the Iroquois and the black slaves. You see, Raymond, the government required the slave masters to keep their servants in at night, packed in small quarters, but because of that the highly contagious disease spread among them like a wildfire. Fences were erected around houses where a case of smallpox occurred to quarantine the people, and one rule stated that all persons were thereby strictly prohibited from pulling down any fences made to prevent the possibility of spreading the smallpox.

"After they discovered more modern methods of handling this disease, the town trustees decided that Doctor Josiah Barrett would have liberty to handle the business of inoculation for the smallpox in Fort Edward from that present time forward," the old man said.

§   §   §

The following evening, Finn entered Rogers' command post to ask for instructions on replacing spent ammunition. Everybody in the dark room was talking and did not pay him any attention.

Behind Finn, Donald MacCurdy barged in with Moses Hazen and pushed him aside. They stopped in front of Robert Rogers' desk.

"I'm here to ask for my men's back pay. My men haven't been paid and are ready to commence suits to collect," MacCurdy said.

The room was filled with pipe smoke and tension. Bottles and glasses of whiskey were on the table. Fire crackled in the fireplace. The three Rogers brothers looked expressionlessly at MacCurdy.

The Stark brothers sat silently, watching. Sergeant Beaubien lay in the corner close to Bill, unconcernedly gnawing a bone.

The atmosphere was touchy, and the men were cagey. Robert Rogers sat behind a table smoking a pipe. "Money is scarce these days. You know that," he said.

MacCurdy stepped forward, pulling a pistol from his belt. The Rogers' brothers and Starks brothers tensed up and reached for their side arms. Rogers waved his hand, and they froze. MacCurdy placed a pistol on the table and leaned over it. He looked Rogers in the eyes.

"You have saved a lot of money due to the recent, heavy casualties that have resulted in a decreased payroll. But the remaining men are still waiting for their pay, sir," he said.

"I need the monies to hire new recruits to replace the casualties. So that you know, I still have not received any payment from the government for my services in the winter of '56. That's the kind of government we're fighting for, lieutenant," Rogers replied.

John and Bill Stark supported Robert Rogers. They

thought the men should be patient and wait for a while longer.

Moses Hazen moved beside MacCurdy. "We don't care about your land speculations. You and William Johnson can stick it where the sun doesn't shine, sir. Men must get paid. Otherwise walking point in the dark might get mighty perilous," he said.

Rogers leaned over the table and pushed the pistol aside. "I will walk the point in front of you any time. Will you do the same for me, lieutenant?"

MacCurdy and Hazen stared at the Rogers and the Starks in turns. Then, without saying anything more, Mac-Curdy picked up his pistol and led Hazen out, past Finn.

After the two men left, the Rogers brothers discussed ways to get reimbursed for all the monies they had paid to recruit the Rangers. Robert Rogers had to stay in Fort Edward and try to collect business debts from his real estate deals. He sent his brothers to demand payment from the government.

Richard Rogers was sent to New Hampshire for new recruits. He waited to obtain pay for Robert Rogers' services for 1755 upon the Boston Government, but could not obtain any, although the Governor generously supported the justice of the claim.

James Rogers took a letter to Lord Loudoun, soliciting his aid in obtaining funds from the Government. It was an order for what was due to Robert Rogers and his men for their services in the winter of 1756. Lord Loudoun replied that as those services were prior to his command, it was not in his power to reward them.

John Rogers then approached General Amherst, asking reimbursement for expenses in 1757, but he gave Robert Rogers a similar answer.

Donald MacCurdy's men afterward commenced suits with Judge Lynch and recovered judgments against Robert Rogers for eight hundred twenty-eight pounds in sterling, besides costs.

In the end, Robert Rogers never received any payment from the provincial government or from London — but that is another story.

On their trips to collect payments from the government, Richard, James, and John Rogers met on the road close to John Morton's farmhouse. They talked quietly amongst themselves, contemplating whether they should seek Morton's assistance in the debt collection effort, but they decided to ask Robert's advice first and headed home.

Watson, Morton's secretary, carrying a briefcase stuffed with papers, passed them by on his way to the Morton house. Once inside, Watson entered the library, where he reported to John Morton the news of his protégé.

"He looked so lost and has no family left. I might consider taking him under my protection, or even adopting him," Morton said.

"But sir, you cannot possibly consider such a thing. You do not even know this man," Watson said.

"I have my reasons, Watson. Sometimes our hearts know better 'Invitis omnibus' than our minds are willing to accept, that is, against the wishes of everyone," Morton said.

Morton walked into his study and paused in front of a large painting that portrayed an older man. "He came here in search of a home and to secure a peaceful life away from the eastern oppressor of his homeland. He has asked remarkably little and risked his life fighting for our cause. I must pay him what is his due. He needs a protector," he said.

"But sir—," Watson's voice faltered.

"Is that all you can say? Finn Morton he shall be from now on! I shall send him an invitation to visit us. Will you see to it, dear Watson," Morton said. Watson bowed and departed.

His wife Ann Justis entered the room, putting her hand on his shoulder. "John, you must do what is right," she said.

"He was searching for Columbia when first we met him. Remember that? How could I not help a young man like that?"

Morton took her hand, and they left the room. At the door, he turned and once more looked at a monumental portrait on the wall. Brass plate on the frame read *'Martti Marttinen A.D. 1654'*. The man in the painting was dressed in a suit from 1650, and his face bore a striking resemblance to Finn.

Chapter 4

APPLE TREES AND CHERRY TREES blossomed in the early, warm summer, and bumblebees were busy flying from flower to flower. Deer were in heat, and their grunting and bellowing sounded across the wilderness. A sawyer, fast in the bed of a stream with its branches projecting to the surface, bobbed up and down with the current. There was still some morning pink and a rising mist on the Hudson River. A stream ran from a beaver pond to the river, and a beaver dove, making a massive splash with its tail. As the pink shroud lifted, the towering hills emerged in the distance.

On the road to Fort Edward (which was more like a cattle trail with two tracks and a plethora of potholes than a proper road), a traveling man wearing a large, black-brimmed hat with a long walking cane paused to rest. He ate a raw apple and watched a farmer fixing a broken double-post pole fence.

Some distance away across the fields, townspeople enjoyed the sunny, open air under towering trees. Women brought little babies out to play on colorful quilts.

A lightning bolt had struck a pine some time ago, and a man took a drink of water from his canteen, admiring nature's handiwork on the tree trunk. Three townsmen wearing brim hats played cards under another tree in the shade on a desk they had carried out. A fourth man stood close by, watching them play.

Robert Rogers had his table brought outside and had a late breakfast as a skillet sizzled over the fire with bacon. He piled mountains of scrambled eggs onto his plate along with thick slices of bacon. He sat down outside of his command post and placed his plate, pistol, and hunting knife side-by-side on the table. A skivvy brought him a large pewter tankard of ale with a foamy head.

"Now this is a goddamn breakfast," Rogers exclaimed, looking at his plate with satisfaction. He took a long drink from the tankard and wiped the foaming mustache on his sleeve. "But, I'm getting a little tired of this same old stuff." He noticed Finn loitering outside. "Ranger Finn, take some men and see if you can catch us some fish from the river."

"Roger that, sir," Finn said and headed over to the quartermasters to collect fishing gear. He saw Fronto. "Hey Dog, let's go fishing again. The last time wasn't truly relaxing, and maybe we'll have better luck this time."

"Sure. Let's get Gus and Catherina. Have you seen Daniel anywhere?" Fronto said.

They found Gus and Catherina tending a broken fence and headed for the river. "Catherina, have you seen Daniel?" Finn asked.

"No, but I think he went to the river with the Mohawks," she said.

On the way to the river, they met Colonial Bill mending fishing nets. He was shaking with his eyes wide. "Be warned of a demon that would engulf you in the abyss where he dwelt," he said to them.

When they had passed him, Colonial Bill looked around and up into the trees, frightened, and ran after them. They found Daniel sitting by himself on the river bank, and slightly further ahead, Mohawk warriors were fishing.

"Hey Daniel, what's up, my Wappinger friend?" Finn asked.

Catherina jumped down to sit on the riverbank next to Daniel, her feet dangling just above the water. Daniel was lost in thought, tossing stones into the water, and did not look up. "Where are all my people? In the earth, they lie. I feel their tombs with my hands. I hear the river below murmuring hoarsely over the stones. What are you telling me, river? You carry the memories past," he said.

Finn, Gus, and Fronto sat down beside them to watch the Mohawk warriors fishing. Two of them pulled off their red breeches and removed their long slips of stroud cloth. Finn put his hand over Catherina's eyes. She giggled and pushed his arms off.

"Hey, I had a brother, and I have lived with these guys all my life. Besides, I want to watch," she said, pleased that Finn had noticed how she admired the warrior's bare, muscular bodies gleaming wet in the sun.

The Mohawks wrapped the cloth around their arms in such a way that it reached down to the lower part of the palm of their right hands. They dove under the rock where the catfish lay to cover themselves from the scorching beams of the sun and to watch for prey. When the fierce fish saw the tempting bait, they immediately seized it in order to eat it. The diver opened his hand, seized the voracious fish by his tender parts, had an intense struggle with it against the crevices of the rock, and at last brought it safely ashore.

Finn jumped up, excited. "Whoa. Now that's what I call fishing. You can take that from an expert fisher, which I am, too!"

Catherina pushed him into the river, and Finn flew backward, landing on his back in the water. "Right, and you're a merry-Andrew! Most Mohawks are in the watery element nearly equal to amphibious animals," she shouted, laughing.

Finn emerged from the water and crawled up the bank, spitting water and shaking his hair.

Daniel snapped out of his dark thoughts and laughed. "I know warriors who lasso giant fish by the tail and drag them with buckeye and devil's shoestring. Others attract fish with torches, harpooning them with lengths of cane, and shooting them with arrows!" He said.

Colonial Bill stepped closer from out of the bushes nearby. "We used fishhooks made of bone, built channels of wood and stone, and perforated shells for sinking nets," he told them.

The Mohawks went splashing in the pools, scaring the fish and whacking their heads with the blows of cudgels.

Sergeant Beaubien appeared, wagging his bushy tail and poking people in the face with his grandiose wet snout, with Bill Stark and John Rogers following him. "When it is cold, giant catfish called the goonch look for places to spawn. Hollow banks, submerged timbers, the rusted wrecks of boatmen's misfortune; anything quiet and dark will do. Once the eggs are laid, the male chases the female off with a snap of his jaws. Then, for days he hovers over his gummy brood, waiting for the first fingerlings to emerge and pouncing on any intruders," Bill Stark said.

John Rogers nodded solemnly and pretended to be serious. "It is told that the goonch has long scavenged the half-rotten human corpses from boating accidents. This diet may have helped the goonch grow to unusually elephantine proportions. It may also have led the goonch to get a taste for human flesh, which may now be fueling frightening attacks on living humans," he said.

Colonial Bill looked terrified because he had heard all the stories and knew them to be true. "There was a ten-year-old, who was dragged down into the river by what people described as an elongated pig! His mother was washing clothes by a stream and heard a splash and a faint yelp. Where the boy had been fishing only a few bubbles were left!" he said, looking at them with eyes wide with shock.

"My mother was fond of saying that the bones of drowned boys lay at the bottom of every pond around here," Daniel said.

Colonial Bill took off his hat and revealed bleached white hair. "Fishing sure holds a different thrill when you are the bait. I had a clear right to judge the river's roaring demon was coming," he said, closing his eyes to pray.

Finn enjoyed the warm sun above the river, and listening to people talking and having a good time. The war and hardships seemed to disappear for a moment. For the first time in a long time, he felt a sense of belonging.

"People spear them with pitchforks or catch them with hooks spooled in by five men, but a few old-timers prefer to dispense with those things altogether. Barehanded, they encounter the beast in its lair," Stark said, demonstrating with his hands.

John Rogers nodded his head in affirmation. "The goonch may not have fangs, but they do have strong rows of inward-curving barbs designed to allow food in but not out. When clamped on your arm, it has an unfortunate tendency to bend down and turn. It ain't but like sandpaper, real coarse sandpaper, but once that thing gets to flouncing, and that sandpaper gets to rubbing, it can peel your skin right off," he told them, making an ugly face.

"Sometimes the men, who look for drowning victims, will fasten a gaff hook to one arm and dive for fish. One of them went down just a few miles from here and came up days later, a drowned man himself. Old man of the river hooked him a giant fish and couldn't get loose. They found them, two or three days later, side-by-side on a sandbar!" Stark continued.

They spent the afternoon fishing on the river with villagers and the Mohawks, when they caught a giant catfish. The fish was ten feet long and weighed over four hundred pounds. It was so powerful that it took twenty minutes from several Rangers to land it. When they finally got it on the beach, they noticed a large bump in its belly.

Finn took his hunting knife and sliced the fish open. People stepped back, repulsed and horrified as a woman's not quite decomposed body covered in gunk sloshed out. Shocked, people pulled back, holding their breath from the stench.

"I think we've found Hester," Finn said, almost throwing up.

Colonial Bill passed out and fell on his back.

§   §   §

Daniel and Shelagh wanted to get married in a Wappinger ceremony and planned a simple wedding party. The Nimham family held a meeting and Daniel's mother pulled him aside.

"Son, are you sure about this? Shelagh is a respectable woman, but she knows only the English way of life, and you are a Wappinger warrior fighting in a war," she asked.

"Mother, I have never wanted anything more than this," Daniel replied.

"So be it. I won't stand in your way," she said.

Daniel's family sent one of the men to Shelagh's family to speak on behalf of the prospective groom. He informed them that Chief Nimham's mother sent a deer he had hunted the day before to Shelagh's relatives.

Shelagh's family were not committed Catholics and knew the local traditions well. The Nimham family was well known in the area, and Daniel was regarded as a reputable provider and protector and after deliberation they decided to accept the proposal. Nobody asked Shelagh anything, and her mother answered. "Go back to his family to announce our acceptance and present them these gifts," she said, handing the man some utensils and hunting supplies.

Daniel's parents accepted the gifts, and the marriage was sanctioned. To mark the occasion, there was a simple exchange of jewelry, blankets, and a belt of wampum to Shelagh's parents.

Shelagh's parents presented the couple with practical presents. The traditional wedding ceremony was to be held in the new church already under construction to satisfy

Shelagh's family. Then, the second part, Wappinger ceremony, was held in a meadow outside the fort with Rangers standing guard. The young bride surprised everyone when she appeared, wearing a traditional, knee-length skirt of deerskin and a band of wampum beads around her forehead. Except for clear beads and shell necklaces, her tanned, slim body was naked from the waist up. Her face was painted with white, red, and yellow clay.

Daniel's mother was pleased with her son's new wife. "This marriage symbolizes the union and connection to the spirits, Father Sky and the natural world of Mother Earth," she said.

Daniel's people blessed the bride and groom with children, long life, and abundant crops. The marriage ceremony was quite informal and the fried bread, venison, corn and potato soup, and fresh berries were placed on a blanket for everyone to share after it was blessed by the Elders. Daniel and Shelagh held a ceremonial washing of hands to wash away bygone troubles and any reminiscences of past sweethearts. The couple then made a joint declaration that they chose to be known as husband and wife, and then they smoked from the pipe.

Catherina gathered the young women to prepare Shelagh's wedding night. They decorated the simple shed that was to be their home. They used tobacco and blue Lobelia to make a small bundle to help with better results of love.

Catherina winked her eye to the other women and placed the love potion under Shelagh's pillow. "Tomorrow, the couple will travel on what we call a honeymoon," Catherina said. Younger women giggled and playfully poked each other.

At the wedding, tiny Shelagh had to get on her toes so she could reach up and gently touch Daniel's face tattoos and scars. Feeling her fingers caressing his skin, Daniel flinched at first, but then he relaxed and looked deep into her eyes. The giant warrior leaned down and took her exquisite, beautiful face in his big, coarse hands, and then kissed her gently.

Men gathered outside to celebrate the wedding. John Rogers rested his foot on a log and lit his pipe.

"One time, my brother Robert was visited by a hideous being called Yule while he was in his hunting cabin. It was so appalling that no person in the entire province allowed the being to enter his house, except my brother. Later, the thing asked to sleep in his bed, and not so unwillingly he agreed, and as the thing got into the bed, it turned into an Elfish woman who was clad in silk; the most beautiful woman he had ever seen," John Rogers poked fun at his brother. "Of course, he screwed her silly."

Gus poked Finn with a long stick. "Finn, tell us which one would you choose? Would you want your bride to be ugly yet faithful, or beautiful yet false?"

"I must free the lady from the predicament entirely by allowing her to choose for her own self," Finn declared.

"A horde of dragons could not help anyone who would harm my Prudentina," Gus said.

Hearing Prudentina's name, memories of the slave ship flashed through Finn's mind, and he looked away, biting his lower lip. He glanced at Gus and started to say something, but then stopped (he wanted to tell Gus, his best friend, that he had had an affair with his sister). Gus looked back at him, wondering, totally unaware of what had taken place between Finn and Prudentina.

Finn took a deep breath, opened his mouth, and again hesitated. Then he said something completely different than what he had wanted to say. "But I tell you also this. The worst kind of theft is to seduce another man's wife away from him. In Finland, if they are caught, generally that man is hung, and the woman is buried alive, unless her husband begs for mercy on her behalf," he said.

"Sounds like what I would do," Gus replied.

"Like once, there were two men who both got married. The first one seduced the other one's wife, and her husband caught them in the act. He got so mad he started punishing his wife so badly that she died. In a court of law, he was found innocent, but the man who seduced her was found guilty, and he was punished," Finn said.

"So, what did they do to him?"

Finn made a nasty face and drew a finger across his throat.

The wedding was concluded when Daniel moved into a family hut with Shelagh built just for them, and the Rangers poked fun at him. Finn got an idea and got some Rangers together to pull a prank on Daniel. Finn, Fronto, and Gus snuck close to their cabin and started making loud moaning sounds under the window. Daniel rushed out of the door with a tomahawk in his hand and sent them running. Finn and the others fell into the long grass, laughing and hollering. Daniel shook his head and went back inside, smiling.

The wedding party went on, and Finn walked around a corner of a barn and found a bunch of Rangers smoking pipes, drinking whiskey, and singing. A simple board had been placed on top of two black ash logs as a makeshift bar for whiskey tumblers. Moses Hazen played the conductor. "We're Colonel Baker's Rangers. We're dirty sons of bitches, and we shove our sharp bayonets right up your fucking ass!"

Bill Stark waved at Finn and filled a tumbler. "Hey Finn, come and join us. Tell us more of your fishing stories," he said, and the Rangers laughed.

"No thanks, I better get going back to the barracks," Finn replied.

"Come on and have a drink with us, Ranger. Have one. It won't hurt," Stark said.

Finn smiled and shrugged his shoulders, then took the tumbler being handed to him and carefully drank half of it. The strong, golden-colored liquid burned his throat, and he made an ugly face. The Rangers cheered him on. He took a deep breath and downed the rest of it.

Just then, Catherina walked around the corner and saw him. She stopped in her tracks and put her hands on her hips. "Oh, there you are. Look at you," she said.

Surprised, Finn first tried to hide the tumbler. Realizing it was too late, he faced Catherina. "Now wait a minute. I can explain. I was just going to leave," he started saying.

"Yeah, right, never mind. You and your buddies," Catherina snapped at him.

"That's not fair. I'm here to get one drink with my men and you-" Finn started to respond, wiping the corner of his mouth. Catherina cut him off by holding her arm straight out at him with the palm of her hand facing him. She looked him right in the eyes and grabbed a full tumbler with her other hand, downed it without blinking an eye before placing the empty tumbler on the board, and walked away. Finn stared after her, flabbergasted, and took a few steps to follow her, but then he stopped. The Rangers burst out laughing, mimicking Finn and Catherina, rolling their eyes, and filling more whiskey tumblers.

Behind the corner, Catherina made sure no one saw her gagging and spitting in the grass. A blue cornflower withered and dropped its leaves from the strong whiskey fumes she exhaled as she wiped her mouth. She glanced around again, did a little butt wiggle, pulled at her undies, and headed back to her farm.

Being in a temper, Finn joined Gus and Fronto. "She had no right to humiliate me in front of the Rangers. And... and... and watching those naked warriors by the river as she did. Her eyes almost popped out, for crying out loud. You are my witnesses," he said, making Gus and Fronto look slightly uncomfortable because they did not know what to say to him. Finn told them that, then and there, he had decided to volunteer again for an expedition.

Finn was determined and marched to the command post. Robert Rogers took a long, appraising look at him. "Well, men are needed for a new attempt to reduce the French fort at Louisburg. Ranger Finn, you were there last time. You will join MacCurdy's men for this mission," he said.

"Hopefully, this time we don't have to walk back," Finn replied.

Daniel's furlough was cut short as Donald MacCurdy and Moses Hazen led the Rangers out from Fort Edward. They stared at Robert Rogers quietly as they passed him by standing at the gates. Finn kept looking straight ahead as they marched past Catherina's farm, and she pretended not to see him. She bit her lip and only turned to look after him when she knew he had gone.

The wedding party continued as a new wagon train pulled into the fort. Wagons were loaded with saws, axes, and grinning lumberjacks. Helen of Magdalena and the whores at the gate camp were pleased to see so many new customers coming in. Selous Claymore and his enterprise arrived in Fort Edward.

§ § §

The old man in the Catskill Mountain House asked Henry Raymond to wheel him to the bar table and lit a cigar. "Fort Edward, that shithole, was growing as more and more drifters arrived, low lives and scumbags transported from England, coming in pursuit of a better life. But amongst the newcomers, there were also men who were determined to improve their life with their own bare hands. Timber was the name of the game, for the King needed planks and masts to build ever more men-of-war for his navy.

"Selous Claymore was one such man, who was born in northern England to a wealthy business man, whose wealth was largely founded on gunpowder production for the Royal Navy, and whose boyhood house was adjacent to the naval dockyard. His older brother took over the family business, leaving Selous wondering what to do with his life. He then noticed how the landowners were encouraged to plant trees to provide timber for the burgeoning British navy, but suitable material was scarce on the islands and the ongoing conflicts with the French made sourcing on the continent many times hazardous.

"Military service did not interest him, and he decided to make a trip to Holland, where he learned that the saw-mill technology was far ahead of that at home where the process remained largely unknown. It left him thinking how to use it on a grand scale. His brother did not want him to stay because he saw a potential competitor, but they managed to come to an amicable agreement. Together they talked with their father who gave him the money, as an advance inheritance, to leave for America.

"In the new continent, he obtained a permit to harvest forests around Fort Edward and hired a bunch of hard-working and hard-drinking woodcutters. He established a lumber camp made of bunkhouses and tents in the outskirts of the fort. Armed with axes and crosscut saws, his crews started cutting down the mighty forests. His men took particular pride in their work. There were only a few women in the camp as cooks. The men worked hard all week and on the weekend traveled to Fort Edward to see the whores, drink hard, and eat.

"Selous Claymore was a self-learned forester and logger. His first mill was taken to the forest near his logging camp where a temporary shelter was built, and the logs were skidded to the works by horses and oxen teams, often when there was some snow to provide lubrication.

"Selous Claymore was a courageous and energetic man, who learned the hard way to be a foreman for the tough lumberjacks. He had to fight them and cut down more trees than the others to earn their respect. He became an expert in using his axe and could also carve statues out of stumps with it.

"Men actually started liking their employer after he came up with competitions for them. Life in the camp was boring. There was nothing besides work. They competed for prizes in climbing trees, cutting logs, and axe throwing. Soon, local townspeople and the Iroquois gathered to follow and make wagers for the winners. Liquor was strictly forbidden in the camp during working days, but at the competitions Claymore allowed it to flow freely, and it always did. Next day he let the men sleep in late.

"First he had some trouble hiring men for his new camp due to the war and because of his new site's proximity to the frontier trouble spots. He eventually sold his idea by telling them that the militia is there only to protect them and that he had already made arrangements for them with Helen of Magdalena, whose pleasure camp practice at the time had already gained considerable reputation. Upon hearing promises of money, whores, and whiskey, the men were quick to line up and signed up for the work detail.

"Selous Claymore was a smart man, and he read a lot about forestry. He thought long term, and as his business grew larger, he intended to build it in more permanent facilities on a river. The logs could be floated down to it by log drivers, increasing his production capacity." The old man paused to smoke his cigar. After a while, he continued. "On the other hand, up north, Louisburg on Isle Royal was a city with a crowded harbor, shipping lumber and fish to Europe, and bustling streets, and block after block of notable buildings. Men of wealth and position gambled and speculated. Their wives and daughters gossiped and flirted. The aristocrats and the ambitious bourgeois strutted and postured like their counterparts at Versailles. Artisans, petty tradesmen, laborers, and servants knew and kept their places in a community as ordered as Paris. Then the day came when we, the Rangers, arrived at the gates and all that ended," he said.

§   §   §

In Boston, the British high command pored over the maps, trying to find a way to turn the war to their favor. The situation looked bleak to say the least. The French domain in America now included not only the Isle Royale, the Isle Saint Jean, and the original New France stretching along the Saint Lawrence, but also Louisiana, the Mississippi Valley, the Caribbean islands of Martinique, Guadeloupe, Marie Galante, Saint Barthelemy, part of Hispaniola, a piece of Saint Martin, and a steamy South American foothold.

Finally, the officers settled to concentrate the efforts on Fort Louisburg, which was an access port, a transportation center, and a hub for ships trading among the mother country, the Caribbean, the Gulf of Mexico, and Canada.

The products of the New World Empire were furs from the continent's woods and streams, fish from the North Atlantic and the Gulf of St. Lawrence, and sugar and molasses from the West Indies. At Louisburg, the trading routes met.

Louisburg guarded the approaches of the St. Lawrence River, gateway to the heart of French Canada, and it also stood sentinel over the immensely valuable cod fisheries of the Banks. It was hailed as another Gibraltar. The guns of Louisburg posed a menace to the lifelines of the New England colonies.

The commander of the army was Major-General Jeffrey Amherst, backed by three brigadiers known for their energy, including Generals James Wolfe, Whitmore, and Lawrence. The charismatic personality and the professional ambition of Wolfe gave him mastery in council, and he took the leadership in the execution of the projects undertaken for the reduction of the town. His army numbered thirteen thousand men and was supported by a heavy artillery train.

Wolfe remained skeptical. "This is a fortress that is considered unbeatable," he commented.

Command of the naval squadron was given to Admiral Boscawen, who knew the American waters. He had twenty-one battleships and fourteen frigates. "Louisburg's merchants fatten on commerce that outstrips all the ports of New England," he said, studying several large maps on the table.

Outside of the headquarters, the air in the crowded military camp was packed with the heat of bodies as Finn carried heavy supplies. He turned sharply around a roaring crowd filled with hard, bearded faces and ran into someone. The man turned around, and Finn realized it was James Cook, who was surprised to see him as well.

"Finn, it is you. It's good to see you again," he said.

"James Cook! You are far away from Bell's alehouse. How are you? And how is Elizabeth?" Finn replied, still astonished at the encounter.

"I joined the navy, and I'm here to perform land surveys. Let me introduce you to my military engineer and surveyor Samuel Holland, who is making a plan of the enemy camp using a plane table. He gives me instructions in the use of this survey equipment," Cook said.

"I'm pleased to meet you, young sir. Mr. Cook has told me about your adventures in England," Samuel Holland said to Finn and handed the plane table to Cook. He showed it to Finn who looked at it curiously, not understanding what it was.

"So it helps you to navigate, I take it? See, I have my compass right here." Finn tapped his head, "Anyways, I've heard that the attack has been delayed by adverse weather and problems crossing the Atlantic," he said.

Finn was eager to hear if Cook had any news of Rosie, but Cook said he had no knowledge of her whereabouts since she had departed London with Finn. He looked terribly sad upon hearing this, and the two men listened in silence as he told them in length why he had not been able to get back to England.

The next day, General Wolfe ordered James Cook to scout the entrenchments along the shore of Gabarus Bay where the French lay to resist landings in force, and Finn insisted on joining him.

Under cover of darkness, Finn, Gus, Fronto, Daniel, and Cook proceeded to a high ground close to the French fort. They lay quietly at the observation post all day, and using the telescope, Cook made detailed drawings of the enemy's fortifications.

The French had seven thousand men in the garrison in the town, and they managed to get five ships of the line into the harbor — more than enough to prevent a naval assault. The fort had over two hundred guns and seventeen mortars placed on the battlements and outlying batteries, and there were forty-four guns in reserve.

General Wolfe had previously contemplated a charge by way of Mire Bay and the little harbors to the east. "It is my privilege to lead the division making the main attack," he said, wanting to set an example for the troops.

Two-thirds of the troops at Louisburg were in the entrenchments waiting for the British. Many of the French soldiers had been in the encampments for more than a week in the crummy weather, and they were ready to take revenge on their enemy.

The instructions from London directed that the landing should be attempted nearer the town. The French had fortified the obvious landing places, and when the English attempted to land, they were close to being disastrously repulsed.

The French positions were protected by skillfully prepared fortifications, and its guns were concealed behind freshly-cut spruce and fir trees, which were not removed until the moment of firing. The French cannon opened fire as soon as the English landing boats came within range.

The fire from the batteries was so powerful that Wolfe's division, in response to his signal of recall, immediately began to pull off.

In the entrenchments, a light breeze drove the smoke from the British and the French fire. The Rangers in boats were on the flank, and the smoke concealed their movements from the French. In the lead boat, Cook and Finn tried to see what was happening around them.

Cook noticed something on the shore. "Finn, look. See that behind the ridge east of the cove? There is a small and rocky creek that the French have not fortified," he said.

Finn looked where Cook was pointing and yelled to Fronto, who was the coxswain, as usual. "Head right into that gap, Fronto!"

Finn and Cook led the Rangers on the amphibious assault on the small boats, and in a decisive move they managed to avoid the French observation and created a beach head. Wolfe saw what had happened and understood the importance of the situation. He ordered the troops to attack to assist the Rangers on the beach. He personally landed on the beach with troops from his ships.

"If those batteries had waited until the troops had landed, a slaughter would have followed," he said.

Crucial time was lost to the French by the fact that they were unaware of what was taking place on the other side of the ridge. One of their sentries saw movement and raised an alarm, but it was too late. The French mounted a counterattack immediately after seeing the Rangers upon their rear.

Moses Hazen led the Rangers in intense action. The first attack by French skirmishers was beaten back by the Rangers. The pole cannons inflicted horrendous casualties on the French ranks. The Rangers' counterattack drove the French forces in disarray into the city.

Several thousand more British troops landed on the beach, and the British quickly established their line of guns on the high ground and aimed at the fort below. After that, most of the town was exposed to an intense bombardment.

The last French hope came from their five ships-of-the-lines, whose guns were able to threaten the siege. One lucky British shot hit the powder store on one of the

French warships, destroying it. The resulting fire spread to two more. The burning ships themselves inflicted serious damage on the town as their loaded guns fired, threatening both the town and other ships. Soon after, the town and soldiers finally surrendered.

When the French fort capitulated, Boscawen and Wolfe were overjoyed and locked arms, dancing around. "The Road to Quebec is open," Wolfe said, smiling victoriously.

§   §   §

The British soon realized that one victorious campaign did not necessarily win the war. In the area of operations, clean-up actions were required to secure the fort from the French. Colonel Monckton ordered Donald MacCurdy and his Rangers to raid a local resistance leader's center of operations. MacCurdy and Hazen were close in their discussion, hovering over a map. "Right there is Sainte Anne's Point, an Acadian village. Your job is to convince the leader to lay down his arms and vacate his family to greener pastures, understood?" Monkton said.

When Finn approached, they stopped abruptly, and Hazen left. MacCurdy shouted after him. "And Ranger Hazen, have one of your men cut down that big snag for firewood."

MacCurdy stood up, studying a map. He paced back and forth, deep in thought as a young private, a cross-eyed, hired hand, started to cut down the mighty oak snag close to him. He sawed it and then started pushing it. "Timber!" yelled the private.

Horrified, Finn realized what was about to happen. "Sir, watch out!" he shouted to MacCurdy, but it was too late. The tree fell in the wrong direction, and it toppled, crashing on top of MacCurdy. The Rangers rushed to help him and tried to remove the massive tree trunk, but there was nothing they could do. MacCurdy's lifeless corpse rolled out from underneath the tree.

Upon hearing about the accident, Monckton shrugged his shoulders, ordered the hapless private to be shot for gross carelessness, and summoned Moses Hazen. "Lieutenant Hazen, you are in charge now. Continue on to Sainte Anne's Point as planned," he said.

MacCurdy's body was wrapped in a tarpaulin and lifted onto a wagon. The Rangers solemnly formed two lines as the wagon drove off between the lines. Then, Hazen gave hand signals, and the Rangers turned on their heels and moved out, followed by a troop of British regulars.

Three hours after sunset, they arrived on the outskirts of Sainte-Anne des Pays-Bas. They encircled the village at night and attacked it from all sides at dawn. A few guards were killed quietly, and the Rangers scalped six Acadian warriors and took six prisoners. The regulars gathered the village people on the village square at gunpoint.

The Rangers kept patrolling the area, searching for any signs of enemy activity while the regulars pillaged and burned the village of over a hundred buildings, two chapels, and all the barns and stables. They burned down a large store-house, and with it, a large quantity of hay, wheat, peas, and oats. They killed about two hundred horses, five head of cattle, and a large number of hogs.

The real trouble started when people inside one of the

farmhouses refused to come out. A soldier standing by the door yelled inside, telling people to come out or burn with it. He signaled with his hand to Moses Hazen that they would not come out.

Other soldiers had captured the local Acadian leader and pushed him in front of Hazen. He grabbed the man by the hair. To coerce his collaboration with the British, Hazen nodded to the soldiers, and forced the Acadian to watch as the house was set on fire.

"While you pledged neutrality to the war, you continued doing business with the French at Louisburg, helping to make it one of the strongest forts in North America," Hazen said. The Acadian screamed and struggled to get free, but Hazen held him down forcefully while flames engulfed the building.

The Rangers rushed back, having seen the smoke from the burning buildings. Upon hearing the people screaming inside, Finn fired his rifle in the air and Hazen let go of the man, seeking cover behind a wagon as he thought the enemy was attacking.

In a desperate attempt, Finn and Gus rushed to open the doors to let people out, but the flames forced them back. In the mayhem, the Acadian leader managed to escape into the surrounding woods with two small children.

The blackened logs were still smoldering as Finn, Gus, Fronto, and Daniel sat in silence, shocked at what they had witnessed. Moses Hazen walked past them and looked back at them with a pitiless impression. "Good job, Rangers. Those were justified kills," he said.

Gus looked at him, stunned, and turned to others.

"Finn bought me my freedom, and for that I followed him to join the Rangers. I wanted to fight for freedom and earn my place. There are tough times that need desperate measures by strong men, I understand all that. But what I have seen today is too much. I have serious doubts about this," Gus confessed.

"I must admit I wonder, too," Finn said, glancing at Moses Hazen.

"This is a white man's justice, not mine," Gus said, troubled.

Fronto tied his backpack so hard he almost snapped the leather strings in two. "So-called justice conducted by the winning side automatically renders only victor's justice. Some men declare war is a crime, while others claim it their mission," he said.

"People do these things because they think that they are on the side of right. But they are no more than the morally weak — the morally deficient brutes," Gus said in anger.

"To an extent that's a controversial claim, because it's a difficult question whether obliterating an entire village inhabited by civilians with the flimsiest of military targets as a pretext should be regarded as a war crime, but the question remains, what is a war crime when there are no laws stating so?" Fronto replied.

"The white man's hatred runs far deeper than any statute or law can ever hope to address," Daniel said.

"It must be possible to infer that genocide and crimes against humanity are considered more serious than war crimes," Gus continued.

"The law falls silent in time of war. It is difficult to

enforce the rule of law on warfare, such as in this case," Fronto said, looking back at him.

"I considered you a learned man, Fronto, but now I think you simply cynical," Finn said.

"Cicero said that those wars which are unjust are undertaken without provocation, for only a war waged for revenge or defense can be just," Fronto replied.

"To withdraw from condemning and punishing evil is to accept evil. To allow evil to be done is itself an evil. Or inch by inch, we shall all be dragged backward into a natural state of war of all against all, where life is painful, brutish, and short," Gus said.

Daniel leaned over to get everybody's attention. "I don't care what others do, but I care for you. There is no avoidance of culpability. We must lay down ground rules and hold each other responsible. We, as brothers in arms, must accept ourselves as each other's keepers," he said.

"You may ask yourself, where has the messenger gone?" Fronto asked, mysteriously.

The Rangers returned to the base, and Colonel Monkton pretended to be shocked. "I'm shocked by your tactics, Lieutenant Hazen," he said, rolling his eyes. "However, I will recommend you for a promotion."

The Rangers in the camp showed the marks of the violent fighting they had been involved in. Drinking water and whiskey had been rationed, and none of them had a chance to wash the grime of combat from their faces. They sat in silence, too tired to speak, as James Cook came looking for Finn, very excited. "Finn, I have been ordered to map the estuary of the St. Lawrence River before General Wolfe's naval attack on Quebec. I requested you and some Rangers come with me for protection," he said.

The Rangers did not complain and embarked with Cook on a survey mission to navigate the St. Lawrence River to Quebec. Cook led the patrol up and down the river, charting every hazard and marking a channel for the warships to follow.

As the expedition advanced on boats, Cook worked at the bow, taking notes and drawings. The Rangers kept a sharp lookout for the French. Four days later, General Wolfe commended Cook for his stellar work with mapping and surveying and noted how remarkably accurate his drawings were.

They camped on the shore, and in the evening, a messenger brought new orders from Fort Edward. Finn opened the sealed letter. Reading it, he turned to face the others. "We have to return to Fort Edward at once. There is a large offensive about to start, and we're needed there," he said.

§   §   §

The Rangers loaded onto a ship and sailed for Boston. The winds were favorable, and the voyage was uneventful. Finn, Gus, Fronto, and Daniel remained silent, sitting on some boxes and sacks, each lost in his own private thoughts. With a cool ocean breeze on his face, Finn began to believe that he was growing older much too quickly for his liking and that he had seen too much already. On the way to Boston, he wrote a letter to Rosie, which he mailed immediately when they arrived in the harbor.

The trip back across the countryside took them several

days. Urgency of the message they had received demanded that instead of taking their regular route through the forests, they should take Boston Post Road, passing through the new settlements at Rye, Mamaroneck, Larchmont, and New Rochelle, all of which were trading posts along the route. Arriving on the Hudson River at Kings Bridge, they turned north toward Albany.

Upon arriving in Fort Edward, they met Robert Rogers pacing back and forth at the gate. He had been called in for questioning about the Acadian incident. He was angry and ordered Finn, Gus, Fronto, and Daniel to follow him. "No time for this bullshit, I've got a war to fight."

They arrived in front of the commander's headquarters, and Rogers gave a hand signal to stop to the Rangers following him, who had their muskets at the ready. He quietly thought to himself, his glance snapping to each man in turn. He felt there was more to the story than what he had been told, but after a long pause, he made a decision.

"We're right here, Major Rogers. What are your orders?" Finn asked. Rogers looked at each one of them and took a deep breath. "At ease men, you stay here. Ranger Finn, you better come with me. I might need someone to witness this meeting," he said.

Daniel, Gus, and Fronto faced out and took a knee as Rogers and Finn entered the commander's camp. They were directed to General Amherst's tent by a fire with a kettle over it.

Amherst was talking with George Washington and John Morton. He signed some papers on a folding field desk and saw Rogers approaching, dusting the sleeves of his coat.

"Major Roberts is reporting, sir," Rogers said.

"At ease, Major," Amherst replied, walking around the stove.

Washington stepped forward readily. "There are some serious allegations. Rules and regulations have been broken. I think you are well aware of what we're referring to, aren't you? Your lieutenant's actions in the Louisburg operation are being investigated," he said.

Rogers turned to face him. "Rules and regulations can kiss my ass, sir! I guess you would like my Rangers to be nightingales or some sort of angels, wouldn't you? When the going gets tough, the tough call the Rangers. My Rangers have balls that clank," he said.

Washington looked infuriated and took a step back and glanced at the General for his support.

"Enough. I have been one of your greatest supporters, Major Rogers. But you have to control your men," Amherst said.

"But sir—" Rogers said.

"No buts about it," Washington said, cutting him off.

"Sir," Rogers started again.

Amherst pointed a gilded quill at Rogers. "As of right now, you will start writing down rules of engagement for your men. And you will make sure each and every man reads and understands those rules. Is that clear?" he said.

Rogers defended the Rangers, saying the bounty was set by higher authority and that the blame belonged directly on the politicians.

"This is outrageous. We all know what this is all about. Don't play your silly games with me." Rogers looked at John Morton and continued, "Tell me one thing, sir. How far are you willing to let me go to get you your freedom? Let's be honest for once, you want freedom, and I want land. That is admirable and amicable, sir, but somebody has to pay! There is no such thing as a free roast, not on this bonfire of vanities you and the politicians have ordered me to light up!"

Amherst cleared his throat loudly. "Watch your words, Major. I'm sorry to say that what I have since heard of that affair has sullied Lieutenant Hazen's merit with me as I shall always disapprove of killing women and vulnerable children," he said.

"With all due respect, do not reproach me, sir, about morals and ethics. This is war. And if I may remind you, sir, it was the Governor who set out a reward for Acadian scalps — for each man, woman, and child, dead or alive!" Rogers said, leaning on the table with his knuckles. "Well here I am and demand payment for services rendered!"

Rogers pointed his finger at Washington and Morton. "If you let loose the dogs of war, do not pretend they are merely your poodles!"

Silence fell in the room. Amherst took a burning stick to light a pipe and remained silent.

"No need to answer, sir, but I have one more comment," Rogers looked at all of them and continued, "I have neither the time nor the inclination to explain myself, or the actions of my Rangers to any man who rises and sleeps under the blanket of the very freedom we provide, then questions the manner in which we provide it."

Amherst hit the desk with his fist. "Enough! Clerk has your new orders prepared. You are dismissed, Major."

Rogers gave a sharp salute and started to leave with

Finn close behind him. On his way out of the doorway, Rogers turned. "Dear Sirs, I hope you are able to sleep peaceably after we're through and the war is over. Have a good day, sirs," he said and barged out, almost tearing the tent door off the frame.

Amherst turned to Washington, and Morton raised his eyebrow. "I'll be damned, but he might be right. We need soldiers like him," he said.

Rogers and Finn met with Daniel, Gus, and Fronto outside. "We ain't dead yet! Keep moving!" he shouted and headed back to Fort Edward.

As they marched, Finn told them what had taken place in the commander's tent. Fronto squeezed Finn's shoulder hard. "Wisdom, whippersnapper, remember that. The lesson is that you should not try to control that which is beyond your control. Precisely, you control your thoughts, your speech, your words, and your actions," he said.

Finn stopped, leaning on his musket, and pondered for a moment. He then looked up, smiling at Fronto, and pushed his caubeen back. "Well, fuck me running sideways butt naked and barefoot through a forest on fire, but for the first time, I think I might have understood half of what you just said, old man," he said.

§ § §

After the unexpected victory, no time was wasted, and after a momentary resupply of food and ammunition, the Rangers moved farther north toward enemy territory. No time to visit family or anything else.

The Rangers advanced in three separate files through

the dense forests. Mohawk scouts in a wedge formation moved two hundred yards ahead of the main patrol. They came out to a sparsely wooded area, and the men automatically spread out. Almost two hundred men passed by them without a sound as Rogers stepped aside with Hazen to study a map. He motioned Finn, Fronto, Gus, and Daniel to take positions close to them for security, and pulled out maps to study.

A few hours later, the Rangers passed the ruins of the old Fort William Henry. This was their first visit to the fort after their return from Halifax. The Rangers now found the old fort a desolate mass of ruin, covered with half-burnt rafters and fragments of exploded cannon.

Rogers wanted to get a better look at the remnants of the old fort and stopped on a small hill. "There we enjoyed many of the pleasures belonging to a Ranger's life. We left the place occupied by a fine garrison, supplied with everything they could want for their comfort and convenience. Now look what's left of it," he said.

The progress to the enemy fort was fast but cautious. The woods were eerily silent, without any signs of enemy soldiers or warriors. It was almost too quiet. As they were getting closer, Rogers stopped and handed his musket to Finn. "Here, hold this," he said as he deliberated on the best route forward. He knew that advancing to contact with the enemy and engaging him on the field of battle must always be a careful operation.

Finn slung his musket on his back and placed Rogers' rifle against a tree as he was going to tighten his high-top moccasin laces. Just then an alarm resounded across the wilderness, some distance ahead of them, and Rogers took off running to see what was happening. Finn and the others followed him, and in his haste, Finn inadvertently left Rogers' musket behind.

The Rangers ran through the woods, hopping over logs and streams and rushing through thickets. Getting closer to the battlefield, they heard drums and bugles sounding as the battle lines were formed, and then bagpipes started playing. Bursting out of the woods just in time, they witnessed how Dugald Campbell and the Black Watch moved forward, frontally attacking the entrenched French positions at Fort Carillon. The enemy was fully prepared, regimental flags flapping in the breeze and cannon barrels ready and aimed.

On the run, Rogers turned to Finn as they were getting close to the battle field. "Ranger Finn, give me my rifle," he said.

Finn looked around and realized he did not have it. "Oh shit. Sir, I think I forgot it."

Rogers stopped in his tracks and looked at him, dumbfounded. "You did what? You dumb son-of-a-bitch. Hand me yours and get a new one wherever you can find one," he said.

Finn tossed his musket to Rogers and looked around to find a replacement. He grabbed a musket, bullets, and powder from a dead British soldier in a shallow hole nearby. A lucky shot from a French sharpshooter had found its mark at the man's forehead, leaving a gaping black hole, and the entire back half of his head was gone.

The light shone an eerie light through the forest, making the scene appear red and golden, like a valley of insanity as the path wound through the trees. Finn heard his feet pounding the ground and blood rushing through his veins. He felt as if he were a dead walker, a stalker of life, with dementia draining the life out of him and all hope lost and only fear remaining.

They crossed a stream on a decaying trunk and went on until the timber dispersed and they came out on a plain that stretched ahead. Advancing through thick, six-foot tall reeds, they arrived to a dried river floor where several streams flowed into the lake, forming reedy wetlands. They crossed another stream, shoulder deep, and held their rifles and ammo pouches above their heads. Finn gazed at the rising sun, veiled behind the hills that boarded the ravine. The rising morning fog was vague and gray, and he smelled the whiff of blood, urine, and sweat drifting from the battlefield. Just as they came out covered in sludge, five French Marines and five Ottawa warriors rushed out of the tall grass, and the Rangers, crouching to fire, cut them down in a blaze of gunfire.

The silence broke in a roar of gunfire and Finn flushed with the high of it. He stared straight ahead and became unaware of the Rangers around him and could see only the enemy in front of him. He fired and reloaded, fired and reloaded, again and again without thinking. He tasted the cold brass on his tongue and thought it was better than any wine.

Finn did not feel anything as thoughts hammered through his brain. *Shit's happening. Shit's happening. Oh man, this shit's happening. Please Lord, don't make this shit happen. I'm here. Save me for I'm one lonely son of a bitch.*

The Rangers were tasked with screening which generally meant sealing off the front so that the enemy could not send reinforcements or try to break out.

The company was lined along on the lower side of a meadow. Rogers told them to stay fast and shoot only if fired upon because it could reveal their location to the enemy. He moved ahead to survey the landscape and disappeared into the woods a few hundred yards away. The sky was turning dark, and the sound of thunder was getting louder.

A Canadian militiaman burst out of the tree line, running like hell across the lush field — a boy really, who sixteen years earlier had come out of the womb into his mother's tearfully loving arms. The Rangers watched him run, their trigger fingers itching, but orders were clear.

Robert Rogers came out from the wood, pointing at the running man and shouting, "Fire!" But over the loud rumbling battle, the Rangers could not hear. The Canadian was running like crazy for his precious life, dodging and turning. He was close to the safety of the woods, now too confident, and even flipped a bird to the Rangers, knowing their predicament.

Rogers hopped on a stump, and cupping his mouth with his hands, shouted, "Shoot the motherfucking messenger!"

In one swift motion, a hundred musket barrels turned on the running man. In a display of superior Ranger marksmanship, a fusillade of one hundred large .75 caliber slugs found their mark and tore through his body, shredding it to pieces. For a few seconds, the man's body seemed to hang suspended in midair as it turned into a bloody pulp of minced meat. Finn shook his head, "Poor motherfucker, a hundred-yard dash to eternity."

The horizon changed from black to gray, then to

shimmering white. Over the horizon, the drum fire of the French cannon began in which no single cannon could be heard or individual muzzle flashes seen. The bombardment and the roar of bursting shells were constant. The bleak, gray desolation of rain seemed like the skies were wailing in never-ending tears. The thumping rain drops fell slowly and sadly, as though the heavens were weeping for the dead boy.

That day there were many, many dead. At one point, Finn drew in his breath, sniffing the rich and putrid air, and spat. "There's a stiff nearby. Is that what the stink means? It's not a French corpse — they stink, but, not the rotten sweet like that," he said. The Rangers could not find the body, so they had to endure the stench till they moved away a few hours later.

The Rangers pushed on in silence until it became too dark to see more than the soil at their feet in the light of muzzle flashes. They spent the night in a putrid mud hole, shivering, wrapping their muskets and ammunition in blankets. The next morning, in the greyish daylight, the sky turned blue and cloudless. The country was glistening ochre. The horror of the scene contrasted with the blackness of the previous night and the unknown it had covered.

Daylight brought no mercy. A sudden explosion and a scream sent them down onto their bellies in the mud. Finn glanced over a muddy knoll to see what he thought were some shattered trees. The ground was so covered with the dead that it would have been possible to walk across the clearing, in any direction, stepping on dead bodies, without a foot ever touching the ground.

The Rangers came under fire, but they had not the

slightest idea where the shots were coming from. It seemed to them that enemy soldiers converged on them from all directions. Then a fresh anxiety rose, that the enemy could see them and their muskets, and they realized that cannons were aimed at them. They could not miss, yet miss they did, and that contributed to a delusion of safety.

In one of his repeated glances over the knoll in the direction of the trees, Finn realized that they were not trees, but the Black Watch advancing in lines. Among the kilted heathens, Finn saw white puffs shot through with white sparks forming out intricate patterns in the pearly light like a gateway to heaven. Curiously, he did not feel fear which might have helped to replace common sense, which by then was totally lacking. He was convinced that he heard the bell ringing at heaven's gate, but no one was home.

Medals should have been awarded in bulk to the Black Watch that day because it was difficult to make distinctions when in valor, all were equal. Standing back to back on a pile of their fallen comrades, the Campbell brothers were the only officers who, by some kinky Caledonian god, survived the massacre. It was later said that Dugald Campbell and his brother needed help rigging a ball-support under their kilts.

The brothers realized that they had no more regiment of their own, so without hesitation, they decided to join the Rangers to continue fighting.

General Howe, riding a horse (which was not a very good idea in the first place), was hit and died in Israel Putnam's arms.

There was a clump that seemed odd, and under intense firing from the Rangers, the grove began to crumble until a

bullet riddled body fell out and was caught in the branches. It hung there for an instant and then crashed onto the
lower branches before hitting the ground. Another French
sniper had met his fate, for there was no such option as being captured alive for either side.

Then the Abenaki warriors were pouring out of the
gap in the thick underbrush on the right, led by Captain
Lignery who pointed his sword at the Rangers. The Rangers swung around and opened deadly accurate fire on
them, each bullet making an execution. Lignery, biting a
bunch of bloody grass after diving for cover, sent a silent
prayer to Teutates for saving his sorry ass from the Rangers' vengeance.

Afterward, Finn remembered little. The battle was
a bloody blur. He dredged up short rushes, tremendous
noise, choking on thick black powder smoke, spitting blood,
hearing his own grunting and heavy breathing, snapping images of Daniel hacking a man to pieces with his tomahawk,
and the Rogers brothers in brutal hand-to-hand combat
with Abenaki warriors. He recalled snippets like the bloody
haze that permeated everything, running the blade through
a Frenchman's soft belly and watching as he shat in his pants
as he died in agony crying for his mother, warm sticky blood
spurting on his hands and face, an ear-shattering flash and a
crash, lying on his stomach with a splitting headache staring
at a blade of grass, Dugald Campbell hauling him by the
neck and the seat of his pants, vomiting into a ditch, and being too stunned to see where the enemy was. Finn covered
his ears and shouted *Stop the fucking noise!* But not a sound
came out of his mouth.

When Finn's senses returned, he found the thinned

ranks of the Rangers sitting around him, exhausted and covered in blood and grime. There were less than one third of them left. So many familiar faces, friends and brothers, had been lost. Gus, Fronto, and Daniel stared at him silently. They were surrounded by mounds of dead enemies in unnatural positions. Many were maimed and hacked to dozens of pieces. Finn did not realize that the screaming he heard was him until Campbell put his blood soaked hand over Finn's mouth to silence him.

Finn kept glancing at the men around him to see their reactions to his panic. To his surprise, from the looks on their faces, he saw that they understood his sheer horror, but more than that, they accepted it, and even further that they accepted him. They too were just as happy to find themselves still breathing. A shiver went down his spine, and a quiet peace settled upon him. He would not let fear overcome him any longer.

That was enough for Abercrombie, who had not even realized the importance of the high ground near the enemy fort. Things went rapidly from terrible to worse, and the British withdrew in haste. John Stark played a key role while managing to arrange a somewhat orderly retreat at the landing area and converted a near disastrous run for the boats into an orderly launch.

Robert Rogers was absolutely livid about the way the operation was conducted. "What a clusterfuck! A fucking French fire drill! Total disaster! This was the bloodiest battle of the whole war! We have suffered over two thousand casualties! Why can't they trust me? We're not regular infantry. They are using us wrong!" he shouted, pounding a tree and nearly breaking his fist.

§   §   §

The infirmary in Fort Edward was full, and many of the wounded had to be placed in tents. Catherina and Shelagh were busy tending the wounded for hours on end until they almost collapsed from exhaustion. The morale in the fort was frightfully low, and the British regulars walked about in apathy. Only the Rangers, grim and unyielding, kept cleaning their weapons and equipment, preparing for another mission.

Finn arrived to see Major Rogers in the command post. "You summoned me, sir."

Having learned the alphabets of freedom from Gus the slave during a sea voyage, and being one of the few Rangers who could write, Rogers ordered Finn to take notes as he started dictating the rules.

"Here are my notes, brothers. They will provide a history with the bark off," Robert said and slapped his arm around Richard's shoulders.

Richard remained skeptical. "I'm not so sure if that's a brilliant idea. Maybe there is some sense in it," he said.

"I shall call them the Standing Orders. As a matter of fact, I'll not only write the instructions to my Rangers, but I will also write on how to fight the war the way it should be fought, in the Iroquois style," Robert said.

James Stark spat into the fireplace. "It'd be a totally different matter if the high command in Boston would ever find any use for them," he commented.

"I should send instructions to the King as a guide to a totally new style of warfare," Rogers said, getting increasingly excited about the idea as he pondered it.

John Rogers tilted his caubeen back and poured himself a drink. "The fancy pants in London hardly even know what war is all about. All they care for is loot and ransom," he said.

Robert Rogers slapped Finn on the back of his head. He leaned closer to Finn's ear and said. "Write this down, numbnut. Lesson number one: don't forget anything! Got that? Now, the title of the article shall be: Plan of Discipline," he said.

Finn wrote everything down. "Yes sir, I got that down," he said.

Rogers paused for a moment to collect his thoughts. "Alright, let's get started." He gave Hazen a stern look and continued dictating. "Rule Number One: All Rangers are subjected to the rules and articles of war, to arrive at roll call nightly, each equipped with a firelock, sixty rounds of powder and ball, and a tomahawk. At which time an officer from each company shall examine the same, to ensure everything is in order, so as to be ready to advance at a moment's notice. Before the men are dismissed, the necessary guards are to be posted, and scouts for the next day appointed," he said.

Finn, leaning close to the paper with his tongue in the corner of his mouth, kept writing everything down while Rogers paced back and forth, smoking a pipe. Every time Rogers walked past Finn, he slapped him on the back of his head. Fronto, Gus, and Daniel worked on their gear some distance away and watched them.

Fronto grinned. "Now, why I didn't think about that? The bullheaded youth will learn much better that way, guaranteed," he said.

Rogers rubbed his chin. "Okay, Rule Number Two: Whenever you move out to recon the enemy's forts at the cutting edge of battle, if your number be small, march in a single file, keeping at least a five-yard distance from each other as to prevent one shot from killing two men. Send one man, or more, forward, and the like on each side, at the distance of twenty yards from the main body, if the ground you march over will allow it, to give the signal to the officer of the approaching enemy, and of their number, and so on," he said.

Rogers continued dictating the rules well into the evening. Food was served, and Rogers ate while he continued. Finn was busy writing and rubbing his head as it smarted from being slapped so many times.

"Maybe you should include something about letting them come close and surprising the enemy," Bill Stark suggested.

Rogers thought it over for a moment. "You're right," he said and turned to Finn. "Rule Number Thirteen: In general, when engaged by the enemy, reserve your firepower until they approach and are very close, and then use the element of surprise. The greatest consternation will give you an opportunity of rushing upon them with your tomahawks and cutlasses to finish them off." He paused to fill his pipe and continued, "Alright, I think that should do for the day. Now, you have done a pretty good job writing everything down, Ranger. But your duty is not done yet. You shall accompany me to the field mass."

Rogers saw himself in Finn, young and wild, and wanted to do something for him. He thought that perhaps a little fear of God might do the trick for the restless man.

There was a knock on the door as a courier arrived and brought new orders, which he handed to Rogers. He read the paper and turned to look at his men.

"And the King asked whom shall I send? I stepped forward and said, here we are, send us," Rogers said.

§   §   §

Rumors were rampant again in the provinces about some sort of French secret weapon. Supposedly, it was a massive mortar system that could fire heavy projectiles over long distances unheard of until then. Then it was said that the French actually had some of these terrifying weapons, highly mobile and ready to be launched against the poor British.

Adding to the uncertainty of the already dire situation, further reports (or stories more precisely) came in, telling about an extensive canal the French had dug that connected the St. Lawrence River and Lake Champlain that enabled swift movement of troops, supplies, and the new weapons system. In the event that this actually was so, the whole British war effort would be jeopardized. Headquarters decided to send a long range patrol deep into enemy territory to determine the location of the canal, discover the secret weapons, and verify the enemy's strength.

The courier brought the orders to Rogers Island early in the morning. Along with the orders, he brought the news that the ship carrying mail to London, including Finn's letter to Rosie, had been lost at sea. Finn was devastated, but he did not have time to write a new letter as the mission preparations started at once, and the patrol was required straightaway.

The mission was estimated to last for three weeks. Bill Stark was named the patrol leader, and he selected Finn, Gus, Daniel, Fronto, and Sergeant Beaubien, of course. Against his protests, he was ordered to take along two British lieutenants.

Finn cleaned and oiled each round of ammunition and his musket thoroughly. "Maybe I'll see that Colonel Louis again. I winged him once, but next time I will make sure I finish him off," he said.

The Rangers knew exactly what to take with them and how to pack their rucksacks. Enough food for seven days was packed in the rucks, including flour, hard biscuits, peas, butter, sausages, sugar, and tea. The rest of the time, the team was to live off the land and, when possible, find their way to cache sites established by independent support teams for resupplies.

Right before midnight, Robert Rogers led a large element of fifty Rangers toward Lake George. The reconnaissance mission was on.

The first phase of the operation, which was named "Red Herring," was to continue to an island during the night with a full moon, camp on the island the following day, and then, as the primary patrol continued on while making noise to draw the enemy's attention, drop off the seven man recon team behind. The recon team stayed on the island, lying low until the next night, and then quietly slipped to the other side of the lake during the night under the cover of clouds. The diversion was a complete success, and the enemy sent a reinforced company of Marines to pursue the first Ranger patrol. Robert Rogers led them on a wild goose chase around the mountains in the opposite direction, and the recon team was not discovered. Two nights later, having marched forty-eight hours almost nonstop across the wilds, the team was a hundred miles as the crow flies behind the enemy's lines, and entirely on their own.

The recon team rested in drizzling rain the third night and the following day. The clandestine patrol base was close to the northern end of Lake Champlain. The day was hot, and the mosquitos were plentiful, forcing the men to blacken their faces and exposed skin with mud mixed with castor oil. In the evening, the team proceeded toward their area of operation. The country turned out to be rough because it was interlaced with bogs and streams with quagmire banks. Several times the team had to make causeways and rope bridges across streams, which slowed them down and wore them out.

The Rangers moved only during the light summer nights and rested during the day. They did not speak, slept little, and ate less to spare the food for as long as possible. The team moved out at dusk one evening, and at about three o'clock that night, they arrived at a small village of a few rough log cabins. The men fanned out to investigate, but discovered it to be an abandoned hunting lodge. They moved on a few more miles and found a spot of solid ground on a peat bog suitable for a patrol base. It was drizzling cold rain again, and the men huddled together to keep warm under a makeshift lean-to.

The next day, the team huddled under a poncho for a meeting and decided to change their strategy slightly. They had not seen or heard any enemy activity and voted to continue their marching during the daytime in order to find the canal.

They observed a cooking smoke rising from a building some distance away and approached it cautiously. Suddenly, Sergeant Beaubien growled a warning a few hundred yards from a small village, but it was too late. They stumbled into two young Abenaki girls gathering berries in the woods. Daniel talked to them, asking for information about any French soldiers, and the girls told him that there were four *Compagnies franches de la marine* soldiers in the village. Finn handed the girls some sugar as a gift (a bribe actually), and Daniel made the girls promise not to tell about the Rangers to anyone.

The team continued scouting the area, moving farther away from the village. Two hours later, disaster struck. Finn and Daniel were walking point, fifty feet ahead of the others, when out of the bushes appeared four French Marines. The girls had sold them out, or maybe it was just a coincidence. Now, at that instant, in the middle of nowhere, life and death was a matter of who was the quickest. Out of the clear blue sky, people had to make a life and death decision in a split second.

Finn and Daniel fired almost exactly at the same time, killing two Marines while the two survivors turned and ran. Fronto and Gus rushed to the scene and shot the two men, who fell, dead, into a boggy stream. The fight lasted only a couple of seconds, and the four shots echoed in the wilderness. But now the enemy was aware of the Ranger patrol deep in their territory. The element of secrecy was lost, and the patrol had been compromised.

The Rangers moved ten miles on the run, covering their tracks and then stopping to reassess the situation. Bill Stark decided to continue the mission, but he figured that they should go farther to the west. The patrol moved another thirty miles until they had to stop to treat their festering feet. During the rest, they heard cannon fire in the distance, like a rolling thunder. Daniel scouted out the area and reported that he saw what might be the canal where they were to reconnoiter and the patrol moved out to check it out.

Closing in during a clear summer night, they noticed from the tree line that the objective was in a difficult location in the middle of open fields, and there were several plumes of smoke rising to the sky from lodges in the vicinity. They low-crawled closer through the wet, tall grass, and to their utter dismay, they saw that the alleged canal was actually a large drainage ditch full of tepid water.

Nevertheless, they continued to observe the place in order to make sure of any traffic that passed by. However, after a few hours, they came to the conclusion that the target did not contain any military significance and it was just a big ditch.

Bill Stark decided that they should move south toward the first cache for resupplies and then start searching for evidence of the French secret weapons. He suspected that the echoing rumble they had heard earlier was from the weapons in action.

They moved out after sunset and marched again throughout the night. They did not stop until almost noon the following day to sleep for a couple of hours. Late in the afternoon they approached the cache site, crouching low and ready for anything.

Bill Stark walked the point with Sergeant Beaubien out front. All of a sudden, out of a bush to his right, a French captain appeared, buttoning his pants. Stark was just as stunned but regained his faculties first and wanted to capture the enemy officer, but the man sealed his own fate by turning and running, and Stark shot him in the back of the head.

"Fuck! We got to get the resupplies. Let's take them and haul ass out of here," Stark said and rushed to the cache site with the Rangers following close behind him. Then, all hell broke loose.

The French were hidden in the tree line and opened fire. Finn saw, from the corner of his eye, that the French had a hound dog with them, and with a quick shot, he killed the dog. They withdrew while fighting and managed to break contact. Luckily, no one was hurt, and they ran through the forest as fast as they could. The deadly hunt was on.

The Rangers kept moving, changing directions frequently to distract the enemy and running in streams in order not to leave any trails. Their tactics paid off, but four hours later, they made a startling discovery. They found a fresh path and a still-smoldering camp fire and realized that they had discovered the tracks of their pursuers and, in fact, were now behind them.

"Contact at twelve o'clock!" Gus hissed between his teeth, seeing a bunch of French Marines and Abenaki warriors fifty yards away. They were completely unaware of the Rangers' presence.

In one swift motion, the Rangers rushed forward, lining up and firing two quick volleys, the first with rifles and the second with pistols, killing five French and three warriors. The ninth enemy, an Abenaki warrior, managed to

fire and hit Bill Stark in the right leg before Daniel's tomahawk found its mark and buried itself deep in the warrior's
skull.

The Rangers reloaded quickly and collected all the rations from the fallen enemy and then retreated, running on
top of pine timbers on the ground and vanishing without
leaving any marks.

The Rangers withdrew ten miles to a coppice of young
birch trees and willows with some fallen spruce trees. They
dug a hasty hiding place a few inches deep, used branches
to cover it, and dressed Stark's injury. They knew that the
French waited for them to continue running, so they lay
still in their hideout. The eight men stayed in a shallow
dugout, twelve feet by twelve feet, for three days.

Then it started to rain again, and under the cover of
clouds, the Rangers moved out, the rain washing away their
tracks. They took turns helping Stark who was using a branch
as a staff to support himself. After twenty miles, he had a hard
time keeping up with the rest. He was feverish; his wound was
getting infected and it had to be treated, or he would lose his
leg. They found a good spot to stop behind some large rocks,
surrounded by a clump of junipers and willows.

Daniel collected some skullcaps and willow bark,
which he knew would alleviate pain. By chance, he then
found some wild yams and threw them in the mixture as
well for good measure to provide some oomph for the
drained man (although usually the herb was used to increase sexual stamina). He then collected some juniper
berries and crushed them with the handle of his hunting
knife, extracting the oil and mixing it into the herbal con-
coction.

Fronto pulled out a flask of whiskey and Stark expected him to pour it on his wound. Instead, Fronto shook his head and just as Daniel unceremoniously grabbed Stark by the jaw and stuffed the bitter medicine mixture down his throat, Fronto poured a generous quantity of 80 proof whiskey in his mouth to wash it all down. Stark's eyes almost popped out and he gagged, out of breath, and huge drops of sweat broke out on his forehead.

Looking nauseated from the treatment, Stark lay back against a tree, breathing heavily as Daniel prepared to treat his wound. From his pack, Daniel took a container made of birch bark holding honey, which he carried to provide energy on long treks. He gently rubbed honey over Stark's wound to prevent any infections and then dressed it with a clean cloth. After a while, Stark started to get back up. "If the enemy doesn't kill me, your potions probably will, Nimham. But whatever that shit was you gave me, I feel better. Now let's stop fucking around and get a move on," he said.

They managed to go another twenty miles and then the forests behind them remained quiet. They hoped the enemy had lost their tracks, but the answer came almost immediately. Barking hound dogs revealed they were being followed. The French search party was hot on their heels again.

Coming to a thicket, Stark dove on the ground low crawled to the other side. He was breathing hard and knew that he was slowing the rest of them down. "Leave me, and make a run for it. You can make it without me. I'll cover you," Stark said between clenched teeth.

"Oh shut the fuck up, Ranger. No one is left behind,"

Finn cussed at him. With grim determination, he grabbed Stark's armpit to help him along.

Daniel climbed on top of a large rock to listen to the wilderness around them in an intense posture. Before long, he told them that there were at least three powerful search parties after them. "There are hundreds of them," he said. They had to move fast and furious to gain distance if they wished to live.

Upon hearing this, the two British lieutenants stopped in their tracks. They told the others that they had decided to separate from the patrol and find a bearing on their own back to the friendly territory. Without waiting for answer, they just walked away and left the Rangers to their own devices.

"Fuck! That's two muskets less if we make contact with the enemy again," Finn cussed.

"Men, you know what happens if the Abenaki catches us alive," Bill Stark said. "Promise me, you will put a bullet in my head if that is about to happen."

The Rangers dressed Starks wound again, and using two sticks as braces, they wrapped his leg tightly with softened willows. His ankle was swollen badly, and the moccasin strings were pressing deep into his flesh. His hands were bleeding from clutching the pole so hard in pain. They had fifty miles ahead of them to the pickup place on Lake George. The last, desperate dash for safety began as the Rangers used all their remaining strength and endurance.

Two agonizing days later, they saw the deep cove ahead of them and felt a surge of hope. They just might survive. They found an accessible hiding place and settled to wait for the pickup team.

Early in the morning, the Rangers woke up, startled by a musket shot. The French had arrived on the lake as well, and not realizing how close they were to their quarry, the French officer had decided to take a shot at a black grouse on a tree. The Rangers realized that the two warring parties had spent the night within a hundred feet of each other. They lined up in a hasty ambush and waited until the French patrol of five men was only twenty feet away and opened fire, killing them all.

The Rangers sighed in relief at first, but then Finn felt his heart sink. Out of the tree line, hundreds of French Marines marched out, flanked by Canadian militia and the Abenaki, Mi'kmaq, Lenape, Ottawa, and Wyandot warriors.

The French Captain Langdale grinned victoriously. "Surrender, maggots! I promise your death will be pretty quick and not so intensely painful," he shouted, and over his shoulder winked to the warriors who were anxiously waiting to get their hands and blades on the hated Rangers.

"Holy shit," Finn said. They pulled out their knives and tomahawks and braced for the enemy's charge that was sure to follow soon.

Then behind them, from the morning mist on the lake, a canoe appeared, and after a few tense moments, the Rangers sighed in relief - it was Robert Rogers. "Hey Rangers, if I were you, I'd hit the dirt just about right now!" he shouted.

For a moment, everybody on the shore, enemy included, stared at him, speechless. He was alone in the canoe. Then, the fog lifted, and four bateaux filled with Rangers armed to the teeth, glided along the shore. Each Ranger gunboat was fitted with two three-barreled pole cannons and a large caliber swivel gun at the bow, loaded with ball and buckshot.

"I second your 'oh shit'," Gus said and tore for cover.

The Rangers on the boats unleashed a broadside with their muskets, and the pole cannon roared in turns. Each gun fired steel balls, and the shock waves seemed to shake the leaves from the trees as the deadly blasts hit the enemy ranks. The boats moved five feet sideways under the recoil of so many weapons. The enemy disappeared in clouds of deadly black powder smoke. In the end, the amount of bloody mess, pieces of human flesh, and gray brain tissue would have made even the most stalwart butcher flinch.

Finn grabbed Bill Stark and helped him up. They rushed downhill to the pickup point with Sergeant Beaubien, followed by Gus, Fronto, and Daniel, and waded into the water with a hail of bullets whizzing by their ears and making geysers all around.

The pole cannon roared again, and Finn and the others were pulled into the boats. They slumped in the bottom, totally exhausted. Robert Rogers pulled Sergeant Beaubien into the boat, and the animal shook his fur, drenching his wounded master. The dog then slumped on his healthy side and started licking his face.

"Hey Ranger, are you happy to see me or is that a musket in your pocket?" Rogers said, grinning ear to ear as the boats glided to safety and left the devastation behind them.

In the meantime, the two British lieutenants searched for a river crossing and hid from enemy patrols. They had run out of food, but close to a village they found a calf which they slaughtered, stuffing the meat into their backpacks. In the evening, they managed to wade across the river and continued toward friendly lines.

The two men moved on roads and trails and took short cuts across fields and meadows. They did not care if they left a trail like bread crumbs behind. They even stopped to build a fire and roasted some of the meat they were carrying. It was one those freak incidents in any war. In four days the two happy-go-lucky chaps managed to get all the way to within sight of Fort Edward without being caught by the enemy. They were happy to see the fort, but noticed also that there were signs of some enemy patrols lurking in the vicinity.

In the darkest hour, the lieutenants crawled closer to the fort, stopping and listening for a moment, then continued. They took five hours to crawl the remaining five hundred yards and were fairly certain that they were safe. Just as the sun was coming up over the horizon, they got up on their knees to better see the remaining route past the enemies, but they also knew that the provincials were quick on the trigger, as well. They moved slowly forward in the morning mist ready to make a run for it when, suddenly, a volley was fired and both of them were hit.

The two mortally wounded men fell side by side. They saw Colonel Louis with the Abenaki warriors approaching them, tomahawks and hunting knives in hand, ready to torture them.

One of the men was in severe pain, and he mumbled a prayer, raised his pistol to his head and pulled the trigger, splashing his comrade's face with bits and pieces of brains and skull, and then he died, as well. The shot alerted the fort, and the Abenaki warriors disappeared into the forest. The two lieutenants were fifty yards from safety when their luck finally ran out.

§   §   §

Two days later, early in the morning, a scrawny preacher held a field mass for troops on Rogers Island. Troops assembled under flags and banners on the field, the Rangers in green and buckskin, Scots of the Black Watch in their dark tartan, Mohawk warriors in rawhide and full war paint, provincial militia in blue uniforms, and the British regulars in red coats.

The wear and tear was clearly visible on the men's uniforms. Muskets needed maintenance and new spare parts. The blades on their cutlasses were tapered from constant sharpening. Their tomahawk heads were blackened from dried blood. A bewildering array of sores, lesions, bruises, and contusions needed healing. Poultices on wounds needed changing. The thousand-yard stare drew deep lines on the men's faces. Only the dead had seen the end of war.

The preacher raised his arms in prayer. "God of all goodness, look with compassion on those who gave their all in the armed services of our King. In faith and hope, we turn to you for support. Grant that we may trust in your kindness and deliver provisions to sustain us as we send these heroes to you!"

Fronto shrugged his shoulders and whispered to Finn. "Bah, we should be addressing our prayers to the god within us. Then we might give peace a real chance," he said.

John and Bill Stark searched for Robert Rogers around the compound. He appeared, unshaven and waving a wad of money in his hand. "That was a pretty decent night!"

"Rangers, post!"

The Rangers got in formation. Upon the detail posting, Rogers marched in front of the formation.

"Report for Ranger Roll Call."

John Rogers unrolled a list and read the names of all Rangers present at the service, and the men answered as their name was called out. Wind blew across the field, and flags flapped on poles. Catherina, Shelagh and other townspeople watched the ceremony and the ranks of solemn Rangers, and they noticed the empty spaces in the ranks.

"Ranger Paige, Caleb!" John Rogers called out. There was no answer. He waited for a reply.

Then, the company commander answered, "He is no longer with us!"

The roll call continued. John Rogers called out more names, and there were countless instances without a reply. It seemed that the list of names without an answer would never end. He rolled up the list and placed it under his arm, made an about face, and reported to Robert Rogers.

"Sir, Rangers who were Eagles once are now reporting as Rangers to a much higher authority!"

"May God bless them all," Rogers replied.

John Rogers turned on his heels and raised the sword in his right hand to the front of his neck, its blade inclined forward and up. "Hand Salute!" he ordered the formation.

The Rangers in formation saluted sharply, touching a clenched fist to the brow as though grasping the brim of their caubeens between fingers and thumb.

"Order Arms!" John Rogers ordered and lowered his sword.

"Rangers, stand at ease!" Rogers commanded.

The Rangers stood at ease as Finn looked around the field. "There are so many volunteers from the Black Watch and the 60th Royal Americans," he took notice.

"There are others from the 44th and 80th, the Cage's Regiment," Hazen said.

"Colonel Cage? He was with General Braddock. We were there, too. Remember that, Gus?" Finn said.

Richard Rogers looked up into the sky. "I have seen many fantastic shooting stars at night, and I have witnessed many marvelous sunrises. I have seen beautiful country far and wide, raging rivers, mountains high and vast plains, and dense forests. I have seen just about all of the King's possessions across this beautiful country and met exotic people, and I have killed many of them."

Finn let out a sight. "I have been always alone and not been able to share with anyone how I have felt, and in the end I will be alone, too," he said.

Fronto seemed to be the only one not affected. "Life is short, and soon it will end. Death comes quickly and respects no one, it takes pity on no one," he said.

The troops were called to attention. Flags were lowered to half-mast. As the commander of the honor guard, John Rogers took position in front of the honor guard. His voice echoed around the compound.

«Standby, Honor Guard - Attention!»

«Port-Arms!» The guard brought the rifles to a 45-degree angle a few inches from their chests.

«Ready!» The men took a step forward with the left foot only.

«Aim!» The squad raised and aimed the rifles, finger on the trigger.

«Fire!» All seven men fired weapons at the same time. «Reload!»

The volley spooked a cavalry horse in full gear that was tied to a hitching rail in front of the Silver Star tavern. It broke loose and trotted across the wooden bridge, hooves pounding on the planks, and it pranced around the parade field without a rider.

A bugler played Scott Tattoo, its sorrowful, wailing sounds echoing in the forests around the fort.

Chapter 5

LATE IN THE SUMMER, the lush, wild forests around Fort Edward turned dark green. In nests, chicks were getting ready to fly, gathering courage and flapping their wings for the first time. Black crows and magpies flew to a forest clearing to feed, next to a herd of wild boar. The crows grumbled to the boars and tried to steal some of their feed. A brave whippoorwill wanted to have its share as well.

Daniel leaned against the stockade and watched a large, all-black raven sitting on the fence across the field. "He is a messenger from the other world. He is the guardian of healing," he said contemplatively.

Finn came by and squeezed Daniel's broad shoulders. "Any news?" he asked.

Fronto and Gus arrived, looking concerned. They pulled Finn aside and headed toward the Silver Star. On the way there they told him about rumors that a vagabond had been arrested for the highway robbery the three of them had done with the Plunkett gang a couple of years earlier. Finn and Gus exchanged glances. The drunken highway robbery gone badly had not been forgotten.

To their utter amazement, this time it was Fronto who started second guessing. His resolve to stay quiet about their involvement was disturbed by his concern over what this would mean to the stranger arrested for something they had done. Finn and Gus reasoned that the right thing to do was to stay quiet, to continue fighting and that way help others. The vagabond probably was not a decent person, anyway.

In front of the Silver Star, things took a turn for the worse as Sheriff Jimmie Dick, acting on a tip, staggered around the corner, drunk. He took a breath, leaned against the column, and stopped Fronto. Curious townspeople gathered around them.

"The same drifter was seen breaking into the storeroom and stole a barrel of whiskey from the Silver Star, and the outlaw was identified as Fronto by an eye witness," Jimmie Dick said, slurring his words.

People looked at each other in shock. Behind the crowd, somebody pushed a small whiskey barrel under a woman's skirt to hide it from the drunken sheriff.

Fronto placed his thumbs under his belt and faced the sheriff. "Why would I steal whiskey when I can go in any time and drink the whole damn place empty? Let me guess who is behind this, the little old ladies of the town who condemn us for having a little fun every now and then? They should know by now that things not under my control are indifferent to me," he said.

Finn pretended to be taken by surprise, as well. "Mistaken identity? Marcus Fronto the Dog? That's like saying we may wake one morning no longer as a human but as giant insects."

Fronto let out a roaring laugh. Then his face sobered and he bowed and scraped. "Sheriff, the charges against me are deplorable and must be spoken of as frightful. Those in particular which refer to the robbing, I will explain in such a way that they reek of vitriol and bile. If I happen to call you an ignorant, little twit, it will not mean war to the death," he said.

"Fuck off, old man. I'm not crazy. I'm still the law around here," Jimmie Dick said.

Fronto gave the sheriff a condescending pat on the back, placed an arm around his shoulders, and squeezed hard. The sheriff grimaced. "But of course you are. Maybe we should create a wall between us and them. A large and long wall, to keep them away from us," Fronto said, and winked at Finn and Gus.

Finn stepped closer to Jimmie Dick. "Listen Sheriff, my friend here has been under the influence of humans for so long that he's been almost alienated from real dogs. He has spent his whole life creating a nice little burrow, which he continues to improve out of a combination of mad obsessions," he said.

Behind his rough and tough bearing, Jimmie Dick was not a brave man. His blurred glance went from Finn to Gus to Daniel to Fronto and back to Finn. They were armed to the teeth and he had only one lousy pistol. He gulped.

Finn pulled an adolescent boy out from behind the crowd. "Fronto, by the way, this young fellah could start paging for you. He could run errands for an old, feeble man like you," he said.

Fronto glanced at the boy. "Aye, lad, what did Doctor Barrett say about the analysis of my piss?"

"The doctor said that the piss is healthier than the patient," the boy answered.

"That's right. And with an answer like that, a smart boy like you should be in school," Fronto said and took a few steps to leave. He turned around, saluted the sheriff, and continued. "There. I feel much better already. I think I shall go and find myself a new wife at Helen's camp." He then disappeared around the corner.

Finn turned to the sheriff. "Tell me more about these allegations against my friend."

Dick had hiccups, and his flask was empty, but he maintained control, or, so he thought. He tried to focus on Finn, but his face looked blurry. "It is darned much sensitive."

Finn motioned to Molly Brant, the tavern keeper, who handed him a bottle and a tumbler. "Maybe this will help you to remember," he said and poured Dick some whiskey. He stared at the sheriff, who stared at the drink and did not respond. Finn pointed his finger at him and reached for his knife.

Dick reached for the glass. "Okay, okay, information about the robbery comes from the honorable Captain Johan Kopf himself," he confessed.

Finn pounded the column with his fist. "Damn it, I should've known."

Dick took the glass and poured it down his throat. "As it happened, he was also the gentleman who witnessed the storeroom robbery," he said, licking his lips.

"Damn it! Anybody know where this motherfucking Hessian Totenkopf is hiding?" Finn asked the people around him, but nobody knew the answer. After all, Kopf was in His Majesty's secret service.

Unknown to everyone, it was a sick twist of irony that

Johan Kopf had not known that the three of them were, in fact, involved in the robbery. He just enjoyed spreading rumors among the provincials. Besides, he was just doing a part of his job. But now, nobody would believe it, even if the truth ever came out.

§   §   §

The Rangers returned to their quarters, just as Selous Claymore arrived in Fort Edward. He was a giant of a man, wearing a red-checkered shirt, suspenders and dark trousers, and heavy boots. He was there to discuss property deals with Robert Rogers and his brothers, Moses Hazen and Mayor Glock.

Robert Rogers met them in front of the Silver Star. He greeted each one in turn and motioned for them to step inside.

They overheard people talking about Yankee Faust.

"A reliable army wagoner told me that Yankee Faust made a deal with the evil spirit and outsmarted him by saying that he would sell his soul to him if the fiend would fill his boots up with gold coins on the first of every month. Yankee Faust found the largest set of boots in all of the Province of New Hampshire. The next month the devil returned to fill up the boots with gold, but no matter how many gold coins he poured in the boots they would not fill. Yankee Faust had cut off the soles of the boots and put the boots over a hole in the floor, and all the gold coins fell into the basement. The devil, after Yankee Faust outsmarted him, burned down his house in revenge and the gold coins disappeared."

"I heard that the ghost of Yankee Faust's dead first wife appeared on his wedding night and took the ring off the finger of his new wife as the two were in bed together."

"And I heard that a pallbearer at Yankee Faust's funeral got greedy and opened his coffin to find it empty. His body had been replaced by a chest of gold coins with the devil's stamp on them."

Molly Brant shook her head in disbelief. "You are fools. He ain't even dead yet," she shouted from the bar. People laughed at the stupid story tellers.

Brant guided the important business party to the table in the back and took their order. John Rogers stood guard for their privacy.

Rogers cracked his knuckles. "Without further ado, gentlemen, I will receive large grants of land in southern New Hampshire in compensation for my services. I am offering these lands for sale. But perhaps first we should get better acquainted," he said.

"I have joined the Saint John River Society, which was created by a group of military officers for the purpose of developing land along the Saint John River, where as you well know, I saw considerable action," Hazen replied.

Selous Claymore leveled a weighted glance at the men around him. He had heard of the Rogers brothers' reputation. "I own some land in the Richelieu River valley south of Montreal and want to expand my holdings," he told them.

Mayor Glock gave a polite nod and raised his glass. "Gentlemen, having arrived relatively recently from Ireland, I am looking into opportunities in fur trading and the shipping business. However, I'm also one of the partners involved in the Cuyahoga Purchase along the south shore of Lake Erie," he said.

Rogers rubbed his hands together, satisfied. "Well, here's my proposal. With all these tracts of land combined, we would have a nation of our own, think about it. I have excellent contacts with other gentlemen in this area who are truly interested in properties. Unfortunately, they were not able to join us today."

Rogers pulled out some maps from his messenger bag and threw them open on the table. Men leaned closer as Robert Rogers pointed out various plots and borders. Ripples of conversation filled the room.

"Land of opportunity . . ."

"—home of the braves."

". . . Once we get the tribes moved . . ."

"—shock and awe—"

". . . and we could join our properties."

"Seize the prospect—"

As evening descended, men lit pipes, and Molly Brant brought them food and more drinks. The room got dark, and lanterns were lit. Finally, Rogers straightened up and flexed his back.

"Alright gentlemen, perhaps we should take a little break from business and enjoy a friendly game of cards?" he said and motioned to Brant, who hurried over to clean the table. Richard Rogers collected the maps, and Brant wiped the table clean. Rogers threw a deck of cards on the table. He shuffled the deck and was ready to deal.

"Our Irish friends are familiar with the game of Poca. However, I'll introduce you to our own American version of this fine game. Who'll join me?" he asked.

"My wife is expecting me home any time now, but I suppose a hand or two won't hurt," Glock said. That settled it, and the men grabbed their chairs and sat down. Richard Rogers cracked his knuckles as Brant placed a fresh whiskey bottle on the table and James Rogers slapped John on the shoulders.

"Leave the bottle," Robert Rogers said and started dealing. "And there I was, wading knee deep in Abenaki blood—" he began, smiling.

§   §   §

The trials and tribunals of Fort Edward continued. One disaster after another was poised to take a terrible toll on the poor folks. On the square, townspeople gathered to hear a runner who had arrived from Boston reporting of a smallpox outbreak. Richard and Robert Rogers and General Johnson urgently joined Mayor Trevor Glock and Doctor Josiah Barrett in front of the infirmary to discuss how to protect the fort from the epidemic. Inoculation of the people in the fort was brought up.

As the news of the disease spread in the area, more people arrived to learn about the latest ordeal. The Helming brothers and Harold Ferrara closed their shops as a precaution. Helen of Magdalena joined Catherina and Shelagh in asking for any details on how contagious the disease might be. Selous Claymore heard the dreadful news in his logging camp and rode in to confirm the effects the outbreak might have on his logging operation and the crew.

"Outbreaks occur with the arrival of ships and cannot be blamed on unsanitary neighbors," Robert Rogers said.

"The situation is serious. Quarantine stations were established in Boston and New York," Johnson replied.

Rogers raised his eyebrows. "Last time when a bloody pox epidemic broke out, many Bostonians fled, and the provincial government was temporarily relocated to Concord," he said.

Colonial Bill appeared, holding his finger high in the air. "Vaccination is meddling with the will of God. Smallpox is His mechanism for controlling the balance between the blessed and the damned."

Rogers gave an angry look at Colonial Bill to shut him up. "We must understand the ravaging implications of a smallpox epidemic within the jammed conditions of the fort. The procedure will greatly reduce the chances of infection, and the benefits of inoculation far outweigh the risks."

Colonial Bill was adamant. "This kind of intervention breaks the covenant between the community and God. If injections began, no longer can the people know for sure if their suffering is a result from their sins or that repentance is the only path to salvation," he argued. One of the Rangers grabbed him by the shoulders from behind and pushed him behind the crowd and out of sight.

Rogers turned back to Johnson. "I suffered the malady myself, and as a result of treatments, every tooth in my head became so loose that I believe I could have pulled them all with my thumb and finger."

Johnson shuddered. "First the fever and then the aching back and bones. Then the rashes and the pustules," he said.

People stepped back as Rogers and Johnson entered the infirmary, holding handkerchiefs on their faces. Inside, the stench, similar to turpentine and rotting onions garnished with a sweaty dirty sock, was overwhelming. One of the victim's faces was horribly scarred as the skin was torn to pieces as the bumps that were filled with a thick, opaque liquid burst open on his face. Other sufferers were left blind and disfigured with circular scars from the disease. The two men glanced at each other. The epidemic threatened the entire Fort Edward that faced yet another dreadful and looming horror.

"The bloody flux is the worst," Rogers said.

Doctor Barrett informed them that survivors of the disease were immune for the rest of their lives. He insisted on commencing vacillation. The process exposed a healthy person to infected material from a person with smallpox in the hopes of producing a mild disease that provided immunity from further infection.

A specially trained nun from Boston was brought in, and she ground up scabs taken from a person infected with smallpox into a powder, and then blew it into the nostrils of a non-immune person.

The people in the fort were so vexed by now that they did not notice Johan Kopf leading a young Delaware warrior, whose hands were tied, into an alley. He pushed his prisoner behind the barn and tied him to a fence post. He guardedly approached the vaccination site. Walking in the shadows, he put on gloves and pulled a handkerchief over his face. When no one was watching, Kopf stole some of the ground up scab and spread it over a pile of blankets. He hurried back to his captive and untied him.

"There are some blankets you can take to your village as a token of our goodwill," Kopf told the warrior.

In the meanwhile, Richard Rogers happened to be walking by and unsuspectingly grabbed one of the infected blankets.

The warrior rubbed his wrists and glancing at Kopf, took off. He stopped to pick up a couple of blankets, and without looking back he climbed over the palisade and disappeared in the woods. Kopf took off his gloves and tossed them away.

Three days later, Richard Rogers fell ill and was taken to the infirmary. Nasty, red lesions appeared on his mouth, tongue, palate, and throat. For the first couple of days, he had no fever and said that he would be back on his feet in no time, ready for new missions. Then, his condition quickly worsened, and he developed a high fever. He lost consciousness as the disease ravaged his body. A rash developed on his skin, appearing on his forehead and then rapidly spreading to his face, arm pits, and groin. Soon it covered his entire body. Profuse bleeding occurred under the skin, making it look charred and black and turning the whites of his eyes a deep red.

Richard Rogers died six days later. Risking their health, John, James, and Robert Rogers lifted Richard's body, wrapped in a tarpaulin, into a rough wooden casket, and nailed it shut tightly. The solemn funeral procession marched between two lines of Rangers, Iroquois, and the Black Watch, as his brothers buried Richard in the new cemetery on a grassy knoll under a towering oak tree, some distance from the main gate. As the coffin was lowered into the grave, Finn, Gus, Fronto, Daniel, and four other Rangers fired three times, honoring their comrade with a final 21-gun salute.

Robert Rogers made a rough wooden cross, intending it to be temporary, and carved "R. Rogers" on it to mark the grave.

The following night, a band of Shawnee warriors came in scouting, sneaking close to the fort, and came by the new gravesite. Seeing the freshly marked cross in the moonlight, they thought the marker belonged to the much hated Robert Rogers, whose uniform coat and commission paper had been found at the battle site. They had the cruelty and brutality to dig the body up and scalp him. In the darkness, however, they did not see the terrible shape the body was in, and in the end, from his grave Richard Rogers paid the contemptuous act back.

§   §   §

Life went on. It had to, because the people did not know what else to do or where else to go. Surviving meant drudging, toiling, and moiling. But at least it kept the mind busy and off of the other possibility: a tedious, agonizing death. The people learned the hard way that the keys to survival were resilience and perseverance.

The Means family, one of the poorest in the area, built a small camp and was busy laboring around a fire in the middle of large maple trees. They were collecting and boiling sap in a large kettle.

The Mohegan women showed the provincials how to reap the maple syrup, which they called 'sinzibuckwud'. The Mohegan drilled holes into the trunks of the trees, inserted taps into the holes and dangled a bucket from the protruding end of each spout. Sap slowly filled the buckets, which were emptied into large barrels, mounted on wagons, then returned to the spouts, and the process was repeated. The Mohegan women tasted the sap for sweetness.

The harvested sap was hauled off to a base camp, where it was boiled over a fire until it reached the desired consistency.

Robert Rogers watched them working and shook his head. "Back in New Hampshire, sap was collected in the spring time. Now it is going to be too tart for any use," he said.

The Rangers were ordered to help the farmers in harvesting. They collected wheat with sickles and tied them up in bundles and then put them in sheaves. Others cut hay with scythes and raked them into piles to dry.

"Last spring, we set some twenty acres of corn and sowed some six acres of barley and peas," General Johnson said as he watched the men working the fields. "Our corn did well, Lord be praised."

Catherina and Shelagh brought lunch in the form of mutton stew, large loaves of crusty bread, and a small keg of hard cider to the Rangers working in the fields. "Men still have to cut, split, and manage upwards of forty cords of wood to keep the houses warm," Catherina estimated.

A group of men worked to cut and strip the woods, pulled stumps, and did the initial plowing to open the area for the next season's crops.

Finn remembered the slash-and-burn technique that was used back in the old country. "Ah, nothing likes strenuous work. This reminds me of home," he said.

Benjamin Franklin arrived on a wagon and jumped down, and the driver started unloading a new stove. Franklin invited Rogers and Johnson to his demonstration. Out of curiosity, Finn, Gus, Daniel, Fronto, Catherina, and Shelagh joined them.

"Open f-fireplaces are tremendously wasteful," Franklin began. "Fully ninety percent of their heat energy goes up the chimney, and the fire tends to draw colder outside air in through poorly insulated walls and windows. I f-figured there must be a better way to keep warmer."

Franklin set up the stove, and the people came closer to watch. "I call it the Pennsylvania f-fireplace," he said proudly. "It is a marvelous breakthrough in wood burning know-how. By the help of this invention, our children may keep warm at a reasonable rate, without being obliged to f-fetch their fuel from over the Atlantic."

Finn noticed how Catherina was listening with keen interest. He gaped at her long blonde locks and at the curves of her neck and stole a glance at her bulging breasts. She pulled a large scarf tighter around her shoulders against the cold.

Acting on the spur of the moment, Finn stepped forward. "Mr. Franklin, I'll take one right away. Catherina, if you let me, it's my gift to you. I will also collect some moss so we can better insulate your cabin for the winter," he said.

People exchanged approving smiles as the young man was not, after all, a totally helpless case. Fronto winked his eye to Daniel and Gus.

Catherina was taken by surprise and did not know how to respond. "Well, this came so suddenly, I'm not sure," she said.

Finn shook his head and smiled. "I'll accept only an okay for an answer. You've supported the Rangers and the whole fort so well by tending the wounded and in many other ways. I think it's only befitting to show you our appreciation. I'm sure everybody here agrees," he said, looking at the people who nodded in agreement.

After the harvest was collected, Johnson sent four men on a fowling mission. "We shall rejoice together after we have gathered the fruit of our labors," he said.

The four hunters, in one lucky day, killed enough waterfowl, ducks, and geese to support a company of Rangers for several days. The men brought in the catch, and the women built open fires for roasting the birds.

While waiting for the mouthwatering feast, the Rangers exercised their arms in the tree line. Finn tossed a coin up in the air and shot it with his pistol. "Now that's what I call shooting," he bragged, winking at Catherina. She rolled her eyes, but actually, she was impressed with his shooting skills.

Daniel arrived with a group of Wappinger warriors to join them. The warriors had taken a shortcut through the woods and killed two deer, which they brought to the fort and gave to Robert Rogers.

"Major Rogers, accept this quarry as a gift from my brethren," Daniel said.

A sturdy staff was tied between two trees, and the deer were swiftly dressed and hung upside down. The people celebrated the successful hunt, and the feasting lasted all day. It was a rare occasion that the war and constant hunger drifted away, if only for a moment.

Everyone else was merrily eating and drinking as

Fronto led a young, beautiful woman to the fields. He had found her, Tamar, from Helen of Magdalena's camp. For a moment, he had wondered how old she might be, maybe sixteen or seventeen. Then, he shrugged his shoulders and led her to a haystack and helped her to a ladder to climb on top of it.

"Come here, pretty lady. There is a lovely view from the top," he said as his eyes swept over her sumptuous body and lingered on the swell of her cleavage.

She looked around to make sure no one was watching and climbed up. When she was not looking, Fronto pushed the ladders down and faked that the two of them were stuck up there.

Fronto, that grey old fox, slick through experience, had a way with women. He promised her a goat in exchange for her services, and the girl nodded, giggling and purring as Fronto dove on top of her in the hay. He pulled open her shirt, exposing her to the waist. Her breasts were full and round and perfect in the sun, the nipples hard. Sweet and innocent, she started breathing faster as he ran his hand down her back, pulling her closer. He pulled her skirt up, and she threw swabs of hay in the air as Fronto buried his face between her legs.

"Haystack hallelujah! I hear His voice! Bless me, dear Lord, for I'm coming!" Tamar shouted in ecstasy.

Finn heard the blissful squeals and realized what was taking place on top of the haystack, though he was unaware of her chosen profession. He cupped his hand over his mouth and shouted, "For crying out loud, you lecherous, dirty old man!" He shook his head in disbelief and thought, *You sly fox, how do you manage to do it?*

§ § §

One of the few, if not the only, breaks from continuous, mind-numbing labor the people had was the farmers' market with a livestock show in the fall. At the cattle show, there were bulls and bull calves, several pairs of steers, milk cows, oxen, swine, horses, and a multitude of poultry. Small boys chased a squealing piglet in the crowd, while Gus and Fronto were watching a plowing match on a nearby field.

In the plowing match, there were several teams with the winner plowing an eighth of an acre in seventeen minutes. Finn and Daniel leaned against a fence, enjoying the hustle and bustle of the market.

Finn was excited, and he pointed out how the oxen and horses were prepared for a strength trial. "How about a small wager on how much the winner will pull?" he asked Daniel.

"I don't like taking your money, but since you're so adamant about giving it to me, I'll bet two shillings on the gray team," Daniel replied.

There were several teams of oxen and four teams of horses in the strength trials with the winner pulling over seven thousand pounds. Smiling happily, Daniel held out his hand and Finn handed him the coins, looking crestfallen.

Farmers sold various products and groceries at their stalls. Catherina and Shelagh admired some textiles at a stand, bargaining and counting their money several times, but in the end they could not afford the fabric.

A bunch of Rangers were hanging out in front of the

Silver Star singing, "Bang, bang Lulu. Who's gonna bang my Lulu when I go away?" They marched toward Helen of Magdalena's camp.

A farmer arrived to pay a town assessment charge of three shillings and three pence. He also registered his ear mark for his livestock with the town. The provincials were not allowed to trade with any other countries besides England, and the man complained loudly of how ridiculous it was to ship trees from New York to England, have craftsmen make furniture and articles of them, and ship them back to New York where the products were sold for extravagant prices and the profits sent to England.

Finn sat down on a big rock beside Fronto. "What's this delightful life you have been talking about, Dog? I'm not even sure anything honestly has a value, am I? Look around. We're in a war. I can't even figure out how to get back to England, to my Rosie. I don't even know what is it that I'm supposed to seek. I guess I should look out for my own well-being, or maybe I should find the best way to live. But that's not possible in a combat zone, is it? All I have are questions. Maybe you have some answers for me, please? Can you tell me what is of primary importance? In the midst of doubts of all sorts around me, when people can deceive me, when an enemy can kill me at any time, when illness can strike without warning, when life is precarious by all accounts, I wonder whether aiming to live well and to be happy makes any sense at all," he said.

Fronto let out a sigh, but he was happy hearing Finn's thoughts. "Look here, whippersnapper. You may think that you will find happiness in wealth, beauty, and personal gifts such as strength, good eyesight, intelligence, or a good voice. Or perhaps you think to find it in noble birth, power, or honors. But I tell you, these things will not bring you happiness by themselves. For under the guidance of ignorance, they are greater evils than their opposites, inasmuch as they are better able to minister to the evil principle which rules them. You will benefit from them only if you learn to use them wisely under the guidance of knowledge, and only that is sufficient to confer happiness," Fronto replied, and gave Finn a close look to see if he had understood what he just said.

"Old man, you sound as if you're asking me to take on the complexion of the dead," Finn said.

"Clever boy, maybe you genuinely should read the writings of the ancient philosophers. Would that be terrible? Long ago there was a young boy who was shipwrecked. When he got to the shore, he sat down to rest next to a bookseller who was reading aloud from a book about an ancient wise man. The boy liked this so much that he asked the bookseller where he could meet with men like that. As fate would have it, a man walked past at that very moment and the bookseller pointed him out. 'Follow that man,' the man said, and the boy became a student of the man and others like him before establishing his own school," Fronto said.

"Ok, whatever," Finn replied, not quite comprehending the lesson Fronto was trying to teach him, and besides, there was so much more to see at the market. A fife and drum band started playing, marching around the fort square. Finn's thoughts turned to Johan Kopf, and he started to daydream, imagining what he would do to the man, slowly cutting him to pieces, slice by slice.

Hardly anyone noticed as a gentleman arrived in the fort on a coach and checked into the Silver Star. Samuel Adams had come to buy cereal grain for his family malt house in Boston. "Friends call me Sam the Maltster," he said, introducing himself.

Local business leaders Harold Ferrara, Selous Claymore, the Helming brothers, and Doctor Barrett held a meeting in the tavern to get to know each other and explore potential business opportunities. Helen of Magdalena and Molly Brant were not invited to the gentlemen's club, and they held a meeting of their own at a corner table. The men smoked pipes and discussed business and politics with the town mayor.

Samuel Adams over heard the conversation as Mayor Trevor Glock addressed the businessmen. "Mr. Smith argues that a preference for the use of native industry over overseas business to obtain personal profit constitutes an invisible and generous hand, which promotes the interests of the populace and the social order at large while at the same time making the individual wealthier," Glock said.

"Everything is worth what its purchaser will pay for it," Adams commented.

"Mr. Smith goes on to say that it is not from the generosity of the butcher, the brewer, or the baker that we expect our dinner, but from their duty to their own self-interest. We call ourselves, not to their charity, but to their self-love, and never talk to them of our own rations but of their recompenses," Glock replied.

"On the other hand, Bishop Butler argues that following the public good is the best way of progressing one's own good since the two remain essentially alike," Selous Claymore commented.

Fronto overheard them as he walked by with Finn toward the bar. He turned to Finn and made an elaborate acting gesture. "And Mr. Pope said that's the way God and Nature have formed the common surroundings and both selfishness and communal be the same," he said.

Finn shrugged and made a dull-witted face, knocking his head with his knuckles like a piece of wood. He fumbled with his moose-head necklace.

Fronto seemed to give up on him and became serious. "What they were saying is that the gluttony of the rich serves to feed the poor," he said.

"Oh, okay." Finn replied, but obviously still did not understand.

Fronto wrapped his arm around Finn's shoulder. "Never mind, let's go back to the market and find us a couple of beers, shall we?" he said.

At the market, a blacksmith set up shop and made horse shoes. Next to him, a cobbler repaired shoes for people. A third man sat on a bench leaning against a fence, playing a violin. People stopped to take a break and enjoyed his performance.

Young ladies delighted in an open carriage ride, using their umbrellas for shade. Shopkeepers offered tea, sugar, spices, cloth, shoes, stockings, and buttons in their stalls. Artisans demonstrated barrel making, fixtures, glass-blowing, and carpentry.

In front of the new town hall, Helen of Magdalena argued with the Sheriff Jimmie Dick who had denied her request to move her wagons to the fort for the duration of the fair. She complained loudly, counting all the money she was losing.

As the Rangers were heading back to Rogers Island, a lone rider arrived in the fort, a day ahead of his supplies. The imposing man dressed in black rode with his gaze fixed straight ahead, ignoring the greetings and invitations by the whores outside the gates. Businessmen in the Silver Star got curious and came out to ask him about his business. Adal Mauser replied, in a heavy German accent, that he had arrived to gather information and to prepare in advance, in person, for the arrival of his industrial machines which he intended to set up in the locality once he had identified a suitable site.

§   §   §

In the Catskill Mountain House, the fireplace crackled and the dining room and lounge were filled with quiet conversation. The server brought a cigar humidor that looked like a chest. It was made from a high gloss elm wood and had a deep brown finish and an arc shaped top.

After much thought, the old man selected an oblong cigar. "A good cigar should be listened to first — did you know that, Raymond?" he asked, and then rolled the cigar between his fingers close to his ear. "The appearance and feel should be nice and smooth, like silky oil. It tells a story about taste," he said.

The server lit the cigar, and the old man quietly enjoyed smoking it. He then grunted in approval as he observed that the ash produced by the cigar was as white as the smoke the cigar produced. "Very nice. Round taste, and rich and balanced aroma," he said softly, like he was whispering sexy things to a woman's ear.

The old man blew a little smoke toward the ceiling and continued his story, "Hardly anyone paid attention at the time, but it was then that the industrial revolution arrived in Fort Edward, in the form of a single man. Adal Mauser wore a black coat with no collar, and hooks instead of buttons, and a broad-brimmed black hat. He had a beard, but no mustache, because the mustache was seen as a sign of belonging to the military. His beard was cut in a particular manner in order to avoid interference with the kiss of peace.

"Adal Mauser was a German immigrant and a self-trained engineer who arrived in Fort Edward with several wagons filled with the machine parts he developed. He needed water power from the rapids and wood from the forests to burn in his furnace and to build a power plant and a cotton mill.

"Back in the old country, Adal Mauser had established a textile factory with the backing of Frederick the Great in Prussia. A religious man of the Church of the Brethren, or Dunkers, he once visited Pennsylvania on a religious mission to sell bibles. Upon returning to Germany, he applied and received permission from the King to build a factory in New England, on an arrangement which was a part of the bigger deal between the English and Prussian Kings. He moved to New York with his wife Margaret.

"Adal Mauser was an independent minister of the Brethren who required their members to abstain from military service, believing that obedience to Christ precluded such involvements. Adal Mauser emphasized consistency, obedience, and the order of the Brethren, and strongly opposed the use of musical instruments, Sunday Schools, and other worldly amusements.

"His congregation was compelled to live a relatively simple life-style, and was discouraged from attending fairs and carnivals, swearing oaths, attending secular colleges, joining secret societies, filing lawsuits, gambling, and using tobacco or alcohol. Always after talking with his people he declared 'Peace is with you', and they'd reply: 'And with your Spirit'. He also founded an orphanage.

"His wife Margaret wore only long dresses in dull colors, along with a prayer covering. She was a solemn and somewhat sad figure, who was always reminded by her husband of her rightful place as ordained in the bible. She was to keep her mouth shut and be the obedient wife and housekeeper.

"As an inventor, Adal Mauser was ahead of his time. His ambitious business plan combined a mill where carding, spinning, and weaving took place in the same mill, which was also used for finishing such as bleaching and printing, which at the time was something totally unheard of. But first, he had to import machinists from Germany to train new local workers. The first factory was to be completed with the aid of a state loan, with the stipulation that the technology employed would be freely inspected by the public to further civic technological advancement," the old man said.

§   §   §

On Rogers Island, Robert Rogers was once again pissed off. He had heard complaints from the old townswomen that his brother James, distraught over his brother's death, was involved in a drunken fight almost every night and was always causing a disturbance. Robert ordered John to get James back in order to prevent any further injuries and even gave John some money to pay for the damages already done. The next thing he heard was that the two of them were raising hell around the fort together in a drunken carouse, causing double damage.

Early the next morning, Rogers ordered everybody on extra duty as a disciplinary action. "Alright you ladies, it seems like we have a little disciplinary problem. That is easily fixed. Ranger Hazen, take these lowlifes on a forced road march."

"It's my pleasure, sir," Hazen replied.

New Ranger privates arrived that morning, with young Martin Severance among them. The new men stood nervously in front of Rogers' command post.

"Take these new piss ants with you as well," he said.

"Roger that, sir!" Hazen said.

The Rangers hastily prepared their packs and gear. They wanted to get out of the fort and out of Rogers' sight as quickly as possible.

Private Severance scratched his head, seeing the number of items he was supposed to carry with him. He had to take a piss, and he left his gear and rucksack open on his bunk. Finn picked up a large stone and hid it in Severance's pack.

Severance returned and lifted the pack on his back. "Oh boy, this is heavy," he said, and staggered after the Rangers already marching through the gate.

It was a hot day in August, and the Rangers sweated profusely under their heavy rucksacks. Finn passed a water canteen to Gus, Fronto, and Daniel.

The Rangers thought they were going for a relatively slow twelve-mile road march, but their hopes soon vanished as they heard a familiar voice from behind, gaining on them. Robert Rogers came following them with Israel Putnam and some militiamen trailed by a British officer. Rogers caught up with Hazen who was leading the marching formation. "Captain, while we're out here, let's practice some immediate action drills," he said.

"Roger that, sir," Hazen replied.

Rogers gave a silent hand signal to the right: hasty ambush. The Rangers moved quickly to the right of the line of movement and took up the best available concealed firing positions. Rogers initiated the ambush by opening fire and shouting, "Open fire! Charge!"

The Rangers fired a volley into the woods at bales of hay that acted as enemy troops. The Rangers also practiced a bayonet charge against the bales.

Rogers ordered the men back on the road, and they continued marching while a horse-drawn wagon followed them. The Rangers practiced several various scenarios and drills throughout the day. One of the new privates collapsed from heat exhaustion and fell by the roadside. Others dragged him into the shade and poured water on him.

"You have to cool him down. If you run out of water, you must piss on him if nothing else. Otherwise, his brains will boil like an egg," Hazen said.

The unconscious private was carried off and tossed on the wagon. His gear was tossed on top of him. "Take this weakling out of my sight. March or die," Rogers said.

Private Severance was hurting under his heavy rucksack. Finn tapped him on the shoulder, smiling. "It's mind over matter, Ranger. If you don't mind, it doesn't matter," he said and winked at Severance.

In the afternoon, Rogers stopped the training so the men could eat. While the men were eating, he paced back and forth in front of them. "Men, some immediate action drills may be used repeatedly with little danger that the enemy can develop effective counter-measures. But remember that habitual use of some immediate action drills can be extremely dangerous! Any immediate action drill must be carefully studied to detect any potential dangers which may arise from frequent use. If these dangers cannot be eliminated, the drills must be varied to avoid setting patterns!"

After marching six hours straight, they stopped for a brief break. Finn pulled off his moccasins and unwrapped dirty stinking foot rags from his feet. The rags were rectangular sections of unbleached linen with raw edges because hemmed edges would cause blisters. He washed and inspected his feet for sores and rewrapped his feet in clean soft foot wraps and thrust his feet back into the moccasins.

§   §   §

In close vicinity to an old, abandoned military camp site, on the other side of a broad ridge line, the Means family continued collecting sap. Mary Means, the twelve-year-old daughter of Agabus and Berdita Means, was working with her parents by the maple trees. Little Mary helped them by collecting sticks for firewood nearby, while her older brother Elias worked with their father at the trees. Mary's mother was tending the fire while keeping a close eye on her.

The family did not realize that there was a small band of Lenape warriors observing them in the backlit birch trees and blueberry bushes. While Mary was collecting firewood near the camp, she saw some colorful wild flowers — poppies, baby blues, and goldfields — a short distance uphill. She glanced at her mother to make sure she was in sight and wandered a little farther into the woods to pick the flowers.

Behind the bushes, a fledgling Lenape warrior known as Maiden Foot took a liking to Mary. "She reminds me of the sister I recently lost. They are about the same age," he whispered to other warriors.

Little Mary was shocked as Maiden Foot appeared in front of her. To pacify her, Maiden Foot handed Mary a small chain of colorful beads. She looked at the beads, then at the young warrior's painted face, and inhaled sharp to scream. Maiden Foot put his hand over her mouth to silence her.

At the same time, Mary's mother turned around to pick up a bucket of sap, and when she turned back, suddenly Mary had vanished from where she had been standing just a moment ago. "Mary!" she called out.

When she didn't answer, the family launched a frantic search, but little Mary was nowhere to be found. Her mother panicked, and her father was in distress.

Elias continued searching, beating the bushes with a stick. "Mary! Where are you?" he shouted. Eventually they found her mop cap with a yellow ribbon and a small bunch of flowers lying on the ground next to it. The Means family felt a strong, chilly wind rustling the trees.

"Savages must have kidnapped Mary!"

Across the dense, difficult terrain, ravines, and ridges few miles away, Mary was struggling in vain as she was carried away by Maiden Foot and taken to a cliff hollow and to their chief, Newcomer.

Back at the campsite, Elias was visibly shaken but managed to gather himself. "Father, mother, I saw Major Rogers earlier heading that way. They can help us!"

Realizing this would be their only hope probably to see their daughter ever again, Agabus and Berdita Means rushed off to alert the Rangers. In a mad dash for help, buckets of sap were spilled. The Means fought through brush and thickets in a desperate search for the Rangers. "Major Rogers! Major Rogers!" they shouted in desperation.

Agabus darted across an opening and ran head on into John Rogers. He then he saw Robert Rogers standing right next to him. Berdita ran frantically toward Rogers to report Mary's disappearance. "Major Rogers, you must help us to find our daughter! Injuns have seized her!"

Only then did the Means looked more closely around the clearing, and saw that they were surrounded by Finn, Fronto, Daniel, and Gus, plus dozens of other Rangers armed to the teeth and seemingly appearing from thin air. Then a few militiamen and a British officer appeared from the forest.

Rogers listened solemnly as the Means tried to all talk at the same time. "She is not dead, if that is what you are worried about. Sixty Livres are the reward for an English male scalp, and female prisoners are sold in Canada at fifty crowns each. Captives are worth more alive than dead. Sometimes, they have a nasty habit of replacing their deceased family members with prisoners," he explained.

Fronto talked to the mother. "Look at the leaves, the wind scattered some on the face of the ground, and the children of men are just like them. Be thankful for the time you had with your child, even though this turned out differently," he said.

Rogers motioned his officers to rally around him. "Men, this is now a hostage rescue mission. Get ready to move out immediately. We must act fast before they get too far. Putnam, you take the lead with the provincials. My Rangers will bring up the rear."

The Rangers decamped at once and began marching. The Means family huddled together as they watched the Rangers disappear into the woods. It seemed like they just vanished into the green foliage, and again they were left alone in the wilderness.

Israel Putnam was glad that he was allowed to take the lead, and Rogers figured it was a good idea to give him a chance to practice forward scouting. He actually didn't see any real chances of catching up with the girl's kidnappers. They would have a better chance of finding a needle in a haystack.

Pleased to be able to show his skills, Putnam led out with a party of militia in front, the Rangers in the rear, and the British officer Captain Dalyell in the center.

The Rangers followed closely behind, moving swiftly and silently through the forest in a long single line, using only hand signals to communicate. The heavily armed men did not make any sound marching through the dense undergrowth.

Putnam was walking the point, a hundred feet ahead of the others, when they set up to rest and drink. Rogers brought up the rear, and he started talking with Captain Dalyell, bragging about their shooting skills.

Their argument was cut short by the enemy. A few hundred yards ahead, the French officer Langdale commanded his troops with hand signals and the men quickly dispersed into the woods, setting up a firing line, and then they just waited, holding their breaths.

Not long in coming, over the barrels of their rifles, the French saw how Putnam and the Rangers approached their position cautiously.

Langdale's hand shook from fear as he raised it, prepared to make a hand signal to fire. "Open fire!" he shouted, just a fraction of a second too early. Most of the shots missed their intended targets, and he noticed how the dreaded enemy Rangers sprang into action.

The French did not hesitate but attacked the provincials in front. Putnam's troops got pinned down under heavy fire. "They are overrunning us! I need reinforcements, quickly!" Putnam called to Rogers.

The Rangers were quickly brought into line, Dalyell taking up position in the center. Trained and ready for action, the Rangers moved on the right to make a flanking movement around the enemy skirmish line.

The enemy rushed in and attempted to take Putnam, and managing to take one lieutenant and two men as prisoners. Militiamen fought desperately, despite being outmanned.

The Rangers returned fire and attempted a flanking movement, but the firing was too intense. They dove for cover behind trees, bullets hitting trunks all around them. The enemy pressed on their attack, and Israel Putnam and his men could not hold on much longer.

The Rangers rallied, and John Rogers, with a wound in his thigh and a cut in his wrist, bravely maintained his ground and encouraged his men throughout the action. "Hold steady and keep firing!"

In the rear, Robert Rogers heard the French barrages echoing in the woods. He ran forward, trying to make sense of what was happening ahead, but the heavy undergrowth blocked his view. He assumed the attackers were warriors, and his main concern was the rear, which was left wide open. The enemy might be leading them into a trap, which was their usual tactic. "Captain Dalyell, take your men to help Putnam. I shall secure the rear to keep us from any surprises from that direction," he ordered.

Dalyell fought with fanatical bravery, occupying the center where at first the shooting was most severe. Then the action moved to the right, where the enemy made four separate attacks upon the Rangers.

Putnam was attacked by Colonel Louis and dropped his pistol in the dirt. In the following desperate hand-to-hand struggle, Putnam was not an equal against the mighty warrior and he was swiftly pinned down under the man. Putnam grabbed his boot knife but Louis knocked it from his hand. His right hand, by pure chance, landed on the pistol he had dropped, and he pressed it against the warrior's chest and pulled the trigger, but the musket misfired.

Colonel Louis took a firm grasp of Putnam with both hands and threw him against a tree like an oversized rag doll, then quickly bound him up.

The Rangers fierce bayonet charge forced the French to withdraw, leaving their dead behind. Colonel Louis dragged Putnam with them, stripped of his gear, coat, vest, stockings, and shoes. His hands were bound tightly together, and he was forced to carry some large packs from the wounded French soldiers.

The Rangers arrived at the place where Putnam was last seen, but found only some torn clothing and a few belongings scattered on the ground. Finn picked up a little book entitled *The Enchiridion* with Putnam's bookplate on it. "One can never be certain, and your station in life might change at any time," he said to himself.

The enemy war party moved as fast as they could, passing through the woods and climbing undulating paths to a rocky outcropping of a mountain top, eventually reaching the summit. After a brief break to make sure they were not followed, they pressed on along the forest trail, which crossed several small mountain meadows. They then passed through more dense pine forest plantations. The sky was a bright blue. The occasional skylark sang, and the trees bowed back and forth gently in the breeze.

The war party stopped for a short rest, and Putnam was again bound against an old elm tree. He pulled and yanked on the ropes but could not get loose.

The warriors started throwing tomahawks at Putnam to see how close they could hit without killing him. Langdale loaded his musket without the ball in the barrel and fired at Putnam, and laughed as Putnam winced. "*Salaud,*" he cursed.

"I'm an officer and I demand you treat me like a prisoner of war," Putnam shouted.

Langdale shoved the end of his musket into Putnam's face. "Shut up, you miserable dog."

They descended downward into the valley, marveling at the spectacular views of the river valley down below. The densely wooded ridgeline provided them concealment most of the way until finally they crossed another ridge and then continued to follow a stream downhill. After rushing through the forests, the enemy war party halted, and Putnam collapsed, exhausted, onto the ground. His feet were bleeding from the rocks, and his hands were swollen badly. "I cannot go on. Loosen the chords, or kill me and be done with it," he said.

Langdale examined Putnam's hands and feet and then removed his bonds and took away some of his burdens. The warrior who had captured him threw him a pair of moccasins.

While others were eating and resting, Putnam kept waiting for a good opportunity to make a run for it. The warriors were bragging about their exploits, and Langdale turned around to relieve himself in the bushes. Putnam saw his chance and ran for it, making a mad dash with his injured feet toward thick bushes across the clearing.

From the corner of his eye, Colonel Louis saw Putnam's escape attempt. In one swift motion, he gave chase and tackled Putnam with half a ton of hurt. The warrior tied him again to a tree and started piling branches at Putnam's feet and lit them.

Putnam shouted and tried to kick the burning branches off in vain, when a sudden local shower of rain doused the flames, almost as if someone wanted to save the man.

The warrior rekindled it quickly, and Putnam writhed at the stake in pain among the smoke and flames.

The French met with another war party led by Chief Newcomer, leading brooding Mary Means to captivity on a leash. The chief intervened, kicking the flaming branches aside, and he cut Putnam loose. "He's more valuable to us alive than dead. I'm taking the prisoner under my care so we can claim ransom for him from the English," he said and gave Colonel Louis a stern look.

Newcomer turned to the other warriors. "Lay him on the ground, spread-eagled, and secure his wrists and ankles to young trees. Lay some poles across his body with one of us sleeping on the ends of them. That way, if he tries any sudden moves again, he will awaken us," he ordered.

Lying on the bare ground and badly wounded, Putnam was in pain throughout the night. In the morning, he was allowed to eat and walk without any burdens.

Four days later, the war party arrived at Fort Frontenac, and Putnam was relieved when he was placed under the French guard. The fort's elderly commander, the somewhat disabled Pierre-Jacques Chavoy arrived to question him. Another prisoner, identifying himself as Colonel Peter Schuyler, changed Putnam's bandages and replaced his rags with clean clothing, as he was sweating and in terrible pain.

"Captain, perhaps it is our lucky day. I heard we might be exchanged for some French prisoners," Schuyler said, handing his water canteen to Putnam.

§   §   §

The British headquarters was in a panic and the last thing on their minds was the well-being of any provincial civilians, let alone an abducted, terrified little girl. The search parties were called back to prepare for more important missions. While others licked their wounds in the aftermath of yet another defeat, Bradstreet resurrected his plan for an attack on Fort Frontenac. He approached General Abercrombie to get his approval.

"Sir, for complete victory, a three-pronged campaign should be launched against the French possessions. One army already was able to reduce Louisburg, and now we must follow through! We should move against Quebec while another should move from Fort Edward to capture forts Carillon and Saint-Frédéric, and then join up with the third army, which is to attack across Lake Ontario from Oswego. The combined forces will then proceed in a short time with the reduction of the town of Montreal," he said.

"I'm not so sure, Colonel. What are you proposing exactly?" Abercrombie asked.

"The army needs a morale booster, sir. We must try to rescue Captain Putnam. I suggest a quick strike against Fort Frontenac as a way to restore the initiative to our dispirited forces," Bradstreet said.

Robert Rogers studied the maps and pointed at the French fort. "Capturing Fort Frontenac would attract a lot of favorable attention on our side. That would mean fame and promotion for you, sir," he said, knowing how vainglorious Abercrombie was.

"And now, it is unlikely to have a large garrison or to be well fortified," Johnson said, realizing what Rogers was trying to do.

"My bet is that the enemy forces are stretched to the limit on various fronts and will not be deployed in strength there," Rogers continued. "The chances that a strong expedition would meet with success are thus very good, if not excellent."

"Only one of our original objectives, the capture of Fort Louisburg, was met with success. I'd rather not talk about the action against Fort Carillon," Bradstreet said.

Rogers whispered to Johnson. "Following that failure, many of Abercrombie's underlings have sought to distance themselves from any responsibility for the disaster."

Abercrombie mopped the sweat from his brow with a large silk handkerchief. "You might be right," he said and hesitated. "This strategy would support General Forbes' pending expedition. You have my permission to proceed with your plans."

Johnson led Bradstreet and Rogers out of the headquarters. They continued planning on their way back to Fort Edward. "Between us gentlemen, I know the area pretty well, and it is swarming with hostile warriors. This is not going to be a walk in the park. We have to sharpen our plan of attack if we want to cross the finish line with our heads held high," Rogers said, pounding the palm of his hand with a fist.

As soon as they arrived in the headquarters, the officers threw more maps on the table and pored over them. "The order of marching of the boat fleet is as follows," Johnson said. "The Mohawks and Rangers in whaleboats as forward element, then the regulars first in the main body of bateau, then the provincials, and detachments forming a rear guard."

"Sir, what about the captured girl Mary Means?" Rogers asked.

"I'm afraid she must wait for the time being. We have a war to fight and not enough time to save young girls from big trouble," Johnson said.

"I understand, sir. However, we will keep our ears and eyes open and maybe we will get lucky. I will have my men ready immediately," Rogers said.

Preparations for the incursion deep into the enemy territory started, and Fort Edward was full of action. Finn and the others were busy getting the equipment and weapons ready. On Rogers Island, solid rowboats with flat bottoms, large birch-bark canoes, and bateau arrived from Albany, all loaded with supplies.

§　§　§

Catherina was stunned after learning that the operation to rescue Mary Means had been aborted. She became furious, and Daniel tried to calm her down, but to no avail. She stormed to Fort Edward, searching for General Johnson. She did not find him, so she ran over the bridge to Rogers Island and confronted Robert Rogers in his command post, pounding his desk with her fist. "Little girls aren't worth rescuing? How dare you!"

"Ma'am, I'm a professional soldier. The decision is not mine. I follow orders. And now if you'll excuse me, I have a war to attend to," Rogers said.

"Alright then, I suppose it takes a woman to do a man's job around here," she said.

"I warn you, lady," Rogers said, getting up behind his desk with his finger up in the air.

Catherina spun around on her heels and stormed out, slamming the door closed behind her. He looked after her and shook his head in astonishment. "Somebody ought to bridle that grumpy woman," he said.

Catherina, hating the feeling of helplessness, decided to launch a rescue mission on her own and ran to the stables. She found a beautiful, gold-coated palomino with a white mane and tail, already saddled with two scabbards that held pistols. Without a second thought, she mounted it. The stable keeper ran out as she galloped off in a fury, shouting, "Don't worry, Aaron, I'll bring her right back!"

Several hours later, she cautiously cantered into a narrow, shadowy gorge with steep cliffs on both sides, searching for any tracks. Suddenly, a shot rang out, and she felt the airflow from a bullet that shattered her hairpin in two and sent her mop cap flying, and her hair fell out loose on her shoulders.

While trying to turn the horse about to escape, she realized that the warriors had blocked her passage back, and there was nowhere to go but forward, deeper into the canyon. Looking up on the towering cliffs, she saw dozens of warriors lined up along both rims, silhouetted against the sky through treetops and leaves. Cursing, she knew all too well that the warriors wanted much more than just her long, beautiful blonde hair, which by itself would be as prized a possession as a scalp. There was only one way out to avoid the obvious, horrible fate.

What was that Finn always says, Catherina thought, *fuck me running?* She drove her heels into the horse's sides, urging the horse to a gallop. As it reared and neighed, she shouted, "Run, girl, run!"

The mare sprang forward as she kept whipping it, urging it to higher speeds. She rode like a maniac in a hail of fire, bullets kicking up dirt and striking sparks from rocks all around her. Arrows whizzed by and broken branches from trees fell on her.

She leaned down on one side so that she presented as small a target as possible and hoped that the horse's body would protect her at least a little. The warriors launched a hail of bullets, arrows, and spears at her, but she kept kicking the horse in a mad charge toward safety, desperately hanging on to the side of its neck. An arrow pierced through the horse's ear, slicing it in two. The horse shrieked in agony and terror, and bolted forward even faster, and Catherina managed to hang on for her dear life.

The horse's mane whipped her in the face, and she reached for the two pistols in pommel holsters slung around the horse's neck. Grabbing one pistol, she took aim at the warriors high on the cliff above. Just as she came out from under the trees, she recited a Hail Mary and fired. As luck would have it, she hit one of the warriors in the head, just as he was ready to take a clear shot at her.

The dead warrior fell down from the cliffs and came crashing through the trees. The body made a loud thumping noise when it hit the ground and bounced several feet into the air. The rest of the warriors (who respected hunting and fighting skills above all else) were impressed with her being such a crack shot and stopped shooting. She galloped away, her long blonde hair fluttering in the wind, and that is how she barely managed to escape, unharmed.

§ § §

On her way back to Fort Edward, Catherina rode along the high ground, making sure she would not get caught in an ambush again. While stopping to tend the wounded horse, she looked down from a high mountain ridge and saw Lake George glimmering in the distance. She witnessed as the provincial taskforce of nearly three thousand men headed for Lake Ontario and the French fort. They had embarked on a journey of four hundred and thirty miles across lakes and rivers through the wilderness, including eighty-four miles of portage.

A large rowboat full of well-armed Rangers was sent in advance to explore the area ahead of the main attack force. Regardless of all the precautions the Rangers had taken, four Mississauga scouts, hidden high in the treetops where they could spot any traffic within miles on the lake, saw the Rangers.

At dawn, the Rangers landed and camped for the day. Two young provincial officers did not follow instructions to stay in the camp and wandered away from the boat and quickly vanished. Within an hour, search parties fanned out, and early the next morning the scalped bodies of the two unfortunate men, their hands tied behind their backs, gagged, stripped, mutilated and robbed, were found by the Rangers.

Seeing the defaced bodies, which by now were covered in ants eating the tortured flesh, Finn felt nauseous. "There is not a man in this forsaken landscape that could be as unforgiving as I feel right now," he said.

Daniel found an empty messenger bag tossed away in the bushes. "The Mississauga seized a copy of the orders."

"Fuck! We have lost the element of surprise," Robert Rogers said.

The Rangers embarked again on boats during a dark cloudy night. Under the cover of darkness, they stayed close to the opposite side of the narrows and managed to pass by Fort Carillon undiscovered, though they were so close as to hear the sentinel's talking. Two Mohawk scouts were sent back to tell General Johnson that the main body should stay close to the eastern shore. Just in case, the Rangers were prepared to make a diversion in the event that the main force was discovered by the French.

The following night, they approached Crown Point, planning to go by it in the same manner, but Robert Rogers judged it imprudent, due to the clearness of the night, and they stayed concealed on the eastern shore throughout the following day.

The next day, a hundred enemy canoes passed by them, and seven came frighteningly close to their place of concealment, obviously planning to land there. The enemy was so close, the Rangers heard them talking. "*Tout juste.* I want to go a hundred and fifty meters farther where we will land and dine," the French officer said. The Rangers recognized the voice. It was Captain Langdale.

The French soldiers landed on the other side, across a narrow cape from the Rangers. Soon they heard a crackling fire and the French engaged in quiet lively discussions, and they smelled a suckling piglet roasting on a spit. Langdale ordered to break out two bottles of wine as the French bon vivant's wined and dined so close to the Rangers, who lay down concealed in the bushes. Finn smelled the crackling meat in the air, and his stomach was rumbling so hard that he was afraid it would give them away.

After their feast in the woods, the enemy's company

moved on, and the Rangers felt relieved. But it turned out to be too early because another thirty boats and a forty-ton schooner passed by the Rangers on their way toward Canada.

"It's rather busy on the lake today," Rogers whispered.

Late in the evening, the lake turned quiet, and the Rangers proceeded fifteen miles farther down, dispatching Daniel and Finn as scouts. Finn felt a little apprehensive about going out in a small canoe as he thought they were fully exposed on the open lake. He kept thinking of the two poor officers who were tortured to death earlier. Daniel assured him, once again, that a canoe was almost invisible on the water, and even on a clear, moonlit night, the enemy would have trouble seeing a canoe silently gliding on the dark water.

They advanced several miles, paddling with caution. They remained alert, always looking around and keeping track of the slightest sign of enemy movements or sounds. When they saw or heard anything, they froze in place and focused on what was happening in the impenetrable, dark stillness of the night. Somewhere, in the heart of the darkness, an owl hooted mournfully.

Finn and Daniel returned to the Rangers six hours later. "A schooner is anchored maybe ten miles from here," Finn reported, somewhat shaken from the tense hours on the perilous night foray.

The Rangers lightened their boats and prepared to capture the schooner, but were prevented by two smaller boats coming up the lake whose crews intended to land exactly where the Rangers were located.

The Rangers formed a firing on the shore line and as

the enemy approached, fired upon the boats. Three men were hit, and their bodies fell backward from the boats into the water. "Surrender and we will spare you if you come onshore," the Rangers shouted.

The surviving French soldiers brashly gave them the finger and pushed for the other side. The Rangers launched their boats in pursuit, trying to catch them. Fronto took the helm as coxswain. "Pull! Pull!" he shouted. The French seemed to gain on the Rangers and were getting off.

"Row, men, row! Pull like you have never pulled before!" Fronto urged the men. "Steady as she goes. Full slides, men, power strokes, pull!"

Men strained as they pulled oars, and the boat picked up speed, the bow foaming. As the Rangers started getting closer, Finn and Gus took positions on the bow and fired at the enemy boats ahead.

The French crews consisted of twelve men, three of whom had already been killed by the Rangers. Two were wounded, one mortally so, and he soon died. This discouraged the French and they stopped rowing as the Rangers caught up and pulled alongside them.

"Steer the boat to the shore!"

"Ease up!"

The Rangers and their prisoners landed on a nearby rocky lake shore with crystal clear water. James Rogers took a quick inventory of the enemy's boats. "Rangers, wreck and destroy both vessels and their cargo. I hate to waste the finest wheat and flour, but we cannot take them with us, so dump them in the lake," he said.

Some casks of wine and brandy were discovered, and the men quickly filled their canteens. "The rest we will put in a concealed cache for later use," Robert Rogers said, taking a long swig straight from a cask and spilling brandy on his coat.

Two privates were left to guard the prisoners until the main force could arrive to take possession of them. The gloomy prisoners eyed the privates warily as they remained at a safe distance and cocked their muskets, ready to fire if the prisoners tried anything.

The Rangers turned their attention back toward the schooner, hoping to discover more tasty supplies and valuable prisoners, but it had disappeared, obviously having heard the shooting.

The following day, the expedition approached Fort Frontenac, which was a crude, wooden palisade structure, located at the mouth of the Cataraqui River. Getting closer, the Rangers in advance boats ran into five French canoes. The Rangers and Mohawks of the advance guard tried to catch them, but the enemy canoes were faster than the Ranger's large rowboats.

"No use. Fuck it, like the white man says," Daniel said. "We're too tired from the earlier sprint."

Bradstreet's entire force managed to land on the shore without resistance one mile to the south of the fort. Luckily, the French had not posted any sentries or listening posts in the area, and the hills and high ground concealed their movements from the fort.

"Ranger Nimham, take a party to secure the woods," Rogers ordered. Once they landed, Daniel took a war party of Mohawks to scour the surrounding woods. He returned a few hours later and reported to Rogers. "There are no French or warriors outside the fort," Daniel said.

Finn observed the fort with a telescope from a high knoll. "The perimeter seems to be sealed with sentries posted on the palisades. I'd guess from here that there are only a hundred or so soldiers in the fort," he said.

Bradstreet studied the countryside surrounding the enemy fort. "I will move closer to reconnoiter the area with an engineer. Captain Thomas Sowers, follow me," he said.

"Sir, in spite of the vastly overwhelming numbers," Captain Sowers said, "we have seventy rounds for each of our guns and only forty spades, forty shovels, and forty pickaxes for building siege fortifications."

The two officers walked up to a hill position to gain a better look at Fort Frontenac. "That spot, on a bluff about a hundred fifty yards north, is very advantageous where a fascine battery can be built," Bradstreet said, pointing to the locations.

"I will inform Captain Stevens right away," Sowers replied.

Bradstreet shifted his attention to the other side of the fort and pointed at some breastworks. "To the west, two cannons and three howitzers are installed in an abandoned breastwork."

Captain George Coventry of the 55th Foot had been attached to Bradstreet's outfit on the late Lord Howe's recommendation. Bradstreet tasked him to oversee the construction of the siege works.

The French fired at the British for the rest of the day, but without any effect. The battery on the bluff to the north was quickly built, and the guns were put in action right away. The British howitzers, under the direction of the artillery officer Captain Stevens, caused considerable damage in the enemy fort.

A number of well-aimed shells landed inside the fort. One shell exploded in the powder magazine, firing some kegs of gun-powder. The flames scorched some of the warriors almost to death and sent burning soldiers running like human torches, screaming until they fell on the ground in a blackened heap. The horrific sight and the smell of burning human flesh seriously intimidated the French troops.

Regardless of their mounting casualties, the French kept firing, but again with little result. Only eleven militiamen were wounded. Clearly, the British artillery was superior, every ball wreaking havoc in the fort.

Finn, Gus, Fronto, and Daniel started sniping at the French on the palisades. Their well-aimed rifle fire, even at a long distance, forced the enemy artillery men to take cover.

Vastly outnumbered and outgunned, Fort Frontenac was not in any condition to endure the siege. Seeing the dead soldiers and wailing wounded men, some without arms and legs, the fort's commander, Pierre-Jacques Chavoy, decided to surrender. The white flag was raised.

"Ranger Finn, get your men and check out the situation within the fort. We will cover you from here," Rogers ordered.

Finn, Gus, Fronto, Daniel, and Private Severance moved across the open field in a wedge formation and warily approached the main gates, the heavy doors broken from their hinges. "Beware, the French surrendered almost too easily. We don't know what to expect inside," Finn said, fully alert.

They marched into billowing smoke and entered the fort, muskets at the ready.

"Watch the rear and don't take any chances," Gus said to private Severance. "We don't know for sure if this is real. We might be walking into a trap."

The five of them discovered fifty French troops waiting for them, assembled and having laid down their arms. Finn went to the gate and waved his hand to indicate that all was clear. The British troops marched into the fort and the French commander, handing over his sword, officially surrendered to Bradstreet.

The Rangers started searching the fort as the two commanders began negotiating the terms of surrender.

"All French ships, arms, and ammunition are turned over to us. Soldiers and civilians are allowed to leave for Montreal, where an equal number of British prisoners are to be released," Bradstreet said, dictating rather than negotiating.

The Rangers spread out to check the fort and within an hour Rogers reported to Bradstreet. "Sir, we have recovered more than sixty cannons, some of them our own cannons the French had captured at Fort Oswego, and hundreds of barrels of provisions."

Gus was at the supply room, counting beans and bullets. "The biggest prizes are bales of furs destined for shipment downstream to Montreal. I'd reckon the spoils to be worth at least thirty-five thousand in sterling," he said.

At sunset, Bradstreet stood in the guard tower, looking across the lake toward Canada. "The French relief force must be on its way by now. I have no interest in risking a clash. We will use some of the captured French boats to help carry the loot. We will destroy what we can't take with us," he said. He thought this victory just might be the turning point in the war. But then again, he realized that Lady Fortune worked in mysterious ways, and the fog of war remained dense across the frontier.

The search party entered the darkest corner of the fort and discovered the jail. Colonel Peter Schuyler and Israel Putnam were freed from their windowless cells. Putnam appeared outside, shading his eyes from the sunlight. He was shaken and pale but in excellent spirits. "Major Rogers, what took you so long? I was getting bored."

Seeing Putnam alive, Finn rummaged through his rucksack and handed back the little book he had found. "Sir, you might want to have this back."

Seeing the worn book, Putnam's face lit up. "You found it! I thought I had lost it forever."

Rogers toasted with his canteen. "With this one, brilliant stroke, the lifeline of the French Great Lakes Empire has been severed," he said, jubilantly taking long drinks.

After they had plundered, burned, and demolished the fortress, Bradstreet's force retreated back to the British territory.

More important than the capture of French provisions at the post was the destruction of the French naval flotilla on Lake Ontario. The resulting blow to French reputation among the native allies started to erode their war efforts. More and more warriors began to consider if they should, after all, start trading with the British.

"I must admit, the French dealings with its more westerly installations have not been cut off, unfortunately," Rogers said, "It is a fact that for a number of years most French supplies and reinforcements have traveled to the west by way of the rivers, Georgian Bay, and Lake Huron.

The impact of this success on our morale, however, cannot be underestimated."

The Rangers were completely exhausted as they returned to Fort Edward. Shelagh rushed to meet Daniel, and Catherina watched them march in. To her, all of them, and especially Finn, looked dreadfully tired and hungry. The last one to stumble in was Martin Severance. He took off his rucksack, and as it fell from his hands and burst open, the stone rolled out. The Rangers started laughing and hollering, and poor private Severance realized that he had been carrying the rock in his rucksack all along.

Finn slapped him on the shoulders. "Private Severance, you've proven yourself worthy to be called a Ranger. The rock represents all your sins as a cherry, fucking new guy. Be a good pilgrim and throw it away now," he said.

§   §   §

Catherina was badly shaken for several weeks after her close call in the woods. She missed Finn, Gus, Fronto, and Daniel, who were constantly gone on missions. She felt truly grateful to have Shelagh as a friend. After all, Shelagh knew all about being spurned for marrying Daniel. Nevertheless, other townspeople still turned away from Catherina and that made her even more inflexible toward them. After all, she had gone out there, risking her own life, to help them try to find the abducted little girl. And now, how dare they humiliate her just because she did not live according to their expectations. What would Fronto say? *Probably something like there's no justice in the world or something,* she thought.

At the stables, Catherina reached to rub her nose against the mare's velvet nostrils. The horse whickered gently in response and pushed at her, blowing a warm breeze against her face. She had made several attempts to purchase the horse that had saved her life. The stable owner would not renegotiate the asking price (he was afraid of losing the other townspeople as customers if he did), and she did not have enough money to pay his demand.

Having been turned down once more, she sat on the corral fence, sad and pensive, watching the horses being harnessed for work. Two working horses, one reddish brown and one white, were not used to working as a team. The horses were trying to get away and separate. However, they were yoked together.

Daniel arrived and looked at the horses appraisingly. "He is but a dray horse that is a farmer's horse to begin with, and for the first two years does practically nothing but grow. In the next two or three years, he will pass into the routine of farm work and get into shape. The gradual process of adaptation averages about two months, during which he is trained to his surroundings and his service," he said.

Catherina did not answer, and Daniel ran his hands over the horse, feeling his muscles. "Well-molded in every muscle, standing not an inch too high on his well-shaped legs, broad and strong, with nothing of heaviness in the chest or scragginess about the neck and head. He is well adapted for the work for which he is chosen, and that work he will do well," he said.

Catherina was quiet and brooding, and then she spoke softly. "Daniel, will you tell me why it is that some of the

Iroquois do what they do? They tried to kill me and abducted a young girl. Why do they fight us? Why do they steal our little girls?" she asked.

"They were the Lenape. We've tried everything, but we just can't get some people to live together in peace. Every time someone wants peace, he's shot right in the head," Daniel replied.

"Well, that one warrior certainly didn't want peace. He was after my scalp, and much more than that. Besides, I recognized some Senecas among them," Catherina said, feeling her temper flaring.

Daniel turned to face her. "The Haudenosaunee have their problems, too, you know. Don't be like the other white people who don't see any differences between nations. A warrior follows his own way. These problems can't be solved by addressing the rank and file, only through a change in people's scorn toward each other, whether Iroquois or white people," Daniel said.

"Some folks clearly are ignorant cretins. You're right, Daniel. We should do something about those issues head on," Catherina replied, biting her lip.

On his way to the Silver Star, Fronto walked by and overheard their conversation. "Don't worry, by the time things really get out of hand, we will see some true ugliness — bickering, backstabbing, and suddenly grownups sound like eight-year-olds, arguing who started it," he said, smirking. "We have more than enough Kings and Queens *and* their loyal henchmen just like that."

"Why is it so hard? Please, oh please, won't someone make these folks just get along?" Catherina said, sounding desperate.

"Young lady, perhaps you should ask yourself why this bickering is stopping you," Fronto replied, looking sympathetic. "You want to change something, why not start from within? That's where all truly momentous renewal stems from, guaranteed."

They were interrupted by a horse-drawn wagon under the command of farmer Thelaball driving by with a pregnant woman lying in the back on a heap of hay. She had an enormous belly and was breathing irregularly. Sweating profusely, she looked frightened and clutched the edge of the wagon. "I'm ready to give birth, but where is Doctor Barrett? Why doesn't he show up? Oh Lord, I didn't even know I was expecting."

To get out of the way, Fronto hopped up effortlessly to sit on the fence, and Daniel and Catherina stepped aside to let the wagon pass. "The Iroquois do have a problem. They don't understand their role in this war," Daniel said. "Maybe that uncertainty is making the Iroquois feel powerless — warriors secretly think they are wasting their time. It only makes sense that this would lead to quarreling."

Fronto glanced at Daniel. "Well chief, maybe that should be *your* mission, to find a way so that the Iroquois come out stronger," he said.

"Again, we're at war, but that's not the root of the problem. The problem is our attitude about the problem," Daniel insisted.

"I don't want to become the grieving person closing my eyes and wishing myself into a state of indifference, meanwhile stuffing the real passion beneath," Catherina said, folding her arms in front of her.

They all remained quiet for a while. Fronto absent-mindedly picked the little hairs in his ear.

"What I want is... what I actually need is," Catherina said, "I must truly feel that what I have is my own and sufficient for me."

Fronto nodded an affirmative, impressed with her words. He then pointed his finger at Finn, who was looking for everyone.

"And you, whippersnapper, should understand that you should not act grudgingly, nor greedily, nor without thinking, nor with conflicting intentions. Don't let pretensions take over your mind. Let the man within be the custodian of a real you. You should always stand upright, not be held upright," Fronto said. He hopped down and placed his hand over Finn's shoulder, pushing him toward the Silver Star.

§   §   §

During the harvest, farmer Francis Thelaball was in town to sell his crops. John stopped his wagon at the Silver Star and Thelaball, tipsy and overly cautious in his steps, came out of the saloon to help his pregnant wife in.

Daniel and Shelagh followed Finn and Fronto, helping to bring a few items belonging to the farmer's wife.

At the bar, Thelaball wanted to take a room. "There has been much enemy activity, and staying in the farm is not safe in her condition," he said.

"The fort infirmary is full of wounded, and it is not a suitable place for childbirth," Catherina said.

Samuel Adams was drinking beer in the lounge with the Helming brothers, Selous Claymore and Harold Ferrara. Religious man Adal Mauser, an almost eagle-like appearance on his face and his expression hard, had declined the invitation.

Finn, Gus, and Fronto made room at a table, and Finn rubbed his hands together as he ordered a drink. Then he noticed that in the back corner, Fat Murray was sitting down with his arms around two barmaids. "I was leading the way on a twenty-mile forced road march when—" he was saying, telling an embellished story.

After being washed out from the Rangers, Fat Murray had left, searching for a place to live the fake life elsewhere. He ended up in Tangier Tavern, a roadhouse of ill repute on the outskirts of the village of Saratoga, where he hooked up with Mary Brazier the proprietor. She introduced him to some shadowy figures and soon he earned his way rum-running and bootlegging along the Hudson River. His contact in Fort Edward happened to be Billy Blue, the young ferryman slave. Nevertheless, while in the vicinity, Fat Murray could not help himself and ventured in to take back a piece of the glory robbed from him, as he thought.

Finn turned toward the corner table. "Shut the fuck up Fat Murray! You're a fucking liar! That was only a two-mile move to a bivouac site!" he shouted across the room. Fat Murray shut up, and meekly looking around, ducked his head down as if looking for a crack in the floorboards he could disappear into.

At the bar, Robert Rogers, his brothers, and the Stark brothers listened as Samuel Adams tapped the side of his nose as he spoke. "The Boston Town Meeting elected me to the post of tax collector, and I have been keeping a sharp lookout for the British plans. Mark my words, the time will come when the British Parliament will look for new sources of revenue and will seek to overload the provincials. We must resist any such plans, by force of arms if need be."

A husky midwife hurried past them with a hot water tub and some linen under her arm. "Out of the way, coming through!" she shouted, using her elbow to force people out of the way.

Samuel Adams had arrived in Fort Edward on business to get cereal grain for malting from Thelaball, but now he found himself suddenly in the middle of a happy family happening. He raised his tankard in a toast. "Children, we need more children! God tells us to multiply and fill the earth! I'm one of twelve children born to Samuel Adams, Senior, and Mary Adams, nee Fifield. Sadly, only three of these children lived past their third birthday, so here's looking at them," he said and took a long drink.

"It's surprising that anybody lives long enough to become adults. Even if they do, there's still war and famine. The infirmary is full of young men dying. What will become of us?" Catherina asked him.

Adams turned to face her and gave a slight bow. "My dear lady, I was married to Elizabeth Checkley, my pastor's daughter, but I'm now a widower. My beloved Elizabeth passed away shortly after giving birth to a stillborn son last year in July. She gave birth to six of our children, but only two, Samuel and Hannah are with me now—," he choked and wiped off a tear.

Farmer Thelaball was unsteady on his feet, holding on to the table with one hand. "Mr. Adams, I think we can now talk business while we wait," he said in a drunken mumble. He drank more beer and continued, "I have your cereal grain finished, sir. And it helps me to keep my mind off what is happening upstairs."

Screams of labor sounded from the room upstairs and Thelaball's eyes popped wide open. He looked as if he were going to faint. The midwife rushed out to collect more clean towels, and going back in she turned on top of the stairs. "I need more hot water!"

A woman's long, wailing yell pierced through the whole building. Thelaball slumped down on a chair and held his head. Then the screams stopped, and the house became so quiet you could hear a pin drop. Then, very quietly at first, a baby cried upstairs, and people cheered and laughed. Adams patted Thelaball on the back and brought him another beer.

Daniel and Shelagh glanced at each other and then stepped forward. Daniel took his hunting knife and made a ting by a small strike against his tankard. People quieted down and turned to them.

"Excuse us, everyone. We have an announcement to make. I think this is an appropriate time," Daniel said and pulled Shelagh closer. Shelagh hesitated, and she looked around the room a little nervously. Daniel gave her a little encouraging push. "Well, as it happens, Daniel and I have been blessed. We're expecting, too," she said and smiled shyly.

Everybody stopped in a surprised silence for a moment, and Shelagh glanced at Daniel over her shoulder. Then people burst into loud cheers and laughter. People took turns congratulating Daniel and Shelagh. An excited Catherina pulled Shelagh aside while the men gathered around Daniel, slapping him on the back and shoulders.

"Hey, Catherina, when is it your turn to make an announcement like that?" Finn asked loudly, teasing Catherina.

"Watch it, buster," she replied, and gave him a warning look. She then turned around to hide her smile.

"Happy events like this revive optimism among all the provinces," Adams said, raising a pint tankard. People celebrated well into the night, free from care for the first time in a long time. Fort Edward bathed in the light of torches, lanterns, and candles. Outside the palisade, the forests were cloaked in a pitch-black night. Lights from scattered farmhouses sparkled in the middle of the vast dark wilderness like tiny silver stars.

Chapter 6

IN THE FALL, the foliage exploded in a blaze of colors. A forest of Allegheny serviceberry trees burst into glorious shades of red, yellow, and orange. Small, round berries turned from rubicund rosy to almost black. A mature, alder-leaved shadbush was pointed and blushed in tones of auburn and golden. Flocks of bobwhite quail gorged on the rich, delicious berry-like pomes, red to purple to near black.

In Fort Edward, a group of men snuck through the back alleys, shuffling through fallen leaves. They stopped to peek around the corners first to make sure they remained concealed before darting through alleys. They took a short cut through the corral, shushing and pushing horses out of the way. Townspeople were too busy doing their humdrum daily chores to pay the men any attention.

The Rogers brothers did not want to be noticed. Robert Rogers kept the back door open as his brothers slipped into the back room of the Silver Star lounge. He glanced around, then followed them in and quietly closed the door behind him.

Rogers chose the table in the corner. James grabbed a seat next to him while John leaned against the door to the saloon with his arms folded to stop anybody from disturbing them. The Rogers brothers' intentions were to explore some land speculation schemes with General Johnson and Molly Brant.

Johnson and Brant emerged from the storage room, still blushing, and pulled at their clothes and joined the Rogers. They knocked quietly on the door, and after they were allowed in, they nodded to John who let them pass by.

Then to everyone's surprise, Moses Hazen barged in, uninvited, with his new and unfamiliar trading partner Christie, a shadowy man in a dark day outfit with minimal decorations and simple buttons, and sought to join the meeting. John stopped Hazen at the doorway by pushing his finger into his chest. The two men exchanged a glance.

"Who's your hobnobbing mate, Ranger Hazen?" John Rogers asked.

"None of your business, John," Hazen replied.

"At ease John, let them in," Robert Rogers said.

John stared Hazen in the eyes, and then smiled. He allowed them to pass. "Just asking, comrade," he said.

Hazen let Christie go first and then pushed past John, deliberately bumping hard into his shoulder. They grabbed chairs, and Hazen pulled out some maps and papers from his jacket. Seeing the maps, John carelessly left the door ajar as the men leaned in to study the properties over the table.

"I happen to know that vast tracts of land are being offered and sold by certain merchants," Hazen commented.

Robert Rogers nodded and pored over the maps. "We stand to make a fortune," he said.

Catherina happened to walk by in the hallway, having fetched some towels for the infirmary. She overheard the men talking and stopped to listen, and quickly realized that the discussion involved several properties in the vicinity, including the Nimham's land. She knew she had to do something about it.

Catherina pushed the door open. "Not so fast, Major Rogers. The Nimhams happen to be my close friends and neighbors. Besides, Daniel is one of your best scouts for crying out loud. You better leave their land out of your plans. Don't you dare even think about my farm," she said, sternly.

Robert Rogers gave his brother a stern glance. "Damn it, John. You must be more careful. Ma'am, this is none of your concern," he said, biting his lip.

Catherina glared back at him angrily and continued on her errand without looking back. Robert Rogers waited until she was gone.

Christie coughed, looking skeptical. "How are you going to finance all of this, sir?" he asked.

"No fear, Mr. Christie, money's not an issue, although I still haven't received any reimbursement from Boston nor London for my services and efforts in this war." Robert Rogers drummed the table with his knuckles and continued, "Richard, on his last job for me to Boston, delivered my earlier inquiries to the headquarters, but those have gone unanswered. I must send someone again to collect receivables from the local government."

"I have to take my company out on a patrol. Maybe John could do something, brother?" James Rogers said.

"Nope, I was told to report for duty, too. And I think any one of us that left right now would attract unwanted attention," John replied.

"I'll send one of my men that I can trust to Boston. I'll also approach the British headquarters directly, in person. We rule around here. My Rangers will spearhead us to victory and then, gentlemen, we can build our own state," Robert Rogers said, his eyes flaring as he leaned on the maps with both clenched fists.

§   §   §

The commanding General's residence was well lit, and sentries were posted at the entrances. General Forbes' Leicester regiment, the 17th Foot, assembled for the regimental ball. High ranking British officers, their eyebrows lifted high in fastidious disdain, drove by the provincials who gaped at the lavish carriages. The lords and their cohorts (and courtesans) and bodyguards were dressed in the proper extravagantly British fashion.

The honor guard stood at attention as a fife player and drum band performed on the front lawn. Important guests, ladies of the night in floral silk brocade gowns trimmed with pleated linen bands and their benefactors wearing formal, flaring shirts and embroidered silk suits, gathered on the porch to watch as the Union Jack and regimental colors were presented.

General Forbes greeted the guests with his wife at the main entrance. The official reception was a dress splendor with perfumed wigs and impressive hand fans that filled the reception rooms. Fine fabrics and lace abounded. Jewelry, diamonds, and gold shone brilliantly.

A small army of servants in colorful uniforms with white gloves attended to every whim of the guests. Silver trays were loaded with sparkling champagne in crystal goblets, sweets, and pastries.

In the kitchen, the steward watched over the scores of cooks and housemaids who prepared meals, marching behind them with a whip in his hands, ready to unleash a trouncing at the smallest mistake. He checked and tasted each course before allowing it to be taken to the dining room.

The seven-course dinner was served, and the well-off people enjoyed the traditional, but joyous, socialite event of the year. The who's who of the provinces was overjoyed to be seen in the mansion among the cream of the crop. Ripples of pretentiously polite, smug conversation and specious laughter filled the building. Some ladies preferred to gather and gossip in the parlor while the gentlemen took turns taking them for a dance in the ballroom.

Robert Rogers stood alone in the library with a drink in his hand, ill at ease in his brand-new, formal British Army uniform. He greeted people properly and pretended to smile, pulling at his awkward collar. He was there to see General Thomas Cage, hoping to enlist his support for obtaining reimbursements for the monies he had spent recruiting and equipping the Rangers.

Seeking a quiet area for privacy, Rogers took a letter out of his pocket. He folded it out to read it one more time. It was an invoice for security services rendered that totaled three tons of Spanish silver coins and one ton of British coppers. At a writing table, he took a quill pen and signed the paper. He folded the note carefully and motioned to a male slave standing nearby. "Take this to General Cage," he ordered and placed the bill on a small silver tray. The expressionless servant bowed and departed.

Military aides circled around the party, informing the officers that their presence in the library was requested. The officers took their time to excuse themselves with the ladies, and at their own pleasure, they drifted to the large library. Rogers sneered when he noticed George Washington among them in full Virginian regalia.

As the officers eventually entered, they were served a refreshing drink by servants at the door. They gathered by the large fireplace, enjoying the pleasant fire. When all had arrived, servants left and closed the doors. The aides spread maps on the table, placing tin soldiers, cavalry, and cannons carefully on the maps to illustrate military unit locations. The British commanders planned to continue their decisive offensive.

"Gentlemen, there has been some discussion on the native way of warfare," General Amherst said. "Jolly, spiffing chaps called Rangers have proven themselves to be highly adept at it and are going to play a vital role in the future. Therefore, I have invited Major Rogers here tonight."

Being the lowest ranking officer in the room, Rogers made a formal greeting to the room full of superior officers. He had never seen so much high brass in one room.

Admiral Boscawen, ignoring the lowly Major, looked smug and extremely pleased. "Thanks to the Navy, the conquest of Louisburg was a smashing success!"

General Forbes took a long look at the setup on the table and moved some tin soldiers to a new position. "Now, in the second offensive to the west, we must eliminate the small chain of enemy forts that extend south from Lake Erie to Fort Duquesne. Major, your Rangers will serve as scouts and provide security," he said, nodding toward Rogers, who tapped his heels together and bowed in affirmation.

Amherst pointed to the top of the map. "Our third objective will be to drive a splendid blow north and push the French out from the valley by taking Fort Carillon."

Rogers cleared his throat and stepped forward, causing some eyebrows to rise at this display of boldness. "My Rangers have considerable experience in this area of operations. Their skills and dedication will be highlighted even more once we go out on these missions," he said.

Amherst motioned to an aide to bring him a goblet. "I'm happy to announce, gentlemen, that in order to achieve the second objective, the War Office has appointed me to lead a combined provincial and Regular British expeditionary force. The expedition will be launched soon," he said, and as approving gasps rippled among the powdered wigs, he nodded again to Rogers. "Major, diligence of scouts is of utmost importance."

"I must say," General Cage said, "of all the measures that Lord Shirley has authorized, only Bradstreet's performance so far has won the unqualified praise of Shirley's successors. Lord Loudoun has ordered that the bills for his bateau service are to be honored, and he shall receive a colonelcy in the Royal Americans," he said.

Rogers was immensely surprised to hear this. What the hell had happened to his invoice?

"We're charmed, indeed, with the spirit and enterprising genius of Bradstreet," Amherst said. "I have recommended him as Deputy Quarter Master General for America."

Upon hearing the news, Washington could not hide his disappointment and breathed in through his nose so loudly that it did not go unnoticed.

Forbes took a long, careful look at Washington. "Rather than repeat General Braddock's disastrous march on Fort Duquesne through Virginia, I will take a new route through the Allegheny Mountains of Pennsylvania!" He said.

Washington jumped up, knocking his chair over. He forced himself to calm down. "Sir, I don't see why we shouldn't use the same route General Braddock took!" he said, trying to stay calm. Seeing his agitation, Rogers could hardly hide his smile behind a goblet.

"Perhaps, Washington, but then on the other hand, perhaps you don't understand what I see," Forbes said icily.

"What I see is that the Allegheny Mountains are deceptively beautiful this time of the year," Washington said in an icy voice.

Rogers noticed General Johnson among the officers and nudged him aside. He lowered his voice to make sure that no one could hear them. "Sir, I don't like spreading my men on too many missions at the same time. They are overextended as it is. Plus I still haven't received any reimbursement for previous years' service."

Johnson listened, but he was paying closer attention to the conversation around the table. "I understand, Major. Getting more warriors on our side would help, too," he replied and made a gesture toward the generals, tapping the side of his nose. "Politics, you see. Let me see what I can do about it."

"We need to convince these gentlemen that I need the money to recruit more Rangers," Rogers said.

Rogers and Johnson turned around when they heard voices raised. Washington was making a point. "Militia, you will find, never answer your expectations and dependence cannot be placed on them. They are stubborn and perverse, and they are egged on by the officers who lead them, to acts of disobedience. When they are ordered to specific posts for the security of stores or the safety of the inhabitants, they may at any moment resolve to leave them. Even the united vigilance of their officers cannot prevent them. Now, in the event that I was to get a commission in the British Regulars..." he said with a hopeful tone.

Rogers stepped forward, outraged, and interrupted him. "I beg your pardon, sir. In warfare as in everything else, the men of the New World are far better than the history-laden men of the Old," said, infuriated.

Washington let out a low growl and looked at Rogers intensely. He forced himself not to respond, realizing that it might not be such a brilliant idea, career wise, to get into an argument with a lower ranking officer in front of the generals. Besides, Rogers was an officer in the regular British army while he was, at least for the time being, in the provincials.

Amherst raised his glass. "Gentlemen, let us raise a toast to the glory of the British crown and to our ongoing success. Victory is within our reach. The King will reward us generously."

The generals raised their glasses and replied in unison. "Hear, hear! To the King! Fame and everlasting glory shall be ours!"

The officers, blushing and excited, returned to the gala. In the hallway, Johan Kopf, in a formal black Hessian pelisse with golden skeleton embroidery on the front, asked permission to speak with General Cage, demanding again for more liberties to deal with "unwanted elements" in the area, as he put it. Cage declined to speak with him at length, saying only that he had his orders. Kopf was to leave the Rangers alone, for now, and focus on finding more intelligence. Anything else would be considered insubordination and result in a swift demotion, if not decapitation. (In fact, Cage wanted more information, which he could blatantly use for his own advantage in the power struggle among the general staff, and he was afraid to draw too much attention to his private, clandestine operations, which the other generals could find a direct challenge. He preferred rather 'discreet' ways in which Kopf was quite proficient.) As Cage walked away, Kopf threw the glass he was holding into the fireplace, smashing it to pieces.

§   §   §

The following day on Rogers Island, outside of the squad cabin, Gus was checking his gear when Robert Rogers approached him and pulled him aside.

"Ranger, you're to carry this message to the headquarters in Boston. Take one man with you for security," he said and handed a sealed envelope to him. Gus nodded affirmatively and did not ask any questions. That was one of the reasons Rogers had chosen him for the job.

Gus fetched two horses from the corral and noticed Finn cleaning heavy weapons at the armory. Finn inspected the three-barreled pole mounted cannons just as Roger marched by him. "Those guns are sixty percent of our fire power, Ranger. Respect," he said and hurried toward his command post.

Gus walked the horses to the armory. "Hey Finn, Major Rogers ordered me to deliver a message to Boston. Want to ride with me?"

"Sure. It'll be agreeable to get out of here for a change. What's the message?" Finn asked.

Gus shrugged his shoulders. "He didn't say, and I'm not supposed to open it, got to keep it a secret. I'll take it to the provincial headquarters."

Finn told another Ranger to take over the weapons. He grabbed the bridles Gus was handing to him. "So, we're cavalry now. Alright, there's nothing to it," he said, laughing.

Gus mounted the horse with ease. Finn had trouble getting on the horse because he was not that familiar with handling horses. He had one foot in a stirrup, but the pony kept side stepping out of the way in a circle. "Whoa, you son-of-a-bitch," he said.

Laughing and poking jokes at Finn, Gus rode off. Finally, Finn managed to get on the saddle, and the horse galloped away, Finn bouncing in the saddle.

They rode through the New England countryside without incident. They crossed a high ridge in the mountains after climbing for many weary hours. Behind them, they could see the beautiful golden tableland of the Hudson River valley and ahead of them, stretching away into the distance, was the seaboard lowlands, looking like the green bed of a vast ocean. Finn held his breath, enjoying the scenery. Here and there they saw scattered homesteads and trading posts, but for most of the way they crossed unspoiled countryside. In the evening, following a rough track leading to the rocky streambed, they found a camp-site at the base of a hundred-foot-tall waterfall on an un-protected overlook with a magnificent view over the sur-rounding landscape.

Getting up early at sunrise the next day, Gus and Finn arrived in Boston later that afternoon, passing the Roxbury Latin School. They mingled in the crowds and enjoyed the hustle of the big city after being in the forests for so long. In the harbor, two large, overcrowded ships, the *Duke William* and the *Violet*, carrying hundreds of Acadians, were docked at the pier and led by a brig of war.

Finn and Gus stopped to watch as the British Marines disembarked, and the commanding officer reported to the Harbor Master.

"Of the thirty-one hundred Acadians deported from Ile St. Jean, I'd say about sixteen hundred and fifty of them drowned or died of disease. Many of them escaped from the north shore to Quebec on French schooners. Others fled to Miramichi, but they have no food and are starving," the Marine reported.

One vessel had a large number of sick people on deck. The men and women and children were seasick and weak because there had not been enough food for the trip. They were not allowed to land.

"City council has ordered that Acadians caught in our provinces be put into the jails," The Harbor Master said.

A merchant named Daniel Launcey took pity on the deportees and their conditions on the ships. He offered to pay the councilman for allowing the Acadians to disembark if only for a day or so, but after much arguing and bargaining, he gave up. There was much wailing and moaning on the decks. A desperate Acadian man yelled from the ship, pointing his finger at the British. "You're murderous English! There is nothing but bones of starved animals and ruins of homes left in Acadia!"

"Lucky for them, Ranger Hazen is not present. He'd probably burn the ship down and them along with it," Gus said wryly.

"Don't even mention it," Finn replied and shivered at the memory of the burning church.

Gus and Finn wandered around the Boston town. On a market square, Finn took notice of some young ladies strolling in the park. He wiggled his eyebrows and winked suggestively at them. They glanced at his worn green outfit and turned up their noses, then turned to smile at a junior ensign wearing a red parade uniform. Finn did not understand what was wrong and sniffed his armpits to see if his smell might be the culprit.

Going through a park, Gus stopped to listen to a black man talking to a group of men. He learned that the person talking was Thomas Prince Hall and the others were all former slaves, now free, like him.

"We're going to get organized and establish a Lodge of our own. Thomas, read the article again," one of the men in the group said.

Upon hearing this, Gus's curiosity intensified, and he stepped closer. "Yes, please do so," he said. "I would be pleased to hear about your plans."

Thomas Hall was pleased to see this black man in a

Ranger uniform — which was quite a rare sight in Boston — join his audience. He took a rolled up paper from his pocket and began to read it.

"To the loving brethren of the ancient and honorable society of Freemasons," he started and paused to let the words sink in on his audience. "And having by virtue thereof congregated and formed a Lodge in His Majesty's Twenty-Eighth Regiment of Foot, to organize a Lodge in said Regiment in North America with Power to appoint Wardens and all other officers to a Lodge and all persons that shall be made masons in such Lodge. Signed by Richard Gridley," he said.

The men talked excitedly about joining Military Lodge No. 441, an integrated Lodge attached to the British Army. Gus would have liked to hear more details, but he realized he still had the message to deliver to the headquarters. "This is all terribly intriguing indeed. I wish you all the luck, but I must now be on my way," he said.

"God bless you. May your good fortune increase and your way be made easy, and may we all be alive this time next year," Prince Hall bade him goodbye.

Gus and Finn found their way around the unfamiliar city, and after asking for directions finally managed to deliver the message to the headquarters. The officer in attendance took the letter at the front desk by the entrance but did not let them in any farther. While waiting for the receipt in the foyer, they overheard a conversation in an adjoining conference room that recently the first reservation in America was founded in New Jersey on three thousand acres, by the New Jersey Provincial Assembly. It was going to be a permanent home for the Lenni and the Lenape people.

"Home is where I lay down my rucksack," Finn commented.

Finally, the officer returned and handed them a receipt for the message. "This receipt shows that the message has been acknowledged. Take this back to the gracious Major, and tell him to wait for further instructions," he said and turned to his books.

On the way back to Fort Edward, Finn and Gus reached the highest peaks of the mountain range by yet another long climb. The view in front of them was impressive enough to compensate them for their labor, and they decided to stop for a quick lunch. Beginning in gray red, range after range of mountains overlapped each other, then faded to a purple and eventually lost themselves in a blue haze.

"Gus, here's an idea. Imagine a rifle that repeats. I tell you, with one of them, I could conquer this land all the way to the Island of California," Finn said.

They sat on a ledge and gazed at the scenery, captivated by the view. Finally, Finn broke the spell by a request for chewing tobacco, and so they moved on.

§ § §

Back in Fort Edward, riding through the gates, they did not have time to dismount as Robert Rogers approached them, furious. His rage very nearly spooked the horses.

"The Forbes expedition went from pathetic to worse! I should not have left Washington to his own devices!"

He ordered the Rangers to prepare an operation immediately to strengthen the expedition. All hell was breaking loose and disaster loomed. "You'll take the horses and pack mules and join the expedition in Fort Ligonier. You've got, let's see, until... yesterday," he said.

There was a burst of activity at the stables as the Rangers loaded supplies, weapons, and ammunition on the mules, and horses were saddled. The Rangers were issued wide-brim cavalry hats that provided more protection against rain than their usual caubeen.

In the garrison, the army horse's life was fairly peaceful and calm, but they had to be ready at all times for action or the pursuit of hostile warriors. No pains were spared to enhance the usefulness of an army horse, and every astute frontiersman knew that meticulous care would decide the outcome of extensive, forced marches or prevent a deadly failure by an unreliable mount in combat. A trooper would rob for his horse, share his bread, and water the horse's nostrils and lips with precious water from his canteen.

The Rangers saddled up, turned their horses around in unison, and drove spurs into the horses' sides. The horses reared up and neighed as the mounted Ranger patrol galloped off in a cloud of dust.

Just as Finn was about to take off, Catherina came running across his field of vision, and in a flashy display of talent, he turned his gelding. She brought him a small box and stuffed it in his saddlebag. "Here, take this. It's not much, but it will help on the road," she said and looked at him, a little concerned.

"Thank you, Catherina. That was very thoughtful of you," Finn replied. His horse took off galloping after the others and Finn could barely hold on as Catherina waved goodbye after him.

The mountains were dark green, lush, and beautiful. Overhead stretched the deep blue of the cloudless sky. The horses they rode were cheap beasts of burden, but still they were small, light, and fast. Mounted Rangers were an unusual sight, and they brought only those parts of the military gear and tools that would suit them. Daniel led the way with beaded scabbards slung across his horse. The Rangers' determined faces were deep in shadow under their hats.

Together, at the head of the column, rode Daniel and Finn, while behind in single file came Fronto and Gus, followed by the rest, sitting loosely in their saddles. Cavalry hats sat well over their eyes, and muskets, raincoats, canteens, saddle pockets, and lassos were at their sides. Strung out behind came the pack mules, trotting along at their own pace. The packers brought up the rear, swinging their whips and shouting at the lagging mules.

After reaching the summit, they had a needed rest. The sight on the crest was remarkably pleasant as the trees there obscured the hot sun, but they quickly left them for the thorny scrub that barred their progress and then began their descent, following the trail that continued more steeply down the ridge.

The Rangers rode as fast as they could without tiring the horses or outpacing the pack mules. But at times they rode like riders of the apocalypse, through the forest trails, over the hills and through the thickets. The Rangers did not like the noise they made, and took the time to stop and wrap burlap around the horses' feet.

Horses slipped and slid on their hind legs during the precipitous descent. The Rangers were afraid of the possibility of being thrown off and quickly overwhelmed by

an avalanche of horseflesh as the result of some wretched
stumble. But the trained horses were sure of foot, except
when treacherous ground gave way.

When possible, they rode hard and fast, whipping
and driving the horses to faster and faster paces. The horses' hooves kicked up leaves and dirt, and Finn was almost
knocked off the saddle as he dodged small tree branches.
Then, the horses were forced over rugged terrain and up
over the perilous mountains all day long and into the quiet
of the long night.

Crossing a meadow, the Rangers were unaware that they
were followed by a musket barrel from the opposite tree line
three hundred yards away. Slightly jutting out from behind a
large rock, the gaping black muzzle was aimed right at them.
A shadowy figure lurked in ambush between a large tree and
the rock. The aiming point moved from Ranger to Ranger,
searching for the right target. It passed the Mohawks and
came back to the Rangers. Then, the menacing gun muzzle
stopped and rested squarely on Finn.

Finn heard the discharge faint in the distance, and almost immediately felt the air brushing his skin as the bullet
whizzed by only an inch from his face.

"Ambush!" he shouted. "Contact at nine o'clock!" He
pulled out his musket from the scabbard and threw a quick
shot at the puff of smoke he saw in the wood line.

Several Rangers stood up in their stirrups and promptly returned fire. Their bullets hit the rock where the sniper had been
just a moment before, sending sparks and chips of stone flying.
Then, in the bushes, he saw a glimpse of a horse he recognized.

"It's Totenkopf!" he shouted, drawing his cutlass and
charging his horse.

The others got ready to follow him, but at that juncture, one of the forward scouts came in fast. The horse skidded on the loose earth as the Mohawk yanked on the reins. He reported that the Forbes expedition was in dire straits, and the Rangers were required straightaway.

"Come on! No time to chase him! We must keep moving on!" Daniel shouted, letting out a blood curdling war cry before galloping away.

Finn felt emptiness as he watched the cloud of dust that pledged bloodshed and combat, but at the same time, Totenkopf was within sight. The Rangers urged on their horses, but Finn hesitated, wanting to attack his archenemy. The others were gaining distance. Cursing, he rushed after them.

Hiding behind the rock, Johan Kopf did not even care that now practically everyone, particularly the Rangers, knew of his intentions to kill Finn. After all, he was a Hessian officer in His Majesty's secret service, and in that capacity he was untouchable by the provincials. He whistled and took his time to reload the special purpose musket. He admired the telescope he had attached to the rifle and was pleased with his new invention, which he considered to be an excellent killing combination. He detached the three draw, leather-clad field telescope, and admired the scope of impressive proportions, running his finger over the engraving, "The Marksman."

§   §   §

On their way to Fort Ligonier, the Rangers arrived in a Pennsylvanian settlement from the east and were riding through the town when they noticed people gathering on the market square. From the south, a Virginian regiment was marching through the town, and some of the locals did not like it as it disturbed their market events.

The Virginians were commanded by George Washington, who had just received a letter from Richmond informing him that his bid for running for the House of Burgess had been accepted. Right away, he decided to tell the troops of this significant event.

On the market square, people were entertained by a multi-piece band and one person with a guitar. People were dancing and singing along. People traded stories and jokes and played various games with darts, cards, and dice.

The Rangers passed by the stables and neared a general store and a saloon. "Alright, let's take a break and grab a bite to eat. We need some more supplies, too," Finn decided.

The Rangers stopped and dismounted to allow their horses a drink from a trough. Finn took out the box Catherina gave him from the saddlebags and walked stiffly, holding his butt, and sat down to eat on a pile of hay by the corral.

The Virginians passed through the town and formed on a nearby field. Washington stepped up to give a speech to the crowd on a podium. He took an imposing stance and delivered an eloquent speech which he had practiced several times earlier. "The King cannot at any time maintain an extensive and complicated war unless we destroy the provincial resources of France and Spain, and further add to our own commercial resources, which must ever be the sole basis of our military might," he said.

Hearing the words, Fronto winced. "He sounds like a politician. Their talk reminds me of a glaring of cats."

"There isn't any other way but the hard way," Washington continued. "This is the first war on a global scale. It is our duty to look after Virginian interests."

The statement, delivered boldly in the Pennsylvanian heartland, drew angry gasps from the crowd. Unexpectedly, down the road a riotous bunch of fifty men appeared, armed with clubs, sticks, and cudgels. Some men wore female clothes. Others were in Iroquois disguise, and some had blackened faces.

"What's with the ugly queens with beards?" Finn asked.

"It's a signal that common rules have been suspended," Daniel replied.

Angry shouts and threats of more violence sounded across the square as the mob approached the gathering. Women in the audience took their children and hurried away. A deputy sheriff attempted to stop the mob, standing in front of them and holding his arm up. The crowd quickly seized him, beat him up, and threw him over a fence and out of the way.

"Maybe we should do something," Gus said, brushing sweat and dirt off his horse with some straw.

"Like what? Join the protestors?" Daniel replied, and handed a piece of dried bread to his horse.

"Nevermind, it's none of our business anyways. Let's move on. I'm sure the good Colonel can handle the situation," Finn said.

Washington took a pose on the podium, leaning on the railing with both hands, and looked daggers down on the Pennsylvanians. "King George is not planning for world dominations, contrary to what the French may think, and he is not committed to destroying the French empire either. There have even been discussions on handing them back Quebec. In the grand scheme of things, we do not want to upset other European powers by being too successful in our endeavors. We have been victorious, and have gained more than our share as it is, more than we know what to do with. There is a chance that if we over-colonize, it might turn against us, as has happened to the Spaniards."

The approaching rioters jumped over the fence and destroyed many plants in a garden. The deputy scrambled up and ran away. Some rioters carried off public pumps while others tore down private lamp posts. Shouting men smashed windows and smeared business signs with tar. The mob stopped in front of the podium, but George Washington did not look concerned.

"We demand our rights!"

"We demand more land!"

"We want protection from illegal land claims!"

The shouts and demands from the crowd seemed to inspire Washington to make a grand, motivating speech. After a while, the mob began to agree with him, and eventually he managed to calm them down. In the end, the angry protestors applauded and cheered the proud man on the podium who graciously accepted the accolades.

Washington looked over the spectators in front of him and turned to the Virginians, smiling victoriously. "In this war against the petty French and their ruthless allies from the north, in which I play a most prominent part, I can guarantee you that no enemy, foreign or domestic, will be able to make claims to your land. And that pertains particularly to the Pennsylvanians."

The townspeople thought they had heard him wrong, but the rioters clapped and hailed him, and pushed the people to scatter in different directions. Once the crowd had dispersed, Finn saw how Washington met with the mob leader in the back and handed the man a small purse. The plan had worked, and a messenger was dispatched to deliver the story, the tale of Washington's spirited defense of Virginian's rights deep in Pennsylvania and how it spread among his future constituency.

Having finished his meager lunch, Finn shook his head. "Yeah, you're right, Fronto. I think I just learned something. All wannabe politicians are like cats in heat. I think we just witnessed a ritual of some sorts where both parties understood their place in it. We better move on, this place stinks," he commented.

The Rangers mounted their horses, and riding out of the town, they resumed their canter. As the evening fell, the camp was pitched by a small mountain stream near a grassy hillside. The saddles, packs, and cargo ropes were laid on the ground in orderly fashion, and horses and mules gathered together on the side of the hill by a Ranger, who sat perched on a rock above them, musket in hand. Finn was totally drained and hungry, and as they sat about the fire and talked, the stories that circulated about a campfire were more fun than real.

Finn stared at the flames, knowing that this march would stay in his memory for a long time, and his thoughts turned to Rosie. *Because of you I feel, because of you I see, because of you I hear and smell, because of you I dream.* He made a mental note to write her a new letter, soon.

As the warm glow of the fire seemed to possess a mysterious quality, it warmed Finn's confidence and he dozed off with a smile on his face. That night, however, sleeping rough deep in the forests on the Appalachian Mountains, Eros — tucked away in Finn's heart — cast a spell and thus the lonesome Ranger dreamed of Catherina instead.

§   §   §

General Forbes convened a council of war at his field headquarters and explained his plan to attack the French stronghold of Fort Duquesne. Forbes general staff represented a notable group of experienced and battle-hardened commanders.

General Saint Clair, the deputy quartermaster, was a veteran of Major General Edward Braddock's expedition. A man of quick temper and no tact, Saint Clair antagonized everyone.

Then there was the Swiss-born mercenary Henry Bouquet of the 60th Regiment of Foot, the Royal Americans, who served as his second-in-command. The man spoke in a thick German accent.

Bouquet listened closely as Forbes reviewed his plans to build a series of fortified camps behind them to protect the lines of communications. The last link was the site at Loyalhanna, only fifty miles from their ultimate objective at the junction of the Allegheny and Monongahela rivers. The base camps would also ensure a safe passage of return, should it become necessary. Furthermore, the mere presence of the camps was intended to make it clear to the enemy that his expedition was not just a foray, but a permanent conquest of territory.

Always so inventive, Bouquet had anticipated his General's assessment. "*Sehr gut*, I have already strengthened the western posts, Presque Isle, and Venango after we captured them from the French," he replied. "I was also successful in recruiting among the Germans of Pennsylvania, though I also, naturally, tangled with Quakers. I must remind you, sir, that Fort Ligonier is still under construction."

George Washington, fresh off the campaign trail, arrived to the meeting fifteen minutes late on purpose. As he entered the command tent, he nodded a friendly greeting to the officers, but then he noticed two Pennsylvanian officers among them and immediately the tent was filled with tension. He took a seat on the opposite side from the Pennsylvanians, the two parties exchanging icy stares across the table. The Pennsylvanians had already heard of Washington's little political trick as they called it, and they considered the Virginian to be no more than an upstart, craving for promotion and currying favors and recognition from the British. They were right, Washington was hedging his bets.

Forbes remained, or chose to remain, ignorant of hostilities between the provincials. "The number of hostile warriors encamped in the vicinity of Fort Duquesne is difficult to determine. The precise size of the French force is unclear," he said.

Saint Clair was worried. "Moreover, even if we take the fort, we're unsure of holding it throughout the winter. The supply lines will be long and uncertain," he said.

Henry Bouquet gave a nod to Forbes. "The risks being so obviously greater than the advantages, there is no doubt as to the sole course that prudence dictates."

Washington trailed the route on the map with his finger. "Nevertheless, General Forbes, you have to decide whether to advance on the French fortress or to settle into winter quarters," he said.

Forbes studied the maps in length. "Where there's a will, there's a way. Instead of using the old Nemacolin trail, we will take a shorter route, using only one easy passage of the Juniata," he finally said, pointing out strategic locations and ordering Washington and Bouquet to start their campaign.

Just as the Forbes Expedition was getting ready to embark for Fort Ligonier, the Rangers rode over the mountains with pack mules. As a colonel rode by them, Finn thought he recognized the man. He turned to a Pennsylvanian militia men standing close by.

"Who was the colonel? Have I seen him before?" he asked.

"That was Colonel Armstrong, the Hero of Kittanning," the man replied, lighting a pipe.

Finn did not recognize the name. "Why is he called the Hero of Kittanning?"

The guy made sure the pipe was lit before continuing. "Colonel Armstrong led us on a raid to capture Chief Jacoby, and we launched a surprise attack on the village near Kittanning. Jacoby set up a defense, holing up with his wife and kids inside their home. When he refused to surrender, his house and others were set on fire, touching off gunpowder that had been stored inside. Some buildings exploded, and pieces of bodies flew high into the air and landed in a nearby cornfield. Jacoby was killed and scalped after jumping from his home in an attempt to escape the flames," the man told him.

The Rangers were pressed into service immediately and were to serve as mounted scouts and a security force for the mission. They were excited for their new role as a light cavalry.

"Ride or die," Finn said, and urging his horse, he led the Rangers across a wide ravine to the flank of the main force.

Up the ascent of the mountains they toiled. They winded among trees and shrubs, scrambled up and down steep slopes, picked paths across fields of shattered rock and steadied their horses over the smooth surfaces of boulders. They climbed straight up hard places.

The air grew cold, and in a gorge, a cold wind blew briskly down to meet the warm air rising from the waters of the creek far below. That night they made camp, and the only place where Finn could lie down was on a broad, flat rock. They were now among the pines, which towered above them.

The advance was a cautious one and slow. The fall weather turned and soon constant rain was turning the touted Forbes Road into one long, narrow slough. Luckily for them, the mounted Rangers rode far ahead as forward scouts and provided security on the sides, riding on solid ground. Finn and Gus talked about the time they were part of the road building crew for the Braddock mission, not far away from their current location.

Washington called the Virginian officers for a meeting out of sight from the others. "We do not want Pennsylvania to open a new route into the Ohio territories that will provide both provinces a claim. It is in our own interests to repair the Braddock road that already gives us direct access to the Forks of the Ohio," he told them, whispering.

Forbes's troops struggled through the wilds of Pennsylvania, and lousy weather started taking its toll. Many troops became ill because they were poorly fed and they started deserting in alarming numbers.

At his command post, Forbes studied rough maps, or rough sketches of a few thick lines, drawn by the scouts on the high ridgelines. Provisions were difficult to deliver by means of the crude road cut through pristine forests and over the four wall-like ridges of the Alleghenies that lay between Ligonier and the supply base in Carlisle. In winter, they would be difficult to achieve, and he was worried for a good reason. He was aching and felt his stomach twitching, and he knew the disease was setting in, but decided to move on as an upstanding soldier to set the example for his troops.

The so-called road flooded repeatedly, its clay and rocky ground becoming impassable. Landslides blocked their passage, and torrents washed the road away where it traversed the mountain passes. Finn started to realize that cavalry was not suited to emergencies in such a situation.

Great numbers of wagons, bearing thousands of pounds of supplies, became stuck, or worse, mud slides propelling stumps and boulders destroyed them.

The Rangers continued to provide advanced security

and covered the flanks, sometimes operating miles from the main force. They discovered several small ambushes and quickly neutralized them. Most of the time, the enemy did not attack them but instead withdrew straight away when the Rangers appeared.

In one instance, however, the Rangers made a cavalry charge to flush out a bunch of Canadian militia and a band of Shawnee warriors from a group of weeping beech trees. The enemy opened fire at them and pulled out across a deep rocky gully to safety.

Only a couple of miles later, another enemy group fired on the Rangers and immediately ran for cover, but this time across relatively open terrain. Finn stopped the others from chasing the enemy. "Watch out, it's the oldest trick in the world. Don't let them lure us into ambuscade," Finn said.

Not being fed adequately, hundreds of soldiers became ill with lung and bowel infections. Many officers became bedridden for long periods of time, and Forbes himself became seriously ill. His sickness cast a shadow of doubt on the possibility for success on the campaign. He called for his aide.

"I'm a dying man," Forbes said. "My disease is turning into a bloody flux, and I suffer from more than one affliction," he said in a weak voice, slipping in and out of consciousness.

A few days later, Forbes was blinded by migraines, dehydrated, and barely able to walk at times. He found no rest, nor could he get out of bed. Soldiers, demoralized as they were by then, witnessed the sad spectacle of their commanding officer being carried along the road in a litter slung between two horses.

The Swiss soldier of fortune, Henry Bouquet remained the only able bodied officer. Hardly a soldierly figure, being plump and looking more like a clock smith, he kept up his cursing, and on several occasions whipped the poor soldiers, trying to keep them moving. "*Verdammte, Deine Mutter schwitzt beim Kacken!* The Pennsylvania Regiment is riddled by contentiousness, desertion, drunkenness, and other totally unprofessional behavior," he said.

Adding to the Forbes's troubles, the Virginians, led by Washington, actively conspired against his decision to open the new road. That included actions and attitudes beyond mere foot-dragging, even to the point of trying to get rid of the general himself.

Washington planned to take immediate action. "It's obvious he cannot lead the troops in action. I should take charge of this expedition, and then I could improve Virginia's interests in this matter," he said.

When Forbes discovered that Washington was engaged in an effort behind his back to have him declared unfit for command, he was furious. "Notwithstanding my anger, I see Washington's plot for what it is, a maneuver to advance Virginia's claim to the western territory and to prevent Pennsylvania from asserting its own."

The expedition slowly continued, like a constipated mule, their haphazard movement toward Fort Ligonier slow but still progressing. The long lines of wretched troops followed wagons pulled by oxen.

Finn, Gus, Fronto, and Daniel stopped on a ridge line by some cherry trees and magnolias to watch as the advance continued along the muddy tracks the officers insisted calling a road. It was a sad spectacle, and the Rangers sentiments were even sadder. After two victories, it was becoming apparent that the British could not take advantage of the situation. Instead, slowly but surely, the war effort was getting bogged down again in a disorder in the western Pennsylvania wilderness. "I'm afraid that we're fucking never going to win this war, not like this," Finn said, disappointedly voicing everybody's thoughts.

§   §   §

Tribulations and squabbles, one after another, began causing serious carelessness. Eager to get to their destination, the provincials advanced without forward scouts. Consequently, Washington's Virginians ran smack into groups of the French lurking around Fort Ligonier, sent to provoke the British and cause all sorts of damage by hitting targets of opportunity. The provincials took some unnecessary casualties, but the enemy again refused to fight them at length and withdrew quickly.

Forbes was getting to be distraught after receiving messengers from his superiors. "We have been charged with the destruction of Fort Duquesne. Yet here I am begging the indigent Assemblies of both Pennsylvania and Maryland to fund the campaign with monies they are so reluctant to give," he said with lament.

As troubles mounted, Henry Bouquet seemed to be in his element. "Sir, we now have five thousand provincials from the two colonies, plus Virginia and North Carolina. I have personally trained them for flexibility and open-order combat maneuvering. We will not repeat Braddock's

mistakes this time," he reported, still confident and determined.

Hardly hearing the news, Forbes suffered a severe attack, coughing and spitting blood. His aide wiped his forehead with a wet towel.

"I have managed to beat one thousand obstacles to
build an army around the Royal Americans. But the provincials must stop quarreling among themselves. Neither
will I take the tardiness of my regulars any longer. Not this
far into the campaign. If that is not enough, the artillery
train is late in arriving. Who needs an enemy with allies like
that?" Forbes said.

Washington counted his war chest and estimated the
number of native allies remaining with the British. "Many
of our allies, Cherokees and Catawba, have drifted away.
The auxiliaries are extra-sensitive and easily offended. I
particularly hate Cherokees being too greedy, and every
service of theirs has to be purchased."

Forbes gave a weak smile. "For once, we can agree
on something, Washington. I tried to meet the demands
of Chief Little Carpenter, but I must admit I did so with
contempt, too, for they are a degenerate and avaricious lot
indeed," he said. He then had a particularly severe bout of
diarrhea, filling the tent with stench. The aides rushed to
help him, opening the tent flaps for ventilation.

After having changed clothes, Forbes seemed to feel
slightly better. "Don't get me wrong, sir," he said, turning
to Bouquet. "I'm still extremely determined to carve an entirely new way through the wilderness to the Ohio's forks.
Major Grant has done a good job in fulfilling my orders
and has actively sought the support of locals. However, you

must be credited for your understanding and patience with the road builders for the ultimate success of our campaign, dear Bouquet."

Washington could not understand what he had just heard. "This is catastrophe. Due to the lack of regimental clothing, I decided to fit out my command in the light warrior hunting gear," he said. "It's hardly fit for professional soldiers but it's the only thing we have left. This outfit is ruined. We don't even have a proper band to play marching tunes for us to improve the spirits. Major Bouquet, your advocacy for this new route cannot be understood."

The advance continued sluggishly in the pouring rain, but after what seemed to be an eternity, they finally arrived in Fort Ligonier. Seeing the fort, it was clear to the Rangers that Bouquet had been rather optimistic about its condition. The fort was hardly more than some logs and earthworks with only a few cannon barrels showing along the palisades made of poles and sticks. The raggedy flag in the center dangled wet and limp. The commanding officer of the fort, Colonel Burd, hollow-eyed and unshaven in his soiled uniform, was waiting for them at the gate.

Forbes was carried through the gate on a pole stretcher. "What is the situation, colonel?" he said to Burd, his voice barely audible.

Burd's voice was shaking as he replied. "Sir, the French have sent a small force forward in an attempt to draw some of my men into an ambush. The ruse did not succeed, and I have repulsed several attacks on the fort."

After attacking the fort a day earlier, the French and Shawnees had remained near the fort through the night, sniping at sentries and probing the defenses. Upon hearing of the approaching British and provincial reinforcements, they apparently withdrew back to Fort Duquesne. The British were all optimistic, but they were sorely mistaken once again, as well.

Taking command of the fort, Forbes and Bouquet urgently required substantial facts. "We need better insight concerning the exact distance to the enemy fort, the extent and condition of its fortifications, the morale of its garrison, and the number of Shawnees and Delawareans encamped about the stockade. How about using the Rangers where we want those most?" Bouquet said.

"I will have none of that, Bouquet! Major Grant, you shall take two battalions and conduct a reconnaissance mission to Fort Duquesne and report to me what you see," Forbes said. "We shall then make our final plans. You may proceed with your mission, Major."

"Yes, sir, right away." Major Grant's eyes lit up as he left to prepare for his recon mission to Fort Duquesne. Excited, he waved for his subordinate officers.

Forbes addressed Washington. "Listen, you will take your Virginians and recon the area around the fort here to make sure that the enemy can no more harass us while we're here. Colonel Mercer, you shall take the 2nd Virginians and follow the opposite route around the fort to do the same."

Washington's unit moved out of the fort in decent order, with the drummers in front, into the surrounding woods, but without any forward scouts. Colonel Mercer's company followed, and once outside the gate turned the other way. Washington's company had moved only a couple of miles when, to his utter shock, they were ambushed by several companies of French troops and bands of warriors, still lurking around Fort Ligonier.

Washington drew his sword, and trying to stay calm, commanded his troops. "Men, stand your ground. Do what you have been trained to do."

The Virginians responded swiftly, and the men let out all their frustrations, launching an attack recklessly over open ground, killing one enemy and taking three prisoners. One of the wounded men on the ground jumped up suddenly with his hands high in the air.

"Don't shoot! I surrender! I'm an Englishman!" he shouted, desperately waving his arms. "I was taken from my home in Lancaster County by the hostiles."

The Virginians severely beat the guy up, just in case he was lying, and dragged him to the fort. His information concerning the poor state of Fort Duquesne was corroborated by one of the French prisoners, beaten and bruised as well, who had been interrogated.

The always unpredictable weather turned as Washington led his inexperienced Virginian unit across the woods. A thick fog descended on them like a blanket of white cotton candy. "Stay strong. The enemy is close. When you see him, you can fire at will," Washington said and motioned the advance to continue.

The soldier walking point, wide-eyed and sweating profusely, nervously grabbed his musket with the attached bayonet, slicing and piercing the fog, which was as thick as pea soup. He froze in horror as he saw flickering movement in the fog. "Enemy is upon us! Fire!" He shouted.

Heavy firing erupted all along the marching formation. Troops fired wildly into the fog, at the muzzle flashes and at anything that moved. A screaming assault came with bayonets appearing from the fog, thrusting and piercing bodies. Men were killed by head shots and maimed in close-quarter fighting. In a blind, murderous rage, men fought each other with bayonets, knives, and axes, severing heads and hands, and smashing skulls with tomahawks. A soldier was knocked down, and Washington heard his ribs crack as another soldier dropped his weight onto a knee, caving in the chest.

Looking down from his horse, Washington realized that all soldiers wore blue uniforms. Shocked, he shouted stop shooting repeatedly, but none of the panicked troops heard him, and the butchering continued. He wavered, not knowing what to do as an increasing number of troops fell down dead. Finally, he collected his courage and rode in the middle of the two formations and struck muskets up with his sword.

"Cease fire! Cease fire!" He shouted and firing ceased. Wind blew the fog away and revealed two devastated Virginian units facing each other at close range. The men killed in fighting, many of them dismembered and decapitated, lay in between them in bloody heaps.

§   §   §

Major Grant, his head held high and an unwavering expression on his face, marched from Fort Ligonier at the head of his troops and headed west to Fort Duquesne. He was eagerly seeking the fame and glory of a quick victory, just like that of the heroic Bradstreet that he secretly admired. Taking initiative, he decided to try capturing the enemy's stronghold on his own. Instead of strictly following his orders to lead the operation stealthily, Grant decided to run the reconnaissance in force, and to deceive the enemy, he split his force in two.

"In one bold move, fame and fortune shall be mine." Grant was excited of his daring plan and said, "Listen up. Let's keep it simple. We shall split in two, and while the First battalion approaches the fort to lure the enemy out, the Second battalion will attack their flank and wipe them out."

Grant's First Battalion approached within sight of Fort Duquesne and baited the French by literally beating their drums. However, Grant had seriously underestimated the enemy's ability, and his meticulous intent to lure out and ambush the fort's defenders went badly awry. By his own design, he had decided to jump from the frying pan directly into the fire.

Fort Duquesne's commander, the experienced Captain Lignery, was running low on supplies because his supply chain had been cut by the British capture of Fort Frontenac. Nevertheless, the captain was not going give up his position without a fight, and he well knew the weak points in the English tactics.

The Abenaki scouts, led by Colonel Louis, arrived to tell Lignery of the approaching British forces. "It's a trick, and a lousy one. There are two battalions of English. The first one we see and hear is only bait," he said.

Lignery, being keenly aware of the lack of supplies in the fort, but not lacking a cunning resourcefulness of his own, was certain that the English did not know about it, and he made a quick plan. "Fools come marching with drums. *D'accord*, we shall oblige. We can sure use their supplies," he said.

Lignery decided to set a trap for Grant. He ordered some of the troops out front to appear to get ready to follow the English out to the battlefield as Grant had hoped. The trick was that in the back of the fort, out of sight, the French quickly made an exit hole in the palisade and a large war party of warriors exited the fort. They circled around in tall grass to wait for the unsuspecting second battalion.

The French plan worked perfectly, and when the British first sighted enemy soldiers, it was all too late. The combined attack force of the French and the Abenaki surprise bayonet charge from the tall grass at close range on Grant's second battalion was more than enough to secure victory.

The British troops were thrown into panic and confusion at the attack. They were surrounded as raging French and screaming warriors descended upon them from all sides. Men tried to seek refuge in shallow holes and were run through and hacked to pieces in place.

Some distance ahead, the first battalion, acting as the bait, attempted to turn around to support the second. The French had anticipated this and launched a vicious attack on their rear. From that point on, the British were at the mercy of their attackers. Grant was captured, caught trying to dig into a badger hole in the ground and cover himself with some straws and grass. More than half his men, the lucky ones, were killed. For the other half, the anguish was only beginning.

The surviving remnants of the British withdrew in chaos and panic. Men ran wildly into the woods, and Colonel

Louis' warriors chased and killed them with tomahawks and knives. Screaming prisoners were dragged out from the woods and bound on stakes along the road to the fort.

In hindsight, it appeared that it was this particular moment in time that Lady Fortuna changed her mind on a whim. Perhaps she was bored.

Nevertheless, inside the fort, the defending garrison was actually far worse off than the attacking British. The French were disappointed when they found out that the British were not carrying many rations on them, and their Delaware and Shawnee allies started leaving, which drastically reduced the garrison. Provisions had run out days before, and now the French had nothing left to eat but their horses. Furthermore, Captain Lignery realized that the formations they had just destroyed were only the advance unit. The main English forces had yet to come and the minute they did arrive, he would have no defenses left.

In the grand scheme of things, Lignery had no way of knowing it, but the French had lost the diplomatic war being waged to secure and maintain the native support. General Forbes's behind-the-scenes maneuvering with the Philadelphia Quakers had obtained the key Treaty of Easton and the Moravian minister John Burnside had secretly negotiated for some time with the tribes virtually within the shadow of Fort Duquesne. Warriors listened to his promises of gifts and peace and prosperity for all, and then accepted his proposal. In the end, formerly hostile Delawares and Shawnees agreed to entrust the British and make peace with them and returned to their homes. Warriors picked up their weapons and departed the battlefield in small groups.

Having lost most of their allies who were crucial to any hopes of success, the French decided to abandon the fort and destroy it altogether. Nothing was to be left to the hated English. A huge explosion shook the ground for miles and echoed through the surrounding countryside as logs and earthwork were thrown high in the air. The fort was successfully demolished to matchsticks.

The Rangers arrived on the battlefield just in time to take part in the final advance to the fort but too late to assist in the fighting. They advanced along the trail, the thick smell of burned flesh permeating the air, where they discovered the corpses of those killed at Major Grant's disastrous last stand. From the smoke, a road appeared in front of them, lined by stakes with tortured bodies, scalped with bloody heads and intestines lying on the ground at their feet.

Arriving at the camp, still feeling nauseated from the bitter stench of blood and guts, Finn dismounted and took a swig of whiskey to wash out the bad taste. He walked stiffly, holding his back. "Man, my ass is sore. Screw this cavalry shit. I'd rather be on foot."

The British troops, who earlier had perceived themselves as being defeated, just below the height of their goal, now experienced joy that admitted virtually no limits. They had suffered, but they persevered and were rewarded, as if by the gift of grace.

§   §   §

The following day, a messenger brought new orders that the Rangers were to return to Fort Edward immediately.

They packed their bags and loaded the mules again and started the long journey back home. Finn was pleased to see that he actually thought of it as home — something he had not thought of for a long time. After losing his family and seeing his home village destroyed, he had been convinced that he would never be able to get attached to any place in the world again.

Finn's horse grunted in its efforts and drew its breath in a long and labored blowing. The chug, chug, chug of his tired horse as they marched along became wearisome, and he felt as though he were not doing anything unusual in puffing and blowing himself. Finn started wondering if it would be possible for a rider to get hitched in his saddle, but then he reminded himself that he must handle the horse at all times and not just lounge on his back.

The Rangers were all exhausted from the long ride, and they did not talk much. Each man withdrew to his own thoughts, yet all eyes kept a sharp lookout around the terrain they were passing through. Finn thought of Rosie, but he imagined arriving back to the fort and Catherina waiting for him at the gate. His unquiet mind kept going between the two women. He figured that the reason he could not focus his thoughts on anything was because he was so tired and worn out.

They cut downward among the masses of rock for some time when they suddenly found themselves on a shelf of rock, overlooking the Hudson River Valley. They sought to avoid a steep gorge by going up and around, but after tedious progress, they were still confronted by a drop of about a hundred feet. The upper half of the trail gave Finn the willies, and he felt the pressure build, thinking the horse might try to buck him off. Going down the steep switchbacks was not an opportune time to get a fear of heights, and Finn let out a sigh in relief as the trail became wider and smoother, and then it leveled out onto the valley floor.

Arriving in a road junction under a towering oak that would take them to Fort Edward, Finn remembered an invitation he had received and after giving it a thought, he decided to go see John Morton. He would catch up with the others later, and let them move past him.

"You just go on, tell Major Rogers that I'm going to take a little furlough," Finn said and headed the other way.

It was a warm day, and Finn took off his green jacket. He remembered all too well the ambush Johan Kopf had set up earlier, and figured that, in his chemise shirt, which had been white but now was grayish brown, and a wide-brimmed hat, he would be sufficiently disguised from a distance.

Finn followed the well-traveled road, seeking safety also from being close to other travelers. The road followed the Christina River, and at the confluence of Brandywine Creek he stopped to get his bearings on a knoll.

In the distance, he noticed a farmhouse with a country porch surrounded by a perennial garden on seventy acres of land. Approaching the house, he saw a three stall stables with tack room attached to a large two-story barn bordering a fenced field. Across the fields, there was a small log cabin under a group of Bald Cypress trees by a trout pond with a swarm of dragonflies skimming the surface.

John Morton, smoking a pipe, met him on the front porch. "It's so nice to see you, Finn. Good to see you're fine," he said, welcoming his guest.

"Good to be here. Thank you for having me, sir." Finn dismounted and tied the horse to a pole by the stables.

"I have invited some guests for a nice little fowling day out. You will join us, I hope," Morton said.

"Sure thing, sir, I'd be glad to help any way I can," Finn replied, already feeling the strain easing up on his shoulders and back.

Morton had invited some government officials and political leaders from the neighboring provinces to go on a pheasant hunt, with Samuel Adams, Benjamin Franklin, and George Washington among them.

Farm hands carried supplies to the log cabin as the guests walked leisurely behind. Finn did not feel comfortable staying with the gentlemen who were discussing politics and such, and he preferred to work to make a slatted fire in front of a large lean-to by the water's edge with the farm hands. Morton noticed his protégé's rather low mood, and as he was a fair judge of character, he knew it was caused by the young man's recent experiences on the frontier. He considered it an extremely telling sign that Finn did not shy away from people, although he remained a little aloof.

The hired hands placed some rocks in a circle and built a smaller cooking fire next to it. The men hung heavy cloaks, gear, and their fowling pieces on the protruding poles. A plank placed on top of two rocks served as a table. Food and supplies were brought in sacks and wooden boxes while tin cups and plates were put out.

A cook prepared bacon strips on a frying pan and a kettle of stew simmered, hanging from the tip of a long pole on top of the fire. Bird dogs lay close by waiting, sniffing the smells from the cooking fire. The gentlemen poured whiskey in cups and filled their pipes, talking shop and exchanging humorous anecdotes.

John Morton nudged Finn's arm and pointed at one of the dogs, a brownish shaggy female. "That's my Bessie, one of the best bird dogs in these parts," he said.

Around the fire, the men discussed the role of indentured servants. There was a comparison between European servants and African slaves, and there was a consensus that both kinds of laborers were needed in order to build the provinces.

"Pity it is that thousands of people should be starving at home, when they may live here in peace and plenty as a great many who have been transported for a punishment have found pleasure, profit, and ease and would rather undergo any hardship than be forced back on their own country," Washington said.

"Perhaps so," Morton replied. "But the courts in England have exported scores of petty criminals to America. Forced servitude in the New World is used as a punishment in the Old World. Out of sight, out of mind, I suppose."

"I visited the southern islands with my brother some time ago, and as an example, Saint-Dominguez, producer of forty percent of the world's sugar, is the most profitable colony the French own. In fact, it is the wealthiest and most flourishing of the slave colonies in the Caribbean," Washington said.

"Gangs of runaway slaves known as maroons live in the woods away from control," Adams said. "They often conduct violent raids on the island's sugar and coffee plantations. The success of these attacks establishes a black, martial practice of violence and brutality to achieve political ends."

"The first court case, M-Montgomery versus Shedding to challenge the legality of slavery took place in Scotland two years ago," Franklin said, taking a long swig from his flask.

"I have heard that a voodoo priest by the name of Francois Mackinder has succeeded in unifying the black resistance," Morton said. "He inspired his people by drawing on African traditions and religions. He was able to join the bands and also established a network of secret groups among plantation slaves, leading a rebellion from 1751 through 1757. Later he was captured by the French and burned at the stake."

Although staying at a distance, Finn was listening, and he actually enjoyed the ebb and flow of the conversation. The men considered various possibilities, and someone mentioned a resolution for the gradual abolition of slavery. The others did not comment.

A game warden in ordinary clothes and a silver badge on a chain around his neck arrived. Finn noticed a limp in his stride and some scars on his face. "Gentlemen, everything is ready. Lock and load your pieces," the game warden said and ordered the servants ahead to spread out to flush out birds. Servants formed a loose line and moved ahead. Men picked up their flintlock fowlers and followed in small groups into the woods.

As fall advanced, the cascading waters of river falls crystallized in rainbow hues of ice, creating a kaleidoscope of brilliant blues, greens, and pinks. The rolling falls, which sent water down a vertical drop, never quite stopped flow-ing, and ice etched the walls behind the falls into sparkling caverns. The valley floor varied with sheer coulees climbing to the grasslands above.

The men stopped to get a drink from their flasks and enjoyed the scenery. "There's a lot of space here and not a whole lot of neighbors," Adams said, admiring the surroundings.

There was a little open grassland coming to the base of the bluffs and coulees that looked down on the river valley. Red willows lined the banks of the river with occasional gaps. The tall grasses ran into sections of solid, prickly, young trees.

"There's nothing like the thrill of a rooster pheasant flushing from underfoot on a chilly fall morning," Morton said, excited. The weather was getting colder, and the sun only showed itself toward the end of the day.

"Fortunately there's no rain," Morton continued.

"The wind is blowing quite a bit and makes for some bitter cold if we're on the wrong side of the hill," Finn said.

"Then we had better stay on the less windy side," Morton said.

Bessie got into pheasants and chased them around, and the men hunted up a hill, Finn taking point almost by instinct. He flushed out more pheasants that ran out of the brush. Washington raised his fowling piece and fired at the flock, hitting one of them. Bessie rushed out in a blurry brown rush to get it.

As they rounded a corner of a hill, Bessie pointed a fairly large sized covey of pheasants and ran ahead. A covey of about fifteen pheasants burst out from the side of the hill. The men watched where they went and headed straight for them, fowlers at the ready.

The men walked along the hillside in a line and finally found the birds. A volley of fowler blasts met a pheasant coming out running up a hedgerow, but none of them hit the fast bird which was dodging and zigzagging in the brush. Franklin reloaded, and taking calm aim, shot at it and when the bird hit the ground, he began a victory dance. To everyone's great surprise, all of a sudden the bird jumped up and took off again.

"Unfortunately, your victory dance was a little premature!" Morton laughed just as the pheasants flew out. A barrage of fowler blasts echoed all over the place and finally men headed back to the campsite in high spirits, laughing.

"Finn, you should take some of these birds back with you," Morton said. "But before you go, I want to show you something."

That evening, Finn enjoyed the first warm, home-cooked meal he'd had in a long time. Not able to restrain himself to proper manners, he wolfed down sweet potatoes and roasted pheasants, washing them down with cold, hard cider. He was stuffed, and Morton poured him some 18-year-old whiskey into an enamel mug for an after dinner drink. Taking a sip, he felt the warm relaxation spreading through his muscles, and in no time, he was out like a candle.

Finn had horrible nightmares, tossing and turning in sweat in his bunk. *He was in his home village again, and it was burning. He saw his mother Missis Marianne walking there among the burning and killing, and he shivered. The shadowy figures were right behind her — stalking her with shining, bloodthirsty blades in their hands. He heard a cry of triumphant shouts from the executioners as his friends Evert, Canut, and Brobus were all sucked into in a swirl of shining blades swinging wildly. Bayonets and lances thrust through bodies, piercing vital organs. Bloody froth spewed from dying mouths.*

Totenkopf's sinister snicker echoed, "You led me to your village, you little faggot! Look, winner takes it all!" His voice rose to an evil, laughing crescendo as he raped Finn's mother.

Finn screamed in terror and desperation, "Mother, I didn't do it!" He was running, but his body wasn't moving and his legs weighed him down like lead. Johan Kopf paddled up behind him. Blood and tissue rained on him from the carnage, and he felt an unbearable, crushing guilt, and just then he spun out from the foggy abyss in terror, sweating profusely and breathing heavy in the darkness, tears running down his face, shouting, "Mom, forgive me!"

His mother's beautiful face appeared, smiling tenderly, and he felt her gentle touch on his cheek, calming him down. "It's alright, my dear. It's alright. You're in capable hands. Now find Columbia," she said and her face faded away.

Finn snapped out of sleep, startled and confused, not knowing where he was at first. Then he realized he was in a warm bed with crisp white linen in a quiet house and saw his clothes washed and folded on a chair next to him, and he remembered he was in Morton's guest room. After getting up, he ventured into the kitchen were Ann told him that he had slept eighteen hours straight.

§   §   §

Two days later, Finn rode back toward Fort Edward, holding a musket ready in front of him in the saddle and keeping a sharp lookout for any potential ambush sites. Ann Morton had packed full saddles bags for him, and John had slung four pheasants on top of them. He wore his green Ranger coat and caubeen after having sworn to himself that he would never take them off again under any circumstances. If Totenkopf wanted to surprise him and his shot found its mark, so be it. At least he would die proudly wearing his uniform.

On the road, Finn stopped to eat under a giant beech tree, and he watched as a farmer was walking a flock of turkeys to a trading post near. He had covered the birds' feet with little booties to protect them on the long journey to the market. It started to rain, and Finn took shelter under the tree while waiting for it to stop. He leaned against the trunk, gazing in the horizon and thinking of the past two days at the Morton's house.

John Morton had led him to the library and pointed out a painting on the wall. It was a portrait of a man dressed in a brown brocade jacket, a white ruff collar, a wig and a hat, and there was a copper plate with a name Martti Marttinen on it. Finn was startled to look at the picture because he felt like he was looking in a mirror.

"Where are you from, Finn?" Morton had asked him.

"It's — or was — a small village called Rautalammi. But it's all gone now," Finn had replied.

"That place is mentioned in my family records as well, and I remember my father and grandfather talking about it," Morton had told him.

"My father was killed in a war, somewhere, sometime, but I don't know," Finn had replied, hesitantly.

"Nevertheless, I have every reason to believe we share bloodlines, Finn."

Finn had just stood there, his mind racing back and forth, not knowing what to say.

John Morton had then continued, "Therefore, I have decided to adopt you, and Ann has given her blessing. If you wish, that is. You're a grown man who can take care of himself, but you do need a protector and a supporter if you will, Finn, and that way you will be able to take my name."

The rain stopped, and Finn continued his ride north on the road, following the Hudson River. He kept thinking about John Morton's words and kept silently repeating the name. "Finn Morton. Morton, Finn Morton. Finn... Morton. Mr. Morton." He felt pretty pleased about it, although it still sounded so peculiar and somewhat strange to be his own. The images of his nightmare also kept interrupting his thoughts, and his mother's words made him feel especially uncomfortable. After all, he thought that finding a new home had been the meaning of her last words to him. But now, he was not sure what to think.

Riding through Albany, passing the *Stadt Huys*, city hall, and cutting through an alley, he ignored the whores who were flaunting their services at bargain prices, and he did not pay any attention to the sound of a whip coming from an open window on the second floor of the building he was passing. Without realizing it, Finn rode right under Johan Kopf's window, but Kopf was tied up in a drug-induced grogginess, engaging in perversions with two women involving whips, monogloves, and hogties. One woman was in agonizing strappado bondage and another woman was chained to a Saint Andrew's cross.

Finn kept thinking about Rosie, and the prospects of his returning to England seemed to be nil. He just could not figure out how it would be possible. His best option was to accept his fate and make the most of the current situation. Finally, reaching Fort Edward and exhausted from constant vigilance, Finn wiped his forehead as he rode through the main gate, putting his musket back in the scabbard. He could hardly wait to see Catherina again.

In the fort, a day was set aside for prayers and celebrations in honor of the recent military victories. Finn returned the horse to the stables and took the saddle off, and started to wipe the horse clean with a pack of straw.

Gus and Fronto came to see him. "It's about time you got back," Fronto said and patted Finn on the shoulders.

Gus noticed the pheasants Finn had slung over the corral fence. "Nice birds. How was your furlough?" he asked.

Fronto grinned. "Good to have you back in one piece, lad. I was starting to feel lonely around here. There is going to be a party in town today. This is the first time in ages there's been plenty of food, and a beer. And a whiskey," he said, laughing with gusto.

The festivities started with a sermon, which was held in the half-finished new church. The latest newcomer in town, Adal Mauser, marched through the fort in his black coat, throwing scornful glances at the festival preparations, and headed straight to the front row and sat down. Based on his observations, this town sorely needed a firm hand to take the wayward flock on the path to righteousness. Across the aisle, Mayor Glock and Judge Lynch greeted the newcomer with a gentlemanly nod from their seats. They exchanged glances with each other — who was this man, a friend or foe?

The Rogers brothers, Israel Putnam, and the Stark brothers marched in, sitting right behind the business leaders. Dugald Campbell with his brother and officers from the Black Watch came in, followed by Harold Ferrara taking off his bonnet. Just as the townspeople started filing in, Sheriff Jimmie Dick pushed through and slumped on a bench, leaving the shaken, old ladies fanning their faces from his boozy breath and demeanor. Then some Rangers pushed the ladies aside, and militia and British regulars filled the wall sides.

Standing behind a column in the shadows, solemn Doctor Barrett had noticed the tall man in black in the front row, considered the stranger a competitor, and made a mental note to find out more about him as he stepped forward toward the pulpit. "Ask of me, and I shall give thee, the heathen for inheritance, and the uttermost parts of the earth for thy possession," he said, his finger held high and clutching the bible firmly under his arm.

Outside, long tables were set up on the square in front of the new church. Helen of Magdalena set up a small booth and had one of her girls there to promote her services and guide customers to her camp, right outside the gates. The Sheriff had not allowed her to bring the camp inside the fort. Once again, she had refused to pay for a license that would guarantee "insurance against vandalism."

The Jewish shopkeepers, the Hellman brothers, did pay for the insurance, and set up a booth outside their store to sell kosher venison.

Finn, Gus, and Fronto followed two little boys chasing

quacking ducks through the crowds. They met Catherina who was getting ready to make roast marinated pigeon breasts with sweet butternut squash on a grill iron skillet. Her falcon had had a remarkably successful hunting day earlier. Finn tossed the pheasants on the table triumphantly. "Here you go."

Catherina was pleasantly surprised to see Finn. "Very gratifying, thanks. And nice to see you, too," she said and blushed as he smiled back at her. His smile could be so penetrating and vulgar — and so exciting.

All around the fort, food was prepared in clay pots and iron kettles over hot coals and preserved by smoking, salt curing, and pickling. Venison, turkey and other game roasted over an open fire, while stews of corn, beans, and squash cooked in clay pots. The butcher processed a whole pig into hams and bacon, and the meat was preserved with salt.

Finn fanned the smoke with his hand to smell the roasting meals just as Daniel and Shelagh arrived with a large group of Wappinger. The women brought with them corn, beans, squash, barley, and wheat that they offered to the townspeople. Catherina invited Daniel and Shelagh to meet them, and soon the table was filled with food.

A little off to the side, a group of bachelor soldiers and orphans had set up their own cooking fire, turning meager rations of dried beans, salted meat and hard bread into soups and stews.

The sermon was over, and the people were coming out of the church, and the band started to play. It consisted of an expedient array of instruments that happened to be available, flute and clarinet players, a sackbut, mandolin and guitar players, and a fiddler. In the town square, people started an English country dance, lining up and facing each other.

Shelagh got tired quickly and was going to retire early, but she insisted that Daniel stay with his friends. Besides, she wanted to be by herself at home for a little while.

"I hear that. It's nice to enjoy some peace and quiet now and then," Finn said.

"Yeah, right, look who's talking?" said Gus.

Music, dancing, happy gabble, and a plethora of lingering food smells filled the fort square. At least for a day, the people were able to drive any haunting fears aside about the war and survival. Important victories had been achieved, and certainly the horrors should come to an end soon. There would be no more bedeviling uncertainty of what had happened to husbands and sons out there somewhere in the frontier and what seemed to be a constant stream of dead, young soldiers would stop finally.

As the party went on, it was Finn who got the idea first. He winked at Fronto, who nodded in response. They grabbed Gus by the elbows, and motioning Daniel to follow them, the four of them headed toward the Silver Star, laughing and jesting.

"Behave, all of you," Catherina shouted after them.

Fronto turned and bowed to her. "Like we do always, gentlemen as we are."

"Yeah right," she replied rolling her eyes, and waved her arm, dismissing them.

As the afternoon turned toward evening, more and more men started drifting toward the Silver Star. There was a group of Highlanders from the Black Watch regiment leading the way, but the Rangers were not far behind.

Selous Claymore marched through the gates in front of his loggers, their sleeves rolled up and eager to join the party after a week of hard work. A few of them took along Helen's women under their arms, giggling and teasing as they passed her camp.

In the tavern, officer brothers John and Dugald Campbell from the Black Watch had already gotten sufficiently drunk so as to be highly affectionate and patriotic. Fronto winked at a barmaid and raising his tankard in a toast started to sing. "From the parlor of the inn, a pleasant murmur smote the ear, the music of a violin."

§   §   §

In the Silver Star, the usual crowd shuffled in, Rangers in green and rawhide, hunters and trappers in furs, Highlanders in their kilts occasionally flashing a bit too much, loggers, whores, Mohawks in a motley assortment of outfits and proudly wearing war paint on their faces, a few British regulars in red and militia in blue, all tippling, toasting, sipping, slurping, quaffing, and guzzling in perfect harmony. Many had started the day with a pick-me-up and now intended to finish it with a put-me-down. Alongside the liquefied mileposts, they had enjoyed a midmorning whistle wetter, a luncheon libation, an afternoon accompaniment, and a dinner snort. The bar was a place where muskets, tomahawks, cutlasses, axes, daggers, pistols and other grim tools of the frontier trade courteously made room for beer tankards, whiskey, hard cider, rum, and Madeira fortified with brandy. Elbows were rubbed while veiled in a dense tobacco smoke.

In the corner, a bony, senior man with blackened teeth pounded away on the harpsichord out of tune, striking tempo as the people got addled, afflicted, biggy, boozy, busky, buzzey, cherubimical, cracked, and halfway to Concord as Ben Franklin so eloquently jotted down later for posterity in the corner table while Samuel Adams gave a slurred, yet fervent, lecture on the horrors of approaching British taxation.

The Dugald brothers, both sitting one leg over the other and so obviously free-balling, were lamenting the misfortunes of their country occasioned by her enormous debt that they could not pay Mary Brant who demanded payment.

"Cough it up. I'm not impressed you men going regimental like that although I must admit you're both well-endowed. I don't care how poor you are or the state of your finances. In King, we trust. All others pay cash."

Robert Rogers came in and learned the basis of their trouble. "What seems to be the problem here?"

Brant folded her arms. "These fine two gentlemen have been drinking all day and all night and now they claim to be as poor as a rat in church."

Rogers turned to the drunken Scots who tried to focus on him. Dugald Campbell turned his empty tankard upside down on the table. "Kingdom for a pint of your finest brew," he slurred.

"Gentlemen, give no more uneasiness about the matter, as I will pay half of the debt," Rogers said and took a wallet out of his jacket and slapped Finn on the shoulders.

"And a trusted man of mine will pay the remainder, and thus clear the nation at once of her difficulties!"

The Campbell's treated Rogers to a drink and pronounced him the nation's benefactor. "One should always pay one's debts as Rogers did that of the nation," they said loudly and ordered another round.

A group of loggers decided to take their whores outside in an alley for a group quickie, and as they left, Finn quickly claimed the round table. Gus, Fronto, and Daniel swiftly joined him, staggering from the bar with glasses in both hands. In defiance of the townspeople and their norms — decent, proper and law abiding women were not supposed to be seen in saloons — Catherina marched in and joined them at the table. The noise was getting louder, and the men had to bend over the table, tankards in their hands, and shout to be heard.

Finn started telling them what had happened in John Morton's house during his short furlough. He had to repeat almost every other word because the tavern was so loud and the others were hard of hearing after copious amounts of drinks. Besides, being in the same condition, Finn got mixed up telling his story and had to start again more than once.

Nobody at the table noticed as the saloon doors opened and a gorgeous woman in a tight-fitting green riding dress walked in. She wore a black felt riding hat with purple ostrich feathers over her long, red hair and had a chained corset in front. The veil she wore did not hide her bee-stung, full lips and high red cheekbones. Men gawked at her beauty as she walked through the lounge looking for someone.

The woman stopped behind Finn, who was unaware of her presence. Others stopped talking and looked up at her, curiously. She took off her gloves. "Finn my darling, I finally found you. I have been searching for you all over the provinces," Rosie said, smiling, and lifted her veil.

Recognizing her voice, Finn was taken totally by surprise. He jumped up, knocking down his chair and spun around to face her. First, he just stood there, staring at Rosie as memories flashed through his mind.

His eyes wide, Finn looked at her and tried to find words. "Rosie! What are you doing here? Where, what... I can...," He stuttered. The memories of meeting Rosie in London and their time together living in Bristol and how the pressgang had bounced on him flashed through his mind. Then he came to the shocking realization that after arriving in America, somewhere along the line, he had given up his wows to work hard and get just enough money to pay his way back to Rosie. He felt a nasty tasting lump of regret in his throat, and he swallowed hard as his eyes became wet.

"My, my, our lives just got very interesting," Fronto grinned.

Catherina stood up, regarded Rosie from head to toe, and put her hands on her hips as she gave Finn an inquiring look. Catherina felt a surge of jealousy, something she was completely unfamiliar with, and it angered her.

Finn stood between Catherina and Rosie, his head snapping back and forth between them. He felt dizzy and held his head.

"Well, why don't you introduce us to your old friend, Finn?" Catherina said, folding her arms.

"But, but, but this is Rosie! I thought I would never see you again," he said.

"Really, is that so?" Catherina said, probing.

"But how can this be? How did you get here, Rosie?" Finn asked.

Rosie gently touched his chin with her fingertip. "When you didn't come back, I went out to look for you and was told what had happened," Rosie replied. "But in the port, I found out that there was no *Hope*. So I decided to come searching for you and made a contract to pay for my ticket."

Rosie pulled out a rolled piece of paper and showed them her contract as an indentured servant. She had been ordered to report to General Johnson's estate.

Now it was Catherina's turn to be stunned. "I'm truly impressed, Finn. This woman sold herself into slavery because you dumped her?" she said, dumbfounded.

Finn was all mixed up and tried to find words. "No, no, it wasn't like that. I was forced into service on a slave ship. Then on the ship I met Gus and his sister, wait, I mean I think I better shut up," his voice faltered as his shoulders slumped.

Gus raised his eyebrow. "What about my sister, Prudentina?"

"Nothing, just forget about it. I mean, she was agreeable to me," Finn said, trying to dodge the subject.

Rosie folded her arms in front of her and turned to Finn. "Really, and who is this Prudentina? Do tell me all about her, Finn. And why is this woman so eager to know about me, Finn?" she said, nodding toward Catherina.

Finn gulped and just gawked at them in turns.

"What, cat took your tongue, Finn?" Catherina said.

"Oh, I so want to hear this," Fronto said, laughing and slapping his thighs.

At that moment, the doors were slammed open, and a boy ran into the tavern, terrified. He tried to say something, but could not get anything out at first. He took a deep breath and then almost yelled.

"There is an unwonted light in the sky! It is a daunting, celestial apparition!"

A loud stir rippled through the crowd. Many of the people were superstitious, and the boy's words drove a spike of fear through them. The saloon emptied as the people rushed out to see the spectacle. Gathering on the square, the people looked up at the sky but saw only some white clouds in moonlight.

"Silly boy, what are you raving about?" Rogers asked.

Finn, Gus, Fronto, and Daniel almost fell out with the Campbell brothers. "What is all this commotion and ballyhoo about?"

Then, a wind blew and the clouds scattered, and as the opening widened, the boy pointed to the sky. People stared in disbelief. "See, just like I told you!"

The crowd gasped, and people pointed up to the sky, as an exceptional, sun-grazing comet streaked across the night sky. It got bigger and began to erupt into a brilliant luster that was brighter than the full moon.

"What is that? I have never seen anything like it," Catherina said in awe.

"It has a tail like a dragon," Rosie whispered.

"The tail of the dragon is like a long sword advancing to the north," Dugald Campbell said. The vibrant, shining comet was now seen clearly against a background of stars.

"Probably just a disturbance in the Earth's atmosphere, I'd say. Whatever it may be, it is mighty pretty," Finn said between hiccups.

The townspeople nervously watched the comet in awe, huddling close together. Some started praying.

"For all we know, it is only a dirty snow ball in a vacuum of nothingness," Fronto said.

"Blasphemy! It will bring disaster. The Lord's wrath is upon us," Colonial Bill said, staring at the comet in horror.

Dugald Campbell staggered forward, raising his tankard to the comet. "Mighty warrior, or whoever you are, maybe you will bring us success in this bloody war! There are armies out there to be toppled! Empires are to be born!"

He took a long swig, let out a loud belch, and threw the tankard away. The clouds started gathering again and covered the comet from sight. The townspeople spread out to go home — their mood for partying had vaporized. They kept nervously glancing up at the sky over their shoulders.

No one noticed a black, menacing figure in the shadows leaning against a tree, edgily observing Catherina and Rosie. When the crowd disappeared around the corner, Johan Kopf lit his pipe, the moonlight catching the dreaded skull and crossbones emblem on his woolen mirliton hat, and he blew a long plume of smoke from his nostrils. *Aaah, the thrill of the chase! I see a double trophy, like two delicate, warm and moist apple strudels,* he thought, *and the winner shall take them both!*